Hardbed Hotel

Andrea Carter

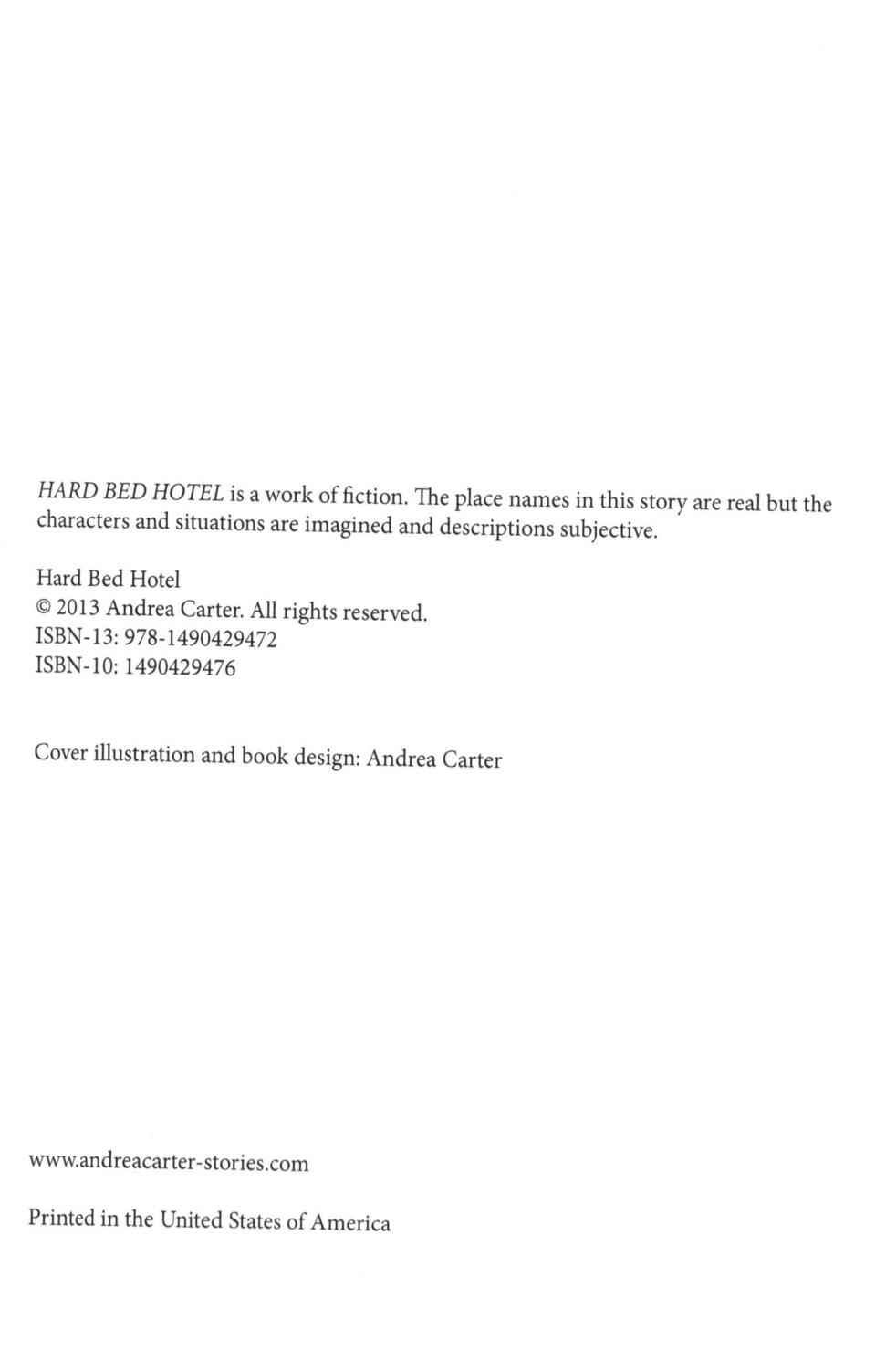

HARD BED HOTEL is a work of fiction. The place names in this story are real but the characters and situations are imagined and descriptions subjective.

Hard Bed Hotel
© 2013 Andrea Carter. All rights reserved.
ISBN-13: 978-1490429472
ISBN-10: 1490429476

Cover illustration and book design: Andrea Carter

www.andreacarter-stories.com

Printed in the United States of America

Many thanks
as always to my husband Alex for the encouragement and motivation that only he can inspire. A special thanks also to my Mom, Dolores Carter and to my good friends Jean MacGregor, Lezak Shallat and Katja Preston for their willingness, positive energy and feedback.

CHAPTER 1
Too late

It was just after the earthquake. The "Mexican Hat Dance" began as a soft vibration and grew increasingly louder from inside the dead man's pocket. It was insisting. Astrid's toes twitched to the beat as she stood, limiting the inclination to dance to inside her shoes, and wondering if the call might be high enough on the list of divine priorities to bring the man back to life. But he remained dead. So she bent down and reached into his vibrating right trouser pocket to retrieve his cell phone.

"Aló?" She answered, her voice betraying her trepidation. Who didn't know that this man had ceased to exist?

A noticeable hesitation. "With Adolfo, please." the woman's voice was brittle.

"Uh... he can't come to the phone right now," was all Astrid could think of under the circumstances.

"Well, I've called him over and over and he refuses to answer. And just now, with this emergency... well, I was lucky to get through at all..." There was an annoyed pause, "And now you! Who are you?" Astrid could almost feel the spray of saliva through the phone as the woman forced angry words from between what Astrid had no doubt were very cherry red lips. "You mean to tell me that even in this dreadful disaster he has a strange woman answer his phone to tell me he can't take the call?" Incredulous, her voice became shrill. "Well then, you can just tell him for me that his excuse better be a good one!" And she hung up.

Astrid pushed the 'off' button, slid the phone back into the dead man's pocket, straightened up and tried not to judge him. Nevertheless she noticed that he was not particularly handsome, nor was he young, and he was overweight by at least 30 kilos. His suit was not expensive and he wasn't wearing jewellery. She wondered why someone would be quite so jealous of this dead man. Whatever the woman's excuse for her interest in him, the man himself definitely had a good one for not returning in kind.

She didn't know much about him other than that two days ago he had died, ceased to exist, become obsolete, was inoperative, kaput, done for. And now he was her new client, the defunct resident of Niche Number 170, Wall 3, Patio Number 62, General Cemetery of Santiago, Chile.

His niche had been made ready for him – a hollow space that receded into the deep wall from which rubble, small chunks of concrete, crumpled paper, empty cigarette packages and broken bits of plastic had been hastily removed. Beyond that, nothing humanly possible could be done to make his resting place less dank and more welcoming. The niche walls in the cemetery were like competitive, low-end real estate developments – pretty and inviting on the outside but barren and cold on the inside. In a sense this made Astrid a public relations professional as well as a tomb janitor because although there wasn't much she could do to the property interior, she was charged with creating cheerful exteriors on those occupied by her deceased lodgers. Her patrons, the surviving relatives paid for the care and maintenance of the family's final resting place.

Unlike more affluent patios comprised of mausoleums and elaborate underground bone hollows, most of the tombs in Patio 62 were rows upon rows of niches, reluctantly butting up to one another inside three-metre-high walls. Each niche was fitted with a locked glass display case, which housed a selection of flowers, ornaments, photos and other sentimental embellishments. More modest niche shelves were minus the glass enclosures but families made an effort to at least buy a nameplate, which was attached to an otherwise desolate concrete wall.

Because everyone is identified by his or her idiosyncrasies and since the personality of the deceased is reflected by what's on their niche shelf, the importance of paraphernalia cannot be understated. Thus, kind strangers often take pity on a barren shelf, donating flowers and small ornaments to help lift it out of its loneliness. And eager to provide amusement in the afterlife, families regularly add to their child's afterlife toy collection, smothering the narrow shelf space to the point where the child's nameplate is hidden from sight.

When visitors drop by, it's the tomb decoration that provides conversational starting points. For instance a football pennant would get things off the ground – "You're looking good today, Señor. Once a fan of Universidad de Chile, always a fan, I see. You're lucky the sun hasn't faded the pennant. God must be doing you some favours. You know they won the championship again this year. Maybe you interceded on their behalf?" The visitor might chuckle and a cordial – often transforming into bawdy – dialogue might ensue. The live visitor will kindly leave space in the conversation should the deceased desire to respond from the tomb. Thus as you wander the paths between the walls, you often see visitors looking up in long, silent pauses at a photo in the niche.

In death as in life, one's home is one's home, to be appreciated for its distinct character and charm, to be welcoming and hospitable, and above all to provoke pleasant memories that will leave all parties satisfied. The visitor is meant to return home full, as though having consumed a hearty meal, one that he can digest until it's time to return for the next visit.

Preparations for this man's arrival – a Señor Adolfo Rodriguez-Rodriguez who had died an accidental death – had been completed only minutes before Astrid's two colleagues came into view. They chatted and nodded to one another as they pulled the trolley with the man's coffin. A few sombre mourners followed in an informal procession, trudging forward, heads down, hands folded at their waist, feet so heavy with grief that even the funeral pace was too much effort.

Astrid's colleagues parked the trolley in front of her, one of them removed his ragged straw hat, and with a sweeping bow and boyish grin indicated that the dead Señor Adolfo was now in her capable hands. "Take over for a minute, will you, my dear?" They headed off for a cigarette and promised to return shortly to cement Señor Adolfo inside the yawning mouth that had been reserved for him in the wall of Patio Number 62.

But that was five minutes ago. Things had changed drastically since then because of the earthquake.

Still trembling, Astrid glanced around at the current scene. A low voice carried on a wisp of jasmine-scented air entered her ear, "Stay calm, my dear. You're in shock but it will pass. What did I tell you? And don't worry, you and your loved ones are safe." It was the voice of the old woman from Santa María Street. More than the voice, it was the scent that triggered the memory of the old woman's wrinkled skin over bones and her haunting dark eyes.

The quake must have destroyed a good number of the two million tombs that populated Santiago's General Cemetery. Astrid was standing in the middle of her Patio, facing the vaults of human remains under her care. Her heart was pounding as she realised the gravity of what had just happened. The unexpected ringing of the dead man's cell phone added to the present shock, increasing the velocity of her pulse and making the situation even more surreal.

Five minutes earlier her colleagues, who had parked Señor Adolfo's trolley in front of her were just out of sight around the corner when the earth started to shudder, and an escalating rumble launched itself from somewhere deep below Astrid's feet. It devoured the ground from bottom up. The rumbling, like a monstrous truck speeding towards the heavens threatened the peace. Trees waved their branches but like giddy children in a school play who were rooted to the 'Xs' marked on stage, they could not abandon the production and had no choice but to continue the dance. They shook thousands of terrified birds out into the open sky. Dust rose from underfoot and billowed down from the surrounding hills to weigh in on the smog that already held the city captive.

Like a dog shaking off parasites, Mother Earth frantically tried to free herself of the countless structures and nuisance artefacts that had, over the years, become attached to her surface without permission. In a determined house cleaning she shook her rugs, releasing the dust – an invasive powder as deadly as any used to exterminate pests. It formed heavy brown clouds that hung over the valley. The sun, who watched from across the heavens flushed an embarrassed, cowardly red. Not that he was inclined to intervene anyway; he was not the omnipotent power of his reputation, but a fraud, nothing but a huge, blustering fireball. Untouchable, safe at his distance, a meek little, "sorry," which could not be heard above his gassy explosions was his only intervention. He shone down, slightly apologetic over the episode, his red eyes squinting past the dense clouds. Then he turned and shrugged because he knew that at least for him, things would still be the same tomorrow.

As the ground shifted violently, the cement and ancient adobe structures of the cemetery wobbled and twisted, glass windows in the niches exploded, giving way to a barrage of personal photos and ornaments that crashed to the ground. Slabs of concrete chunked off the walls and collided in the air before smacking the earth at Astrid's feet. She jumped back, instinctively positioning herself in the middle of the wide passage between the rows of niches. The long cemetery dwellings cracked open at irregular intervals, revealing dark, brooding secrets that sloped, slid and crashed into one another – decayed coffins on angles, bony hands reaching out from under shattered lids, calcified fingers accusing no one and everyone, arthritic knee joints exposing themselves to the warm air, hollow skulls with gaping eye sockets looking joyously up into the open sky for the first time in decades. Voices that had been recorded and trapped inside the molecular structure of the walls for more than a century saw their chance for escape and they released a gigantic symphony of sighs, moans, screeches, ferocious yells and doleful whimpers.

Suddenly the trembling stopped. The tortured, silent reprieve was followed by another light shuddering as Mother Earth relaxed her shoulders and more concrete and wood finally let go and clanked into place on the ground. Astrid remained fixed to her spot on the path as the world began to breath normally once more. The sounds of crashing porcelain, exploding glass, collapsing tin awnings, splintering wood, crumbling concrete, wrenching ground, rupturing pavement, human screams and deathly groans from amongst the patios were all swallowed into an eerie silence that echoed in extended seconds somewhere beyond time. The sun receded sheepishly into the dark green sky.

Señor Adolfo had been dumped precipitously from his coffin, which had been hurled off the trolley. He landed on his side at Astrid's feet, his stiff body settling into a shallow concave blemish on the tarmac. His eyes were closed, he had a sort of blissful grin on his face, and although his hair was slightly dishevelled, he was no worse for wear. Astrid stared down at him for several minutes, the part of her brain that triggered logical thought having seized up like a set of rusty old cogs. That was when she answered the first phone call.

There was no sign of Señor Adolfo's family. Common sense must have sent them running to one of the main passageways, clear of the walls. Perhaps they had been hurt or were too frightened to move. Nevertheless, it occurred to her that they should have informed the lady with the cherry red lips of Señor Adolfo's permanently indisposed state.

Astrid had barely recovered from Cherry Red Lip's call when the defunct man's phone rang again, the incongruous "Mexican Hat Dance" playing foolishly into the post-quake air.

Astrid felt an obligation once again to take the call, partly because the tinny music was mocking the disaster, like someone laughing aloud at a funeral, but also because she was Señor Adolfo's caretaker, and ironic as it was, someone wanted to know that he had survived the quake.

She fumbled into Señor Adolfo's pocket once more. "Aló?"

"I want to speak with Adolfo, please. This is Sergio. I'm calling from Arica."

"I'm sorry but he is permanently indisposed."

"That's not a very classic excuse. I don't know what you have to do with him, but I suppose he didn't tell you that he owes me one million pesos. I may be two days away by bus, but I can still get there and break his legs. You tell him that for me."

"Si, Señor. Good day." She looked down at the man who failed to be alive. His legs were the least of his worries.

She pushed the 'off' button but couldn't bring herself to turn off the power. Even though the man who in life was known as Señor Adolfo Rodriguez-Rodriguez, now found himself among the non-living, the ringing phone seemed to prolong his relevance, bring him back to where people needed him. She didn't know if he would have wanted it but decided not to second-guess his wishes or those of the family. They must have left the cell phone in his pocket, perhaps deliberately, perhaps not. Like him, his phone would stop ringing when the battery died. So she deposited the apparatus into his trouser pocket once again and hoped it would not ring again soon. It was one thing to take care of him after he had passed into his current state, but quite another to be the messenger of his fateful news.

Yesterday Astrid had been tipped off about the planned arrival of the new Patio Number 62 resident when cement workers had come to survey the niche. They were accompanied by Señor Adolfo's brother, who was drunk – "...out of profound grief," he said.

He introduced himself as Señor Carlos and explained to Astrid how Señor Adolfo's passing had been entirely unexpected. They had just been together in his very own garden, drinking wine, slapping their knees and laughing, enjoying the true story about a fat woman on a bus.

The inebriated Señor Carlos saw fit to go into detail about the story, assuring Astrid that it was relevant to the cause of death. He began somewhere near the beginning, where he was saying to his brother "...the bus stopped and the rush hour crowd crammed in the door. The bus was so packed that this fatso was forced up against the bus driver... other people were still hanging outside the front door when the bus took off. Crammed in there like sardines falling out of a net."

"Yeah, I heard that her huge ass was like an overstuffed pillow against the back of the driver's neck." Adolfo was already red with laughter.

"With her weight against him, it took all of his strength just to turn the wheel, so you can imagine what happened when she farted."

"He must have felt a warm gust, maybe even some debris. And what about the vibrations coming off of a pair of buttocks like that?"

She apologised, "Ladies and gentlemen, I'm so sorry. It escaped. It simply escaped."

But her apology was not heard over the din of rude retorts from passengers — "Señora, you should have let it escape before you left home this morning," —"Señora, how do you expect us to breathe in this atmosphere?" — "She doesn't need a tuba, she is a tuba!" — "We have no room for buskers, Señora," — "Yeah especially someone the size of a tuba!" By now the driver was weeping and groaning and sweating profusely.

"Lucky his head wasn't separated from his body."

"Forget about the headless horseman. What about a headless conductor?"

"Señora, have mercy!"

The imagery was too much and the brothers were beside themselves, spittle and bits of pastry from their empanadas blowing from between their lips. Tears from helpless laughter streamed down their cheeks.

"The driver must have been in shock. The strength drained from his arms and he froze."

"Yeah, but his neck must have been on fire from such an explosion."

"And that's when the bus hit the building on George's Avenue."

"Yeah, demolished by a fart!"

"Not only that..." Señor Adolfo's red face grew even redder as he forced out the last bit of the story. "Not only that..." he sputtered in between guffaws, "Three people died in the accident! And one of them wasn't the fat lady. She survived to fart again."

They both howled.

Señor Carlos slapped his thigh and through his own stream of tears he watched Señor Adolfo roll out of his chair and onto the grass in a fit of merry hysteria.

As Señor Adolfo flailed about on the ground, red-faced, and sputtering, a very drunk Señor Carlos continued to embellish the fat lady story, exaggerating the details and laughing even harder. It was out of control.

Anyway, the truth of the matter is that as Señor Adolfo was rolling on the ground he was actually choking to death on an olive pit. And Señor Carlos continued howling uproariously as his brother, flailing about, finally ceased moving and fell deathly still.

After that horrendous experience, Señor Carlos vowed that he would never again permit anyone to use the expression, 'he laughed himself to death' in his presence. "It was very traumatic for me and a sad situation all round and, as you can see, a shock to have to deliver my dear, beloved brother to his final resting place so early in his life, God bless his soul."

After this comprehensive account, which moved him into a state of visible despondency, the drunken Señor Carlos pressed 3,000 pesos into Astrid's palm and promised to pay her the same each month for the watering of flowers and the general care and cleaning of Señor Adolfo's post-mortem place of residence.

But now the earthquake had eliminated that need for care, along with its associated potential income. Once they steadied themselves and came out of hiding, the family would not leave Señor Adolfo on the ground in front of his cart. Nor would they bury him in the ruins. They would be wise to cremate him. In this case they would take his ashes home and they would try to sell his niche. But since it was in ruins, it would be a long-term real estate challenge. Even if they succeeded, Astrid would have to wait for a member of the new buyer's family to die in order to make up for her lost income. She sighed. Business was going to be slow.

Under the circumstances, she knew that her monthly earnings would be suspended. The patrons would not pay to maintain ruins. The bodies of her muertitos (her little dead ones) would all be temporarily relocated while the patio walls were reconstructed. It could take months but probably more likely it would be years before she would be able to make a living from her patch in Patio 62 again.

Perhaps she would accept Señora Ruby's invitation to share her Patio. Señora Ruby was the sole caretaker of Patio 35, which consisted of a stretch of niches in the outer wall and several older, more upscale family mausoleums. Señora Ruby had tried to convince Astrid to transfer to her sector so they could work together because she was getting too old to care for the entire Patio herself and she complained that she had no children to apprentice and inherit her post.

Today Astrid looked up to the heavens and prayed that Señora Ruby's Patio had not suffered serious damage. At that moment, the earth gave itself another strong shake and Astrid crouched down, absent-mindedly leaning on Señor Adolfo's large shoulder for support. Her weight was apparently all that was needed to disturb his own fragile balance and he suddenly rolled over, nose to tarmac. Startled, she jumped back. She would have to abandon him this way. He was too heavy to roll back over again.

After a time, the putrid smell of death and decay began to filter into the air. She estimated that it was only a matter of minutes before Señor Adolfo's brother would be back to demand the return of his 3,000 pesos. So Astrid hustled away from the prone body lying on the path of Patio 62. She kept her head down, intent as she picked her way over the ruins. But she was aware that she was successfully sneaking past Señor Adolfo's family. They were huddled in the centre of a path, shaken and muttering about the end of the world. She stopped to watch when Señor Carlos' cell phone rang, sending out a ring tone that interrupted the silence of disaster with its rock organ version of 'Stairway to Heaven.'

Señor Carlos fumbled for the phone and then stood frozen, staring at the small screen.

"It's Adolfo! This is a call from Adolfo! What?" He pushed the button and raised the phone to his ear, "Adolfo? Adolfo? Adolfo...?" He choked and held his cell up to the sky. Then he announced to his stupefied family, "Adolfo called but I can't hear what he's trying to tell me. God help me, I can't hear him!" He broke into desperate sobs and sank to his knees as the small group bent around him. They all stared trancelike at the square screen on his phone, a disconcerted human sculpture in the midst of the broken path.

In awe of the mystery of such an unlikely event, one of the more religious sisters sank to her knees, raised both arms, gazed up towards the heavens and coughed into the dusty air, "Holy Virgin, you've made us witness to a miracle. It's a miracle. Adolfo is a saint. We must tell the bishop." Another woman – a more practical soul – turned around, palms up to the sky in a gesture of gratitude. "Thanks be to God for Telefónica. He has given them an exceptional network. God bless the Spaniards and their technology."

With the 3,000 pesos jammed deep into her pocket, Astrid scurried past them like a guilty cat. It was her fault. Why hadn't she just turned the phone off? Señor Adolfo must have rolled onto it when she leaned into him and now the autodial, which happened to select his brother's number, was activated. The call would be repeated until the battery finally died or until Mother Earth shook Señor Adolfo enough to roll him back, which was extremely unlikely. Señor Carlos better be prepared for a lot of calls from heaven.

No doubt because of Señor Adolfo's powers from the afterlife, his family would declare him a saint and they would set up an altar for him in the cemetery, perhaps not far from the rock of the 'poor Christ.' Strangers would come to visit him and repeat the story of the miraculous telephone call from life beyond, gaze into the faded eyes in his photo, and return to petition him for favours. Soon he would be known as Saint Adolfo. "And all for what?" Astrid answered her own question, "For choking on an olive pit and for being so overweight that pressure from his dead gut pushed a button on a cell phone that someone left turned on? Who am I to judge?"

As she approached Señora Ruby's shack at the corner of Patio 35, she was witness to another disquieting scene. The tremors served to evict groups of cemetery squatters. They were scurrying about like rats blinded by daylight.

As was customary in many cemeteries, indigents made their way inside the gates to bed down and take shelter beside tombs and inside mausoleums, staying for days or months, sometimes even years. The cemetery, being what it was, was affectionately referred to as 'Los patios de los Callados' ('Patios of the Mutes'), or 'Hotel Cama Dura' ('Hard Bed Hotel').

Today's tragedy would make many squatters homeless once again. Astrid paused to watch as they hobbled helter-skelter away from the stench and disaster, having hastily slung plastic bags stuffed with limited creature comforts over their shoulders. Some would not have escaped at all on that day and only later would the authorities discover several unidentified bodies huddled under rough woollen blankets, crushed beneath the ruins. The death of these homeless people would never officially be recorded because cemetery regulations prohibited anyone from actually living within its walls. Therefore they had never officially existed but the administration would make room in a common grave and, in death as in life, their bodies would be overlooked.

In spite of the strict no-squatter regulation, most cemetery caretakers took pity on the homeless and turned a blind eye to the rules. Less sympathetic caretakers could usually be convinced by the occasional gift of a cigarette or a 100-peso coin offered up by the grubby hand of someone in greater need than themselves. Señora Ruby did not accept gifts but if she granted anyone space in her patio, she insisted that they pick up their own garbage, donate one or two empty bottles a month for use as flower vases, and above all, discreetly use the approved cemetery toilets. She would not tolerate the sacrilege or stench of urine on tombs and pathways.

So squatters snuck in each night before the gates were locked. After the gatekeeper became familiar with them, he would permit them to wander in at later hours in exchange for a cigarette or a few ounces of wine. The next day, they tidied the space outside of their quarters and either left to go about their business downtown or they lounged around the passageways and sprawled on mausoleum steps chatting with neighbours and playing with homeless dogs.

In relation to squatters, but unknown until it actually investigated, the administration had, on occasion, received complaints from residents of a neighbourhood upwind of the cemetery. They objected to the offensive odour of night-time cremations, claiming it ruined otherwise peaceful meals and family evenings in front of the TV and they demanded it be stopped at once. The administration insisted that night cremation was not a cemetery practice. However, the barbecue odour persisted and finally several elderly ladies with thinning, coiffed hair, dressed in their Sunday best with large butterfly broaches and strands of pearls, went to protest with placards outside the cemetery offices. Their presence and persistence drew television cameras and bad publicity, forcing the administration to look into the matter.

Reporters followed cemetery officials as they uncovered and displayed the evidence. Their cameras panned across three barbecue grills, two half-barrels with wood charcoal and soot and two dozen empty wine bottles. The hangdog, stubbly faces of 20 squatters were flashed across the news with intermittent images of the dismayed, well-coiffed ladies with pursed lips, one of whom suggested the homeless people were very likely cannibals. All of the squatters were evicted and three caretakers were reprimanded and threatened with losing their Patios. However, several squatters returned after a few days, offering every spare cigarette and coin in their possession to non-conformist caretakers. Having regained access, they reduced the size of their fires and eliminated barbecues from the menu. From then on, the only safe options were stew or fried fish.

Under normal circumstances, the night-time population of the General Cemetery increased by several hundred souls, all locked safely behind the tall gates where they slept side-by-side with the muertitos.

But as of about five minutes ago, as a result of the earthquake, these were no longer normal circumstances.

CHAPTER 2

The Old Woman of Santa María Street

It had been more than a month since the earthquake and Astrid and Señora Ruby passed the days in stops and starts at Patio 35. They were still surrounded by destruction and much of their time was spent hunting for lost tools, reorganising and marvelling over small mercies, such as how the decaying virgin statue on the abandoned tomb of Mercedes de la Fuente was spared the lamentable fate of toppling and smashing into a million pieces. Señora Ruby was disconcerted by this particular phenomenon but did not discuss the inner anxiety it caused. Instead, she redirected her thoughts, and the conversation to a different one – one they had had at least a half dozen times since the quake – that of the old woman of Santa María Street.

Señora Ruby planted her feet firmly at the base of the concrete wall beside her tool shed and leaned back into it. She was hunched over, her shoulders rounded so much that her torso looked like a big mitt ready to catch anything that came at her. She rolled her back into the wall as she listened, eyes closed, arms folded across her chest, face tilted up towards the sun.

With her light blue smock, her short, dusty grey rubber boots, grey hair and complexion the colour of cement, she resembled a wrinkled lizard. Astrid affectionately thought of her as the cemetery chameleon.

It was Señora Ruby's custom to develop an itch between her shoulder blades when she and Astrid relaxed to gossip or when she stopped to listen to a romantic bolero on the radio at the door of her shed. Sometimes her eyes watered in nostalgic bliss and she hummed softly. Who knows what came to mind from decades gone by? She claimed that her rocking motion relieved the itch in her back and helped her to concentrate, but Astrid attributed the habit to advanced age – something always itching and aching.

Although Señora Ruby said that as far as her age was concerned, she could never count higher than the number 68, Astrid estimated Señora Ruby to have lived through at least 74 or 75 summers. She was a well-seasoned fixture on Patio 35, having inherited this caretaker post from her own mother, who inherited it from her mother before her, which, if you added it up, meant that she was from a line of cemetery caretakers who dated back to its inception. Therefore, Señora Ruby knew everything there was to know about the Santiago General Cemetery.

Today, as Señora Ruby's lids drooped heavily over her eyes and she chewed on the inside of her right cheek, Astrid noticed how the fingers of time had scratched and blended their years across her weathered canvas. Her cheeks, which she dusted heavily every day with coral-coloured powder that, in Astrid's estimation, only served to attract flies, were sallow, and the creases in her forehead appeared deeper in the afternoon light. Her lips curled downwards in a frown that didn't mean she was unhappy, just concentrating. Her grey eyebrows, from which occasionally leapt one remarkably long hair, came together in a furrowed V at the bridge of her nose. The wrinkles that spidered out into her cheeks from her upper lip, and especially those around her eyes were oily and attracted black particles of smog, making her face look like a charcoal drawing, black on white with two uneven round daubs of coral. Recently, her grey hair had thinned rather drastically and strands fell out when she ran her fingers through it. But she refused to cut it and it hung to the middle of her back in straggly, often oily tresses.

Today Señora Ruby was listening to Astrid's account of the mysterious old lady from Santa María Street. Señora Ruby's opinion was that the old lady was one of Astrid's guardian angels. She was one of her muertitos, who had come to her rescue, as some are known to do.

"Yes, Astrid. There is little doubt." She opened her eyes and took a moment to focus. "But tell me again and don't leave out a single detail."

Astrid took her time. She extracted a cigarette and offered one to Señora Ruby, who declined. Astrid sucked in one long drag, exhaled slowly as she thought, inhaled again and then expelled the smoke forcefully out the side of her mouth as she began a recount of the events.

....

"On the day of the earthquake – of course I didn't know there would be an earthquake – I went to the bakery, as usual... you know, the one on the corner of Santa María Street, to buy a bun for my lunch. I had a few extra pesos, so I thought I would stop for a slice of cold cut meat at Siete Pelos' corner shop. I always think it's worth it to go the extra distance because his meat is cheap. It's because he cuts from the outdated pressed ends, but I don't mind that. Anyway, even though his shop is a block off my route, I still had time. The only thing was to make sure I got there before Siete Pelos disappeared on one of his hair repair interludes. You know Siete Pelos ("Seven Hairs"), don't you Señora Ruby?"

Señora Ruby nodded. "Who doesn't? Go on..."

Siete Pelos was baptised Omar Marco Lopez-Parra but most people forgot his true name upon the launch of his new hair style, which he invented to cover up premature hair loss when he was only 23 years old. At that age, Omar's scalp failed to produce new hair and what hair he already had, began to fall out surprisingly rapidly from the centre top area of his head, forcing him to take drastic measures. Among other things, he began to pray to San Expedito to help him grow at least the one essential lock of hair he needed to achieve the style he had seen atop the heads of several distinguished, albeit older, gentlemen. "That's all I ask, San Expedito. It's not much considering most men my age still have a full head of hair. All I need is this growth. Just in this one spot. If you grant me this, I'll be your humble servant until I die."

San Expedito, the patron saint of all who need to expedite events – in Omar's case, hair growth – is a popular saint, not only in Chile, but also in all of South America. The story behind San Expedito is worth knowing:

He was a Roman legionnaire in the 4th Century AD and according to one of the common versions of the story, he was walking along a road one day when the spirit of God touched him, encouraging him to convert to Christianity. But an evil spirit in the form of a crow intervened, cawing "Tomorrow, tomorrow, tomorrow... leave your decision for another day. You should be in no rush to convert to Christianity." In response, San Expedito stepped on the crow, crushing and killing him, and declared, "There will be no postponements!" He therefore became known as the saint who answers those in need of an urgent solution and he is most often seen in his Roman uniform, one foot on a dead crow, and sometimes with a clock in one hand. Of course his original calling was to help others approach God and to become good Christians without delay. But he has evolved to entertain petitions that include help with business dealings as well as almost any other project considered to be urgent or that simply has to be completed at some point before you die.

The Catholic Church in Chile, having initially rejected a request to build a chapel in San Expedito's honour, ended up themselves praying to the Saint and within the expeditious period of only nine days, decided to give it the green light. So there is now a chapel just outside of Viña del Mar that houses a large San Expedito statue. It has come to be known as San Expedito's home in Chile and a priest organises heavily advertised annual pilgrimages to the site.

Anyway, Siete Pelos negotiation with the Saint was satisfactory to both parties – in exchange for his long strand of hair, Siete Pelos would close his shop each year to travel to the San Expedito chapel, where he lit a candle at the foot of the larger-than-life icon. More importantly, in addition to the annual pilgrimage, Siete Pelos' secret pact with the Saint was that he would source, stock and sell San Expedito pennants, photos and trinkets in his shop. Each year, expedited by the priest of the chapel, Siete Pelos set in motion new deals with an ever-expanding list of foreign suppliers of holy gift items and he returned home, excited about his motley collection.

He even managed to source San Expedito handkerchiefs. Not a practical item, when you think about it, since people would end up blowing their noses in his face. Nonetheless the Saint was there to help turn a peso and, if necessary, to catch nasal mucus. Siete Pelos had the largest collection of San Expedito paraphernalia in Santiago and he shamelessly promoted it at every opportunity. His sales were so successful that he and the priest realised the sky was the limit and they arranged for the production of yet more rare San Expedito branded goods such as underwear, soap, hair pomade, embroidered insignias, belts, neckties, earrings, cell phone cases, toilet paper covers and air fresheners (to name a few) as well as the standard saint cards, candles, framed photos and lighters. He and the priest ran a booming business but there was no doubt about who was really responsible for their success.

But, back to Siete Pelos and the point about his hair… It took about four years to grow this single thin strand to a satisfactory length. The initial witty estimate was that the strand consisted of only seven hairs and even though this was a gross exaggeration, the name, Siete Pelos ("Seven Hairs") stuck. The sad tress grew out of the left side of his head above his ear and just below his part. At its optimum, it stretched about 60 centimetres and with that, Siete Pelos was able to maintain his distinct look. Each morning he stretched out the strand and, coating a comb with San Expedito pomade, he stroked it a few times from the root to the tip before winding it back and forth over his bald cranium and patting it in place.

Over the course of the day, because he constantly bent and stretched as he served his customers, the strand slowly unwound, revealing more and more of Siete Pelos' greasy scalp until it reached the point where he had to fling it over his shoulder to keep it out of his way. This did not go unnoticed, and more than one customer threatened, "If I find one of your seven, long greasy hairs in my sandwich, I'll come back and pull out the other six!" Therefore three or four times a day it was necessary to hang a sign that said 'I'll be back in five minutes' so that he could run to his room next door to re-wind and re-grease his precious plait of hair. Most often, the five minutes extended to thirty.

The morning of the earthquake, Astrid was spared the concern about this extended five-minute hair recess because the mysterious old woman of Santa María Street discouraged her from going to Siete Pelos' altogether.

Astrid glanced at Señora Ruby to check if she was still awake and then continued with her story. "When I left the bakery, before going over to Siete Pelos' place, I saw an old lady shuffling along on two legs as thin as raspberry canes. It looked like she was curling her toes hard inside her pair of pink Adidas so that they wouldn't fall off. The shoes must have been three sizes too big. The old girl hesitated at the edge of the sidewalk. I remember she was wearing a pair of white hand-knit socks that had fallen down around her ankles; it reminded me of the plumage around the neck of a condor and I thought to myself that maybe she was hiding a beak and a pair of beady eyes under her skirt." Astrid laughed at the image, but Señora Ruby remained expressionless, flipping her wrist as a signal for Astrid to get on with it.

"Anyway, like I told you before, but just so you remember... you know, in case it triggers a memory... the old lady was wearing a light beige sweater with holes in the elbows. The sweater was stretched out of shape and it hung down past her hips. She had on a faded flower cotton skirt. Her hair was a dull grey and it was pulled back into a loose bun and there was a big red double dahlia sticking out of it. She was wearing a huge pair of long, dangling silver earrings, her cheeks were caked with powder and she wore heavy red lipstick. My first thought was that she was on her way to an early morning fiesta. But she looked worse for wear, so maybe she was just coming back from an all-night one. I mean I didn't know what to think of her. She was a rare old bird and you never know what some of these ancient types get up to."

Señora Ruby looked at her sideways.

"Sorry, Señora Ruby. I didn't mean anything by that."

Señora Ruby just nodded for her to carry on.

"You know, I was afraid she was going to lose one of her big shoes on the street, so I approached her and offered my arm. That's when I noticed a fresh jasmine scent around her. I mean – I was surprised that she smelled so nice considering the state she was in. And this changed my perception of her. The aroma created the impression that she was more elegant. She just looked up at me, didn't smile or anything, and she slipped her hand under my arm. Her fingers pinched my elbow and I noticed her long fingernails had been freshly varnished with bright red nail polish. Really odd, don't you think, especially so early in the morning?"

Señora Ruby nodded in agreement and squinted up into the blue sky as though she was going to respond with something wise. But she didn't. So Astrid continued.

"Where are you going?" The old woman's voice was raspy.

"I'm going over to Siete Pelos' for a slice or two of meat. Are you going that way?"

"No. I'm not. And you shouldn't either." The old lady snapped. "You must get away from here. Go home instead, or go and visit a friend." She stopped walking, looked up into Astrid's face and ordered, "Now!"

Astrid was shocked. It was like an order delivered from a sergeant. She paused in the middle of the road to look down at the old lady, who stood staring back intensely.

"Why should I do that?" Astrid decided to humour her, patting the old lady's shiny red fingertips.

"Because there's going to be a tremendous earthquake this morning. And soon. And you shouldn't be on the street alone." The old lady's eyes drilled into Astrid's. Astrid rolled back on her heels, feeling the need for more distance between them.

"Oh, Señora, I doubt if there will be an earthquake. Where would you get such an idea?"

To dismiss the notion, Astrid gently tugged the old woman's arm and they resumed their trek towards the other side of the street.

The old lady's fingers tightened, her sharp nails jabbing the interior softness of Astrid's elbow. "Now listen to me. Go wherever you're going then but forget about stopping for the meat. Go, I tell you!" She pressed her bony shoulder into Astrid, forcing the two of them to halt again. The old lady just looked up, her eyes penetrating Astrid's. Astrid felt the hairs on the back of her neck prickle.

Now it was the old lady who tugged at Astrid to continue.

When they reached the other side of the street, the woman unhooked herself from Astrid's elbow, wagged one red-tipped index finger up at her face and repeated. "Forget the meat, Señora. Get away." Her eyes were fierce but had an unnerving background stillness, which Astrid found vaguely familiar but was unable to identify. She wanted to ask the old lady's name but in an instant the leathery stick of a woman was gone, bones clattering off in the opposite direction, her big pink shoes slapping the pavement and her oversized dahlia flopping loosely out of the grey nest of hair on the back of her head. She faded off before Astrid's eyes and Astrid turned away, her empty stomach beginning a sick dance.

Trying to forget the old woman's warning, she continued along the sidewalk. But she kept her head down, alert for the slightest vibration or groan coming from the street, and when she became suspicious of irregular cracks in the pavement – perceiving one or two to have lengthened and broadened as she passed them by – real or not, she was unnerved and she stopped and turned around. The old lady was nowhere in sight.

Maybe she'd eat jam today instead of a slice of Siete Pelos' cold cuts. She did an about-face and avoided the cracks as she strode onward, increasing her pace with each step. By the time she reached the cemetery gate she was in a flat-out run, her knees and ankles grinding under her weight.

Safely at work, she calmed down, unlocked her tool shack and donned her dusty blue caretaker smock. She wandered round to the front of the main wall of Patio 62 to do a quick revision of her muertitos, and headed over to inspect the newly prepared niche. She estimated that it had only been about 20 minutes from the time the old lady on Santa María Street had disappeared to when the two caretakers pulled up in front of her with Señor Adolfo on their trolley, just before the earthquake struck.

....

Señora Ruby's eyes were still half closed and she resumed rolling her back against the wall. "Well, if you and no one else in the neighbourhood has seen the old lady before or since, then my professional opinion is that she is one of your muertitos. But I can tell you she doesn't sound familiar to me. And if she appeared to you, it's because she knows you from your patio."

"About a week after the earthquake, I asked Norma, at the bakery... you know Norma... she's the biggest snoop on the block, always watching everything. She knows everyone in the neighbourhood and nothing gets past her. Anyway, Norma saw me help the old lady across the street. But she said she doesn't know who she is and hasn't seen her since that day either."

"Do you recognise her face from any of the niche photos?"

"Well, you know that so many of those muertitos have been there since before my own mother's time, long before I took over, and some of the niches are too old to have photos. But, Señora Ruby, there was something about the old lady's eyes... something I recognised. I don't know if it was the eyes themselves or just their expression. Maybe I've seen the expression before. There was something disturbing there... behind her eyes, you know... like she saw from far, far away."

"This is the look from beyond the grave."

Astrid stared at Señora Ruby without seeing her. She knew she was right. She was always right about these things. She was old, had lived through countless unnatural experiences, and was a good judge of things that happened between one reality and another.

Señora Ruby continued to make her case, "There can be no other explanation... and she accurately predicted the earthquake. I mean... how? And she was a stranger to our streets. No one knows who she was. And no one has seen her since. She appeared for no other reason than to warn you."

"So in my opinion," Señora Ruby was closing the conversation, twisting her back, stretching, preparing to return to work, "she was one of your muertitos who came out to protect you."

"Yeah." Astrid took a last drag on the remains of her cigarette and squinted through the smoke. "Maybe she even saved my life, Señora Ruby. You know that Siete Pelos' shop ended up in a complete shambles? He was crushed under the rubble."

"Susana told me."

"Did Susana also tell you that a good portion of his floor collapsed into a sink hole, like it had been bombed?" Astrid shuddered and ground her cigarette butt into the dust under her loafer. "And everything on his shelves either went down with it, or was blown out onto the sidewalk. When things calmed down, Señor Oscar's youngest son – what's-his-name? – ran over to steal candies that had scattered across the ground. If he hadn't been such a little thief, Siete Pelos could have died."

"Yeah, Susana told me that too. She said that the little bugger was scared out of his wits because he thought a snake had slithered out from under the rubble to bite his grubby little paw when he reached into the candy jar. Thought it was Satan himself. A miracle the kid didn't die on the spot from fright." Señora Ruby laughed her throaty laugh.

Astrid picked up on the story, "I heard that he dropped all the candy and stood there shaking like a leaf, pointing at the snake and screaming. When Señor Oscar ran over he recognised that the snake was not a snake at all, but Siete Pelos' single strand of hair. It was like it had taken on a life of its own. Señor Oscar said that when he tugged on it, Siete Pelos yelped.

Anyway, that's how he knew for sure he was alive. But Siete Pelos begged him to spare his hair. Poor Siete. Can you imagine? So Señor Oscar dug him out with his bare hands. They say he'll be okay but he'll have to walk with a cane."

"Saved by a hair." Señora Ruby commented under her breath.

Astrid was more serious now, "I understand he's already rebuilding the front of his shop... and without government help. Imagine! I heard he made a new sign for it and it says, Conversé con los Santos ("I spoke to the Saints"). Of course he's stocking even more San Expedito cards. And he gave Señor Oscar a sample of every single San Expedito item that he has. You should see Señor Oscar's taxi now. With all the knickknacks, there's almost no room for passengers."

"Yeah, I heard someone say that there are so many San Expedito images in the taxi now that you feel like you're being escorted to your destination by the whole Roman army. And apparently the air fresheners are so strong that by the time you get out, your skin turns green and you smell like a pine tree."

"Yeah, but you know what I heard? I heard that Señor Oscar actually started to re-sell the gifts from Siete Pelos. In fact, he almost forces them on you. Susana said it's so bad that he locks the door and doesn't let you out unless you buy something."

"Oh, do you really think so, Astrid? I mean you know the stuff Susana comes up with."

Astrid shrugged.

"The point, Astrid, is that the old lady saved you from being buried alive with Siete Pelos. Had you not turned around and walked the other way, you could have died there, or at best, been seriously injured, or maybe even discovered strangled to death by Siete Pelos' hair."

Astrid rubbed her throat and shivered. She recalled that she had heard the old woman's voice again after the quake when she was standing alone in the eerie silence of the path. The voice was telling her not to panic. And she had been conscious of the calming scent of jasmine, if not the coolness of a ghost brushing past her in the gloomy air.

"But Señora Ruby, I'll never find the old woman of Santa María Street now. My patio's been torn down and they're rebuilding. All of my muertitos were removed to the temporary services area. If there was a chance to recognise the old lady, it would have been while her niche was still intact."

"Then it is as it is. We can't explain things the dead do, my little heart." (Astrid was particularly touched when Señora Ruby used this pet name.) "Whoever she was, she did what she wanted to do and has gone again now. God knows that many of my own muertitos have saved me through the years. And you know it too. I've told you. I can't even count how many times they've protected me from delinquents within these very walls. Don't ask questions. Just call up these things that you will never forget and be grateful."

CHAPTER 3

One Side of the Coin

Astrid was humming 'Everything Changes' as she ambled through the west gates towards her shack. This morning she had awakened with an unusual amount of vigour, happy with the world. She had lain in bed smiling up at the fine cracks in her ceiling, which, when she squinted, sketched trees and brooks and smoke from old trains that dragged themselves over one mountain after another, across imaginary bridges that eventually disappeared bravely into the broken sea that was her roof. Something good was going to happen today. She could feel it in her bones.

She didn't notice Juan Bonifacio Maluenda-Valdéz drive up in the 1975 Volvo Amazon and she didn't hear the brakes squeak as he pulled in across from the cemetery gate. He extracted from his pocket the loose cigarette that his friend Mario had sheepishly bestowed as a going-away gift, lit it, leaned back and inhaled. For a moment the smoke obscured his gaunt face, the handsome features faded behind years of hard living, grey eyes once a steel blue that drove the girls wild. His fine nose had a knuckle dent in it and there was evidence of a fist having hammered into his slightly deformed lower lip (possibly more than once) and one of his bottom molars was missing. He tossed his hair, running his fingers through it several times, ignoring its dull, brittle ends. Juan loved the length and thickness of his hair, denying its less than healthy condition. He insisted on the 70s' style, feathered and long at the back, because it made him look so damned handsome. "Watch," he predicted, "the rest of the world will come round full circle because this is a classic 'do' and I'll be the first one to say 'I told you so.'" He was lost in the past, stuck in the groove, like a needle caught in the vinyl track of his most popular hit song whose title was 'This is the Moment of Forever.' Juan studied the entrance to the cemetery, absent-mindedly watching a woman with huge hoop earrings and big leather loafers, her short, slightly waddling strides carrying her along the outside wall of the graveyard.

Mario had apologised, saying that a cigarette was the most he could offer because his wife had threatened to divorce him. "If you don't boot that ill-begotten, blue-eyed loser out the door now – yesterday – then I'll throw you out with him! And don't think I won't." Mario, being basically honest and lacking in diplomacy, confessed to Juan what his wife had said. Nothing he could do. "So sorry, amigo. But, here... have a cigarette." Juan didn't hold it against him. He accepted and cleared out.

He squinted through the smoke. His last option lay inside those gates – specifically, in the family mausoleum. He tried to remember exactly where it was located. Patio number 46 came to mind, but who knew? It had been so long. He tossed the cigarette butt to the sidewalk just as the woman bustled around the gate and disappeared from his consciousness.

On his way over to the cemetery, he had detoured past his old apartment building in the centre of Santiago. It was still in shambles. The earthquake had sealed its destiny – it would finally be demolished next week along with most other buildings on the street where he had lived the last twenty unlucky years of his life.

Long before he had made it his home, half of the building had been burnt out by a fire and it was legally declared unfit to inhabit. But at the time, he was desperate and the landlord was greedy, so they made a deal. The landlord removed the tape from across the door and with a toothless grin trenched across heavily whiskered cheeks, ushered Juan in with a sweep of his arm. "Welcome to the palace. Just be careful. I don't want any legal troubles here. So we don't know each other and I'm not really renting this to you," he had told him. The walls were still charred, soot clinging to everything, but Juan improvised and, although he could not call it home, this hovel was a place to lay his head. Before he knew it, twenty years had gone by.

The day he found the burnt-out rooms, he was kicking aside some soot on the kitchen floor when he stepped on a rock. Nudging it with the toe of his boot, he saw that it was a smooth, polished gem that had come loose from its setting. He bent down to examine it and discovered a precious lapis lázuli stone clinging for its life to a single clamp on a long silver chain. He picked it up, dug it out of what was left of the pendant, gave it a quick shine on his sleeve, kissed it and christened it his 'ojo azul con suerte' ("lucky blue eye") before dropping the rare, blue rock into his trouser pocket. Why he should believe the stone to be lucky after it was ill-fated enough to fall out of a pendant into the soot from a disastrous fire was a mystery, but probably the answer lay somewhere in the fact that he needed something, anything at all, to give him hope.

After all these years, he still had his lucky blue eye and every morning he pulled it out of his pocket to perform the ritual that called up its good fortune; he rolled it between his fingers, no less than three times – back and forth, round and round, over and out – and then raised it to his lips to kiss it twice with the respect one might give the pope's ring. His luck, which had gone bad somewhere around the year 1978, hadn't changed much since he found the stone. But he was optimistic because the discovery of his lucky blue eye was 20 years ago and someone had told him (he couldn't remember who) that bad fortune never lasts for more than 21 years in a row. So if he could guard it carefully, then this year was bound to be his year of fortune.

Juan never considered that maybe his kisses and affectionate fondling of the lapis lázuli – the repeated whispered pleas for something good to happen, anything at all – might be such a nuisance to the stone that it would result not only its ability to perform magic, but its psychology, its very desire to be lucky. In fact, all of this unwanted attention could even cause a stone (depending on its disposition) to become quite depressed. That Juan himself was the source of his own bad luck, and that the care he gave the stone actually served to perpetuate the negative energy that hovered around him as a grey aura, never entered his mind. He was fiercely determined that his blue stone brought him luck, even though it stubbornly refused to do any such thing.

Juan had convinced himself that the earthquake was the last bit of misfortune to perpetrate itself upon him before the all-important twenty-first year rolled around. It was the turning point and the stars would now begin to shine down upon him as they had once done. He was confident.

The day of the earthquake (now three months ago) Juan had been performing a little romantic number at Slaughterhouse Square in front of a bleary-eyed audience of exactly eleven. It was early. All seven of them were all either too shocked, too scared, or too hung-over to move, so they clung to each other as the earth jostled them about on the wooden bench until eventually, with the pressure of the group all leaning in the same direction, the man at the end fell off. From there, it was a slow-motion domino effect. As the earth continued to tremble under their sprawling bodies, mouths hanging open, jaws trembling in time to the karaoke tune in the background, they all looked up at Juan for answers because he was, after all, the man with the microphone. He stopped singing but managed to remain on his feet, wobbling on the spot, microphone making a hollow sound as it repeatedly clunked into his bony chest. Perhaps it was really the sound of his heart. Whatever it was, it reminded him that he was still alive. When the tremors finally ended, the audience stumbled over one another and staggered off in shock, leaving Juan standing there with an empty hat that had bounced at least two metres away from his feet.

What does one do after an earthquake? One goes home, hoping to be able to sit down peacefully in one's familiar surroundings and sigh with relief, grateful to be unharmed. But as he made his way on foot from Slaughterhouse Square to the city centre, clambering over rubble and through the turmoil of the streets, he knew long before rounding the final corner, that his building was a lost cause. What chance did its charred timbers and twisted rebar have against such power? He reached into his pocket to fondle his lucky blue eye and as fortune would have it the Salvation Army was on the scene. "Well, my friend," the Salvation Army sergeant announced as he placed a hand on Juan's shoulder, "You have no choice but to abandon everything in your room. It's been crushed and lost under someone else's floor." So with just the clothes on his back and his lucky blue eye, Juan followed the kind volunteers to the Salvation Army shelter.

After more than three weeks of not much else other than sleeping on one of the cots that lined the main room of the sparse accommodation, eating two meals a day, hanging out on the streets, lounging against the walls and watching the world go by, Juan was told he'd have to leave to make room for new people in need. Either that, they said, or he could agree to don one of their Salvation Army uniforms and make himself useful by collecting funds on the sidewalks in the more fortunate east end of the city, which had not sustained much damage from the quake, and where, as the whole world knew, people had more money.

Juan opted for the uniform. He had to admit that it suited him well, the navy blue making him look taller, picking up the few remaining celestial sparks in his eyes. He arranged his hair around the collar and stood erect, chest out, buttons shining, tilting his head and smiling a crooked smile. The suit would help project his natural charm to the ladies, warm their hearts and open their wallets. He would do well with a suit like this for his act. He looked so suave, cool and sleek that he was certain his appearance alone would result in a few extra pesos being thrown into the hat at the end of one of his musical interludes.

He collected more than 18,000 pesos the first day and returned to the shelter with coins jingling in the Salvation Army pot. The next several days were about the same. But on the fifth day, the irresistible urge for a drink, coupled with the coins in the pot, got the better of him and he removed his tie and jacket, thoughtfully folding it inside out over his arm. He bought twelve boxes of wine, and settled down under the bridge where he felt obliged to share his booze with five other homeless men. They whiled away the evening, all reliving their unique experience of the quake and several times they were sent scrambling out from under the bridge by more aftershocks.

Juan returned to the Salvation Army shelter at dawn, banging on their door, crying that he had been mugged by a group of young, godforsaken delinquents who knocked him unconscious and locked him behind the gates of a liquor shop, and that it took several hours before the owner arrived to release him. The shelter volunteers ignored the stale stench of wine and gave him another chance. They served him soup and sympathy and offered him a bed for the next night. He gratefully accepted and promised to be more careful in the future. The following day he went out onto the street and produced excellent results, collecting the remarkable sum of 22,650 pesos. He managed to walk the straight and narrow for another couple of weeks, returning obediently to the shelter each evening, bounty in hand like a proud hunting dog.

But on the fourteenth night he could no longer resist temptation. Fourteen boxes of wine and two nights beyond that, and he knew the Salvation Army sergeant wouldn't believe his story again. So with a stolen X-Acto knife, he removed the Salvation Army insignias from the fine blue jacket, he spit and rubbed until the ghosts of their stitching had all but disappeared, brushed down the suit with a damp cloth, straightened the tie and went back to Slaughterhouse Square dressed in his semi-military, and he had no doubt, extremely attractive new look.

His fans, lined up hodgepodge on the wooden benches, gazed up at him as he swanked to the far end of the patio and they murmured to one another before throwing out the odd compliment. "Jhonny, you're positively dashing today. What have you done to yourself?" "Jhonny, march on over to my place!"

He rehearsed with the suit to check its ease of movement, bending a tad here and stretching a little there, being forced to hold up a hand in order to quell imaginary heavy applause that arose because of the Salvation Army vogue. He whispered under his breath as he pivoted in tight circles, his arms fluttering overhead to silence the enamoured crowd. "Thank you. You've been wonderful, as always. Don't hesitate to contribute to the cause."

It turned out that the Franklin market sector, where Slaughterhouse Square was located, had escaped the quake with a mere warning. Mother Earth had shaken her fist but had not visited her full wrath upon them. The place was electric with stories and excitement. Saved. Everyone said they must be doing something right, must have been spared for a reason. But just in case, they were all on evacuation alert, fearing one big aftershock would loosen a vital cornerstone somewhere (who knew where?) that was capable of causing it all to tumble.

Juan liked to describe Franklin as a 'less refined' sector of the city. It had its own culture, a coarse, pugnacious synergy that flowed through its veins. It was mean and bustling on the surface, but it was friendly if you knew your way around. It was home to the famous Persa Bío Bío, a market area that covered multiple city blocks with a mish-mash of stores in old, adjoining one- and two-storey brick and adobe buildings. Since the sector's awakening as a market decades earlier, it had grown like a jungle, too fertile to be contained indoors. Its merchandise sprawled and wound its way out of the narrow doors and crept out of the tall windows. Multifarious goods crawled along sidewalks and into empty lots, expanding into the spaces under tents and then reached up to display themselves from hooks and improvised hangers that had been hurriedly stabbed into walls. The market was a paradise for things – things under multiple layers and over numerous levels. As if by magic, unlikely items were pulled out from behind other even more implausible articles. Discarded products were tossed up onto roofs and into forgotten pigeonholes. It was a place for foot traffic, where delivery trucks, if they must enter at all, had to inch along behind streams of browsing pedestrians, meandering dogs and busy vendors. Narrow passageways were crammed with all nature of new and used goods from nuts and bolts, perfume, pliable two-headed dinosaurs and plush toys, machetes and rifles, live tarantulas and kittens, large appliances and autos, sandals and beach balls. Whatever you needed. If you couldn't find it elsewhere in the city, you would find it somewhere in the Persa. It was a well-known fact that an unspoken quantity of the market's products had been stolen directly off the backs of trucks on some hapless highway. But even if the authorities were so inclined, there was just too much activity to monitor.

After the quake the vendors rearranged and rebuilt their pyramids of radios, shoes and telephone parts, posters, clothing and batteries, bags and boxes of plastic toys, second-hand tools, firearms and books, ironing boards and plants, televisions and car parts, refrigerators and industrial stoves. They dusted off their hands and repositioned themselves on their tall stools, one foot on the ground for balance at one corner of their merchandise. Using a long, hooked pole they jumped up to snag anything you showed the slightest bit of interest in, holding it up to detain you while they rattled off sales spiels about why you couldn't live without it. Persa Bío Bío, always open for business.

At the curbs, delivery men in oversized, stained jogging pants and too-tight t-shirts over spongy paunches slept across their sloped, dual-wheeled wooden carts until someone whistled and, like firemen called to an emergency, they jumped awake. Piling furniture and appliances onto their planks on wheels, they danced like ballerinas between sleeping dogs and street sellers down roads and around corners. Vendors threw up their arms and yelled at each other; music blasted out of every entrance; an auctioneer shot words into his microphone, pulling in curious browsers; fruit sellers with portable wagons stopped to weigh bags of fresh fruit on their fraudulent scales, blues buskers against red brick walls wailed out tunes, young boys scuffled with each other here and there as pretty girls stood by, ready to take the arm of the winner; a family of chinchineros (street drummers) danced – twirling and jumping to the beat of the drums and cymbals on their backs; men with the Polaroids stood beside haughty llamas who batted long eyelashes from behind bright green and pink tassels; puppies scrambled to escape cardboard box prisons as their owners quickly snatched pesos offered in exchange for 'giving away' their pets.

Persa Bío Bío was the kind of place where you could conveniently lose yourself between countless stalls and passageways that spidered off the main streets but it was relatively easy to find your friends if you knew where to look. Both things made it the perfect hangout for a guy like Juan Bonifacio Maluenda-Valdéz. His place of business was Slaughterhouse Square, the plaza with a gazebo behind the old meat packing plant. Over the years it had morphed into an informal performance stage for washed-up singers who were down on their luck and in need of a drink. In general it attracted the same class of fans – their glory days either a thing of the ancient past or nothing but dreams for future greatness bottled in cheap wine.

Juan took turns singing to the background music of the karaoke system shared by the performers. He appeared in sets between the likes of Roger, who sang old romantic tunes made famous by Charles Aznavour, Marlen who had a Mexican ranchera act, the gay Ramirez Duo who were favourites with their flamboyant performance, which included tossing metallic confetti from their pockets so it fluttered into the faces of adoring patrons, and Lizbet who purred like a kitten between stanzas. There were others on weekends. Sometimes the regular performers got lucky and booked wedding gigs or community parties, leaving an opportunity at the plaza for less-known artists to step up and show their stuff. The truth is that most of the performers at Slaughterhouse Square were extraordinarily gifted individuals and if you were lucky enough to catch them on a good day, you would be entertained like a king for the price of a peso.

Juan was not a bad person; his lot was simply the accumulation of a series of unfortunate events. For years he had coasted along in survival mode believing that one day his luck would change. Over the last couple of decades his life revolved around crony has-beens and up-and-coming karaoke artists at the plaza. He tried not to dwell on the sharp, downward spiral in which he was captive and he managed (for the most part) to drink himself into a state of ignorant bliss. He was, however, capable of a certain discipline when it came to singing, especially on weekends. These were the most profitable periods. He liked to be at the plaza for both the money and the camaraderie. After their gigs, he and his fellow performers partied late into the night. During weekdays they all took it easy, doing whatever came naturally whenever the spirit moved them.

Jesica, whose car Juan now sat in outside of the cemetery, was one of the plaza regulars. She used to sing but found her true calling as technical support, operating the karaoke machine, burning and organising CDs for sale, ensuring the sound system was in working order. Juan and Jesica had a fling and he even called her his girlfriend once, but for how long he couldn't remember. The affair blew itself out naturally, coming to a mutually satisfactory end when they intuitively followed different drinking partners. No hard feelings.

The one thing Jesica still had that Juan sometimes needed, and that she occasionally conceded, was her mustard-coloured Volvo Amazon. She had inherited it from her father along with his little house. The car was her father's prized possession and he would have sooner let the house go up in flames than let someone scratch his Volvo. So Jesica hung onto it tooth and nail, never once being tempted to sell it for a fortune worth of wine. 'The tank' came in handy to haul speakers, CDs and an accumulation of sound equipment, some of which had been in the trunk so long she thought it was part of the car body. She sometimes rented out the tank and spent the extra money on tasselled and sequined Saturday night outfits. Everyone at Slaughterhouse Square, by fair means or foul, made ends meet, and in comparison, Jesica was a successful businesswoman.

Juan promised to pay Jesica for the use of her car today. He told her that he had suddenly remembered where there were a few valuable family heirlooms and that she could take her pick when he returned, which would be the next day, since it was an overnight trip. The truth was that he didn't need to drive far, but the errand would take time – perhaps a day and a night. It wouldn't have been necessary at all if Jesica would have allowed him to stay at her house.

At the best of times, Jesica's house was packed like a can of sardines with Slaughterhouse Square regulars, but during these days in which the earth shook under their feet and people were forced to flee from between their own walls, there was neither a spare place on the floor nor enough room to hang one more hammock.

After he failed as a Salvation Army resident, and given the crowded circumstances at Jesica's, Juan managed to charm Mario, who ran a small restaurant at the edge of Slaughterhouse Square, into providing him with a blanket and a spot on his living room floor. Mario's hospitality lasted less than two weeks because Juan's raucous, late-night arrivals and the rancid smell of wine permeated the little house and over-saturated Mario's wife's patience, who threatened to throw them both out on their ears if Mario didn't do something about it.

So here he was, outside the cemetery – his last chance – absently watching a short, stout woman as she disappeared beyond the gates. Juan took a long drag of the cigarette, sucking the last bit of flavour out of it. "Bless you Mario, it was a pleasure." He tossed the butt out the window and gathered his wits for his approach to the cemetery guard. He knew that he would need permission to enter under the current health restrictions.

He had no trouble convincing the cemetery guard that he had legitimate business in a family mausoleum somewhere on Patio 46. This was mostly because of his rather fine, new navy blue suit and tie, and a skeleton key that he withdrew from his pocket as evidence of a right to enter a door somewhere. The guard checked his map and confirmed that Patio 46 had not suffered much damage, gracias a Diós. "And here, exactly here," he pointed with military precision to a spot on his map, is the location of the Maluenda-Valdéz family tomb. Am I right, Señor?"

"Yes, absolutely. That's the one," said Juan. He breathed a heavy sigh of relief and fingered the lucky blue eye in his pocket as he looked up to the heavens. The guard whistled and a one-legged cemetery guide in a heavy blue smock and a white mask over his face emerged from the shadows of the same shack. He handed Juan a mask, indicating with a hand that had only three fingers that Juan had to put it on before they could proceed.

Juan followed him in silence. Clutching the skeleton key inside one pocket and his lucky blue eye in the other, he beat out a rhythm in his head in time to the click-clack of the crutches and the flopping pant-leg, which was loosely pinned around the man's stump. The one-legged guide turned around four times to ensure Juan was keeping pace.

Juan had come across the skeleton key under a bench at Slaughterhouse Square the day before, just after he received the unfortunate news that he was no longer welcome to sleep on Mario's living room floor. Fingering the old key, the cogs in his head slowly began to turn. It reminded him of something. It wasn't the key to the mausoleum, but it could be. He immediately formulated a plan to take advantage of an almost legitimate family refuge. He kissed the key. It could possibly become a second lucky talisman.

"I understand entirely and without reservation, your desire to be left alone at your family tomb, Señor," said the one-legged guide. His eyes misted over. "I guess it's been a long time. But don't worry. These souls escaped the tumult of our recent disaster." He gave him a three-finger salute and clacked away down the path leaving Juan to slyly pull the wire cutter out from his trouser waistband and open the mausoleum door. He stepped inside and looked around.

There was less space than Juan remembered. He hadn't been here since he was a boy and childhood memories always made things appear larger. The walls to the left and right of the wrought iron gated entrance were lined with built-in crypts, stacked four-high, floor to ceiling. He didn't know who was buried in them. No doubt they were great-uncles and aunts of whom he had no memory, let alone sentimental attachment. His grandfather, the family patriarch, was entombed under the marble altar on the back wall. His name carved in elegant letters reminded Juan that he was born into privilege. He pursed his lips and exhaled in a semi-whistle. The privilege had long since been squandered.

On top of the altar was a tall crystal vase, its expensive cut still obvious through the years of dust and neglect. Two brittle, barren rose stems leaned out of it. Clinging to the altar at a sad angle was a soiled, yellowed cloth with appliquéd edges. He remembered it had belonged to his sister, who donated it to the family crypt when their father died. His sister, now dead and buried too, was in the basement along with his parents. Colours from the stained glass window on the back wall streamed across the altar. A couple of panes were shattered allowing scant yellow rays of sunlight to warm the shoulders of a small bronze statue of the Virgin Mary that sat opposite the vase. He noted the brushed silver urn in the floor near his grandfather's tomb but couldn't recall whose ashes it contained. Outside of several distant cousins, Juan was the lone surviving member of his clan; there was no one left who could inform him about the ashes. Juan had allowed the mausoleum to fall into decay when he stopped paying a caretaker more than 20 years ago and he didn't remember the urn being there then. He felt a twinge of guilt for his lack of responsibility. But just a small one. He decided the urn contained the ashes of an unrelated person, someone who needed a free place to rest, a squatter like himself, a kindred spirit.

 The trap door to the basement level was as he remembered. He bent down and tugged on the brass ring until the old door creaked open. He threw it back and gaped into the underground darkness, then pulled out some matches and crawled down the sturdy wooden ladder until he reached the concrete surface below. His family's private catacombs. The walls were lined with tombs here too, and there was one with his name on it. Bless his mother for always being prepared. He shivered. She had really outdone herself. She had always vowed that the family would remain together. She had made it as pleasant a dungeon as possible. The tomb façades were marble and the floor had been painted dark green with specially treated chemicals to protect against the damp. There was enough space down here for a narrow mattress and a box of clothes, maybe even a small bedside table. He circled around slowly, nodding to himself with satisfaction. This would do nicely as long as the trap door allowed for a bit of fresh air. He'd have to arrange a wooden frame for the mattress. It might also be possible to make minimal use of the upstairs if he could pull it off inconspicuously. He smiled, content, and he dared to imagine a small portable radio or maybe even a miniature TV with antennae. He wondered what sort of reception they got in this neighbourhood. He'd have to pirate electricity from one of the cables that ran along the wide path leading to the crematorium, but anything was possible. It was just a question of getting around to it.

Unfortunately, rather than a solid door, his mother had chosen an ornate wrought iron entrance gate, which allowed a virtually unobstructed view of the main floor. But if he placed a box and cloth there for odds and ends, it would simply be shrugged off as some sort of family idiosyncrasy. No matter, it would work out. He turned in slow circles on the spot, nodding and grinning with satisfaction.

Astrid didn't see Juan Bonifacio make his entrance to the mausoleum that day and she didn't notice when he walked back down the path towards the cemetery gate. She was oblivious of his gift of a few peso coins, which the guard at the gate accepted with a sideways smile and a discreet nod. She wasn't aware that he returned ten minutes later with a boxful of CDs, two blankets, a pillow and a worn leather case. She didn't know that he attached a new padlock to the iron gate of the Maluenda-Valdéz family mausoleum and that he left the grounds with a crystal vase and brushed silver urn packed in a ragged cardboard box.

CHAPTER 4

The Aftermath

Astrid yanked at the weeds that flourished alongside the lovely but rarely visited mausoleum of the Cruz-Lopez family. By mid afternoon, the premonition about good things to come had dissipated and the contentment from that morning had disappeared along with it. She felt irritable without being able to identify the source of her disgruntlement. Señora Ruby had gone off to conduct a vase-making workshop, taking all of their glass coca-cola bottles and leaving the shed in disarray after rummaging the shelves for plastic flowers and recycled ribbon. Maybe that was the problem. More unnecessary mess in the midst of her dishevelled life. Now nearly three months since the quake, she was still trying to find where things belonged. She felt she had been uprooted. Sometimes the ground still swayed under her feet and she experienced a feeling of seasickness. She identified it as such even though she had never seen a real boat, much less sailed on one. She questioned whether it was indeed a light aftershock or simply a psychological leftover and she decided she would never know.

Astrid gave up on the weeds, pulled the garden hose around and just stood there like any other zombie in a cemetery, water trickling out over the vines. The sound quietened her anxiety somewhat and she allowed her mind to wander.

A week after the disaster, Susana her overweight neighbour had rolled down the street wearing a sweater with sleeves that stretched far beyond her hands, so that she flapped her way through the air like an albatross unable to take flight, announcing that only 61 people had died and most of the 720 injured were given a positive prognosis. "Gracias a

Diós the quake hit in the morning when people were awake and able to escape in the daylight." What Susana didn't optimistically bellow out was that, according to the news reports, the quake had registered 7.7 on the Richter scale and this part of the city had been particularly hard-hit.

But Astrid measured it by degrees of heartache and wondered how much a heart could withstand before it shattered and caved in.

Walking home the morning of the quake, she could see that the destruction had been random. There was no obvious pattern. It struck at the weakest points. That was all. There was no why or wherefore. It was not selective sabotage. No payback for miserable sinners; no sanction for saints. No justice in earthquakes. Maybe some places were more vulnerable because of their cobbled together add-ons or rough construction but that was not their fault. Where there was no money, you had to cut corners. And at some weak points where the earth jarred and forced and cranked harder than in others, even more solid structures had been destroyed.

When she arrived at her own door, Astrid was afraid to face what was inside. So she turned her back and looked at what lay in front of her house. Directly across the street, appearing through a blanket of dust was a jagged chunk of Señor Sanchez's blue wall that had come to rest outside his door. His yellow metal sign squeaked back and forth from a rusty nail in the bottom corner so the words, "Tire repair" read upside down. On the street, a red car had sunk through the asphalt and only its roof remained above ground. Astrid dared not look inside the vehicle. The neighbour's gate had been wrenched from its hinges and now pierced the ground in her front garden. Bricks from the wall were helter-skelter. The water had stopped running now, but the odour of damp earth, plywood and cement and the pungent stench from sewage testified to broken pipes. Frightened chickens, dogs, cats and rats scurried in and out of the rubble, unable to find safe harbour from the continuing frequent tremors.

Astrid stopped breathing for an unknown length of time and the fierce beating of her heart rocked her back and forth as she leaned into her skewed doorjamb. She bent forward and vomited onto her shoes and then laid her cheek against the wooden frame and stood, knees locked, body rigid, and cried without knowing she was crying. That's how her son Hector found her.

Some time later (Astrid wasn't sure how long), her daughter Constancia jumped out of the back of a taxi. She was shaking and crying as she ran towards Hector's ample arms and the three of them stood leaning into one another for support.

Like the majority of her neighbours, for the first two nights Astrid, Constancia and Hector lay on mattresses they had dragged out onto the sidewalks in front of their house. Not much sleep was had.

On the third day, the sun rose, marking the resurrection of life in the neighbourhood in spite of the continuing aftershocks, some of which were almost as strong as the quake itself. Astrid's small house seemed to have found its balance on the warped ground and on the third night she would sleep in her own bed, teetering as it might on the floor, within the cracked walls of her room. I

t had already been decided that Hector and Constancia would sleep there with her – everyone together for safety's sake. They agreed unreservedly that the family should either all die under the weight of the roof in the event of a strong aftershock or they should all live to celebrate together.

Constancia, now 28 and Hector, 33, were products of her youthful marriage to the organ grinder. Astrid had seen to it that the organ grinder wound out his last tune under their roof more than twelve years ago. In his absence Constancia, Hector and Astrid stood together, each one being essential to the balance and well being of the others. As the youngest, Constancia was the most dependent, the least easily appeased and one could even say that she was spoiled. Thus Astrid and Hector, perhaps underestimating Constancia, bore most of the weight.

Constancia spent the interminable first day of the resurrection in childish outbursts until Hector grabbed her by the shoulders. "For God's sake, Cona, pull yourself together. Grow up. Do you see us flying into a tantrum with every broken bit of glass we find?"

She let out a wail but he had no pity. "Por Diós, shut up. Quit crying. Things can't get any worse. Just clean up so we can move ahead. Nobody else is going to put this place back together for us." He turned her around brusquely and pointed her towards the kitchen.

Constancia shuffled forward, her wails diminishing to soft whimpers as she resumed the cleanup in slow motion, piling waste into corners, occasionally jumping back to allow cockroaches to scurry across her path into a dark crack.

Astrid ignored the commotion as she surveyed and prepared to attack the shambles in her bedroom. She tried to avoid thinking of him, but the organ grinder pushed his way into her thoughts because the last time a quake had disturbed their house, he had been there. After the safety of the children, their biggest concern had been for his wooden organ on wheels and the small inventory of related products that they stored beside it in the far corner. She remembered the boxes of colourful pinwheels, plastic moulded toys and hard, tasteless candy that were spared when a roof panel fell and came to rest above them, between the wardrobe and the floor. The organ and its contents were scratched and dusty but otherwise intact.

She still could not bear to pronounce the organ grinder's Christian name, which she tried to forget was 'Jaime.' He pushed his colourful wooden music box, children's pinwheels, flags, plastic toys and candies out the door and onto the street for the last time after she confirmed that he had been grinding more than just his handcrafted music box.

Astrid had not considered herself an unattractive woman nor had she been an unreasonable, overly demanding wife. She was a diamond in the rough and even now, after all these years, she knew that in spite of not being cut and polished, she had a certain, special sparkle. She had been satisfied with what the organ grinder offered on all accounts and assumed he had been also. But she was wrong. Life with her had not been exciting or melodic enough. Perhaps after 23 years of marriage, life was simply too serene and ordinary and the organ grinder had a desire to spice up his end a little bit, like when he decided to put a new paper music roll into his box because he'd listened to the old tune too many times. Since organ grinders were known to be mostly tone-deaf, it was surprising that he paid attention to the current song at all, let alone be inspired to change it. And this is what made his infidelity all the more painful. During all that time, Astrid assumed he was satisfied with her tune. His desire to exchange her for a new set of notes or even to add something to his repertoire (where she had rightfully taken her place as his one and only song) was not only heartbreaking, but a shock. In all her years with the man, she had not seen it coming.

But rumours about him had begun to drift past her on the street, and although they made her ears involuntarily perk up and a small stew begin to cook in her head, she didn't want to stir the pot. It was only when she was presented with undeniable physical evidence that she decided to turn up the heat.

One day, young Lidia's unique, perfumed, hand-painted rose scarf turned up in the organ grinder's suit pocket. It was the same day that Astrid encountered a long chestnut-red hair wound possessively around his shirt collar. Jaime had brushed it off as hair from a horse's tail but Astrid quite unexpectedly put two and two together when she made a trip to the bakery that same afternoon.

As Astrid approached Lidia, who stood nonchalantly at her post by the scale behind the counter, she detected a strikingly familiar perfume drifting over from Lidia's vicinity, conspicuous above the natural aroma of freshly baked bread. Well-known for her constant whining, which Astrid had come to ignore, this morning Lidia was droning on as usual as she absently placed the buns on the scale. She was fussing about how she had misplaced her favourite hand-painted scarf. Normally Astrid would murmur something sympathetic but the mention of the scarf assaulted her like a missile finding its mark and when she looked up at Lidia, who was tucking a stray lock of long chestnut-red hair under her cap, Astrid felt that missile explode in her chest. She was unable to offer the babbling girl so much as the hint of a wave before she turned and left the shop and she didn't hear Lidia call after her sarcastically, "And thank you too."

She marched home and ordered the organ grinder to accompany her to the bakery, where she loudly accused the two of them in front of a long queue of customers waiting to weigh their bread for afternoon tea. Her discourse was short but penetrating. Words such as "shameless" and "unfaithful," were the warm-up, followed by "whore," "son-of-a-bitch," "sons of the devil" and "stinking, disgusting, pieces of evil animal shit." The customers were delighted with the unexpected entertainment and rushed home to serve the gossip for dessert. Astrid turned on her heel, the organ grinder's ear twisted firmly between thumb and forefinger and she announced to Lidia over her shoulder that the organ grinder would be back within the hour with all of his music. On the road back to their house, he first pleaded innocence and then realising she wasn't going to buy it he begged forgiveness. Curious neighbours appeared one at a time outside their front doors as the couple passed by, Astrid marching like a soldier to war, her eyes not veering from the horizon and the organ grinder scurrying around her in circles, imploring her to listen. But Astrid was firm in her resolve. She could see no other choice but to have him gone. She stonily crammed his clothes into two large paper bags with twine handles and pushed him out into the street, followed by his music on wheels. As it turned out, apparently Lidia wouldn't have him either. Word was that she moved to another community to live with her aunt. Whatever happened, she was never seen again.

Every so often over the weeks that followed the organ grinder showed up and knocked meekly on the door, begging to be allowed to return. But Astrid silently double-locked it and closed her curtains without acknowledging him. After several months he stopped asking. She cried herself to sleep each night long after he stopped appearing but during the day she attended to household chores, fussed over Constancia and Hector, performed her caretaker duties at the cemetery, and no one ever knew how shattered she really was. She developed a thick, outer shell. That was when her heart, already weak, transferred some of its malady to her outermost organ; her skin began to dry and it took on a grey tinge, her fingernails became brittle and the ends of her hair split and broke off. The light from within flickered and waned and her eyes lost their earlier intensity.

That was a lifetime ago. As if coming out of a trance, Astrid turned and picked up the large jagged piece of the bedroom mirror that the earth had shaken free and that she planned to salvage for use until some extra money fell from the sky. She tilted the irregular shape to reflect her face, then her torso and so on, down to her feet. Her dark eyes looked back at themselves, somewhat tired but still kind. She noticed the deepening crows' feet at their outer corners. More than telling her age, they testified to a propensity for laughter and she didn't mind that. If anything, it was her skin that exposed her 53 years. Having never recovered its youthful glow, it now looked sallow. She wouldn't have been defined as beautiful and maybe not even pretty, but her features were pleasant enough – a round face with plump lips ready with a smile and a small dot of a nose that wriggled involuntarily when she was amused. Her shoulder-length hair that she habitually pulled back into a bun at the nape of her neck had surprisingly few grey hairs, saving her the decision of whether or not to do without lunch a couple of times a week in order to pay for hair dye. She liked to wear long earrings that jingled when she moved or giant hoops that tickled her neck. This type of accessory had become just as much a part of her persona as her socks and leather loafers.

Astrid could not be considered petite because her short stature gave the impression of carrying extra weight even though she was not fat. This was accented by her movements, which over the past couple of years, had stiffened around her hips making her waddle a bit side-to-side. Years ago her doctor told her that she had a mild arrhythmia and recommended a diet light in salt and fat, but she found it hard to comply because of lifelong habits as well as limited income, which did not allow for 'healthy' considerations. Therefore, she carried on as usual, reassured by the fact that her work provided her with plenty of fresh air and exercise.

She tilted the mirror to look at her feet. She loved her feet. She kept them safe within woollen socks, and stuffed them into protective leather loafers. She was so careful that she rarely wore pantyhose with dress shoes and never, ever wore open-toed sandals. The skin on her feet was finer than that of her hands, which unavoidably grew more and more calloused and chapped as she toiled. She took pleasure in rubbing her feet when she climbed into bed at night not only because the massage was pleasant but also because her feet were the only real virgin territory left on her body. Although they had taken her thousands of miles back and forth through pathways, stepped on the same stairs that had been used generations ago for purposes both good and evil, her feet had retained their virtue and innocence.

Astrid carefully leaned the jagged chunk of mirror against the wall on the back of her antique dressing table. She caressed the surface of the table and thought about her mother, who had survived the big earthquake of 1985. This house had been damaged during that earlier quake and the scars, having never really disappeared, would now be buried under these fresh wounds. Her mother had chastised the organ grinder for being such a wimp in the face of the disaster and stopped short of telling Astrid, "I told you so." From the moment Astrid first introduced him, her mother judged him as a lazy sort with an eye for pretty women. Astrid's mother was a good judge of character, bragging that she had seen so many of them, both dead and alive, that she was seldom mistaken. But Astrid was head over heels, convinced this was one of the few times her mother was wrong. In the end, it was a blessing that her mother didn't live to see that she had been right. Under the circumstances, there was little satisfaction in it. Today Astrid longed for her, yearned to hear her voice reminding them there would be a reward at the end of the day, imagined her calling them to the table for a cup of tea and some fresh bread. Her mother would bow her head, say a brief word of thanks and then would waste no time initiating gossip about the neighbours, inserting dry, witty quips in order to make them laugh and take their minds off their own immediate troubles and the fact that they had no meat. Astrid was sad for the loss of her mother, for the loss of her home such as it was, for the loss of her Patio 62. But she thought about Hector and Constancia and wouldn't allow herself to heed the call of a pending dark depression that the earthquake had brought to her door, lest it swallow her up.

Like Señora Ruby, she had inherited the caretaker post from her mother and for all intents and purposes, she had been raised in the General Cemetery. What else was there? As a toddler, her little feet pattered across the sacred ground behind her mother, lifting the garden hose over small bushes and trying to help as she sprinkled patches of dry earth in front of someone's tomb, frolicked with the kittens, danced in and out between the crosses, played hide and seek behind tombstones, raked dry leaves, discovered lost treasure. She picked wild flowers and stuck them behind her ears, talked to the stone faces that were carved in tall statues and sidled up to visitors at the altar of the Poor Christ, watching them bend down to light candles. She stood silently, hands held in prayer, staring into the flames and wondered what the visitors were talking to Jesus about and if he was paying attention. She held private conversations with photos of the deceased, making friends with children her own age who had left this world to live in heaven. Even during her failed marriage to the organ grinder, she hadn't travelled far from these walls. Their house was only minutes from the cemetery and everything she needed could be found between here and there. Astrid knew there was another world out there somewhere. She'd seen some of it on TV. But she didn't need to venture into it.

Her hopes for Constancia to apprentice under her had to be abandoned when she realised that Constancia had an unhealthy fear of the dead. Instead Constancia helped with promotions and sales in a small clothing shop in a commercial sector known as El Patronato, only a short bus ride from home. Now Astrid would have no family to follow in her footsteps and her patch of the cemetery was destined to be inherited by a stranger.

Her son Hector, who never had illusions about being an organ grinder like his father, or a cemetery caretaker like herself, had used his own ingenuity to get a good job in the tourism trade. He left the house to go downtown each morning dressed in a suit and tie. She was proud of him. Her disappointment in the fact that neither child followed in her footsteps eventually dissipated when she saw how satisfied they both were with their lives.

She and Hector and Constancia spent the days immediately following the quake, clearing a path through their house and hauling rubble to the front gate. Most of the furniture, except for three light chairs and two shelves, was salvageable. Dishes, windows, and porcelain ornaments fell, exploded, or were shattered on the patched linoleum and oiled wooden floor. Curtain rods were bent, ceiling panels had given way, great patches of plaster had fallen off the walls, and finally bricks crumbled to expose pipes and wiring and the interior of adjoining neighbours' rooms. At first glance, the damage to the floors was minimal, but just as in washing dry blood from a wound, the extent of the injury made itself known with a little more cleaning. They found two large sinkholes under the floor – one in the living room and one in the main hallway. Romanticising about something clandestine, Constancia mused that the hollows were the remains of ancient escape tunnels but Hector said that was an outlandish theory. Perhaps then, they had been used as hideouts for drug runners. Putting a damper on her notions, Hector reminded her that this had been their grandmother's house, and great-grandmother's before that. The holes, he said, were simply left over from an old piping system. The immediate solution was just as unremarkable as the problem itself – some salvaged lumber and a couple of throw rugs.

Water and electricity service to the neighbourhood had been fully restored. Hector appeared one day with cement and yellow paint and they patched up and repainted the exterior walls. Constancia and Astrid hung pictures in strategic locations and arranged furniture to mask superficial damage that could wait for another day, knowing full well that it would probably remain in the same state for her lifetime. The roof was patched and might leak in the winter but they would deal with that if and when it happened. For now, their place was holding together. Bright patches of hope.

Her house, like the neighbours', was still ailing and torn, but everyone knocked things back into place, improvising, invoking good humour to help see past the lopsided walls and caved-in streets. They made jokes about the disaster, teasing Siete Pelos while admiring his new signage. They nudged elbows and forced a smile out of rotund María, who, all her life, had fainted on the spot at the first sign of a tremor. They said she would be assigned the duty of filling the holes that she, herself created on the sidewalk every time she fainted and they told her that if the municipality caught wind of this, she would be charged with filling in all of the potholes on the entire street. When she laughed, her two oversized front teeth appeared from behind her upper lip and she crossed her arms good-naturedly under her ample, bouncing bosom.

The neighbourhood was wounded, and would remain so for years. Damaged roofs here and there, tilted sidewalks, never-repaired fences, flimsy walls thrown up out of immediate necessity, some last-minute rubble piled at street corners – these would all remain forever and become part of the everyday landscape. Children born after the earthquake would never know the neighbourhood had once been more orderly. They would grow up playing between the disfigured walls, hiding behind mounds of cement chunks and throwing garbage into wide crevices – never questioning the reason for the existence of such landmarks. They would not know the nightmares that woke their parents. Nor would they see the scars that healed over their souls. Everything was covered with humour and the desire to forget.

Astrid brought her thoughts back to the present and, rounding the mausoleum, she saw that Señora Ruby had returned from her workshop and was leaning back in her chair in front of her shack, mouth hanging open, eyes closed. She snored into the music from the radio. Astrid tugged the hose and considered a light-hearted spray in Señora Ruby's direction but thought better of it for fear of stopping the old lady's heart. Not knowing when it had happened, Astrid realised that her hours of discontent had vanished. She stood still, a half-smile on her face, water from the hose carelessly splashing into the low foliage at her feet as she surveyed the patch of ground she now shared with the kind old soul who was sleeping in the sun.

CHAPTER 5

The Other Side of the Coin

It rarely rained in October. At this time of year, the sun generously dispersed his rays across the cloudless atmosphere, transforming it to pure sky blue from here to forever. Except for the occasional feathery white trail of a jet, there was a clear view to the heavens, and prayers travelled first-class, non-stop, from the sacred grounds of the cemetery to the saints who lounged at the impeccably manicured perimeters of the heavens beyond.

But this afternoon held an extraordinary surprise. Heavy clouds blew in from the west and the sun, suddenly rendered impotent by the stubborn winds, cowered away as the skies darkened and it began to rain. At first, it pattered down slowly, a random heavy drop landing here or there on a leaf and then on the sidewalk. The frequency and rhythm gradually built up – patter, patter became splat, splat, splat – and Astrid could see it wasn't just a small spring shower that was toying with them but a freak cloudburst that meant business. She rushed to help Señora Ruby coil the garden hose and close up the tool shack just as it began to pour down in sheets.

From the steps of the Gomez family mausoleum, under the protection of thick rubber tree leaves tangled with magenta bougainvillea that wound over to the roof, the two of them huddled together and listened to the rhythmic sound of the world lost under rain. Astrid thought it was beautiful and said so to Señora Ruby, who agreed with silent nods, her dark eyes, wide, slowly scanning the panorama from beneath the foliage. Mesmerised, it was almost an hour before they exchanged another word.

And then all that was said was, "It's beautiful, isn't it?" "Yes, and refreshing too." The rain continued. It was magic.

Quiet streams materialised at the edges of passageways and joined into others along the main path, forming miniature rivers with wild currents that flushed leaves and small pebbles to secret destinations. Captivated, the two women watched the drops, watched the rivers, watched the heavens above and waited for the sunlight that they expected would stream through holes in the sky's dark mantle to bestow rich green shrubbery, lone palms and wet marble staircases with fresh golden promises and fluorescent dreams. But the sun's capacity was limited that afternoon.

The rain didn't stop but it diminished in intensity as the drops continued to fall over the valley, sometimes augmented by short, ferocious bursts that cascaded across the roofs and the tangled cemetery jungle before settling back into a steady, beating rhythm. It persisted all afternoon.

Finally Señora Ruby sighed and prepared to go home. She tied a motley collection of plastic bags around her body and over her shoes, transforming herself into an extemporaneous waterproof package, and slowly slopped through the rippling pathways towards the gate. Astrid said she would stay late to do a revision of the patio before leaving for the night. She adored the rain, especially when it caught them off guard as it had today. The patio smelled of fecund soil and fresh flowers. She could almost taste the green shoots that would unfurl with newborn grace amongst the moss at the edges of the darkest walls.

Astrid scrounged around and found a large garbage bag to pull over her shoulders. Ripping a hole for her head but leaving her arms tucked inside, she set off in this plastic straight jacket to patrol the patio. Except for the music of the rain, the place was deathly quiet. The sky was unusually dark for this time of day. But it smelled of tranquillity and she took pleasure in it. This was a perfect opportunity to wander beyond her usual perimeter, to explore patios outside of her responsibility, something she hadn't done for years, and certainly not since the earthquake. She would become reacquainted with the state of things in this rejuvenated world awash with surprise and hope.

As Astrid squished around the northwest corner of Patio 46, she skidded and fell on the muddy passageway. One elbow pierced the plastic bag and she rolled onto her back, large drops of rain falling onto her face. She yelped when the pain shot through her arm, across her shoulders and up her neck, after which she was forced to remain sprawled on the ground, moaning, one elbow jutting out of the bag and the other arm still tucked inside. Unable to move, she squeezed her eyes shut and listened as soft raindrops danced across her plastic exterior before sliding down and dripping into the puddle beside her. She would lie there and allow her muscles to rest before attempting to move again. As she blinked up into the sky, the drops eventually won out over her lids, forcing them to stay closed. A fog filled her head and made her woozy. She opened her mouth to drink a few drops of rainwater but it didn't help and the agony caused her to faint sooner rather than later. So she laid in the puddle, wet from top to bottom, her head resting on a small pile of leaves accumulating at the edge of a ferocious little eddy. She lay absolutely still and could have easily been mistaken for one of the cemetery's own misplaced bodies or lost souls, something shaken up by the quake and overlooked.

When she opened her eyes a few seconds later (or several minutes, or maybe even hours later – she couldn't be sure) she saw the unmistakeable figure of Jhonny Pretty rippling past her beyond the sheets of rain. The cascading water between them warped his image but his face was clear enough for her to identify. He glided silently over the watery path only about three metres from where she lay and he disappeared around the corner. Perhaps she was dreaming. Astrid swooned like a soaked schoolgirl, her eyes involuntarily closing once more for who-knows-how-long and she thought about Jhonny.

Jhonny Pretty and his band of Rockeros had disappeared from the face of the earth after their epic popularity in the 1970s. She still had vinyl copies of all of his songs – 'This is the Moment of Forever ' and 'Softly,' two of his big chart-toppers as well as a mountain of his mediocre sellers, which for Astrid were all phenomenal hits because Jhonny Pretty had the most spectacularly sexy voice in history.

She recalled the day more than twenty years ago when she first heard the tragic news about Jhonny Pretty. Susana had knocked her over when Astrid was latching her front gate on the way to work. Susana, the fierce gossip whose rubber ears stretched around the neighbourhood (they said her capacity was beyond measure) and who was unable to contain for more than three seconds even the tiniest tidbit of news, was bursting with something big. That morning she was carried away by her own heavy inertia, knees unable to hold her back, giving out along the slow downward grade towards Astrid's gate. Gaining speed at a dangerous rate, she finally rolled violently into Astrid, sending them both sprawling onto the sidewalk.

Susana, who was of short stature and weighed no less than 90 kilos, had never been a thin or dainty child and Astrid instinctively had pity on her mother because she couldn't help envisioning the day of Susana's birth. Perhaps that was why her mother, named 'Oy, Me Dolió' ("Ouch, that hurt") a quiet woman of medium height, wore an expression of perpetual pain. Apparently, upon delivering her huge baby girl, the midwife nicknamed Susana's mother 'Oy, me Dolió,' and since then her given name became a thing of the deep past.

That day, more than two decades ago, when Susana knocked her off her feet and before they could even get back up and brush themselves off, Susana was waving her arms, trumpeting to everyone within earshot about the terrible bus accident. Jhonny Pretty and his band of Rockeros were gravely, probably even fatally injured on a road near a small town out of Valparaiso and there was little chance they would survive! The whole country was devastated. That night Astrid heard the news repeated on the radio, the reporter himself apologising for breaking down in tears as he read the unthinkable. "Excuse me, listeners, for my obvious emotion, but this is too much to bear, let alone to report. Excuse me while I cry." The silence across the airwaves was peppered with soft squeaks and a few deep sobs and then after several seconds he continued his lament.

But a couple of weeks later, the story mysteriously went cold as they sometimes do and, like the Rockeros themselves, it simply died away. Astrid stayed tuned, but nothing followed. Months passed and even Susana had no news. So she speculated and finally stated unequivocally that Jhonny Pretty and his Rockeros had agonised for months before God invited them to pass through the gates of heaven. No doubt their families wanted to avoid a public spectacle (Susana assumed this was because the bodies were terribly disfigured) and Jhonny was entombed with his parents, sister and a couple of aunts and uncles who were already resident in the family mausoleum at the General Cemetery. One of Susana's acquaintances had seen his name on a tomb in the basement level of the Maluenda-Valdéz mausoleum.

Eventually, even Astrid could no longer resist the truth and she allowed herself to mourn Jhonny Pretty. She visited his family mausoleum, an elegant structure that resembled a tiny chapel. She tied a bunch of carnations to the wrought iron entrance with a carefully hand-written note that said simply, "Rest in peace, Jhonny. You will never be forgotten." Of course, over the years, she had grown to accept his fate, but she still questioned God's logic in depriving the world of this incredible talent at such a young age. Although she rarely visited, if she ever did happen to just pass by, she crossed herself and whispered, "May the Virgin watch over you." She had never been lucky enough to happen upon it when the mausoleum was unlocked, but Señora Ruby confirmed what Susana's friend had seen. Yes, indeed Jhonny's name was on a tomb in the basement.

And now Astrid had just seen his ghost. Her eyes popped wide open at the stunning realisation. Leaning on her bruised elbow and then using her other hand to punch through the makeshift rainwear, she twisted her torso and planted both palms on the slippery path to try to get to her feet. With her heavy, rain-soaked loafers sliding over the muddy surface, which itself moved in solid steams underfoot, she took baby steps towards where Jhonny Pretty had disappeared. She lost her balance a few times, teetering above puddles that bubbled like a fresh mud stew. Rain continued to penetrate the tree canopies, bouncing off the steeply angled roofs of mausoleums, and pelting directly to the ground. Her view was obscured by the torrent but she thought she saw Jhonny Pretty move in front of a flickering light inside the Maluenda-Valdéz family mausoleum. As if she wasn't already soaked to the bone, a cold wave of regret for not visiting this mausoleum more often over the years washed over her and she shivered. She had gotten caught up in her own small, everyday concerns and had neglected to pay him the respect he was due. She berated herself, especially considering how conveniently close his resting place was to Señora Ruby's Patio.

One controlled step after the next, she advanced across the mud, the crinkling sound of her now ripped and useless plastic outerwear, muffled by the rain. She eased closer and stepped up to the back wall of the mausoleum, peering through the broken stained glass. The flickering light was gone. Everything was still. There was no sign of anything out of the ordinary. Shadows from tree branches waved at her mockingly and an owl turned his head to stare at such childish hope. She shuddered but persisted.

The mausoleum had two floors – the main one and an underground chamber. She knew without having to enter that the top floor had an altar below the stained glass window but from her vantage point she couldn't see what kinds of vases, ornaments and photos were displayed. She would have to return tomorrow.

Meanwhile, Juan Bonificio Maluenda-Valdéz, also known by his professional name of Jhonny Pretty, arranged his blankets and pillow in the corner near his own branded sepulchre in the basement. He reached over and ran his fingers across the letters that spelled his name and he smiled in the dim light. His mother had always been one to think ahead. "Gracias Mamá, for preparing this resting place so far in advance. It turned out to be very convenient." As he fumbled his way into the warmth between the blankets, he accidentally blew out the candle. No matter. He would sleep away the rest of the evening. The sudden storm brought the entire city to a standstill and there was nowhere to go and nothing more to do because of it. Grateful for the shelter, he fell asleep to the sound of the water streaming past the walls above.

Sliding on thin layers of mud and sloshing through puddles, Astrid ignored her injuries in the rush to get home. She arrived at her door like a wild package undone, dripping and soaked to the bone. Kicking off her loafers and clawing at her soggy apparel, she squished across the living room floor and pulled out her vinyl copy of 'Softly' by Jhonny Pretty y los Rockeros and she set the needle on the perimeter of the black magic disc before peeling out of the wet clothes. The melody, its introduction strummed and plucked by his perfectly orchestrated background guitars, filled the room. She wrapped her arms across her chest and, grasping her shoulders, she swayed to and fro as Jhonny's rich voice crooned, "Softly, love me softly, hold me gently…"

As Astrid closed her eyes that night, she considered confiding in Señora Ruby or asking one of the guards at the gate what they knew about Jhonny Pretty and his family. But she resolved almost immediately that were she to bring him to their attention, word would get out and soon a host of unwelcome fans would sit vigil at the mausoleum. No, thank you very much, she would guard this secret very carefully.

CHAPTER 6

Destiny

The Andes, having captured and finally released the evening's rays to the Pacific horizon stood vigil in the blue dusk. The mountains, in their wisdom, understood that yesterday's sighting of Jhonny Pretty as he drifted behind the curtain of rain was just a prelude. Today they would witness a subsequent, more important encounter.

In the few remaining moments of natural light, the mountains cast an eye over the valley, watching and trying not to judge as Astrid gazed upon Jhonny Pretty through the magic of twilight. He was still gorgeous, albeit in a rugged, older, supernatural form. She looked up into his face from her position on the steps below the Maluenda-Valdéz mausoleum and her knees went weak. The ghost of Jhonny Pretty stood frozen, looking back at her from the other side of the very same wrought iron gate to which, years ago, she had tied her forlorn bunch of carnations. She was so close to him, yet so far – nothing to separate them other than a few short steps and the thin veil that hangs between the living and the dead.

Juan stopped in mid-step to look down at her. The woman had startled him. She had padded silently to his door in a pair of ugly, scuffed, brown leather loafers and now she stood only a few metres away, looking like a silly, slightly stout statue. Her appearance was undone, like she had dressed in a hurry. How long had she been there? She had the look of a crazed fan gazing up at her idol. Something he hadn't seen for years. Something that simultaneously thrilled him and yet produced a knot in his stomach. Too late. He had been recognised and his new digs were in danger of being compromised.

Astrid was surprised the ghost didn't simply disappear. She didn't know what to say. He allowed her to see him for a reason. Ghosts do that. Perhaps he had a request. She leaned closer to peer inside, beyond his wrought iron shield and he leaned backwards to the same degree. The little building's interior was in ruins. Clearly the family had not left a caretaker in charge. She noticed that the altar was barren except for some dried twigs that had been dumped onto the old, worn altar cloth. She was drawn to a yellowed photo of Jhonny Pretty y los Rockeros in a flimsy wooden frame that leaned against the back wall above the altar.

Juan studied her, waiting for her to make the first move. He wanted to say, "What do you want? Say something or walk away." But he refrained. The woman's wiry black hair was drawn into a bun at the nape of her neck and her long, pink feather earrings almost brushed her shoulders. She wore a light blue smock over an unhemmed, flower cotton skirt that hung to mid-calf. One of her green socks climbed up her leg to meet the bottom of her skirt. The other rolled down sloppily onto itself around her ankle, revealing a hairy calf. Juan shuddered. Her shabby shoes were firmly on the bottom step. She was looking at him through the smoke of a filter cigarette that hung loosely between her lips. The woman was leaning forward slightly, hands on her hips, squinting at him, the sallow skin around her eyes giving way to deep laugh lines. But she wasn't laughing. In fact, her eyes were filling with tears. She was infatuated with him – just like that. Juan recognised an adoring fan when he saw one. Well, he was, after all, Jhonny Pretty, the Chilean heartthrob of the 70s. Hard to resist, he imagined.

He stepped back into the shadows and she politely leaned back in response, stepping off the bottom stair and onto the path below. He was grateful for the reprieve offered by the increased distance.

And Astrid breathed easier for having moved out of the range of his electrifying charm. It was so powerful she felt it would short-circuit her heart. She reminded herself she would have to be careful. The doctor had warned her about her heart. And about her smoking.

Juan was attracted to her filter cigarette. But he would deny himself this luxury, opting instead for the thin protection of the dark mausoleum. He was aware that although this was his family tomb, he was trespassing in the cemetery at night, and he could see by her smock that she was a cemetery caretaker, perhaps with a will to turn him in. But it wasn't only that – he shrank back from her, as he remembered doing towards the end of 'his golden era' in response to the ageing, touching, scratching, and clawing female hands. You never know where they've been, and worse yet, where they might want to go.

Astrid observed in privileged silence. Jhonny Pretty's ghost was looking back at her. Their eyes were trained on one another like cats who had surprised each other in the night. Suspicious and entranced. Astrid was honoured by his presence, his tranquillity and undivided attention during these scant seconds. She wondered when he had last ventured up from his underground crypt. Maybe he climbed upstairs every night to look out at the stars or to smell the fresh air. It was probably impossible for a musical genius such at himself to tolerate the eternal suffocating darkness he had been sentenced to. Surely even beyond the grave he would occasionally need the starry sky for inspiration.

Her gaze still squarely on Jhonny Pretty's face, Astrid took another step backwards. She could sense that he needed his space. She could grant him that much. After all, seeing him again, confirming he was here, was enough for one night. She was not the expert in ghosts that Señora Ruby was, but she knew they could be unpredictable. Therefore she had to be cautious if she hoped to visit Jhonny Pretty again. And again, and again. Without a word, or so much as a nod, she turned around and walked away, towards the west gate and left him standing in the shadows. She was trembling with excitement and anticipation.

After she disappeared, Juan waited a few minutes before resuming his earlier activity. He understood now that the woman was merely an interruption, not a threat. Before being startled by her, he had been looking for a place to stash coins and he found it in a wide crack of the marble top of his grandfather's tomb. He adjusted the old photo of himself and los Rockeros to cover it. The fact that he would probably never have any coins to stash was something he chose to deny. There was never anything left over after a day at Slaughterhouse Square but moving to the cemetery was a new phase in his life and he was hopeful about picking up a few new good habits. After all, this was the year his luck would change. He instinctively inserted his hand into his trouser pocket to fondle the lucky blue eye.

It was easy for him not to be distracted for long by the face of a strange woman who gawked silently in his direction. But not so for Astrid. Her thoughts wandered back again and again to the man who was the subject of her attention. On her way towards the cemetery gate, just thinking about the encounter, Astrid was lit up like a human lantern, whereas Juan dismissed her almost immediately.

Other than the desire to smoke a filter cigarette, he never gave the strange woman another thought. He wasn't even flattered that she was enamoured with him. He didn't feel the need to carve another notch in his belt (God only knows how many notched belts he had gone through in his heyday), and it didn't occur to him that she might try to see him again.

He picked up the old photo of himself and los Rockeros and angled it so the faint light reflected each of the band members' faces. With the exception of one, they had been a handsome group. This was the only photo that Juan still owned. It had been taken outside of their tour bus, an old green Volvo with Jhonny Pretty y los Rockeros painted across both sides in an unfolding, script typeface where 'los Rockeros' formed the shape of a guitar. This was the bus that had rolled down the bank that night, interrupting a major tour and sending them all to hell.

Mauricio, los Rockeros manager bought the bus from one of his contacts and insisted the abundance of grinding and squeaking was not due to any type of serious mechanical failure, but to the normal wear and tear of a used vehicle. As it turned out, because of so many failing bits and pieces, it was impossible to know exactly which one caused the accident.

After the fact, they discovered that Mauricio had paid only half of what he told them the bus would cost and he had pocketed the other half. In addition, they came to understand that this particular bucket of bolts was supposed to have been sold for parts, but at the last minute, Mauricio rescued it for their tour. He apparently had 'woman trouble' and needed some extra cash.

Had it not been for the fact that Mauricio had been following the bus in his Peugeot that night (delayed by the woman troubles in question), the authorities would never have been alerted to the accident in time to pry them out alive. It was a lonely highway and Los Rockeros would have bled out and perished right there at the bottom of the steep bank. But Mauricio had driven back for help. This and his pleas for forgiveness were his saving grace, and Juan convinced the other band members to let him stay on as their manager. But no one was thinking clearly during that time and things were never really the same after that anyway. Mauricio attempted to coordinate rehearsals and gigs but the band members drifted off, each into their own broken world. Sometimes one or two of them would wake up to their responsibilities, but no one was entirely capable of maintaining the roles that melded them into the incomparable group they had once been, so it fell apart without any conscious effort either to stay together or to split up. It was the ultimate, dark turning point for each individual member.

Although Mauricio had not been physically injured, after it became apparent that the band no longer existed, and when rumours of his corrupt practices starting buzzing around the industry, he was sent headlong into a black, managerial abyss. Ironically the only option that arose for him was to make a living in the customer service centre of a large auto repair shop, where he would be reminded forever of his most grave of sins.

Pato, the bass player had several teeth knocked out in the accident and his jaw was wired shut for weeks. They nicknamed him 'Traintracks' about which he uncharacteristically lacked a sense of humour. On top of that, he lost his short-term memory, consequently forgetting what songs they had just finished playing and he couldn't make it through a rehearsal without destroying equipment out of frustration and then breaking into sobs. Word had it that he eventually became an outstanding ice cream vendor on the beaches of Viña del Mar, never tiring of chiming his one and only sales pitch or pounding back and forth along over the same stretch of sand. Juan thought of him like a gold fish whose short memory span means that by the time he laps his bowl a few times, he thinks he's experiencing life anew.

'Fish Face' (whose Christian name no one in the group remembered) was the drummer. Not so miraculously, his eyes still bulged and his oversized lips remained unaltered after the disaster. During their heyday, Mauricio always said it was lucky that Fish Face was a drummer because they could sit him back in the shadows, arrange the lighting to showcase his hands and avoid his face, which was much too un-rockero-like. Unfortunately, Fish Face developed a serious tic in his right arm after the accident and he could no longer be trusted to pound out a steady beat. Juan had seen Fish Face only once after the band disintegrated. He was one of a group of illegal parking attendants on the street outside of a strip joint, where he also sometimes worked as a bouncer, and where, even less frequently he was allowed to jump onto the stool behind the drums and hammer out heavy rhythms. Inevitably his drumming challenged the dancers to keep up, their loose buttocks bouncing uncontrollably and breasts jostling to an impossible beat, until the women reached such a point of frustration that they all ganged up on Fish Face and kicked him off the stage with their stilettos.

'Gringo', the pale-skinned keyboard player took the longest to recover from the accident. He had been on the toilet when the bus rolled. For him, the expression, 'getting caught with your pants down' had a near fatal meaning. He was unable to prevent his private parts from being crushed when, after being thrown into the air and tumbling back down onto the toilet, his testicles were slammed under the toilet lid, resulting in almost total castration. He was literally hanging by a thread, and the doctors did what they could to reunite his manhood, but he would never be the same again – neither physically nor mentally. In a humorous attempt to bring him round, Gringo became known simply as Menos (Less) by the rest of the group. Although he played along with the joke, trying to ease into the reality that it reflected, he was never able to fully accept his new condition. He sang with less enthusiasm, became depressed and immediately began to put on weight, which eventually earned him the added nickname, 'Más' (More), before finally and forever becoming became known as Más o Menos (More or Less). Some time after that, Más o Menos converted to Christianity and joined an evangelical group, with whom, on Sundays, he could be heard singing soprano on downtown street corners.

Juan suffered internal bleeding, broken ribs, a broken collarbone and overall bruising. The doctor said that his brain also got knocked about inside his cranium. He was told that he would be as good as new after the bones and muscles healed and the swelling went down. But Juan sometimes heard voices echoing in what he was convinced was hollow space in his head. He demanded a more careful scrutiny of the x-rays, but they couldn't find anything outside the norm of such an occurence. The doctors were never able to help him with the problem of voices from the hollow, so Juan coped as best he could, initially getting lost for hours inside the void and arguing with the voices. He discovered that rum was a good mediator between himself and the voices and he stopped performing for years. He became what is known as a vividor (live-in scrounger) and a paracaidista (literally, a parachutist, someone who drops in, unannounced and uninvited, especially at meal times or to weddings and funerals). He did well as a vividor for the first few years because women were happy to show him off as their celebrity trophy. But he slowly lost his shine and the women became bored with their tarnished showpiece, such as he was. He also grew tired of the control they exerted over him so he drifted towards individual parties, weddings and funerals where food and drink were plentiful and where he was free to come and go as he pleased.

From there, he followed the crowd over to Slaughterhouse Square and before long, he became one of the fixtures, performing songs and selling his own karaoke CDs at rock bottom prices. His only fans were those whose memories were so compromised by drink that they didn't have high expectations and his popularity, such as it was, remained a secret amongst the usuals at Slaughterhouse Square. In spite of himself and his audience, Juan began to rediscover his unique, romantic style and before long his confidence and charm had risen to a semi-healthy level.

Under the individual and collective circumstances, it was understandable that los Rockeros would have passed into oblivion. One by one, they wandered off down their own path, never feeling the need to keep in touch with one another. In fact, at first they were not even aware that one or other of them had wandered off. Jhonny Pretty y los Rockeros were forgotten even to themselves. New bands replaced them. The dial on the radio slid down to the next station, easily bypassing a frequency that, as far as the world could remember, never existed. The band evaporated, was sucked up into the heavens, and once in awhile, when a radio jingle pirated one of their tunes, it got sneezed out of the airwaves and landed in someone's ear like a bit of pigeon poop.

Juan tapped the photo a couple of times with his fingers and replaced it onto the altar before disappearing beneath the trap door for the rest of the night. He fell asleep thinking about the strange woman's filter cigarette.

As she bounced down the path, Astrid couldn't help but reflect on how handsome Jhonny was in the navy blue suit, how tall he looked and how he had maintained his enviable erect posture. Such admirable physical condition and clothing for a man who had been dead for more than 20 years. Ghosts always appear in the clothes in which they were buried. Someone had taken care in his final appearance, dressing him in a suit that never dates itself, something eternal, disciplined, with a hint of military about it. His face showed signs of ageing but no doubt this was a result of damages caused by the bus accident rather than by the passing years.

To say she was extremely happy with the day's events was an understatement. On her way home, Astrid barely touched the surface of the silt left behind by yesterday's rain. She floated along, etching a light trail in her wake – not unlike a satisfied slug, her invisible antennae wriggling overhead, seeking signals from Jhonny Pretty's ghost. He must have chosen her to communicate something. Otherwise he would not have revealed himself. She was to be his spokeswoman, his publicist, his companion, perhaps his spiritual lover. She shivered with anticipation. Life was good.

Unable to concentrate on anything else, when Astrid arrived home, she sat down with a cup of tea and a sandwich and, through a thin stream of smoke, listened as the vinyl 45s spun out Jhonny's smooth-as-silk voice and brought him to life once again. Then she tore apart the low cupboard in her kitchen, until she exhumed several copies of El Ritmo magazine, the popular, number one music publication from the 60s and 70s. She leafed frantically through the pages, pupils enlarged, fingers aflutter, until she uncovered everything in her possession about Jhonny – photos, articles, interviews. She spread them out over the kitchen table and stood back to study them. Sadly, there were huge gaps in her collection that she would need to fill. She would organise the magazines chronologically, tagging and highlighting the pages where he was mentioned. In order to fully engage herself in his life (or afterlife, as it were), she would become better informed, rediscover every known detail. If she visited flea markets, she might even unearth other Rockero paraphernalia. Perhaps she could also bargain with Susana. A tangible library of photos and articles would allow her to design an altar to Jhonny. Yes, this collection would be essential – a touchstone for the shared reality that belonged only to herself and Jhonny's ghost. The most appropriate place for such a private altar would be in her bedroom. So intimate. To have Jhonny Pretty in her boudoir! She'd have to clean out a corner, probably transform her mother's old dressing table into the altar. Her mother would understand. She'd build it tomorrow.

She climbed into bed with her pile of magazines and fell asleep with the centre spread of El Ritmo resting across her face, Jhonny's enchanting blue eyes gazing directly into hers, their noses touching. Her jaw dropped open and she snored into Jhonny's crooked smile, drawing his lips in and out with each breath. Her precious virgin-like toes stepped into a slow dance with Jhonny as he wound himself across the floor of her dreams.

CHAPTER 7

Divine Intervention

Siete Pelos was looking particularly debonair when Astrid stopped in to buy two slices of cold cuts and a loose Derby brand filter cigarette. He turned to serve her, reluctantly interrupting his rendition of 'Eternal Secret Love,' and the tune faded away into a glow over his head.

"And would you consider a San Expedito lighter?" He extracted one from its cardboard stand and held it up between thumb and forefinger only centimetres from her nose. His attempt at nonchalance was betrayed by his ears, which twitched like a dog who hears food being slopped into his dish. She knew this was no ordinary day.

She leaned in and squinted at him. His cheeks were flushed and the strand was wound around the top of his head with extraordinary pizzazz – a touch of je ne sais quoi. There was something festive about his swirl of hairy pomade. Siete's teeth even sparkled. Could he have rinsed with mouthwash? And was that a blast of Brut cologne that just assaulted her head-on? She chose to ignore it.

"No, thank you. San Expedito has never done anything for me."

"Have you ever tried him? I mean, really given him a chance?" Siete Pelos talked as though San Expedito was a brand of soft drink. 'Enjoy San Expedito, a new refreshing taste experience.'

Astrid brushed aside his enthusiasm. "No, it's just that I prefer the Virgin Carmen. She has always come through for me. And I already have a statue at home, thank you." Maybe she would have to buy her cigarettes and cold cuts elsewhere; Siete Pelos' new hard sales approach was annoying.

Trying to discourage more of it, she kept her head down as she inserted her loose cigarette into the hard leather cigarette case Constancia had given her three Christmases ago and she stuffed the slices of meat into the bag with her bun. Anxious to leave, she slid several coins across the counter, avoiding eye contact because now his odd behaviour was making her uncomfortable.

Just as Astrid turned to make her escape, Susana careened into the shop, face aglow, eyes shining, a San Expedito pendant bouncing merrily above her ample bosom, which was doing double time. She rushed headlong towards Siete Pelos, barely acknowledging Astrid.

"I beg your pardon, Susana. You're too good to say hello?"

"Oh, sorry, Astrid." She shot her a half glance. It was all she mustered before twisting her head around to breathlessly address Sieto Pelos as if they were alone.

"Oh, Siete Pelos, your gift is beautiful. Thank you, again." She was holding the cheap San Expedito pendant between her fingers and smiling across at Siete Pelos. His face flushed, he cleared his throat and blinked his eyes in Astrid's direction. Astrid, who was poised with one foot already out the door, stopped to watch, one eyebrow raised.

In her cloud of pubescent-like puppy love Susana was oblivious to any improprieties. She gushed, leaned onto the counter and pushed her bosom forward until it swelled dangerously close to Siete Pelos' nose, her jiggling breasts whetting his appetite for a taste of this fleshy jelly. Astrid thought his entire long strand of hair would unwind and fall to the floor where he would be in danger of tripping, either on it or on his tongue, whichever he couldn't draw in fast enough. He really had to learn to curb his enthusiasm, at least in public.

"So, what's going on here?" Astrid addressed them both, pretending to be stern, but she couldn't conceal her grin.

"It's the work of San Expedito." Siete Pelos murmured absently, unable to remove his eyes from Susana's bosom and barely able to talk due to the current tongue problem.

"I doubt that." Astrid challenged him. "You two have known each other all your lives. And it's obvious what's happening. Surely it doesn't take San Expedito's powers a lifetime to kick in. I mean how effective is he, Siete Pelos?"

"No, no, it's true." Susana came to his defence. "Siete," she pronounced his name slowly and with feeling, without removing her gaze from his eyes, "gave me this pendant less than a week ago, and I prayed with it close to my heart every night." She flushed and finally turned to look at Astrid. "I don't know if you know that for the past four years, I've been looking for a boyfriend. It turns out that I was just praying to the wrong saint. San Expedito brought results right away. I mean, look, here I am after only a few days, with the very man who gave me the pendant. How much more expedient can you be? I mean it's a miracle." She beamed across at Siete Pelos who by now was so weak with desire that he was wilting over the counter, his forehead dripping with sweat.

"Are you sure you haven't been planning this for years, Siete Pelos?"

He tried to pull himself together. "No, I assure you. It's a surprise for me too. San Expedito brought us one to the other. Ourselves, we had nothing to do with it. Well, you know... up to a point." Now that the truth was out, he was less self-conscious. He wiped his brow and regained enough composure to coordinate a light stroking of the back of Susana's hand. He swallowed and straightened, reminding himself that he owed it to San Expedito to do a proper job.

"You see, Astrid, you need a San Expedito pendant too." Siete Pelos reached behind and unhooked one from the shelf and handed it to her. "Take it today. I'll add it to my ledger and you can pay me at the end of the month."

"What do I need one for? I'm fine the way I am."

"Well, maybe you don't realise what you're missing. I mean, we didn't..." he shot a meaningful glance at Susana and detached himself to make the sale. "Anyway, take it and you'll see." He pressed the pendant into Astrid's palm.

An image of Jhonny Pretty materialised from where it had been waiting in the shadowed windows of her mind. She closed her eyes and watched as Jhonny's face floated through the air and superimposed itself over that of San Expedito, transforming San Expedito into a Roman rock star. Or perhaps it was Jhonny Pretty – become Roman soldier. Either way, he was the one. Astrid closed her fingers around the pendant and felt Jhonny's supernatural heat. She would take it.

"Okay then. Thank-you, Siete Pelos." She looked across at him. "Maybe you're right. But just so you know, I don't need it for love. You can mark this in your book." She carefully dropped the pendant into a small nylon change purse, inserted it into her skirt pocket, and patted it against her hip. Suddenly feeling awkward in the atmosphere that had become unbearably saturated with Susana's and Siete Pelos' mutual desire, she nodded her head and left without another word.

San Expedito was an unexpected player on the scene. But if he was going to do something for her, then she would just let it happen. Perhaps she could say a test prayer or two when she got home at the end of the day. She tapped her skirt where the pendant was stashed and walked straight up to Señora Ruby's shack to prepare for the day's work.

All day long, the pendant burned into her hip. She could feel the heat of Jhonny's spirit fused with that of the saint and it became so unbearable that she couldn't concentrate. Finally, she closed her eyes and reached into her pocket to extract the little pendant, half expecting Jhonny to wink up at her, daring her to flirt back. But when she uncurled her fingers to look down at it, she was met with the pious, static features of San Expedito with his foot on the dead crow. She sighed and yielding to common sense, hung the pendant around her neck. Saints like San Expedito deserve to be seen and not shoved away into the fabric darkness at her hip. She patted him into place on her collarbone and decided she might as well test his powers. She whispered into the air between the tombs.

"My Dear San Expedito, who is of just and urgent causes, intercede to our Lord, ask him to come to me in this hour of need. Help me to overcome difficult times, protect me and grant my wish." She paused here, unable to define exactly what she wished San Expedito to do about Jhonny Pretty. She must try to be precise because when saints come to your aid, they grant exactly what you ask for, nothing more and nothing less. "My dear San Expedito," she began again, "I'm sorry that I have interrupted your busy day. I know that I need your help but I don't yet know how to ask for it. Please be with me as I search for the right words and I'll get back to you tonight. Muchas gracias." She raised the pendant to her lips and kissed it, "Gracias, my most dearest of Saints." She felt a twinge of guilty towards the Virgin Carmen and turned to whisper up into the air, "And you my most beloved Virgin, you are my one and only Virgin, to whom I pledge constant love and loyalty. Don't worry about San Expedito."

With that, she felt a certain tranquillity that allowed her to concentrate on the muertitos in Señora Ruby's patio.

She and Señora Ruby devoted themselves to opposite ends of the patio that day. Señora Ruby said she felt the need to visit some of the older tombs on the wall. Although it was not officially within the jurisdiction of Patio 35, she was tempted to remove and repair a chipped and filthy miniature bust of the Virgin Mary that was perched on the barren concrete ledge of a tomb belonging to a certain Mercedes de la Fuente, deceased 1937. Each time she approached it, she was filled with a deep sorrow and a compulsion towards a charitable good deed. The cracks in the concrete niche were filled with dirt and the only sign that someone had once cared about Mercedes de la Fuente was that they had wiped the marble nameplate, leaving a smear. A low wall of pigeon droppings was encrusted along the ledge and around the base of the little statue, making it look like the Virgin grew out of a pile of bird droppings. Señora Ruby could not recall one single person ever visiting this poor, forgotten soul. She was not even certain if the decayed statue, which must have been placed there decades ago by a caring relative (who else?), had any life left in it. How could it possibly provide even a drop of comfort to the brittle bones of Mercedes de la Fuente? Several times in the past, Señora Ruby had reached up to brush dead leaves and small twigs from the statue but each time she felt something like an electric shock striking her fingertips and coursing up to her shoulders. It was like a slap across the knuckles, warning her away. The faded eyes of the virgin, now largely chipped paint, observed aloofly from the faint lines that still defined them and on more than one such occasion Señora Ruby thought she saw a fierce flicker of something snapping like a bolt across the bridge of the eroded plaster nose.

The result of today's half-hearted attempt ended the same way so Señora Ruby promised herself once again that she would not interfere. But even as the electric barrier warned her off, it acted like a magnet, pulling on her heart, calling her back to attend the tomb at a future date. She knew her relationship with this disfigured virgin and Mercedes de la Fuente was not over but today, as on every other occasion she was forced to go about her business elsewhere.

Meanwhile Astrid had set to work pulling weeds and sprinkling water around the edges of the decades-old mausoleums at the outer edge of Patio 35, moving closer and closer to the path leading to Jhonny Pretty's tomb. She looked up at the sun, still high in the sky and willed it to make a faster than usual descent. Restless, she fingered the peso coins in her pocket and decided to make a quick trip to Siete Pelos to buy another loose cigarette. She tucked the watering hose into a corner and abandoned the patio, heading towards the west gate.

On her way back, she passed an adjacent wall of children's niches, obvious because of its narrow depth – small coffins slid into cramped spaces, niches all heavily decorated with pinwheels, stuffed toys, sentimental plastic name tags and ribbons. One of the children's walls had been destroyed by the quake, but surprisingly, most survived. She wanted to attribute this to a sort of justice for the innocent, even though deep down she knew it had been spared out of random luck. The occasional barren niche with only a name inscribed on a dirty plaque interrupted the noisy colour that ran across the rest of the wall. The lonely tomb was like a shy child in a playroom full of boisterous others, an uncultivated, timid little life left on the sidelines with no toys of his own. The children's walls were at once happy and sad. The bright ornaments and doted-on niches demonstrated the joy in a continued celebration of a little soul but also reflected the sorrow of its amputated life. As she neared the wall, she saw balloons and fresh flowers left from a recent birthday party. The family had come and gone. She wondered if it had been a big party, lots of relatives, or perhaps just the dead child's mother and maybe a brother or sister. The niche window had been cleaned and no doubt these were the new toys that had been arranged inside. The child was named Arturo. He died three years ago, October 2001, at the age of five. Astrid looked at his photo. A happy boy with chapped cheeks and twinkling, mischievous eyes. "How did you die?" she asked under her breath. She looked around at his balloons.

"Happy Birthday, little Arturo." she spoke aloud now, touching the glass in front of his photo with her fingertips. "It looks like you had a party, received some new toys. You're one of the lucky ones here, you know – your family coming all the time, never forgetting. They keep you alive this way, doing what they can for you, spoiling you like they never would have, had you remained alive. You must be a very good boy, very special." A breeze carried the lilt of childish laughter through the bushes. She hesitated before joining him, unable to suppress a giggle as she looked into the eyes of the photo. "I think maybe you are a little imp. Have you gotten into some trouble lately?" She interpreted the lightness in the air as agreement. She felt kinship with the spirit of this little man who would never be, and recognised him as a playful accomplice, probably already wise beyond his short years, which had stretched well past this reality.

On a whim she said, "Let me have some of your balloons, Arturo. I need to make someone else feel special too." Astrid untied the ribbons that anchored two red balloons and one blue one to the awning above his niche window. Arturo did not object. "Thank you." He winked at her as the sun glinted off his glass window, "You're welcome, Señora."

Astrid turned, half skipping down the path towards Jhonny Pretty's home which bordered a long series of low tombs, all with trap doors to subterranean bone depositories. They were sunken concrete structures, rising above the ground by a metre or less. Some were finished with colourful ceramic and inset flowerbeds, others plainer, but all had large, carved headstones, most with protective angels and ample surface for vases and ornaments. Being an expert in respectful dealings with the dead, she knew how to graciously help herself to carnations and irises from vases that were full to overflowing. She reassured the owners that the flowers were a humble offering to a great musical genius. She was confident they believed her and she bent in mock curtsies, quick gestures of gratitude on Jhonny's behalf. "Thank you very much. Thank you very much, ladies and gentlemen." Astrid, an ordinary matron in tattered apparel gracefully dipped and straightened; she, the caretaker with blue smock over crinkle-cotton skirt and faded striped socks in brown leather loafers, who wobbled slightly with each step, her dangly earrings chiming from her ears, was transformed into an oversized garden fairy. She was happy. She barely noticed as she sailed through a waft of air carrying the faint aroma of jasmine. It all seemed to belong.

Early that evening, just after the cemetery gates closed, Astrid finished tidying the grounds around the Maluendez-Valdéz family mausoleum. She had tied the flower offering neatly to the centre of the entrance gate and two red balloons and one blue one hung beneath with a semi-festive inclination. She couldn't decide whether or not to wait and see Jhonny in person tonight. She would love to approach him but she didn't want to be too forward and scare him away. Maybe she could just say a few words into the air of this, his familial space. Perhaps he would be close enough to sense her presence and agree to be seen. Once this thought occurred to her, she was unable to push it aside. Compelled to communicate with him, she sat down on the top step of the mausoleum. She twisted around to peer past the balloons and into the interior before she ventured an introduction.

"Jhonny Pretty, I am honoured you allowed me to see you. I mean I know I can't see you now, at this moment but I have seen you. And you have seen me. I wonder when you first saw me? Did you notice that I work here? Did you maybe cross paths with some of my muertitos? Maybe they told you that I am trustworthy and capable. I am, you know. I'm very well respected here. And I have two children and many friends who will also testify to my good character. But you probably know all you need to know about me, at least for now."

She paused thoughtfully. "Maybe you have some specific news you need to distribute, like about your terrible accident or about a song you had in your head when you died, or maybe a new one that you've composed from beyond?" She had so many questions but couldn't resist bringing the conversation back around to herself. "Did you maybe choose to talk to me because I am conveniently here or did you want someone in particular, someone special, maybe just my type?" Her cheeks heated up at the thought of being sought out by Jhonny Pretty and she fumbled nervously for the cigarette in her leather case. She had been saving it for a special moment. Well, that special moment just happened to be now. "I don't know what you know about me, Jhonny. May I call you Jhonny? I imagine that's what your friends call you." She lit her cigarette and tilted her face up to the sky as she exhaled her first puff. "My friends just call me Astrid. I don't have a nickname. I don't know if that's good or bad, but it's okay with me either way."

Once she started talking, Astrid realised she had a lot to say. Although she always confided in Señora Ruby and in Constancia, she was suddenly aware that she had never shared many truly intimate things about herself. And now, here she was, in the presence of none other than Jhonny Pretty, Chile's famous 70s rock musician, feeling the need to spill her guts. She dragged deeply on her cigarette, her eyes darting about as she tried to decide where to begin.

"Jhonny, there is probably not much point in me telling you that I have always been one of your biggest fans. I mean, well, everyone is one of your biggest fans." She giggled and was sure she could feel a slight swelling in the air around her. Jhonny had every reason to be proud of his musical accomplishments. "But since you have decided to trust me it's fair that you know some of my own peculiarities. And I don't mind telling you so you won't have to worry about being disappointed in your choice of confidante." She liked that word – 'confidante' – a confidante to Jhonny Pretty, no less. She took a drag on her cigarette and watched as the smoke drifted behind the wrought iron gate towards his altar. "It's satisfying..." She raised her voice as though she was shouting through the bathroom door at someone who refused to come out. "It's satisfying, don't you think, to have someone in whom you can place all of your trust?" She unconsciously reached for the San Expedito pendant and rubbed it between thumb and forefinger before jumping into the deep end. "Jhonny, I am not an unhappy woman but I am not entirely content either. It's been a long time since I've had a sentimental relationship with a man and that's one thing that's missing from my life – as much as I hate to admit it. It's been like this since my ex-husband, in fact. He hurt me deeply and I haven't let anyone close to me since." She paused, allowing the silence to punctuate the point. "I don't know for sure but there have probably been more than a few who have been interested in me. It's just that, well, you know, I don't pay attention. Since you approached me, though, I've been thinking about it non-stop. I'm reconsidering the idea of being close to a man. I mean, for me, a purely spiritual relationship would be most desirable. It's more than virtual. I mean since you're really here, and all. I don't see how we can hurt one another under these circumstances. I mean it's not like I have to worry about you being unfaithful to me." She took one final drag on her cigarette, enjoying the taste. "And you won't have to worry about me." She laughed a throaty laugh and tossed the cigarette butt to the ground at the base of the stairs. Out of nowhere in the deepening blue of the night, she felt very sexy, very unique – like one of Jhonny's chosen ones. Now she suddenly understood that she was the only chosen one. The responsibility was overwhelming and she was suddenly very nervous.

She must make him understand that for her, he was also the only one. "I'm absolutely loyal. And of course, I'll do anything you ask." She winked boldly into the dark air of the mausoleum. "After all, you approached me for a reason. There must be something you need. Could it possibly be just my companionship? Jhonny, if that's it, you know I'm more than willing, I am honoured." Her chin high, she primped her hair with both hands and then lightly brushed each of her sleeves. She had forgotten she was still wearing her cemetery smock. It wasn't the most enticing outfit in the world. Oh well, she had already confessed to Jhonny that she worked here. Besides, there was probably not much she could keep secret from a ghost, especially one as worldly-wise as Jhonny Pretty. She blushed as she thought about how experienced he was, not only as a musician and a man of travel, but as a woman's man.

She waited for a response from Jhonny's spirit. Maybe he was absent. Perhaps he was out for a stroll with some of his spirit friends. He certainly had his pick here – from dead presidents to other famous musicians. But maybe he was here with her all the same, sitting silently on the steps, testing her, becoming better acquainted before opening a private portal to his own soul.

Meanwhile, the only portal Juan was opening was his mouth. He was still over at Slaughterhouse Square. They'd had an unpredictably successful weekday because a group of tourists from the north swooped down on them after a shopping spree at the Persa Bío Bío and then settled in on the patio of Mario's restaurant. The tourists, feeling they had conquered the local vendors with their negotiating skills, were already high on themselves. And they positively beamed with excitement at the good fortune of having run across the one and only Jhonny Pretty, exclaiming loudly that he was still able to croon and rock with the best of them. Wait until they told their friends at home. How much did he charge for an autographed CD? And could they take a few photos? When they invited him for a drink, Juan was pleased to oblige. One of the women – the prettiest, middle-aged one with the bleached blonde hair– admitted that she thought he had perished in a bus accident years ago. "What a great surprise and even greater pleasure to sit across the table from you, in the flesh, see that you are alive and well, and gaze into your very blue eyes, Jhonny. How fortunate that you still have your voice, and your looks..." He acknowledged her statement with a wink and a crooked smile. Even when someone else was talking, she kept her eyes trained on him. He noticed when she pulled out a full packet of Derby filter cigarettes and set them on the table.

"I hear you're from the interior of Iquique. I've been there a few times, myself." He pointed at the Derbys. "Do you mind?"

"Be my guest." She smiled as she slid the packet towards him with one hand and with the other she reached over to rub his thigh. Nothing subtle about this northern specimen.

Juan stroked the lapel of his Salvation Army jacket and leaned across the table, his hand lingering over her fingers for a second, the fingers that would surely bring him pleasure later in the evening.

He was right. The woman, whose name he never did ask, fell asleep beside him in the bed of a hotel that she paid for. He woke up in the middle of the night, confused, missing the dankness of his private dungeon, unable to remember why he was not there now.

It would be the next night before he returned to his squatter home in the cemetery to see the deflated red and blue balloons, as shrunken as he was after a drunken tussle with the unknown northern creature, dried flowers tied to his door as a reminder of his dehydrated state after so much whiskey. Without questioning their origin, he yanked the flowers and shrivelled balloons free and tossed them around the side of the mausoleum, letting them fall where they may, like so much discarded nuisance. He failed to notice that someone had tended to the weeds at the base of the walls and he let himself in, locked the entrance gate, stumbled down the ladder and snuggled in to sleep beside his silent relatives, ignorant of their disdain. Peace comes to those with a hangover.

CHAPTER 8
It all Works Out

Stars teasing their light through the strings of time play a silent symphony across the midnight blue Santiago sky. All over the city, innocent stargazers make wishes on this cosmic array of exhausted suns – blazing gases that ceased to burn thousands of years ago, but which, through the trickery of time and distance, punch through the darkness into current reality. Dreamers and desperate people put their faith in these stars, in their power already long gone, faded crescendos, ghosts of sound, echoes in darkness. "Sorry," the sky says, "but you missed the deadline." And how were you to know? These lights that hang helter-skelter in the heavens are a glittering invitation for people with unfulfilled desires. Besides, who lives according to distant deadlines? Even tomorrow comes too soon.

Sometimes wishes are granted outright and sometimes they appear in an alternate form – days, weeks or years after the fact. Sometimes one magic star gets confused with another and it seems that wishes are not granted at all. But watch. As sure as the stars shine in their seemingly haphazard pattern, life unfolds as it should in Santiago.

In spite of numerous and unexpected delays and sudden changes of plans (or lack of them), life in this city plays its own symphony, often missing a beat, sometimes in disharmony, occasionally holding its breath as it fingers its way around to the full chord or searches to strike the single, defining note, playing and re-playing through rests and staccato, sometimes taking days and weeks until it reaches its glorious (or disappointing) finale. But end it does. Things manage to fall into position, all the notes hovering over the places they've been, their final passage resounding into the sky like the lost lights of the celestial bodies that hang over them. A symphonic outcome reached, mission accomplished one way or the other (at least for now), every mortal is an unwitting player in the grand orchestra.

In a city of six million souls (and at least two million more if you count the dead and buried), all existing under the same sky and gazing up at the same stars, destinies meet at unlikely junctures and intertwine.

....

The big downtown retail stores open their doors at 10:30 or 11 a.m. and the little ones across the river in El Patronato, where Constancia works, open up one by one at no particular hour in spite of attempts to be consistent.

Each morning, like a giant stage play during an uncoordinated scene change, graffiti is trundled up inside metal roller blinds on storefronts that line the narrow streets. Shop windows exposed, the morning light illuminates freaky mannequin torsos, some with plastic hair and others with straw-like wigs that look like they haven't been adjusted since 1970, some with frozen half-smiles and heavy, triangular eyebrows pencilled over dull, painted eyes whose colour has flaked off, leaving them to stare cross-eyed at passersby. Some have no heads at all, or have handless arms. An eerie sight. The latest styles of sequinned t-shirts, coloured stockings, thong underwear and stretchy denim trousers are drawn over the mannequins and around black wire frames. All of it shouts for attention. Large letters are scrawled directly on the glass in front of the mannequins' brittle faces as each shop lays claim to the lowest prices in El Patronato. The mannequins stare past in cold wonder at such bargains, as if even they can't believe the irresistible deals on offer.

Like her mother, Constancia had a responsible nature. Because she was prompt, she was assigned to open the shop each morning. She proudly surveyed the window dressing as she raised the metal shutter. Designing enticing window displays was a flair she inherited from her mother's side, a talent that came from generations of women naturally skilled at bringing life to the non-living.

This morning she would introduce some of the newly arrived, sexier items into window arrangements, which would no doubt produce an immediate increase in sales. She knew her clients. The window dressing was everything. That, and the price scrawled in large pink-glitter letters on oversized yellow cards attached to each garment. This was her trademark. Several other shops had copied her unique price tag protocol but no one could pull it off with the same flamboyance. Only yesterday, she had sold a striking outfit to a performing artist named Jesica, who had blown in from Slaughterhouse Square.

The little bell above the door jingled and Jesica had breezed into the shop. "Buenos días." She bellowed her greeting to Constancia who was attempting to ignore customers while she painted metallic purple swirls on her fingernails. Constancia always felt that her hands were her strong point. She knew that her round, dark eyes and thick hair were attractive but she had always been self-conscious about the rest of her face, specifically her nose and lips. Unlike her mother, Constancia had a rather long nose, some would say, even sharp. Her lips were not full and she had to pencil extra width around them when she applied her lipstick. She secretly planned collagen treatments but up to now had not been able to put aside enough cash. Besides, she had heard horror stories about the cheap but illegal clinics where innocent women looking for sex appeal walked in, and misshapen beings clinging to some semblance of humanity walked out. Therefore, as she saw it, the only immediate choice was to emphasize her hands. She had developed a habit of fluttering them when she spoke, her fingers always in motion like she was plucking a harp, often distracting to the point of being annoying.

Constancia looked up slowly, irritated by the brash intrusion – a customer coming into her shop to look around – and she waved her fingers through the air like two foppish butterflies to dry the polish.

Jesica ignored that. "I'm interested in the blue satin blouse and stretch pants in your window. Do you have a size 36?"

Without bothering to greet the woman, Constancia's professional eye sized her up as a 48. She sighed and, taking her time, she carefully twisted the cap on the nail polish bottle. She pushed it aside, sauntered around the counter, stepped over to the window and leaned in. She didn't really need to refer to the window display. She knew very well which outfit the woman wanted, but making the woman wait increased her own importance. It was a valuable lesson she had learned years ago.

"Let me see what we have in stock." She deliberately studied her nails as she brushed past the woman on her way to the back room and she emerged with three bags, one each of size 42, 44 and 46. She knew the first two were unnecessary but thought it best to humour the customer. She clumsily kicked aside several empty boxes from behind a curtain with a toe of her baby blue pump. "You can try them on here," she said from behind her butterfly hands.

After several minutes, during which the shop air filled with grunts and sighs, the woman twirled out from the behind the curtain in the size 46, looking like a loaf of bread with too much yeast. She embraced herself in front of the mirror and raised her hands in victory as she posed to view herself from various angles. She coquettishly dragged her slightly puffy, pink fingers over her bosom and hips. "What do you think?"

"Maybe a vest, too." suggested Constancia. "I have a nice pink, fringed number. Here, let me show you." Constancia could smell commission and she suddenly came to life, willing to give a little bit of herself over to this blue stuffed sausage who was definitely going to buy something.

Jesica beamed when she tried on the vest. "I love it, my dear, I love it!" Apparently it was just the panache she needed to liven up an evening's musical set. She twisted and turned in front of the mirror that was shoved behind the curtain of the cramped cubical change space. The fringes of the short fake leather vest did a good job of hiding the rolls that raged around her hips but left her plump, luscious bottom exposed. The v-neck top lunged into her cleavage and she said she would wear a long pendant to emphasise the area. "And my pink leather cowboy boots will finish it off perfectly." She was excited. "You're a true genius. I can't wait to wear this!" She posed and twirled a couple more times in front of the mirror. "Maybe a scarf?"

Constancia dug out a wild paisley purple one and hooked it onto Jesica's waiting fingers. Jesica waved it coyly in front of her face several times. Then suddenly a salsa hit the airwaves from the transistor radio on the shelf behind the till and, unable to resist, the stuffed blue sausage broke out in dance. Startled, Constancia stepped back, and watched as Jesica wound her hips to the beat, the fringes of the vest whipping up a breeze in the otherwise still air of the crowded little shop. Watching herself in the mirror, this crazed, fringed creature twirled and gyrated until her broad hips finally collided with the bald mannequin that was dressed in the bold cotton print top and tight jeans. The defenceless mannequin wobbled and Constancia grabbed for it but it was too late. All three of them landed in a jumble of plastic arms, sequins, exposed bosoms and rolls of flesh under fake leather fringes and blue satin. The paisley scarf floated softly down to cover Jesica's face.

"Díos mío!" Jesica puffed through the scarf. "Are you all right?"

Constancia raised her nose from where it had wedged itself in Jesica's sweaty bosom (she thought she whiffed industrial silicon) and coldly looked her straight in the eye before disentangling herself from the pile of flesh and plastic.

"Yes, I'll be fine," she huffed.

Jesica raised her hand to Constancia's as much to get a hand up as to introduce herself. "I'm Jesica."

"I'm Constancia. A pleasure." As their eyes met, it was like they were only now seeing one another for the first time. Constancia judged Jesica to be bold and clumsy, but she was nonetheless a magical creature and Jesica recognised Constancia as a gifted young woman with a bright future. They both smiled, astonished by the sudden mutual amicability. It would be the beginning of a charmed, and long-lasting friendship that confused even the stars that shone down upon it.

Across the river, near the centre of the city, just off the Plaza de Armas, Hector smiled up into the clear blue sky and thanked the invisible stars for sending him so many tourists this morning. Why foreigners couldn't sleep in a little longer, he would never understand. They were on holiday, after all, weren't they? Their eagerness forced him into an inconveniently early start but like Constancia, he had become accustomed to being on the job well before noon.

This was going to be a busy day. He brushed off his shiny, pinstriped suit and straightened his blue, llama-print tie. Soon he'd have to buy a bigger jacket or ask Constancia to alter this one. The fabric was worn and pulling at the seams. It was imperative that he maintain a loose fit, something that his growing gut was threatening to do away with.

Although Hector had inherited his father's chiselled features, broad forehead and sparkling brown eyes, he had also inherited his mother's short stature and propensity to grow heavy. He secretly purchased shoes with lifts to increase his height but had made only half-hearted efforts to rein in his appetite. His girth continued to grow. He gave his mother credit for his thick, black hair. Due to his belief that female foreigners were attracted to Latino stereotypes (but also because he, himself, was drawn to the mode), he slicked his hair straight back from his forehead with extra-firm hold, wet-look gel until, from a distance, you might say he was wearing a shiny black helmet. Hector's cheeks were always clean-shaven but he carefully groomed a heavy moustache in order to draw attention to what he was sure were sensuous, masculine lips above his square chin. Dark glasses with mirrored lenses protruded from his jacket pocket in front of a carefully folded blue polyester handkerchief. When Hector moved forward down the street, he didn't just walk; he strutted with a slight bounce, shoulders back, head high, exuding the confidence and style of a brawny rooster after a battle in which he ran the risk of dirtying his claws but from which he never failed to emerge victorious. In spite of his convincing exterior, Hector was always the first to cower around a corner at the first sign of conflict.

He had a gift for languages and over the years he had managed to pick up more than just the essential phrases in English, French and German. This allowed him to snatch information from strangers' conversations, introduce himself and enter into their private worlds at appropriate moments. He was fascinated by the innocence of foreigners. It took very little to impress them and even less to predict where they would go and how they would react to his presence.

"Good morning, Madam," and a woman who thought no one around her could speak English, would turn her face to him, startled at first, and then break into a smile. Always the polite response, "Good morning."

"What lovely blue eyes you have." This never failed to flatter, especially if the eyes were actually dull grey or heavily-lidded and bewildered for having awoken at the far end of the world after a long flight. The woman always blinked her eyes hard several times, instinctively dusting them off to allow him to see more clearly through the windows to her soul. He looked deliberately and deeply into them, sometimes having to rise up onto his toes, but only for a second, and just high enough to spark a flame she forgot existed. Hector knew very well that if the balding, red-faced male companion with the big feet didn't grab her elbow and pull her along, she would accept his invitation for a coffee and likely even pay for it. And who knows what would come out of that? Such was the effect of well-applied Latino charm on gringas. But Hector preferred to keep a distance with his work. Although he had friends who were gigolos, that was not his chosen business. His was less involved, more that of a general practitioner. Besides, he preferred not to come and go at the whim of someone else. He advanced at his own pace and in the direction of his choice, his antennae picking out a fresh tourist like a farmer harvesting a ripe tomato.

This morning he spotted a likely mark from the other side of the plaza and he followed the group of three middle-aged British couples to a café. He settled into a table at the perimeter and with just a nod of his head, ordered his usual espresso. It would be easy to approach and offer to help them discover places they would not otherwise become acquainted with but he was careful not to interfere with their independent plans. Although he had once considered becoming a freelance guide and although he knew the secrets of the city, he discarded the idea because of the time and patience required to please unworldly and unreasonably demanding tourists.

Hector was always well-dressed in suit and tie and he carried a briefcase, which, by the end of the day was full of watches, wallets, passports and anything else people were careless enough to make available to a pickpocket. Unlike many of his counterparts, Hector preferred to work alone. He was skilled, which meant he didn't need to pass off the goods to a colleague who would scurry around the corner and out of sight. Hector didn't like partners or middlemen. Besides, he had several reliable contacts to whom he sold valuable documents and jewellery. Most of them were fences who did business out of their second-hand stores in the Persa Bío Bío, in close proximity to Slaughterhouse Square.

This morning there was no need to apply his full-on charm to a middle-aged female foreigner. One of the British women had purchased a bright, souvenir Andean-weave bag and she was anxious to put it to use. He watched her admire it as she removed it from her shoulder and set it on the ground at her feet. The corner of her wallet was visible from under the top fold. Her partner had slung his jacket over the back of his chair. Hector could bet the life of his mother that the man had left his passport tucked into the inside jacket pocket. He observed smiling as they craned their necks to peruse the one and only menu handed to them by the waiter. They weren't used to sharing. They struggled and failed in their attempts to order a full English breakfast. Hector still wasn't sure what a full English breakfast consisted of. But whatever it was, he knew they were going to be disappointed with Chilean-style, half-cooked, semi-scrambled eggs that were served with runny whites and small bits of cold ham. This is where his English language skills came in. He approached the group.

"Good morning." He smiled, exposing his polished teeth inside his sensuous mouth that was tickled at the top by his straight black moustache. His slick hair glistened in the sun.

The pink faces turned up towards him in unison. He saw them glance approvingly at his hair. They all replied politely, "Good morning."

"I couldn't help but notice you seem to be having trouble ordering breakfast," he said in his beguiling Spanish accent.

The man with the jacket chuckled. "It's that obvious, is it? Yes, actually, we could use some help with the language."

"No problem. I am happy to translate." Hector crouched so he was at their eye level, knees bent over the woman's purse, right hand on the back of the man's chair. He indicated for the waiter to give them a moment. He pointed with his left hand at an item on the menu and they all leaned forward, their eyes following his finger. As they did so, he slid his right hand into the pocket of the jacket that was draped on the chair and pulled out the passport, quickly shoving it into his belt. Then he shifted, bouncing a little on his heels, as he recited the list of fresh juice choices and reached his left hand into the woman's lovely bright new bag and deftly removed her wallet. He slid it into the other side of his belt and patted his jacket over top.

After explaining that it was next to impossible to find a full English breakfast in Chile, Hector recommended the soft scrambled eggs and a croissant. "Tea is never a problem here. We are a country of tea-drinkers, just like you."

They laughed. Amicable people, these Chileans.

"Well, I am late for a meeting. I hope you enjoy your holiday in our beautiful country." He stood up, briefcase in hand and they thanked him ever so much for his unexpected kindness.

"Such a nice man to go out of his way to help us like that." he heard the woman with the bright bag comment.

On the way out, Hector winked and paid the waiter three times the cost of his coffee. It was only fair that he reward a compadre for his cooperation. His glossy black hair shone up into the morning sky and the sun winked back at him as he strode out of the plaza towards his next tourist stop, the presidential palace.

....

When Juan sauntered into Slaughterhouse Square late that afternoon he was so taken aback by the ample, heart-shaped, blue satin, pink-fringed derriere swaying behind Jesica's speakers, that his jaw fell open and his cigarette, which hung loosely between his lips, flipped end-over-end to the ground. Maintaining his concentration on the gyrating blue bottom, he crouched to retrieve the cigarette and fumbled to put it back between his lips. He stood up and took several short puffs, squinting through the smoke at Jesica in her new outfit. He inhaled the last of his cigarette, dropped it on the patio, crushing it under the toe of his recently spit-polished black loafer and he opened his mouth to comment. But there were no words. Anything that came to mind would, one way or the other, be an understatement. Suffice to say that her outfit made an impact and would not soon be forgotten.

He drew his fingers through his hair a few times and spun around on his heel to survey the individuals who straggled in for the evening's entertainment. He noticed that their eyes were all trained on Jesica's blue satin bottom. No small wonder. He kicked a pebble and walked over to Mario's restaurant, plopped himself down onto the plastic lawn chair at the entrance and ordered a beer.

Mario was talking to a man with a briefcase about buying a one-pound English coin. Mario bragged, "I collect coins. I'm not expert but it's a small hobby of mine. I have a few from North America. And, I also have Swedish, French and German ones, including a couple of new euro coins, but somehow I am still missing the British pound coin. If you want, I'll give you a beer for it."

"Oh come on, my friend. You can do better than that. At today's exchange rate, I can probably buy four Cristal beers with it." The man in the suit with a llama-print tie and hair like a shiny black helmet smiled a crooked smile as he rolled the coin between his fingers.

"Well, okay, maybe three beers."

"It's yours." The man flipped it into the air and Mario caught it.

"Where did you get it?" Mario asked as he turned it over in his palm. "Do you travel a lot?"

"You could say that." The man grinned. "I travel back and forth across the water that divides the city." He removed the dark glasses from his breast pocket and used his blue handkerchief to clean the lenses before glancing around. He winked at a young girl who was observing him and leaned back in his chair, grinning like a greasy Cheshire cat in a worn suit.

Juan figured this guy as a clandestine king of creep but had to admire his finesse, sleazy as it was. He was not a man you would trust, but he was amusing to watch. There was something familiar about him. Perhaps he had seen him here before. Slaughterhouse Square attracted this type of character, and he had little doubt that their paths would cross again.

....

Meanwhile, back at the cemetery… Astrid and Señora Ruby finished the tasks they had assigned themselves for the day and for the first time in ages they prepared to walk together to the gate. Señora Ruby hobbled. She said her back bothered her. So Astrid slowed her pace, tucked Señora Ruby's arm in hers and kissed the straggly hair on top of her head. "It's been a long day."

"Yes," Señora Ruby looked straight ahead, "And it seems to me that they're getting longer."

They strolled silently down the path beside the wall that divided the Patio of the Dissidents from the cemetery proper. Walking here never failed to remind Astrid of her mother, who had instructed her on the history of this place, the country's first cemetery outside of Church grounds.

The Patios of the Dissidents were where the first Protestants were buried, clearly separated from the Catholics. Initially, the large majority of Protestants in Chile were European foreigners and it took decades after the cemetery's inception in 1821 for them to be allowed in the sacred grounds at all. When they were finally given permission, it was under the condition that, in order to prevent them contaminating the pure Catholic souls, a wall must be constructed to divide them. In those days, this overt religious discrimination was one of the least of all indignities imposed upon the dead, so very few people questioned what nowadays would be considered a grave injustice.

Astrid recalled the stories her mother told her of how, before the cemetery existed, Catholic churchyards were the only burial grounds in the country. Catholics complained of the clandestine burials of bodies from 'unqualified' families, which not only took up precious space but also polluted their grounds with undeserving souls. If they were caught in the act, the non-Catholic perpetrators were forced to exhume and expel the rejected human remains. In Santiago, for lack of anywhere else to leave the bodies, they were hauled up and then thrown down from the top of Santa Lucia Hill in the centre of the city and the bodies were left to rot wherever they stopped rolling and were picked apart by animals. The stench and spread of disease was intolerable but it still took ten years to convince the national congress to put a stop to this ignominious and unsanitary practice by finally passing a law that would create an independent holy ground. They agreed that the perfect location for this sacred bit of earth would be out of the way, across the river and downwind from the city centre.

The problem of how to pay for such a project in a country as poor as Chile (which had just financed its independence) was major. Initially, they could only afford to construct adobe walls around the perimeter to keep animals out. Finally, one of Chile's founding fathers, Bernardo O'Higgins came up with the solution. The cemetery infrastructure would be financed through the sale of ice. In those days snow was hauled by mule from the eastern Andean slopes into the city where they converted it to ice. It was a precious commodity and while everyone else paid dearly for it, privileged municipal bosses received theirs for free. O'Higgins simply decreed that city officials would pay for their ice and with this enough funds were found to build the cemetery infrastructure.

When Astrid was a child, she used to ask her mother to recount this story of ice over and over again. She imagined ice angels suspended over graves, their huge wings slowly melting, forming drops that fell like tears over the tombs until the angels themselves were transformed into water and they would seep inside. Then they would freeze again and be left hugging the muertitos in the eternal safety of their cold cocoons.

The creation of the cemetery was a huge accomplishment but for years the authorities still complied with the Church's demand to maintain a strict division between Catholics and Protestants. It took the death of a famous national war hero from the War of Independence Don Manuel Zañartu for the powers that be to allow integration. Although he was Protestant, his loyal followers insisted he be buried with no less dignity than his military counterparts – in the cemetery proper. Thus it was that after his death in 1871 he unwittingly fought and won a most important but forgotten battle – one against the Catholic Church.

Astrid was pensive and she squinted up at the sky, remembering something about how some stars were so old that they didn't exist anymore, yet their lights continued to shine. This was something incomprehensible. She would rather contemplate something closer to home. She lowered her gaze to watch her own worn leather loafers plod along the path. Over the years thousands upon thousands of other footfalls had echoed against the same walls and countless souls had proceeded past, in boxes atop a trolley or balanced on the shoulders of six strong men and they ended up staying forever in this place.

On one hand, in struggles for important changes, time drags its feet. Correcting social injustices can never come soon enough and yet it seems to take forever, usually more than a lifetime. Yet Astrid's own lifetime seemed short. Her children had already been with her for three decades but they were babies only yesterday. The cemetery was a reminder of how relative everything is. Trying to put it all in perspective was impossible, especially if she tried to think in universal terms, which did nothing but cause a headache. It was hard enough understanding her own life.

The smell of freshly turned soil, or the fleeting odour of stale urine at the corner of a wall, or the sight of chipped paint on a worn and ragged cross, or prayers sprayed like graffiti at the door of someone's father's tomb, or a shiny pinwheel glistening in the sun, or the snippet of a melody from a song her mother used to sing, called up memories from the deep that played with her emotions in a way that often left her confused. So she brushed them aside.

This afternoon, however, small aspects of the world around her glowed with fresh importance. Because of her mother's stories, cemetery landmarks and secret places had always been embedded with special meaning and now these same familiar places had added significance because of recent events around Jhonny Pretty and San Expedito. Another layer to her existence. Within only days of seeing Jhonny Pretty's ghost, her universe had expanded and she was exploring what lay around new corners. She reached up to rub her pendant. "Thank you, San Expedito."

She was more than uplifted by her unexpected, direct communication with important, even wise historical figures. When it came to Jhonny Pretty, she was elated and she had to suppress the urge to skip like a schoolgirl and leave Señora Ruby in the dust. The very real prospect of a sentimental relationship with Jhonny Pretty was at hand. And because of his ghostly condition, he was unable to inflict heartache, as had the organ grinder. Astrid was bursting with anticipation. Her universe had indeed opened up but she must be mindful, keep a good balance. She glanced over at Señora Ruby who was muttering something under her breath – perhaps a prayer, perhaps a conversation with one of her cemetery spirits. It was something about being rocked gently in the cradle of a crescent moon as the stars sang lullabies. Astrid chose not to interrupt. Señora Ruby was getting very old and she had to grant her these eccentricities.

As they approached the cemetery entrance, Astrid glimpsed another old woman. This one wore bright pink Adidas that were three sizes too big. The woman motioned up to the sky with a brittle index finger before disappearing behind the gatekeeper's shack. There was jasmine in the air.

CHAPTER 9

The Encounter

Juan was approaching the morning's thin edges of sleep when the hairs on the back of his neck stood straight up, pricking his skin like a million cold needles. He gasped awake as though he had been thrown into an icy pool, his ears alerting him to the sound of rodents scrounging and bustling around above him on the main floor of the mausoleum.

He came up for breath, his eyes staring crazily into the darkness towards the trap door, unable to see anything other than some hazy light that streamed down through the narrow cracks. His ears were now like finely calibrated machines, detecting each rub, each scrape, measuring exactly how close the wiry-haired creatures were to invading his subterranean abode. He pictured their naked, pink tails slithering around the iron bars and their red eyes shining up towards the virgin on the altar, perhaps asking for permission to enter. She would grant it, of course, leaving him vulnerable because she didn't approve of his late nights with the stench of rancid wine and telltale signs of licentiousness.

The sharp claws were near the main entrance. He could hear them winding around the wrought-iron gates. They were after him. How many could there be? Perhaps a platoon. How did they find him? He cringed, trembling under his blankets and waited for what seemed an eternity. When the scratching suddenly stopped he was suspicious. He was frozen with fear and loathing, his body a rigid antenna, ultra-sensitive. Other than his quivering and harried breathing, he was unable to move a muscle.

Astrid was practically floating in her own pleasure at being able to offer her services to Jhonny. She leisurely set the broom aside and bent down to extract small branches that had grown around and had snagged at the base of the Maluenda-Valdéz wrought iron gate. Too bad she couldn't get inside to do a proper cleaning. She used a twig to scratch into the corners, pulling out old leaves and dust that had accumulated over who-knows-how-long. She stretched, poked and rubbed, taking such joy in the privilege of performing this small act of kindness for the one she loved. Her trained eye could see the smog-encrusted corners and soot that had caked into the grooves of the marble altar. The extra dust that arose as a result of the recent earthquake had been lightly brushed aside here and there. She must make a note to find out if an extended family member visited, because as far as she knew Jhonny Pretty was the end of the line for the Maluenda-Valdéz family. The virgin statue was covered in years of film and the stained glass on the back wall looked like it hadn't been touched in a century. Astrid shook her head and sighed. It would only take a minute to give the entrance one more quick brush with the whiskbroom.

Finally, she turned around and descended the stairs towards her tool cart where she had placed some rice pudding. Cradling the bowl like it was a holy chalice, she tingled with anticipation. Jhonny was going to love it. She had planned to leave it at his gate but at the last minute she decided it was best to wait until the end of the day so that nobody would be tempted to steal it.

Last night she happened across a Jhonny photo in an El Ritmo magazine in which he was dipping a spoon into a bowl of Spanish-style rice pudding and puckering up as if to throw a kiss to the camera. Astrid closed in on the image, rubbing her nose against the page and cooing as though to a child, "Oh, Jhonny, you're so irresistible." The caption read, 'Jhonny Pretty enjoys his favourite dessert with friends at El Club Loco.' Spanish-style rice pudding just happened to be Astrid's speciality. She took it as another sign of their destinies intertwined. 'Astrid, the humble cemetery caretaker enchants the famous rockero with her home cooking.' Astrid and Jhonny Pretty, who would have thought? The idea brought a silly smile to her face, which she had worn unaware all morning. Colleagues had stopped to smile in return, men tipped their hats, women waved with enthusiasm. She attributed the special attention to the silent presence of Jhonny's ghost, who must be following her in his invisible cloud of negative ions. Señora Ruby had educated Astrid about the effects of negative ions and said it helped to explain the peace and harmony felt within graveyards.

She placed the bowl of pudding back in the corner of her pushcart and then gave the bottom stair one quick brush before advancing down the path towards Señora Ruby's shack, hips swaying to Los Rockero's "We'll Meet in Paradise." She looked down past her faded skirt at the worn argyle socks in her brown leather loafers and thought about her feet, protected inside like two pink, vestal jewels. Last night she had painted her toenails with passionate red nail polish, each tip a bright little beacon lighting its way for Jhonny. She and her virgin feet would be back tonight with her gift of rice pudding. This would be a most unusual Monday – two trips to the cemetery when she normally took Mondays off. She flushed with anticipation and the possibility of having Jhonny appear to explain why she, of all people, is his chosen one. Her smile broadened.

Juan remained alert on the corner of his bed. The mice had retreated, perhaps attracted to a bigger feast further down the path. Sharing his hovel with mice was out of the question. He could sleep beside dogs or cats or lie down on sweat-soaked blankets beside drunken men. He could even tolerate cockroaches. But he could not abide mice. His inordinate fear of these gnawing mammals was intense. Adrenalin coursed through his body, preparing for flight. In the gloom of his subterranean space, as his pickled brain percolated with defensive plans, his head bobbed on his shoulders and he resembled one of those silly plastic toys in the back of a car driving through a black tunnel. He grinned into the dark as the final solution took shape and he could see the light at the end. There was a way out.

The first step – a somewhat cowardly one – was to wait a little longer, until he was sure the army of revolting little scavengers had moved on. Once he felt safe he sprang to his feet and in the darkness, shook out his blankets like a man gone mad, stood his mattress on end and pummelled the hell out of it with his fist. He was nearly asphyxiated by the dust but he finished the job by stuffing every stitch of clothing he owned into a sack. Heart pounding, he dragged it up the ladder and peered cautiously out from under the trap door. He stepped up to the main floor and crouching, sack thrown onto his back, he scoped the area for a lingering pink tail protruding from a crack. There was none. So he unlocked the gate and dashed around the side of the mausoleum to twist free the end of a pine branch. He returned inside and used the branch to sweep every square centimetre of the altar and the floors. He even used his shirttails to dust the brass handles and grooves of the individual marble sepulchres. He reached for the virgin statue to give it a quick rubdown but he was stopped by her cold stare. Thinking better of it, he left her untouched. "No wonder she's a virgin," he thought, "with a glare like that." He would have stayed longer to admire his handiwork if he had had time, but he had things to do. He rushed to the nearest public washroom and slipped into his Salvation Army suit. It was early in the day for that but he had no choice given the rodent emergency.

Juan hopped onto the first bus that stopped outside the cemetery gate, smiling apologetically for dropping less than the required fare into the box. The cranky bus driver waved him on, too lazy to insist. He slumped down onto the cracked vinyl seat with his sack of clothing. The bus lurched and stalled several times before rattling on towards El Patronato at a speed that would see it drop vital engine parts before too long. The windows clattered and when the bus barrelled through deep potholes, the noise became deafening. Feeling not only rattled, but injured, Juan jumped off before the bus came to a complete stop and he jogged down the narrow alley leading to the Peruvian washerwoman's place, sack pitching on and off his back.

Slaughterhouse Square was slow that afternoon. Besides, his day had gotten off to a foul start, he just wasn't in good form and he was thirsty. So as soon as the coins in the hat netted him enough for beer, he ignored Jesica's questioning glare and called it quits. He slogged over to Mario's restaurant, fell into one of the plastic garden chairs and slammed his coins on the table, "Bring me all the beer this will buy, okay amigo?" It amounted to three pints. He slugged them down in silence, his mind on the mice. He'd have to return to the mausoleum to see if it was still habitable.

After another bone-jarring bus ride back to the cemetery, he walked nonchalantly past the guard at the gate but the beer he had guzzled was still sloshing in his stomach and it added to the queasiness at the thought of the naked pink tails from that morning. He ducked in behind the nearest treed wall and vomited before giving himself a pep talk, emphasising each word with each step. "I am Jhonny Pretty, for Christ's sake. Where is my courage? When have little pink tails had power over you?" He thought better of that one. "Well, if truth be told…"

He hesitated before climbing the steps of the mausoleum, unlocked the gate, tried to ignore the fear that prickled over the goose bumps on his skin and he crossed the floor to the trap door. He opened it and squinted into the darkness below the stairs, alert for signs. It would be impossible to sleep down there tonight; the only solution would be to move his mattress up onto the roof. He stepped back outside and glanced up at the clear blue sky. The fresh air could be rejuvenating. He crossed the path to get a broader perspective of the Maluenda-Valdéz mausoleum. Its façade extended nearly a metre above the roofline. With two short pillars topped with crosses on either side of the slow, central curved wall, the structure had been designed like a miniature chapel, a peaceful house of prayer, a sanctuary for a family full of saints. His mother had achieved her desired effect. And its decorative roofline was a protective barrier behind which he and his mattress would be very comfortable. "Thank you once again, Mother. You outdid yourself."

Mondays were usually quiet days at the cemetery. Even the caretakers took the day off so he had no concerns about a witness questioning his actions. It took great effort and several colourful curses to install the mattress on the roof, but he finally succeeded. As a reward, he rolled a cigarette and lay back, puffing circles of smoke into the intense blue sky. Other than to brush cigarette ashes off of his Salvation Army jacket lest they burn a hole, he had no concerns. In the security of his new location, and with the afternoon heat and a satisfying sense of accomplishment, he fell into a peaceful slumber.

It was dusk before he stirred. The place was uncommonly quiet. Muffled sounds of faraway traffic reminded him he was in the city, but the immediate smell of plants, the palm and pine branches that brushed the roof, birds that flitted and fraternised amidst the foliage and the musty smell of ancient adobe diminished the urban reality of the smog that hung overhead. He woke up feeling pure as a saint, so much so that he could feel righteousness running through his veins. Since absolute sobriety was an unusual condition, it didn't occur to him that clean blood was not a saintly, but rather a normal state of being. Drifting in and out of his siesta and basking in his own virtue, he watched as the sun disappeared behind the hills and the half-moon blessed the earth with her presence. Everything was celestial, larger than life, holier than thou, including himself. He held up a hand and watched the moonlight create an aura around it, five fingers painted in divine light, capable of anything.

Into his otherworldly ambience entered a sound, a hint of the presence of another human being below him, possibly at the steps of the mausoleum. He rolled over onto his stomach and inched himself forward on his elbows to peer down. He was mostly in the shadows. But streaks of moonlight splayed across his back, silhouetting his head, which was all that protruded above the façade. He watched as a woman neared the entrance to his home.

She was carrying a small bowl of something and she slid it past the rungs of the gate to place it just inside his house.

"This is a gift for you, Jhonny. I made it myself. Spanish-style rice pudding. I don't know if you are home at the moment, but this is fresh so I hope you find it and eat it before long, so you taste it at its best. It's exquisite if I do say so myself. It's my speciality." He could hear the smile in her voice.

The woman looked familiar. Curious, Juan raised his eyebrows as he leaned down, careful not to alert her to his presence. The woman's black hair was gathered loosely at the nape of her neck and she wore fluorescent green hoop earrings. Leaning one way and then the other, she peered into his sanctuary with eyes that were lacklustre, out of sync with her enthusiastic tone. Like a friend who nudges you under the table to warn you of an approaching evangelical with an open bible and his hand out, something kicked him fully awake. As his grey matter was wedged open, the image of a woman crawled out of the crack in his brain. He caught a peek of the day he had been surprised by her at the gates of his new home. And he remembered with growing interest something about a woman holding a filter cigarette.

A loose-knit sweater hung over this woman's hips. She sat down on the top step, tucking her skirt under her legs, and she twisted sideways, renewing her efforts to discover what lay amongst the shadowed outlines of his home. She spoke softly, "May the Virgin protect you, Jhonny. I see that she was not damaged during the quake, which is a good sign. I also noticed that someone has cleaned up inside your mausoleum but there is no caretaker assigned here, so maybe a distant relative is visiting you. You deserve many, many visitors. But if truth be told, I prefer to be one of the special few. I mean, I assume you don't show yourself to just anyone. It's rare for ghosts to reveal themselves and it's commonly understood that when they do, it's for a reason. So I want you to know that I feel privileged, Jhonny. I really do." She hesitated, "May I call you 'Jhonny?'" She nodded affirmatively, giving herself permission.

He could see that the woman was becoming emotional, close to tears. She must have a screw loose or her brain short-circuited. First she wanted to feed him and now she infers that he is a ghost. Amused, Juan observed as she rolled back slightly on her bottom and reached into her pocket to extract a leather cigarette case. She pulled out a filter cigarette and in what appeared to be an accomplished performance, twirled it expertly between her fingers before positioning it at right angles to herself on the stair. The cigarette's non-filter end pointed towards the mausoleum. She pulled out a single match from another small box and placed it above the cigarette, forming a 'T.' Taking her time, she returned the cigarette case and matchbox to her skirt pocket and sat erect. Focusing on the cigarette and match, she raised both arms straight above her head as though she was about to make an offering. Then she bowed down slightly, arms still outstretched, fingers tips touching. Juan barely heard the whisper of her voice as she muttered several short phrases. She could be a witch. Who else does this sort of thing? The woman suddenly spoke out loud, "Jhonny," she said, "Let's share a smoke."

Juan's interest was definitely piqued. For a filter cigarette he could go along with this woman, be she 100% witch or not. He forced himself to remove his eyes from the tobacco cylinder to focus on her. Suddenly he remembered that the filter cigarette memory was associated with this very same woman – and not so long ago. Naturally, the image of the Derby cigarette was etched more clearly in his mind than the woman herself but the recurrent presence of the cigarette in her hands meant that the woman deserved more serious regard.

Astrid leaned over, plucked the cigarette from the stair, and held it between thumb and forefinger, her other three fingers fanned up and out, movie-star fashion. She struck the match against the bottom of her shoe and lifted the flame to her face, squinting and grimacing with anticipated pleasure. She took a long drag and blew the smoke into the dim interior, watching to see how far it would go before disappearing into the dusky air.

"That one was for you, Jhonny."

Then she rose to her feet and, facing the entrance, assumed a wide stance. With a few minimal, yet dramatic circular movements of her arm she then rolled the cigarette gently between thumb and forefinger and raised it to her lips again. "And this one..." she said on the intake as she looked up past the roof, "is for..." her voice died.

Her jaw dropped. She gasped in surprise, choking on the smoke that shot back into her throat. Her eyes, as big as saucers, burned with sudden tears and she blinked past them, trying to see through to the beautiful pair of dark eyes that were returning her stare from the roof. They were set in a shadowy face that was illuminated around the edges by a halo, an ethereal, otherworldly aura. If she were to think about it later she would remember that the aura halted and flickered, as though tarnished. But she never did think about it later, and at the moment, it was pure magic. Her first impression was that he was an angel, perhaps one of her guardians watching over her at this late hour. She relaxed a bit but was afraid to bend down and pick up the cigarette that had slipped from between her fingers, fearing that if she removed her gaze, the face would disappear. So the cigarette smouldered at her feet, sending weak wafts of smoke into the mystery under her skirt.

Astrid alternated between squinting and gaping wide-eyed at the face as she tried to identify her angel.

Juan, regretting the waste of a fine cigarette, looked on helplessly as it burned towards the filter. He wanted to scramble down and rescue it, put it to his lips and suck for all it was worth.

Against his will, and perhaps his better judgement, and without knowing what provoked him to sing the words aloud rather than to play them in his head, he began to croon, "Fumar es un placer, genial, sensual. Fumando espero la mujer que quiero..." (Smoking is a pleasure, cool, sensual. Smoking, I wait for the woman I love..."). His own father used to sing this song and all of Latin America knew it. He stopped after the first phrase and let his voice drift into the night. He continued to eye the burning tobacco on the cold floor beside the leather loafer on the woman's left foot.

Astrid stood frozen, allowing the voice that sang the classic tango tune to play across the chords of her willing heart. Of course the song was an old standard, so familiar that the singer could have been the ghost of anyone. Given the darkness of the hour, this could even be the face of any number of her muertitos. But it was not the voice of just anyone. And they were not the eyes of just anyone. It was the voice, and these were the eyes of Jhonny Pretty! Now he was singing to her. To her! "Be still my beating heart!" She felt her pulse pound out a dangerously uneven rhythm and she grabbed at her chest, sinking into a state of wobbly bliss, her feet very close to the glowing butt. When she swooned, she squashed the life out of it with her right foot.

A small light was immediately snuffed out in Juan's world. He groaned. Half of a perfect filter cigarette crushed under a dirty layer of thick cowhide, wasted under the weight of this woman's heel. A shameful way to go. Disappointed, he shook his head and inhaled heavily, hoping the air would at least carry a trace of the ember. He was about to shrink back behind the protection of the façade, like a worm retreating to the safety of a hole he has just eaten his way out of, when the woman's voice shot like a bullet in the crisp air, whistling past to his ear. Her accent revealed a lack of formal education and he knew she grew up in the streets and rows of tombs in which they were now surrounded. She spoke plainly and without inhibition, almost as though she was talking to herself.

Astrid gazed up into Jhonny Pretty's eyes. He was truly a vision from heaven. The moonlight around him glowed with distinct rock'n'roll purity. The night danced out from its darkness and into his radiant presence. He was the fusion of this world with another. And the echo of his voice singing "Fumar es un placer, genial, sensual..." floated down seductively to wrap itself around her shoulders and warm her pulsing heart. She was dazzled by the choice of song, that he should be 'waiting for the woman he loves.'

Meanwhile, as he watched, Juan began to fantasise about smoking.

"Jhonny," she began, "I've been waiting a long time for you, too."

Juan's smoking dream screeched to a halt. What? We've been waiting for each other? This crone is crazy.

"Jhonny, after all these years wasted with others... it pains me think about it, the others, I mean. Probably because you've had so many. I saw you with all those girls in El Ritmo magazine. I don't know why I looked at them. It enrages me. I ruined a whole bunch of pages one night, tearing your face away from theirs. It was stupid, I know. I'm not a violent woman. Just ask anyone. But I made sure that your face always remained untouched... beautiful as it is. I poked their eyes out first with the tip of my scissors and then chopped their bodies away. It might sound foolish but it's done now and I have to try not to think about it, try not to think of you with other women. Well, anyway, I guess it isn't a problem any more, given your current condition. Do you miss the touch of someone, Jhonny?" She paused and stared up at him.

Juan remained silent, contemplating the situation. Was she really expecting a response? She believed he was a ghost. The cogs rotated slowly, turning up fragments of unscrupulous possibilities and laying them out in his mind's eye, waiting for him to construct them into something useful. Thankfully, she didn't leave him much space to respond. She appeared to be on a roll now, beyond stopping.

Pouring out her heart to a man like dead Jhonny was a great privilege. He would not argue, he would only listen and maybe he would offer some wisdom, something he learned from 'the other side.'

"I'm honoured that you allow me to see you, Jhonny. You could have made yourself visible to anyone else. I mean you can have your pick of any woman, just like when you were alive. And look. You chose me!"

She moved to make a curtsy. It was uncoordinated and she stopped half way through the motion. Even through the obscure evening air he could see her blush.

Her face upturned in a happy puppy expression, she primped and fluffed her hair as though she was looking into a mirror. She did her best to conjure a confident, come-hither look, praying that she could pull it off with as much skill as some of Jhonny's El Ritmo women.

She wasn't very successful. Juan was lost for words and continued to stare silently back at her. "Holy Mother of God. I could really use a cigarette," he thought. He lamented the squashed butt at her feet.

Astrid continued. "I guess I know way more about you than you know about me, Jhonny. And since it appears that you have chosen to be with me, it's only fair that I tell you something about myself." She straightened her shoulders, flicked at her hair a couple of times, stood erect, looking upwards, her eyes searching his face as she told him about the organ grinder, how she had hidden the depth of her pain all these years, how she had been unable to trust another living man.

Juan was wilting. His bones ached, he could use a massage, and he was bored. This was like sitting in a front pew at church, trying not to squirm as the priest delivers a monotone sermon in Latin. He knew he wouldn't remember a word she was saying. But it was obvious that her loco solution was to set her sights on a ghost. It was definitely an original approach to protecting a broken heart. But it wasn't really going to do any good with him.

He wanted to retreat behind the façade but the lure of a cigarette prevented him from doing so. He rested his chin on his hands and prepared to wait her out. It was getting late and the woman droned on, her words no longer penetrating his uncaring ears. Even if he took the cigarette out of the equation, he worried that if he pulled himself away, this crazy feline would scale the wall and join him on the roof. If she wasn't desperate, then he didn't know who was.

Astrid's face contorted as she tried to hide silent drops of self-pity that seeped from the corners of her eyes. They dribbled down to her upper lip and she tasted the gratitude she felt towards Jhonny. He had changed her life. But he already understood that. She wanted to explain why she welcomed a dead man into her life. She began in mid-thought. "And that's why you're so perfect, Jhonny. You're not a living man. You can't cause me sorrow by committing sins of the flesh with other women. I know where to find you every night. Even if you don't show yourself to me, I know you're here. You'll always be here. I like the certainty of that, you know? I'm not interested in sex anymore, Jhonny. I missed it for years after I got rid of the organ grinder. But it seemed a small price to pay and besides, I've been conditioned to do without for so long now... then the other night I realised that the Virgin has been saving me for you. Saving what's left of me, what remains of my purity." She caressed her belly and glanced furtively at her virgin-like feet. She decided not to mention them. At least not yet. "I just want your love and companionship. I have to admit that I would love to feel the warmth of your arms around me but to have you – you Jhonny, I will sacrifice that. I mean because... well... being with you now, in whatever form, is more than I can ask. It's more than anyone can ask. Your simple presence feeds my soul." She dropped her eyes at last. "I'm in love with you, Jhonny. You are my dream come true."

Drained but satisfied, Astrid was finished. She felt a twinge of guilt for the one white lie – the one that said she wasn't interested in sex. Of course she was, but under the circumstances, she was willing to forfeit that – at least until she informed herself more clearly about the possibilities of physical interaction with a ghost, under special conditions, of course. She drew the remaining cigarette from the packet that was hidden in the folds of her skirt pocket and prepared to light it. "I'll do anything for you, Jhonny," she said with the cigarette between her lips.

The smell of freshly lit tobacco ignited a spark in Jhonny and he blurted, "I'll accept a cigarette."

Astrid looked up at the halo around Jhonny's head and marvelled at his desire for a smoke. "Still so alive!" she thought. "So real. So manly. And so bold." His blunt request excited her and she felt desire flow through her body, weakening her arms. She licked her lips.

Juan would kill two birds with one stone. He would do it gently. He softened his voice and pronounced his words slowly, deliberately, like a magician, a hypnotist. "Place the cigarette in the grate of the door and walk away very quietly. Don't turn around until you are at the end of the path. This is the first test of your devotion. I will think of you as I smoke." As an added incentive for her expedited exit, he would reward her. "If you are able to do this, you will feel me in your bed when you go to sleep tonight." His grin lit up the night air with such intensity that the Cheshire cat would have been jealous.

....

She obeyed. And that night, as Astrid leisurely massaged her feet before slipping between her sheets she remained alert for Jhonny's presence in her bedroom. Laying on her back, she closed her eyes, took long, slow, even breaths and waited until she felt soft wisps of cold air brush back and forth across her face. She smelled the smoke on his breath and drifted into his invisible arms. "Jhonny, oh Jhonny..."

CHAPTER 10

Exchange of Wealth and Knowledge

Over the weeks that followed, Juan Bonifacio Maluenda-Valdéz didn't talk much and he kept his distance behind the wrought iron entrance of the family crypt. Even though touching had been eliminated from the woman's list of prerequisites for their relationship, he understood that if he was going to benefit, the maintenance of his ghostly veneer was paramount.

In fact Astrid de las Nieves was so fully satisfied with her status as Jhonny Pretty's girlfriend that she radiated the blush of a new bride or perhaps even that of a pregnant wife. Susana and Siete Pelos commented that San Expedito must have come through for her. "She's over the moon." And Siete Pelos agreed, "Yeah, and swinging right off the crescent." They winked and nudged but Astrid wasn't going to give up the best-kept secret of her life, especially to Susana, the most zealous gossip on the planet.

Astrid was not unaware of how Constancia and Hector nodded and rolled their eyes when they thought she wasn't looking. She knew they were curious. But if she revealed her love affair, they would chide and make fun of its unorthodox nature. She decided that if they discovered she was serious about Jhonny Pretty, they might go so far as try to commit her for insanity. They would each grab an arm and force her to wait for hours in the queue at the University Hospital until a haggard nurse from the psychiatric ward would usher them in. They would sully her love affair with their pedestrian misunderstanding. They would be unable to grasp the importance of this relationship, not to mention its convenience. And what about its passion? Oh, the ethereal passion! Something beyond imagination – she in her bed, awaiting the almost nightly visits of the ghost of Jhonny Pretty. She admitted the affair was somewhat maverick but the nonconformity was part of its allure. This, to some degree, was responsible for the perpetual secret smile, which is what gave her away. Despite appearances, she knew she was not insane. But for privacy and security, she had installed two padlocks on the outside of her bedroom door as well as a deadbolt on the inside, and she kept her bedrooms curtains drawn, day and night. Jhonny's altar must not be exposed to curious eyes and probing minds. If Hector or Constancia saw it, they would subject her to serious interrogation because although it was not uncommon to help clients with altars at the cemetery, she had never created such an elaborate, ever-evolving one at home.

Hector noticed the locks and commented to Constancia, "She's probably hiding a stash in there, Cona. I bet she's taken to robbing graves." To which Constancia replied, "Well, all the credit to her then. It's about time. She works hard and I can count on one hand the number of her patrons who pay on time, if they even bother to pay at all. Let her take what she needs."

Relieved by their apparent lack of interest, or at least by their silence, Astrid realised there would be no cross-examination and she stopped imagining scenarios in which she wandered the dark green, urine-stained hallways of the psychiatric ward, avoiding wild-eyed, bearded men who were lusting after her feet.

Astrid became so badly smitten in the days that followed that she was unable to curb temptation and she found herself at Jhonny Pretty's front door at least once a day, sometimes three times, depending on how strongly she felt him calling and how much she burned to see him. She preferred not to go empty-handed. An offering from one lover to another was always a nice gesture. Given his supernatural condition, material gifts from Jhonny to her were not expected; to reciprocate, he sang to her – priceless snippets of songs – his own voice, half whisper, half baritone – causing her knees to go weak and her pulse to race. Less often he acquiesced to a special request for one of his old tunes, which, for a reason not understood by her, he insisted on limiting to no more than a stanza. But no matter, Astrid's cup runneth over.

Astrid regularly delivered Derby filter cigarettes to Jhonny's mausoleum, mostly just one loose one at a time, but if she could afford it, she dropped by with two. Three were beyond her daily budget but she promised herself that if a fortune dropped from the sky, the first thing she'd do would be to buy him a whole packet, still sealed. Jhonny had thoughtfully installed a wooden box, which he referred to as their 'private vault,' just inside the rungs at the entrance gate. He pointed it out, "My dear heart, I arranged this for you." He was going to address her by name, but couldn't remember it. To compensate, he continued with, "Mi amor... I thought it would be convenient and secure. I hate it when I miss your visits, but if you do happen to come by to leave a cigarette or two when I'm not here, you can slip it inside, confident that no one except me will have access."

Given that ghosts sometimes have resources beyond our understanding, she didn't question how he had arranged it. Besides, the use of such terms of endearment distracted her. She didn't care that their private vault was actually just a mailbox with a wide, hinged portal that Juan had ripped off from Jesica's neighbour's gate.

As it happened, one day as he left Jesica's, Juan noticed the mailbox's loose hinges and addressed it directly. "You look like you need rescuing." And with one thump of his fist and barely a pause in his stride, he dropped it into a shopping bag. Jesica said her neighbour had gone berserk when he discovered his mailbox was missing and he cursed the no-good, lowlife son of a bitch who took it. A series of events followed.

Unfortunately for the neighbour, the postman on that route was a conscientious type and he refused to deliver the mail 'just anywhere.' This resulted in the CGE Power bill not arriving. Since CGE ran a zero grace period policy, after three days, a technician was sent up the pole to disconnect the neighbour's power. This happened right in the middle of a do-or-die Colo-Colo football match and the incensed neighbour ran out with a baseball bat to chase the goddamned CGE technician back up the pole where he remained trapped for two hours. Then the neighbour threatened everyone else in sight, all of this, wearing nothing but his Colo-Colo t-shirt.

Now he had to pay a reconnection fee and adding insult to injury, the police dropped by to investigate claims of indecent exposure while threatening a paid employee of a reputable power corporation, and he was fined 50,000 pesos, nearly a week's income. Pay up or go to jail. He tried to borrow the money from Jesica but she refused. "I can't help you out. If you can't even pay your power bill, why would I believe that you would pay me back? And besides, even if I were to show you this kindness, what's to stop you running over here some night, half-naked with your baseball bat just because something else has gone wrong? No way. I'm sorry, but I can't help."

Jesica complained to Juan that her neighbourhood was becoming more and more dangerous. He showed no interest. "Spare me the details, Jesica. You need to concentrate on getting this machine working properly." He motioned to the speaker that had been cutting in and out during his last set. "Besides, what have I got to do with your neighbourhood? Maybe if you had room at the inn, I could help, but under the circumstances..." he let the thought go, shrugged, and walked over to Mario's for a beer.

Anyway, the mailbox was perfect for Juan's purposes. It was a superior model; it even had a trap door for small parcels. He pointed it out to Astrid, "And look, there, on the top left, you can see a special little hinged part that opens and I think it's just the right size for a bowl of your delicious rice pudding." He winked, "Of course, my love, it could never be as delicious as you..." His intimation took her by surprise. The instant it rolled off his tongue, Astrid imagined him licking her ear, his voice whispering soft nothings, and she could feel his hot breath on her throat, even smell his hair. The fantasy had such an impact that she took a careless step backwards and fell down the steps. Bottoms up. Timber! Fore! One brown leather loafer flew from her foot as she landed in a heap, skirt above her waist, exposing more of her upper thighs than Juan cared to see. But before he could avert his glance he noticed her black and red satin panties. Were those two little hearts that were embroidered into the lingerie or were they really twin images of San Expedito? He blinked and made a conscious effort not to care. Curiosity could lead you into dark places you would rather not be. Feeling at odds, he thought maybe he should say something to prove he didn't notice that she had just turned herself upside down, but there is no appropriate comment for such a thing – neither for the unsightly spill nor for the outlandish panties. Averting his eyes, he did his best to ignore the inelegant tumble and, in his most velvet of voices, affirmed from the back of his dim shelter, "Your generosity will always be appreciated by me and me alone, my darling."

Disconcerted by of her own lack of grace and control, Astrid grabbed her loafer and hugged it to her chest. Uncomfortably aware that she was behaving like a schoolgirl, she bent down and scrambled to wriggle her toes back into it. It ended with the heel of her sock protruding into a lumpy pyramid out of the back of the shoe. This went unnoticed as she hastily re-arranged her skirt, whacking it repeatedly as though beating the dust from a rug until it stayed down around her knees.

The simple fact that he referred to her as 'my darling' left her extremely satisfied with this, their latest tryst. And as she made her hasty retreat down the path towards home, she convinced herself that the unfortunate mishap on the stairs would not be remembered.

When she reached her bedroom door and fumbled with the padlocks, she was still euphoric. Jhonny's last uttered phrases resounded in her head – 'my love,' 'delicious,' 'my darling' – offering her a hope and a prayer. She lit three candles and gazed into his centrefold face before peacefully curling up into a ball and succumbing to a rapturous, Jhonny-induced slumber.

Meanwhile, Juan waved a congenial salute to the cemetery gatekeeper on his way back to the nightlife of Slaughterhouse Square. He shook his head in disbelief. If ever there was one, his was a perfect arrangement. Santiago's most accomplished playwright couldn't have written Juan into a better script. The only thing this crazy bat required of him was that he occasionally made an appearance from a safe distance – each of them on opposite sides of his door. He discovered that if he paused to sing part of a verse or if he lingered awhile, simulating interest in one of her daily accounts, she would be so grateful that the next day he would receive two of the Derby filtered babies in his mailbox rather than just one. He was unaware of, and would have been unsympathetic to the sacrifices made by Astrid to afford this small luxury – it meant a bun without meat or cheese for lunch, and forfeiting a cigarette herself.

Juan grew accustomed to the encounters in which he played the ghost and she played the lover in a pairing that would never be consummated. He had never fancied himself an actor, but he began to think that perhaps he had missed his calling. Masquerading as a ghost and feigning transcendental love came easily, at least in this situation, which, when he wasn't bored with it, amused him. The best part was that he was regularly rewarded.

Their occasional meetings grew into an unexpectedly pleasant habit and he admitted to himself that during the past weeks, he had even come to await them with a small amount of pleasure, in the same way that, as a child, he used to anticipate the hot soup that his mother's maid placed on the table in front of him when he returned home from school. He related certain maternal warmth to this particular ritual. Now he had to admit that he took the maid and her soup for granted and it was with nostalgia and regret that he remembered the routine. Therefore, in an attempt to make amends to the maid he had ignored (although she would never know), and to derive lasting benefit from Astrid's visits and award her the attention she craved, he promised himself that he would endeavour to participate more fully, try to concentrate on the woman herself, and not just on the cigarettes and rice pudding.

However, honest reciprocity was, in practice, beyond Juan's emotional capacity. He vaguely recognised this truth because more than one woman had accused him of being cold-hearted and distant. Countless times he had tried to get beyond the emotional fog that had enveloped him since the bus accident but he couldn't fight his way out. He floated around inside the grey, nothing to hang on to, no hooks to grab, no stairs to help him climb up to the clear air that he knew existed somewhere in his brain. He was helpless inside his cocoon void. And now, in the specific case of the caretaker, rather than over-exerting his brain and ending with the inevitable pounding headache, he employed his limited power of concentration to plot methods of extracting additional rice pudding and cigarettes from her.

Before long he hit the jackpot with a major brainwave and made a subtle suggestion to Astrid. "Mi querida, as a ghost there isn't much I can hold onto, save the affections demonstrated through gifts such as those that caring relatives leave at grave sites." He worked up a wretched expression, something he had practised, albeit unsuccessfully, many times with Jesica. "But as you know, my family have all gone before me." His index finger circled to indicate the tombs around him and it punched the air a few times towards the floor, indicating those who rested in the darkness one level below. "People who visit other mausoleums, especially the damaged ones, assume that most of their sentimental ornaments were broken or buried during the quake, so they've written them off and they bring new ones. I see them carrying in gifts day after day. I'm sure you've noticed it too. It makes me sad because I'm left out." He exaggerated the furrow in his brow. "But what can you do?" He shrugged a couple of times, head lowered, eyes discreetly reading her face. Yes, she was sympathetic. Her eyes had grown misty. He continued, "The cemetery, and especially the sectors that are to be renovated, are rich in treasure. People are walking over it, unaware that it exists, oblivious to the valuable items that are trapped under a chunk of cement or buried under just a few centimetres of sand, and these things are crying to be displayed again. Now you have the chance to give the forgotten things a new life in a home where they will be appreciated." He motioned to his immediate surroundings. "I know they are material things that a ghost such as myself has no use for. But they serve a vital purpose – reminding us that even though we are dead, we are valued. I mean that's why your job is so important in the first place, right? Here's an opportunity to satisfy several needs – those of the 'disappeared' ornaments and those of a forgotten rock star." Observing the woman's reaction, he congratulated himself on his rehearsed presentation.

Astrid nodded, inflating her chest and lifting her chin. She totally understood and didn't need more convincing. In fact, that very afternoon she ventured out on her mission. Initially she went only to those sectors that were slightly damaged but as the days passed she became bolder and ventured further into the demolished patios. She shook her head, wondering why she hadn't thought of this herself. Surely it would explain why she had seen a few other caretakers skulking about in the dust and rubble of restricted areas and then scurrying back to the main path when they thought someone was watching. It made perfect sense to recover what had been given up for lost, especially for her noble cause. And it fit in well with the city's new re-use and recycle campaign.

It wasn't long before she began to drop small ornaments into Jhonny's private vault. If an item was too big even for the vault's special door, she manoeuvred it through the bars, and then, using a stick that Jhonny had so thoughtfully left for this purpose, she shoved it in beyond reach.

Juan was impressed with his own artful supplication and with the woman's immediate and fruitful response. It was necessary for him to renew his friendship with Milo, a well-known fence at the Persa Bío Bío. If Milo refused to buy an item, Juan moaned to Astrid the next day, "Oh my dear, these are lovely but at this time, I can't accept your generosity. You understand, don't you? I feel that I am taking advantage... perhaps you have a use for it yourself? I hate to see it discarded again." The truth was that he threw most of the useless items into a bin at the Persa Bío Bío but there was a benefit in offering to return some of them, so he took the trouble to carry them back home. It would make him appear unselfish, winning him more respect and admiration and quite possibly more determination on her part to search out things of greater value. Outwardly he was kind and thoughtful. Inwardly he was jubilant at how easily most of the treasures converted to cash. This relationship had indeed blossomed into a rewarding one.

Of the gifts that Jhonny solicitously returned, Astrid joyfully selected lonely muertitos whom she felt would be most appreciative. She even occasionally bypassed Jhonny, deciding beforehand that something was not good enough for him. These items she added to the sparse, sometimes non-existent collection at the tombs of strangers, "Here, this one looks good on your shelf. I don't know if it carries any personal meaning, but I'm sure you'll enjoy it." She gave the muertitos no choice because she knew that even if they could protest – "Oh, no I really can't accept such a lovely gift" – it would only be out of courtesy, so many of their shelves had been barren and dusty for decades.

Uncharacteristically, Señora Ruby didn't question the origin of so many unexpected adornments. As her patio was gradually transformed into a magical garden of highly decorated tombs, the muertitos became unwitting recipients of stolen goods. Tourists began to flock to Patio 35 with their cameras and subsequently, images of the spruced up tombs were emailed all over the planet, often with Señora Ruby and Astrid in the foreground, arms wrapped around one another, hamming it up as they smiled broadly for the camera. The foreign photographers tipped them a few hundred pesos each time, which for Astrid, added up to extra cigarettes each week. Everyone profited.

Juan tried to feel grateful. He really did. But that damn cloud that hovered around him made it hard to reach anything beyond fleeting, fluffy emotions. Every so often he attempted to channel positive energy towards the woman. A ghost might do that, mightn't he? And sometimes he experienced a fleeting curiosity about the woman's situation, which prodded him to consider reciprocating her attentions in some small way because by fair or foul, her crazy ramblings, like the little treasures themselves, rattled within the rough interior of his brain. The thoughts dangled around at random along the edges of his consciousness and every so often he found himself trying to remember things she told him about her own life. But in these years since the accident, Juan's brain was not fully functioning and his memory often failed him. Even her name, which she had mentioned only during their early meetings, escaped him. He did, however, manage to recall her accolades about his music – his creamy voice and irresistible blue eyes, the way his hair glistened under filtered television lights, the way his hips undulated so seductively to salsa rhythms. In his narcissistic condition, it was normal that he would be unable to recall anything she said about herself. He was aware that she had rambled on at length with stories of her family but as God was his witness, they vanished from his consciousness as if they had never entered in the first place.

Astrid admitted to herself that she had begun to steal from tombs. God forgive her, she was a grave robber. And she had even enlisted San Expedito. She crossed herself. "Dear Jesus, forgive me. Perhaps it is a sickness." She tried to justify it, "You know that everyone is out looking for what they can get and besides the rightful owners believe these things have been lost. Even if they knew where to look, they're not allowed in the sectors that are being reconstructed, so the things would be lost eventually anyway." She turned to San Expedito, "You're the one who has helped me the most, dear San Expedito. I trust this is just another miracle you have, by your grace and goodness, performed. Thank you, I am truly in your debt." Not to alienate the Virgin, she offered a few words to her, too. "Dear Mother of God, thank you for your understanding. We both know what it means to love someone of such greatness and talent, someone who has made a grand contribution to humanity. I know you sympathise with me in this." Truth be told, no matter what Jesus or San Expedito or the Virgin Mary told her, she knew it was more important to provide comfort to Jhonny. She didn't plunder the tombs of her own muertitos; only those that had been destroyed or severely damaged by the earthquake and had not yet been renovated, as well as those she judged to have been deserted by family. The resting place of a certain Mercedes de la Fuente was outstanding for its drabness and lack of attention. Although Señora Ruby did not mention this particular niche, Astrid knew it had a significant hold over her, that it was untouchable; so she respected it and didn't go near. Besides, she could see no value in the distasteful, bird dung encrusted virgin statue that stood on its shelf.

Astrid estimated that her tomb combing would go on for a long time to come since many demolitions were delayed. The cemetery renovations were hampered by bureaucratic entanglements and also because of administrators who spent much of their day partaking in lengthy gossip sessions about prominent members of the local archdiocese and their surreptitious ties to deceased lovers. Therefore, they simply did not have enough hours in their days to sign documents. Or else papers were lost amidst piles of more papers, and the process moved at a snail's pace.

Astrid initially targeted grandiose mausoleums. She sought only precious ornaments that had somehow survived either absolutely intact or with miniscule flaws. She found tall crystal vases, blown glass shapes wrapped in silk ribbon inside glass cases, small porcelain virgins, miniature marble ashtrays, copper picture frames, ornaments and tiles inlaid with silver and lapis lázuli, a few original paintings and even tiny golden birds. Some of the treasures were found teetering at the edges of an altar or balancing on the sides of a disinterred coffin as though they were about to dive in and join the bones of their owner. But mostly they were partially embedded in dirt or under rubble that had not yet been removed since the earthquake.

One day as she lingered in the dusk of a quiet afternoon, she discovered a small but elaborate bronze cherub statue at the corner of the Errazuriz mausoleum. The cherub's perfectly extended wingtip pointed directly up at the name of the architect, which had been inscribed into the granite in 1934. Astrid gasped, "Que Díos le bendiga." God bless the muertito who had chosen to give this to her. She kissed the tips of her fingers and lightly laying her fingertips onto the inscription of the damaged structure, transferred her gratitude to the generous muertito.

She shoved it deep into her pocket and dashed over to the Maluenda-Valdéz mausoleum with this carved personification of love. Fortunately Jhonny Pretty was awaiting her on the day of this acquisition. Her gift and Jhonny's acceptance of it would seal their mutual devotion. He was perched cross-legged atop the family altar, looking pensive, his face accented by the light filtering through the stained glass behind and to his left. He was such a beautiful man, like an angel himself, what with the golden halo that seemed to encircle his coiffed hair. His ethereal charm never failed to stop her heart. She flushed.

"Jhonny, mi amor." She greeted him breathlessly, failing in her endeavour to portray a measure of feminine dignity as she charged up the steps towards him, her leather loafers falling heavily on the marble stairs.

Juan glanced down at her dusty shoes and slouching socks and cringed inwardly, as only ghosts can. When had she begun to refer to him so intimately? And her showing up uninvited this afternoon deepened his already bad humour. He was in a miserable state because of what had happened last night. Now he was going to have to tolerate the caretaker.

"I'm so happy you're here today." In her excitement she failed to smooth her smock. He noticed it was soiled and that the rip under her left arm had lengthened so that the whole seam was almost entirely unstitched, exposing a perspiration stain on the armpit of her blouse. Her cotton flowered skirt hung unevenly below and was muddy at the hem. Yet, here she was, bright as an old bird could be, fluorescent feather earrings tangled in strands of her thick hair that had come undone. She was exceptionally animated. And, being in a dark mood, he found this particularly agitating.

"Jhonny, look what I've found!" She was so close to the iron gate that he saw the dirty smudges on her nose where she had scratched with a muddy fingernail. He tried to conceal his disdain as he leaned back, nose twisted with displeasure.

She ignored that. "I've come to give you the ultimate gift. You won't believe it, Jhonny. You'll love this. It defines what we mean to each other. It's a creature of love, an angel to protect our bond. Look..." She drew the bronze figure out of her pocket and presented it between her two smeared, open palms as though they were a silver platter. The cherub lay asleep on its side, cradled in its lower wing, the other wing extended upward in a gentle, protective curve, carved cloth falling demurely around the genitals, hands folded in prayer under the cheeks. Diamonds were inset at intervals along the edges of the wings. Astrid dropped her eyes to marvel at it. Suddenly overwhelmed by its significance, she burst into tears and Juan just watched her – a sobbing silhouette, head down, shoulders shaking, arms extended – a dishevelled, almost ragged, middle-aged, humble and somewhat stout cemetery caretaker, with fabulous offering in hand.

The sun, always a cynic, was amused by the encounter and he tried to delay his descent as he leered at Astrid. But the gigantic coastal mountains that formed Mother Earth's crown, were sympathetic to the smitten, misguided caretaker and were embarrassed by the sun's callousness, so they towered and reached into the deepening blue sky to hasten his disappearance. As the universe would have it, the moon continued along her path and the mountains were helpless below her rising crescent grin. Although at first she appeared more sympathetic than her daytime counterpart, when the sun threw her a parting wink, his light reflected the grin on her half face and revealed a smile that extended to the other side as she snickered into the darkness of the heavens.

Juan saw the last of the sun's rays glance off the bronze where Astrid had polished it with her sleeves and he squinted at the glitter of several small diamonds. As much as by its estimated value, he was silenced by the beauty of the piece.

Juan was fickle, and in this condition – where, for a second he felt a flicker of compassion for the woman who stood there weeping, in the next instance his softness was replaced by more than a glimmer of greed. And as he vacillated, he relied on his newly found skill as an actor to maintain a consistent tone of appreciation for the splendour and significance of the gift. Meanwhile, part of his imperfect brain had already begun to negotiate with his fence at the Persa Bío Bío.

Concentrating on the moment, "Mi amor," he began, "You have found such an eloquent way to express our love. Surely, this gift is something to be held close at night, to be guarded as we guard our feelings for each other." He was anxious to feel the weight of the treasure in the palms of his own hands.

Yes. The woman was nodding, her head bobbing up and down in a large, repetitive motion. If she didn't stop, it would come unhinged and he'd be looking over at a headless woman in a ratty blue smock. He imagined her head tumbling down and settling onto the soft toes of her big leather loafers, her eyes pleading up at him through her tears. It was necessary to calm her down.

"Mi arco iris," he allowed a long silence to encourage her to look up at him. "Mi canto es para ti. I will sing for you, and only for you." A tune from Leo Dan, his Argentinean contemporary conveniently came to mind. "This is my song of devotion." He began softly, "This woman is my love and I live happily only for her. I know that I can never love anyone else because it's only her I want." The melody drifted into the deep blue obscurity until he forgot the lyrics, at which point he allowed the song to recede to a throaty hum. Astrid closed her eyes and relaxed, swaying side to side ever so slightly and she involuntarily loosened her grip on the treasure. Fearing it would go crashing to the ground, Juan interrupted his soft hum, "Watch the cherub!" and startled Astrid back to the moment. She caught herself in time to save her precious offering.

Their eyes locked through the distinct realities – his the spiritual and hers the terrestrial – and they froze for a few seconds as the moon turned her face to allow time to stand still.

The mountains witnessed the willing victim in the stained flowered skirt relinquish the bronze treasure to the pirate. She had entirely surrendered herself in an earlier battle and today she freely offered this exceptional booty. For her, his acceptance of it was another important sign of their mutual commitment. Astrid's heart and soul lay wasted at the scene. But she felt the utter joy of one who gives over to their true destiny.

Whether he was aware or not, Juan's only weapons were his velvet voice and steely blue eyes. No need to burn and plunder. For him, the statue was proof of his full victory. He was like a cruel marauder who takes only the ivory and leaves the body to rot, the memory of it naturally decomposing.

Happy tears stained Astrid's cheeks as she made her departure. She saw Jhonny in her mind's eye; he would be bending down to touch the bronze angel she had so carefully placed on his floor. She was certain that like her, he was left yearning. She pictured him cradling the little statue at his breast and gazing after her, desiring the touch of her hands and the sensation of her fingers through his thick black hair. He would wish he could caress her from head to foot, lingering over her virgin toes, and running his fingers up the length of her legs, around her waist and the curve of her breasts. She sighed into the moonlight, oblivious to the scorn that wrapped itself around the moon's dark side.

Then the moon turned her face to watch as Juan lunged at the little statue and jammed it into his left jacket pocket, determined to examine it in detail in the morning. He needed this treasure to make up for yesterday's devastating loss. It was only last night that Juan had discovered his lucky blue eye was missing.

CHAPTER 11

Change of Fortune

The night before the caretaker had shown up with the bronze cherub, Juan had finished his final set to the usual spatter of applause from the dwindling crowd. Tipping his non-existent hat, he bowed away from the performance area and bumped into Jesica, who sat smiling absently into the ground as she twisted the knobs on the karaoke control panel. She nodded and mouthed, "Good show," and pressed some small denomination peso notes into his palm. His take for the night. Better than a cup full of coins. Satisfied, Juan wandered towards Mario's to guzzle back a few beers before closing time. As usual he reached into his pocket to roll the smooth lapis lázuli between his fingers. The stone wasn't there. He stopped in his tracks, frozen, in the no-man's land between Mario's restaurant and the emptiness of his pocket.

Juan's lucky eye had vanished. The shock and insecurity this caused overwhelmed him. The cold grip of fear wrapped its bony hands around his neck and punched a hole in his chest. A lump rose in his throat. His heart raced and shaking like a leaf, he plunged both hands into his right trouser pocket and fumbled for the stone. Then the left pocket. Nothing. He pulled the pockets inside out, running his fingers along the seams looking for holes. All intact. He unzipped his trousers and rummaged around inside. Underwear was next. Still nothing. With his trousers roughly down to his knees, he sank onto the edge of the path, buried his head in his hands and sat motionless, wracking his brain. But with such poor short-term memory, he was defeated before he began.

For twenty years Juan had habitually slipped his hand into his right hand pocket, relying on the presence of his lucky blue eye. Several times a day he solicited its protection and good fortune. All he had to do was feel the polished surface of the lapis lázuli to be reassured that life would continue and that he would one day again be favoured in the eyes of the universe. Its loss was a sudden tragedy that meant he would be exposed to all manner of misfortune. He felt naked and cold without the stone.

He tried to retrace his steps in his mind but it could have gone missing during the several hours between when he first arrived at Slaughterhouse Square that evening and when he slipped his hand into his pocket after his last set.

Such was his state of mind that, beyond stepping onto a city bus, empty except for the driver, he couldn't remember going home. He lay awake for hours on top of his mattress, staring into the darkness. Perhaps his mother would intervene somehow, show him where his lucky stone had gone. He prayed to her, but she showed no signs of hearing him. She was probably still too busy playing bridge with her friends. No doubt, after all these years, she had succeeded in making her bridge parties the talk of the heavens. He forgave her that and finally drifted off. He dreamed he was chasing his lucky blue eye down a steep mountain. It rolled over the ground, under bushes, bouncing off rocks; it refused to be trapped and, like a rubber ball, it rebounded in and out of crevices. He got close to it several times but just when he bent down to pick it up, it began to roll again, slowly at first but then at top speed, teasing him, cavorting and jumping down the hill. Juan couldn't descend at that rate. His knees jarred and his legs turned to rubber. The lucky blue eye didn't stop until it reached the bottom, where it lay, glinting up at him from beside one of the still-spinning wheels of the Rockeros wrecked bus. The stone spoke to him, "Do you want to go inside? Do you want to see what's left of your famous band?" Juan couldn't comprehend why his lucky blue eye, knowing how much he had trusted it all these years, would be taunting him. He looked down at it and began to cry, his tears landing all around the stone. "Don't you try to win me over with your crocodile tears." the stone said to him. "I have no sympathy for what you have become. I can't take it anymore and I'm leaving."

"But I didn't cause the accident. It wasn't my fault. Don't go."

His lucky blue eye glinted up at him once more with feeling. Then it jumped inside the broken window of the bus and disappeared into the wreckage.

"Don't go. Don't stop. Keep rolling. Don't stop there. Not there!" Juan stood helpless, listening to the laboured breathing of Jhonny Pretty y los Rockeros.

When he awoke, it was into a feeling of profound desolation. He reached his hand up to the side wall and traced his fingers over the engraving of his mother's name on the cold marble. "Help me, Mamá. I seem to be lost." She didn't answer, though he could swear he heard the shuffling of cards.

After a sleepless night, he returned to the Square to retrace his steps once again. He scoured the grounds of the plaza and the linoleum floors of Mario's restaurant and everywhere in between. He sat on a bench at the outer edges of the performance area for several hours, eyeing the usual suspects. But there was no evidence of his lucky blue eye. By early afternoon, he gave up hope and trudged back to the mausoleum. Forlorn, he felt he was on the verge of a depression as deep as when his grandfather died, abandoning him to the pressure from his father who had tried to force him to become a dentist. He could still feel bile rise up from his stomach at the thought of leaning in to look closely at a stranger's rotting teeth, slimy with saliva, mouth full of sores and gums swollen from growing decay.

He was too desolate to sing that night so he told Jesica he didn't feel well and that he was going home. She didn't question him, simply nodded and waved in one of the eager hopefuls.

A few hours later, after he settled on top of his altar to brood and watch the sun go down, the female caretaker appeared on the steps with the bronze and diamond cherub. Initially he was elated by the perceived value of the gift but after the woman left, it struck him that this good fortune should not be possible without his lucky blue eye. He was so discombobulated by the irrationality of these events, one on the heel of the other, that his head began to spin. He climbed down the ladder to his basement abode and lay back on the mattress. The fact that he was on the receiving end of something so positive immediately after the loss of his lucky talisman did not make sense. One of the cornerstones of his existence – his lucky blue eye – had just been made redundant.

It was akin to discovering that God did not exist. He debated with himself for two full hours, trying to incorporate this incident of good fortune into the philosophy he had lived by for the past twenty years. With the loss of his lapis lázuli, such a turn of good fortune (in the form of the valuable cherub) was quite simply impossible. It wasn't supposed to work that way. Bad luck had turned to good luck and his lapis lázuli had nothing to do with it. Searching for the answer made him so tired that he fell asleep holding the cherub to his chest, thus unknowingly fulfilling Astrid's fantasy.

Given his unwavering faith in the lucky blue eye, it would take several more extraordinary events to convince him that in living without it, bad luck was not his worst enemy. And he might be forced to accept the incomprehensible – that when good fortune knocked at his door it, in fact, had everything to do with the loss of his lucky blue eye.

The day after the acquisition of the bronze and diamond statue, Juan sashayed into the Persa Bío Bío. Outwardly he was deliberately nonchalant but in reality he felt vulnerable without the lucky stone in his pocket. It was as though everyone would see, not the confident, magnetic Jhonny Pretty who lit up the lives of so many women and was the envy of young would-be rockeros, but the forlorn, confused Juan Bonifacio whose pockets were empty and who struggled each day to remember important events and who still, from time to time, heard voices from the past shouting out of that mysterious hollow part of his brain.

He wondered what Milo (whose front was an antique kiosk in the open-air sector behind the electronics warehouse) would say to his asking price. Surely the little cherub would fetch at least 60,000 pesos. On a whim, Juan decided to approach three different merchants to ensure a fair valuation of his prize. He would show it to Milo last. His hopes were raised when the second merchant offered him a good price and the third offered more yet. He swaggered confidently up to Milo's antique counter, trusting his long-standing relationship with the man would mean an even better price than the other two had offered. But he was taken aback with the measly sum Milo was willing to pay.

"But Milo, surely you know these are diamonds set into the wings. We're not talking about glass here. Look at the shine. You can see these are quality rocks." Juan brushed his fingers along the edges of the wings that folded lightly over the angel body. "And feel the fine craftsmanship of the bronze carving. This is one of a kind, Milo."

"What do you know about art and diamonds, Juan? Leave it to a professional. The best you'll get for this is 25,000 pesos. You know I never steer you wrong. Besides, I need to make something on it too." He noted Juan's darkening face. "What's your problem today?" His problem was clearly that the longstanding trust in this man had been misplaced.

"My problem is that you're a thief. That's my problem. I'm taking my business elsewhere. Weep as you watch me go. You'll miss me. You're nothing but a stinking, tired old shark."

Juan sold the cherub for a full 80,000 pesos. It was a bittersweet transaction because it proved him wrong about Milo. But it was also a sign that good luck had rounded the corner to shine on him when least expected.

This good fortune unnerved him again because of the doubt it cast on the power of the lucky blue eye. It meant that he had been dangling dangerously at the end of a thread of misplaced faith all these years. He wasn't prepared for the irony or to admit to being a fool. He needed a drink. He became even more unstrung when Mario unexpectedly offered him a free one. "My butcher made a huge mistake on his bill today. In my favour. Let's celebrate. I'll treat you to a beer. Here's one on the house, amigo." Mario plunked a bottle of Cristal onto the table and ruffled Juan's hair. "Enjoy it while I'm feeling generous... and lucky." Juan rolled his eyes as Mario whistled his way back to the kitchen, the recent gifts being reason to fall into a depression.

Juan mulled over the last few days and tried to convince himself that there was less luck in the air this morning than the last two-week span, during which he had still had his lucky blue eye. In that two weeks the cemetery caretaker delivered so many gifts from tombs that without counting the money from the cherub, it added up to more than 120,000 pesos. Of course, never being one to hoard, he spent what he earned. It was money in, money out. But if people continued giving him gifts and free beer, he'd have a hard time spending anything. Mind you, he wasn't complaining, just confused.

He pondered Milo's highway robbery; it was as though the items had been stolen twice, once from the graves and once from Juan himself. But that wasn't the end of it. Having moved into tourist season and because the Persa Bío Bío was one of Santiago's cultural experiences, the place was bustling with naive foreigners who were willing to pay ten times what Milo had paid Juan for the cemetery prizes. Not unexpectedly, most of these same tourists made the rounds to the usual places – the Presidential Palace, Cerro Santa Lucia, the Plaza de Armas, the Virgin Mary statue on the summit of Cerro San Cristobal and El Mercado Central. This was where accomplished pickpockets and small-time con artists, not unlike Astrid's son Hector, carried out their business.

Thus it happened that Juan's collectibles circulated several times through the Persa. First Juan sold them to Milo, then a tourist bought them, then the likes of Hector stole them from the tourist's bag and sold them back to their fence at the Persa. Different tourists purchased them, Hector stole them again, and so on. 'What goes around comes around' had a slightly different meaning in the Persa. It was an active economic cycle, where everyone played a role.

"So how much do you want for it this time?"

"Well, how much did you sell it for last time?"

"Tell you what... I'll make you a deal. Bring it back to me a third time and I'll buy it for double your asking price."

"Deal."

Juan was unaware of this cycle and it wouldn't have mattered anyway. What would have had an impact, however, was if he knew that it was Hector who had stolen his lucky blue eye. He wouldn't have cared that it was Hector per se because he didn't know Hector personally. But falling victim to a pickpocket would have been a blow to his ego. Juan regarded himself as too astute for that. He was, after all, a man about town, himself a fixture in the Persa, one of the biggest nests of petty crime in the city. He knew his way in and out and he could con along with the best of them – or so he thought. Having recently been enlightened because of the scam Milo had perpetrated on him, he was forced to re-examine his own skill and savvy. Being all the wiser about Milo just added to the insecurity of walking around without his lucky blue eye. Juan had to admit he was in a miserable state.

For Hector it had been easy pickings. Although he was accustomed to working early in the day, he never passed up an opportunity when he saw one. The night before last, after a good day on the job and feeling satisfied with his negotiations at the Persa, he enjoyed a meal of fried fish and rice with some tomato and onion salad at Mario's restaurant. Satisfied, he leaned back to survey the patrons as he picked his teeth and sipped on a cold Cristal.

Hector had his eye on Jhonny Pretty when he stumbled over to a corner table and raised his hand to order 'the usual.' He recognised Jhonny from the plaza, he'd heard about the tragedy of Jhonny Pretty and his band of Rockeros. It was a bit before his time but the music had been popular for good reason and he had to admit to liking it himself. He'd happened on the plaza a few times when Jhonny Pretty was performing and he usually paused, hummed along and tapped a toe. Oddly enough, Jhonny

Pretty seemed to have a cult following that included younger people – too young, Hector thought, to fully appreciate Jhonny Pretty. He wasn't the heartthrob he used to be but still, he managed to attract a limited group – so limited that it was almost secret. He was only at the forefront of the minds of the Slaughterhouse Square crowd. Take Constancia, for instance – although she didn't make it over there very often, when Hector mentioned Jhonny, she admitted to being a fan. "Oh yeah, I know who he is. Thought he was dead though. Are you sure it's him? I'd take him any day. He had such style back in his time – Mom's time. And his voice... oh, his voice. I know you agree, Hector." And she whined, "I'm always working. I never get over there. Why are you the one with all the luck? One day soon, I'll show up there. You'll see. I'll check out the old man for myself."

He observed as Jhonny fumbled in the trouser pocket of what appeared to be a recycled Salvation Army uniform, pulled out coins for the beer and slapped them on the table. Hector spied a quality lapis lázuli stone among the small pile of silver and his eyes glinted. It could easily be set into a pendant and sold as something of value. Jhonny didn't notice he had extracted the stone along with the coins. Mario delivered him a couple of litre bottles of Cristal and before he scraped the coins into his hand he playfully slapped Jhonny up the side of his head. "Hey, man, do you plan to pass me your good luck too? If I wasn't your friend, I could easily steal away your lucky blue eye and then you'd trip and die on your way out of here without ever knowing why."

Juan scowled, annoyed at the brutish cuff. But Mario's warning registered in his beer-soaked brain and he lunged forward to cover the blue stone. He kissed it before sliding it safely back into his right hand trouser pocket and leaned down to blow at the foam on his beer. Hector ordered another drink. There was no rush; he would have the lapis lázuli in his own pocket before the night was out.

Jhonny Pretty finished a third litre of Cristal and wandered out the door towards nowhere in particular. Hector was right behind him. Jhonny stopped under the nearest tree, one hand on the trunk to balance on the two legs God had given him, unzipped the fly on his Salvation Army trousers and proceeded to relieve himself, the recently processed Cristal cascading down the bark. Hector sauntered over to do the same. He sidled up to Jhonny's right side and wobbled, pretending he had to catch his own balance. In doing so, he bumped into Jhonny, deftly sliding his hand into his right hand pocket. He knocked him again with his shoulder – insurance for the distraction. No apology. "This is good spot. Looks like it's been well-used." Jhonny didn't respond. He didn't even look over to see who had bumped into him. He zipped up, turned and staggered off to disappear through the plaza.

Hector unfolded his fingers to look at the smooth blue stone. He rolled it between the palms of his hands. It was soft to the touch and bigger and heavier than he had estimated. He would examine it more closely in the morning.

CHAPTER 12

As Luck Would Have It

The same morning in which Juan, agitated and trying to fend off an impending sense of loss and vulnerability, went out in search of his lucky blue eye, Hector sprang out of bed, yawned, stretched, showered, shaved, gelled his hair, forced the button through the centre buttonhole on his suit that was still too tight, and headed to his favourite coffee shop at the Plaza de Armas. He was feeling vital and ready to conquer the world. The sun shone down on him. Surely he was blessed. It was a day for incredible capers that would more than blow the lid off his usual take. He could just feel it in his bones.

He was also pleased with an idea that had occurred to him on the way home last night; rather than selling the lucky blue stone, he would offer it as a gift to Astrid. It was a long time since he'd shown her the gratitude and love that a mother deserves from a son. He would surprise her, presenting the gift before the Day of the Dead, the biggest holiday of the year, which was only two days away. The more he thought about it, the better he felt. If she wanted it set into a silver pendant to hang around her neck, he would arrange to have it done for her. Hector was so inflated with the idea that the centre button on his suit popped off and sprang into the coffee cup on an adjacent table. He pretended not to notice, rose to his feet and pinched the edge of his jacket between thumb and forefinger as he wedged his way past the table in question, "Excuse me Señores. Have a good day." He had hoped to swipe the bills they had placed under the sugar shaker but just then one of the men extracted them, ready to pay the approaching waiter. Bad luck.

That day Hector's intuition was misguided. First it led him to the Presidential Palace where he was confident of scoring some unusually valuable loot, after which he planned to kick back early with at least a couple of well-deserved beers, or, better yet, a scotch whiskey or two. His nose caught a scent that led him to the subterranean art gallery, where several expensive gift shops adjoined the common space. The current exhibition was by the Chilean 'anti-poet,' Niconar Parra. It consisted of a hundred small box stands on which the anti-poet had positioned common household objects and labelled them with witty titles. The centrepiece of the exhibition was a series of life-size cardboard cut-outs of current and past presidents who were hanging by their necks from the ceiling. Hector was amused. He manoeuvred his way past other observers, in search of the right opportunity.

He found it in the form of a gentleman from Germany. A corner of the man's dark red passport protruded from his jacket pocket. Hector would have to go beyond his usual connections for the sale, but the going price for a German passport was easily $1500 American. Hector wound his way through a small group of gallery hounds and approached the man straight on. He looked directly into the man's eyes, nodded and ventured a half-smile, which was not reciprocated. As he brushed by him, Hector's quick fingers lifted the passport and as he stepped away, he pushed it up into his own jacket sleeve.

He refrained from skipping out of the gallery. Keeping a cool head, he headed up the ramp that inclined towards the exit. When he reached the door he impulsively looked back and he saw the German tourist waving his arms over his head. The man had succeeded in getting the attention of a security guard and was pointing at Hector. Hector pushed his way out the tall glass door and rushed up the stairs, two at a time, to the street. His heart was racing as he attempted to melt into the crowd at the crosswalk. The guards would alert an undercover policeman up on the street. Hector spotted one of them running towards the curb. He knew the policeman would be ruthless, even going so far as to draw his weapon, and had the power to detain everyone on the corner if necessary. So instead of waiting for the light, he hailed a taxi. It pulled up immediately and he jumped into the back seat, flushed and breathless.

"Cerro Santa Lucia," he ordered. The driver nodded and spun around, taking him towards the hillside park in the centre of the city. "A hot day, Señor." The taxi driver was reacting to Hector's flushed appearance. "Yes, very. And so early." Hector twisted around on the seat to watch the plain-clothed policeman rough up a tall gentleman with gelled hair who was waiting for the light at the intersection. Poor sucker. He wouldn't want to be in his shoes during the next few hours.

He remained silent until the taxi reached Cerro Santa Lucia, where he paid the driver and walked over to a bench to calm down. That was close. It had been ages since Hector had been hauled into a police wagon and since then he had honed his craft to perfection. This was the first time in years that he had even been suspected of anything illicit, let alone having been identified as a thief. Today had indeed begun as an exceptional day, but not in the way he imagined. He shook his head and muttered under his breath, "Shit, Hector, you better get your act together." He looked down at his hands. "You let me down today." They were still shaking. He inserted his hand into his left sleeve to retrieve the precious passport and then opened the briefcase to slip it into one of the pockets before turning the combination lock and closing it securely.

He needed sustenance after the near miss, so he bought a sandwich from an ambulant seller and devoured it, feeling the calming effect of the food almost immediately. Right. Back to work.

By noon Hector's mood had changed from one of optimism to one of frustration. For no apparent reason, something was stabbing at his neck and his stomach burned with a growing rage. He was tempted to grab innocent people by the throat and throttle them or swipe them over the side of the head with his briefcase. Pickings had been very slow in the park over the last couple of hours. Hardly anything worth pursuing. He could count the change on one hand. "Might as well beg for coins." He tried to console himself with the knowledge of the passport in his briefcase but even with that, he was agitated and unsettled.

He walked back towards the old town to get a proper lunch in the Plaza de Armas, where he should have stayed in the first place. Once settled at a table in the sun, order submitted to the waiter, he leaned back in his chair, crossed his legs, stretched them out under the table and looked up at the sky. He sighed and briefly closed his eyes, seeing the golden orb under his eyelids. He didn't hear the shuffle of little feet approaching his table. He didn't hear the swipe of his briefcase across the plastic tabletop until it was too late. He opened his eyes to see a young boy running at full speed, the briefcase swinging at his side. The boy was out of sight before Hector could take three steps. He turned and slunk into the chair. His soup arrived and it was cold and he noticed a long hair weaving its way around a potato and under a carrot. He growled, knocked the bowl to the ground and walked away without paying.

In the course of the day he had nearly been arrested and in spite of subsequent efforts he had earned less than a beggar on the stairs in the park, he had caught the shoulder of his jacket on a thorny branch, ripping it beyond repair, and then the German passport, which was the largest single score he had pulled in several months had been stolen out from under his own nose (briefcase along with it) by some young cabro who was barely old enough to wipe his own ass, and lastly he had been served greasy soup flavoured with hair. The only thing that remained of the day was the lucky blue eye that was still tucked safely in his pocket. It was small comfort but at least he would be able to deliver it to his mother as planned.

CHAPTER 13

The Day of the Dead

With the Day of the Dead fast approaching, Astrid de las Nieves and Señora Ruby, anticipating the needs of their most demanding patrons, dedicated themselves to their tombs. The cemetery was abuzz, all of the caretakers on their toes, toiling to win the approval and extra tips from families who would be especially appreciative of their help at this time of year. An obviously unattended, unkempt or, worse yet, dilapidated tomb demonstrated lack of respect and compassion by family, and it was shameful and distressing for the population at large. If a family's schedule did not include habitual (often weekly) visits to their tombs, its members were out in full force during the week of November 1st to make up for it, and possibly upstage a neighbour... keeping up with the Jones', cemetery-style. The caretakers eagerly carried out instructions and participated in preparations, often picking up new clients.

The vase-making workshops and flower arranging demonstrations that Señora Ruby delivered to other caretakers throughout the year paid off this week. Using Señora Ruby's techniques, the caretakers decorated tombs and niches of less affluent families with vases made from cleverly decorated coca-cola bottles. They thoughtfully filled the vases with fresh flowers and arranged knick-knacks around the photos, which took centre stage.

Families added special touches, reaffirming the continuing relevance of their deceased members and acknowledging their ethereal powers of intervention with sheets of hand-written poems, entreating the departed ones for a sign or a favour. These lovingly prepared documents were positioned between ornaments, eventually slumping down and shyly folding in on themselves so that the faces and messages were hidden from passersby. Stems of single plastic roses were jammed into crevices, their flowering heads bending artfully to peer into the faces of photos that were propped up at wooden crosses or on cement niche shelves. Worn-out toys and ceramics were propped at edges or crammed into cluttered spaces. Simple, poignant, hand painted messages on concrete frames – "Dear Mommy, we miss you" – were so new you could still smell the lacquer and feel the pain. Plastic Disney ornaments were set onto the ground and sometimes, as if rising from the tomb, a gauche plaster head, the likeness of an unknown person could be seen on a patch of grass. Cats and dogs wandered between crypts, their tails caressing the corners of lives that were no more than memories but who, by virtue of insistent relatives, remained engaged in the world of the living.

People usually arrived a day or two before the Day of the Dead to thoroughly wash and prepare the graves for the day of the big fiesta. They came in droves, carrying buckets, brooms and dust cloths. Grandparents walked down the paths, hand-in-hand with children and grandchildren. It was a family affair, all generations participating. In spite of this, because of the devastation caused by the recent earthquake and with much of the sacred ground still deemed unhygienic by the authorities, activity was muted. Several informal 'visiting gates' had sprung up on fences surrounding patios that had not yet been reconstructed. The unfortunate families with deceased relatives in these prohibited areas visited from outside the gate nearest their gravesites. Here they attached balloons and photos, tied cards and flowers with ribbons and peered inside for some signal from beyond. At a few such gates, mounds of rubble from the quake served as informal altars. People donated miniature Virgin, Santa Sara, San Cristobal and San Expedito statues and balanced them on narrow flats amidst the chunks and splinters. Candles flickered on the mounds, illuminating hand-scrawled petitions on rough slabs of cement or wood and the prayers on scraps of wrinkled paper that were weighed down by rock and debris. Some had colourful ribbons attached to them; they looked like kite strings fluttering out of a tragedy.

"Please, San Expedito, keep the bones of my father safe as you see to the work that needs to be done. We pray that he will once again rest in peace."

"Thank-you for helping them locate my cousin's remains. We thought they were lost, but you found them. We promise to visit and say prayers to you every week for the next year."

"Dear Mother of Jesus, help us to rebuild our family crypt. You have always been kind, and for this we thank you."

Smoke from candles whispered these prayers to the heavens. And here at the gates the unfortunate families conversed with loved ones – hundreds of visitors at the vertical wrought iron bars through which they were not allowed to pass, looking in towards the flattened patios, hundreds of voices murmuring stories and asking after the state of affairs on 'the other side'. A multitude of arms trying to reach across, like a mass visit to a prison, hoping to exchange words with someone back there somewhere.

Astrid and Señora Ruby bubbled with energy in their patio that had been, gracias a Diós, saved from the quake. It was vital that they be alert to the needs of their patrons so they abandoned their usual banter and positioned themselves at opposite ends of the patio preparing to take mental notes about family gossip so they would compare stories at the end of the day.

Astrid was nearly whisked off her feet by a set of twin boys as they chased each other down the path, one holding onto strings attached to balloons. Their cheeks glowed with excitement and their laughter pierced the air. They turned and ran towards her again. One of them bumped into her and exclaimed breathlessly, "Excuse me, Señora." The other child followed close on his heels. He was laughing so hard as he approached Astrid at collision speed that he stumbled. She faced him, ready for the assault, feet firmly apart, hands on hips, bracing for impact. But instead of colliding, the boy ran right through her as though she wasn't there. But it was he who wasn't there; he was nothing but an illusion, molecules organised into colour. She recognised the ghost of Arturo, the little boy who had allowed her some balloons from his niche so that she could give them to Jhonny Pretty. Arturo and his brother had escaped the family luncheon to run wildly through the crowd. Arturo stopped short, turned sharply on his heel and winked up at Astrid before continuing the chase. She would see him again and she grinned down the path after him.

This was an exceptional year for Señora Ruby and Astrid. The patrons whose family graves had been spared by the quake demonstrated their gratitude to God and it was as if they fell in love again with the deceased relatives. They transported themselves back, releasing memories that had long ago been locked up around the kitchen table. There was an urgent need to talk it all over, to show them that they cared, to insist on making them more comfortable, and ultimately, to bring them back to life within the limited rules of death. They set about small renovations, paying extra attention to detail, retouching chipped paint, adding new decor and more flowers. And it all meant more money for the caretakers. For Astrid, it translated into a few extra Derbys for herself and Jhonny Pretty. She planned to make up for the fact that she had not had time to scavenge for more ornaments lately. However, she was content with everything she had given him to date, especially the cherub. She pictured the items displayed on the floor of his subterranean bedroom and Jhonny himself humming and hovering over them as he dreamed of her.

For his part, Juan avoided the cemetery as much as possible lately because it was like having a circus in his back yard. Over the past weeks, he had become accustomed to the people who routinely and quietly came and went but on the Day of the Dead, people arrived in droves, and it was anything but as quiet as a graveyard. The burial grounds were packed with all manner of creatures – good and evil, dead and alive. Juan remembered seeing the crowds on television news last year, where they estimated that the November 1 visitors reached 1.2 million. He wanted none of that, thank you very much. As it was, he had recently been witness to one or two strange witchcraft rituals. It sent shivers up and down his spine as he watched a middle-aged woman wrap several strands of hair around a thin slice of raw beef steak, seal it into a plastic bag, and bury it at the foot of a wall. She touched the name on a grave and recited a curse. Later that very same week he observed from a distance as two caretakers took it upon themselves to dig up this same plastic bag, build a small fire and offer prayers as they unwound the hair from the rotten meat before burning it all and then burying the ashes, rendering the curse, itself, null and dead. He heard them complain of physical and mental exhaustion after the exorcism. Next time they would call a priest, they said. But he doubted that they ever would and for the first time he fully appreciated caretakers.

The General Cemetery, being a city within a city was home to and attracted thieves and angels, murderers and saints, patrons and tourists. It was rank with superstition and ritual. Stories of ghosts spread freely. It was not for the meek or faint of heart. Juan had heard that even Pinochet's military entered and exited as expeditiously as possible when they were ordered to dump bodies into mass graves during the early days of his dictatorship. Given what they were guilty of, they did not want to linger and feel the wrath of a power even greater than their own.

On the other hand, it was common knowledge that many ghosts watched over caretakers and other well-meaning souls within these walls. Señora Ruby swore that her muertitos had protected her from being robbed and beaten on more than one occasion. The protection was felt in the form of warnings where she was physically prevented from walking in the direction she had intended, as though an arm was braced across her chest, stopping her short and turning her around. Later she would discover that an unlucky visitor had been assaulted for nothing more than small change in the very spot she was heading. Other times, she was aware of being accompanied to the gates at the end of the day by a contingent of friendly spirits, shielding her from unsavoury characters who dared not approach.

Ghost stories were abundant. One of the most famous tells of a young man who was in a bar one night just across from the cemetery grounds when a lovely young woman in a pink chiffon dress sat down at his table and engaged him in lively conversation. She said she liked to dance and so he danced with her until well into the night. The enchanting encounter came to a reluctant end just before sunrise and she insisted on leaving unaccompanied but asked to borrow his jacket, saying she had only a short walk home but that she was cold. She said her name was Martina and she gave him her telephone number and home address and suggested he go there the next day to pick up his jacket. So the next day after work, anxious to see her again, he made his way to her house. An older woman answered the door and he asked for Martina. The older woman frowned and stepped back inside, preparing to close the door in his face, "Señor, please don't come to my door to play games with me."

"What do you mean, Señora? I have no bad intentions. I have just come to pick up my jacket, as Martina invited me to do."

"This is a cruel joke, Señor and I will not tolerate it." She was suddenly angry. "I am Martina's mother." The older woman's eyes filled with tears, and she blurted, "Martina died three years ago."

Astonished, the young man showed the mother the paper on which Martina had written the address and phone number. "But she gave me this, Señora."

"Well, someone is playing a very cruel joke on both of us." She motioned for the young man to follow her into the house where she picked up a framed photograph and held it for him to see. "This is my Martina."

He was aghast. "But that is the young woman, Señora, the woman I danced with last night. The woman I have almost fallen in love with. She was wearing a light pink dress and had a string of pearls around her neck."

The colour drained from Martina's mother's face and she slowly folded to the floor, fainting in front of his eyes. When the young man finally managed to revive her, she asked, "Please describe her to me again."

"Well, as I said, she has the face of the beautiful woman in your photo and she wore a light pink dress, very airy, like a dancer maybe. And she had a single string of pearls around her neck."

"Yes," the mother was sobbing now, clutching the photo to her breast. "It was my Martina. She was a dancer and we buried her in her favourite dress and the single string of pearls, just as you described."

Moved to tears himself, the young man said, "Well, Señora, I had the great honour of dancing with your daughter last night. Perhaps she wanted me to visit and tell you so."

The mother composed herself, somewhat comforted by the idea that her daughter wished to communicate. "Come with me, young man. I will show you where Martina is resting."

They made their way back to the cemetery and the mother led the way into a patio filled with trees, where the flowers were in full bloom. When they approached the girl's tomb, the young man stood speechless and pointed at the ground. There, at the foot of Martina's grave, was his jacket, folded and waiting for him.

Señora Ruby's favourite story was not a ghost story, but more of a miracle. It was about the love between a mother and her daughter. As the story is told, there was once a beautiful young woman, the only daughter of a wealthy couple. She was about to be married and she was walking down the aisle, her husband-to-be, gazing lovingly at her from the front of the church, when without warning and for no apparent reason, the beautiful young girl fell and died instantly at the foot of the altar. Of course there was a mad frenzy as the grief-stricken parents and husband-to-be tried to revive her. But it was in vain.

The young bride-to-be was buried in the family mausoleum in one of the cemetery's most prestigious patios. As in a fairy tale, they placed her into a glass coffin. The parents were crazy with anguish. After the daughter's funeral, the father was in too much pain to return ever again but the mother simply couldn't go home without her baby and she bribed the caretaker to be allowed to sleep there. It is said that at dusk, she raised the girl's body into an upright position and combed her hair and then she sang to her all through the night before gently letting her settle back into her glass bed. All this time the body of the beautiful girl did not decay but remained in a lifelike state. Finally years later, having lived in the mausoleum since her daughter's death, the mother died of grief herself and was buried with her. Only then did the girl's body decompose. Several years later, the father died too and was interred with them and they became like any other family resting together in peace. But everyone who worked in the cemetery knew that they were exceptional and it wasn't long before strangers attended the mausoleum to light candles and pray to them.

Although Juan had heard all of these stories, he had never been frightened by anything but rodents. The only weird thing he had seen in the cemetery was a photo shoot with young Gothic transvestites posing in different outfits as though preparing for a magazine spread. They stripped down for quick clothing changes, pranced around under poinsettia trees and frolicked in groups between hibiscus bushes. Half naked in black leather thongs and feather boas, some of them imitated condors and others leapt gleefully in their pink tutus, clapping and waving their wands as still others peeked coyly from behind paper masks on the ends of twigs.

Initially the transvestites had attempted the photo shoot in the gypsy sector but were threatened with death by two large gypsy men with long sticks. So they moved on. The gypsy sector was by far the most vibrant part of the cemetery but the gypsies demanded respect and privacy and did not tolerate fun-loving antics by Gothic transvestites. From a distance the gypsy neighbourhood was colourful mayhem and with the Day of the Dead on the horizon, life there was ever more abundant. Tombs were being redecorated with whirling, oversized pinwheels planted under orange and green striped awnings, which stretched the length of the graves. Photos and pendants were pegged like clothes on a line around plot perimeters. Bright, plastic birds were attached to more lines and long streamers danced around them in the breeze. Flamenco music rose into the air from numerous ghetto blasters. Families in bright cotton print shirts and multi-layered skirts moved amongst the graves, concentrating on preparations.

Juan was right about the Day of the Dead being circus mayhem. Ice cream sellers strolled the paths inside the gates and outside the flower vendors worked up a sweat trying to keep pace with demand. Owners of the dozens of flower kiosks that lined the exterior walls of the cemetery enlisted extra family members to help them on this day. Bunches of gladiolas and irises leaned over their tall buckets, dripping down onto the shorter arrangements of roses and tight groups of tulips, daisies, and heavy-headed chrysanthemums. Huge wreaths hung on the back walls of the plywood kiosks and helium balloons were tied to stands at the corner. Locals dragged barbecues made of sawed-off metal barrels to street corners where they sold meat and vegetable kabobs on skewers, the heavy smoke signalling that they were open for business. They promoted plastic cups brimming with mote con huesillo, the sweet national juice known for quenching even the fiercest of thirsts. Fresh oranges, mangoes and papayas were also on offer.

It was on the morning of the Day of the Dead that Astrid decided she would 're-gift' to Señora Ruby the lapis lázuli stone that Hector had given her the night before. He had presented it with bravado, explaining in detail how he had negotiated for it, convincing the downtown merchant that his price was inflated. He bragged, "In the end, the real value is much, much more than what I paid. And that," he winked, "will remain a secret between me and the merchant."

"The moment I saw the stone, I knew it had to be yours, Mamá. Look at its blue purity and feel how soft and smooth it is." He added, "If you want it in a pendant, I can arrange to have it set for you."

Hector was obviously excited and Astrid didn't want to dampen his enthusiasm or appear ungrateful. She examined it, one finger flipping it over like a delicate rose in the palm of her hand. "It's lovely, Hector. You shouldn't have." And then, "No, I prefer to keep it in my pocket. I don't want people to see it and desire it for themselves. You know that'll put me in danger on these streets." She stretched her arms up, inviting him to bend down and kiss her.

"Okay, well if you change your mind, tell me. I'm glad you like it. I want you to think of me whenever you look at it." She nodded. Deep down

Hector was glad to get rid of it. There was something evil about the way it shone up at him. Perhaps it cursed him because he stole it. But his mother didn't know that and since she was innocent, he reasoned that she would be immune from any such curse. He didn't ponder the question for long. He bent to hug her again, his gesture rising more from a sense of self-congratulation than a demonstration of love.

Secretly Astrid wanted to get rid of it too. She had never liked lapis lázuli. She found it crass and, overall – well, just too blue. It had always seemed false. She remembered a letter opener with a lapis lázuli handle that someone had given her mother. When she was a small child she wanted to use it as a knife to butter her bread but her mother grabbed it and reprimanded her, "This is not a real knife, Astrid. Don't tarnish it with butter." After that Astrid used to look at it hanging on the wall beside the kitchen towels that her mother never used either. "They are for 'show', Astrid, to add some class to our kitchen." But to her they were just useless. Who keeps things they can't use? Besides, she now owned several small San Expedito charms that she had been buying one by one from Siete Pelos and when she inserted her hands into her pockets she could jingle a number of trinkets, identifying each of them by touch. These charms were different; they were useful. They played a role. One of the oval ones showed San Expedito's kind face, close up. She prayed to this one just before she stepped off the path close to Jhonny's home. The other oval one had a tiny image, San Expedito in all of his Roman splendour. She had a larger double-sided charm, obviously created by a different artist. You could see the tiny brush strokes in his hair. And on the back was a little prayer, which she had memorised. She also had two pendants with relief images forged into the tin-silver alloy. They had holes at the top so that she could hang them from fine chains, which she did not do. And of course, there was her handkerchief with a full-colour stamped image in the centre. She never used it of course; it was not something to soil. She blushed, realising she was, at least on this account, the same as her mother – owning something she would not use. Looking up to the heavens, she rationalised, "Mamá, it's not like it doesn't really have a purpose. It really does do a job, invisible as it is." She was even the owner of two small embroidered, saintly likenesses that she stitched to her special red satin panties. She seldom wore them and if she did, they were washed gently in soft sudsy soap after each occasion.

The lapis lázuli wouldn't mix well with her San Expedito charms. Besides, its presence irritated her in a way she could not explain; it made her feel off-balance. She was conscious of it in her pocket and, like a pebble in her shoe, she felt that she had to keep shifting and twisting to avoid how it seemed to push its way into her skin. Its very presence was trying to invade her with its blueness. She was out of step with herself. She also had a ringing in her ear. The stone was weighting her towards hell. In fact, she had stumbled twice this morning on the sidewalk just outside the cemetery gate, once almost falling right onto her face. She escaped with only scraped knees and skinned elbows and, although the injuries were just on the surface, the aggravation from it cut directly from the blue stone into her gut.

Astrid was unsure about what to do with it. Somehow, although it irked her, it defied being simply tossed onto the ground. She couldn't give it to Constancia because that would hurt Hector's feelings. It occurred to her that Jhonny Pretty might like it but the energy of the stone itself left her in doubt. Although she was convinced that it was more than just a mere stone, its significance escaped her. In the end, she decided that after she and Señora Ruby sat down for their afternoon cup of tea and sandwich, she would go over to Jhonny's place and discreetly sound him out.

As she sipped her tea in the shade of Señora Ruby's shack, Astrid remarked on a funeral she had just witnessed. It was a poor family from Peru who lived downtown in slum housing and they were burying a teenage son who had fallen to his death after a rotten stairway gave out. The topic turned to the living conditions in the downtown core, after which Astrid discovered something rather astounding about Señora Ruby. As a young woman, Señora Ruby had once lived in Santiago Centro. "Odd,"

Astrid said to her, "I always assumed you lived nearby. I never would have pegged you as a downtown type of woman."

"Well, I did live downtown," replied Señora Ruby. "But I moved from there more than years ago. The place went up in flames. Can you imagine?"

Astrid saw pain in Señora Ruby's eyes. She waited.

"It was a very pretty colonial building. Why I ever thought I could forever live in an apartment downtown I'll never know. I guess I had a different idea of myself back then. I guess I thought I was a downtown kind of girl." She crackled at the idea. Brightened by the memory, she straightened her spine, which made her taller by about three centimetres, "I did live there for more than 15 years though. Before the fire, that is. The building was condemned after that. I lost everything in that god-forsaken apartment. They were going to knock it down and I wonder if they ever really did."

"Oh, I'm so sorry, Señora Ruby. I had no idea."

Señora Ruby was looking off into the distance. "Well, it was a long time ago now. But I remember a lapis lázuli pendant I had back then. I used to wear it all the time. But for some reason – I don't remember now what it was – I wasn't wearing the pendant the day of the fire and I lost it. It was one of the things I treasured most and I never laid eyes on it after that day. It probably fell down into the rubble and was buried there. It was originally a Christmas gift to my mother from her favourite patron. She passed it down to me when I was only in my thirties. My mother said it would bring me luck. When I stopped to think about it later, I realised that there probably wouldn't have been a fire, if I had been wearing the pendant. But that was so long ago." her voice drifted off into the blue of the sky.

Astrid perked up. Beaming, she reached into her pocket. "Look. I have a gift for you." She drew out the lapis lázuli and held it in the sun for Señora Ruby to see.

Señora Ruby leaned forward, her nose almost touching the stone in Astrid's palm. She wiped her hands across her thighs a couple of times, preparing to be worthy of holding such a gem. Knuckles cracking as she straightened her fingers, she reached over to caress it before picking it out of Astrid's hand. She tossed it lightly to feel its weight. It was identical to her old stone.

Señora Ruby looked up to the heavens, her eyes had gone misty, "Gracias, mis muertitos. All of you." And then she looked at Astrid, "And thank you, too. What would I do without you, Astrid?" she coughed into her sleeve. Then closing her fingers around the stone, she held it to her breast. "I can't believe it. It's the same size as the stone I remember. And the same shape too." She laughed. "And of course it's the same colour." She shook her head. "If I didn't know better, I would say it's even the very same stone."

Like a ghost lost on the path to heaven, the stone, belligerent and cursing everything in its wake had been on a crusade to find its way back home. And now, in the wrinkled, old hands of its rightful owner, it would curse no longer. Content at last, it could retire. Its harsh blue colour softened and picked up some of the warm magenta from the sky and like a baby in its mother's arms or a bird coddled under the feathers of its parent, it snuggled into Señora Ruby's aged palm.

Señora Ruby felt colour rising in her cheeks and when she reached up to stroke her own hair, she felt it smooth and strong, like that of a woman twenty years younger. Astrid watched in wonder as Señora Ruby transformed before her, wrinkles softening around her lips and the light in her eyes intensifying. She suddenly sparkled of youth. The two of them looked into each other's faces and, unable to contain the delight, laughed aloud for several minutes. The air around them echoed their joy and when they meandered down the path to attend to client needs, they could hear the muertitos gurgling softly from within the niches and tombs across the patio.

CHAPTER 14

Luisa Rocio Suarez

Everyone knows that especially in cemeteries the line between life and death is very thin. It merges and intertwines. But rarely do people pretend to be dead. For this reason, the old woman of Santa María Street had her eye on Juan Bonifacio Maluenda-Valdéz. She watched him from across the way – from the tomb out of which she slipped every morning and into which she absconded each night. Although they both lived at Hard Bed Hotel, there was one big difference between them – she was pretending to be alive and he was pretending to be dead. She was therefore, suspicious of Juan Bonifacio Maluenda-Valdéz, aka Jhonny Pretty.

She observed his advances towards Astrid de las Nieves and she was aware of how he poured on the charm, taking full advantage of her infatuation. Up to now, she, Luisa Rocio Suarez, had been unable to scare him off. The problem was that she had never received proper haunting training or spiritual conduct guidance and she was not in full control of her ghostly powers. Sometimes she executed them to a T but in general the technique and finesse required to enter and exit the earthly realm at will were beyond her.

She had once successfully manifested herself as a messenger when Astrid de las Nieves needed her on the day of the earthquake. It had required great effort and although she had subsequently followed the woman along the paths of the cemetery and through the streets of the neighbourhood, she had, up to this point, failed to achieve the tactile human quality she had summoned that day. What an accomplishment it had been – she had succeeded in dressing herself in the outfit of a recently deceased young woman about whom she knew nothing. She had stolen the clothes without so much as a backwards glance, abandoning the naked bones without a twinge of guilt. Granted, the clothes were not a great fit – especially the shoes – but they served their purpose. So she decided to keep them, and had no intention of changing her wardrobe.

Luisa Rocio Suarez flushed with ghostly pride as she recalled her grand success on the day of the earthquake, having saved Astrid from certain unpleasant death by strangulation with greasy hair. But her warm glow was replaced with the cold blue breath of frustration whenever she turned her attention to the opposite side of the path, the path that separated her from the sanctuary of this man who called himself Jhonny Pretty. He had become a serious threat to Astrid, the woman she had chosen as her 'project,' for whom she had named herself guardian angel. This Jhonny Pretty was not just a passing ship in the night; he had an ideal arrangement with poor, innocent Astrid de las Nieves and Luisa could see that there was no way he was about to give it up. He was proving to be a permanent nuisance.

She admitted that on the day of the earthquake, her abilities had reached far and beyond, an otherworldly adrenalin having kicked in, for which she now realised she should have been more grateful. Juan Bonifacio Maluenda-Valdéz was, in comparison, nothing but a pesky menace, unworthy of the necessary powers. Even so, she wanted to exert her control and put the fear of the devil into the man. She had expected that as a ghost, she would automatically be given the facility to appear to, and disappear from, the living at will. But this was not the case. There was more to it and up to now, it escaped her.

The crowds had disappeared after the Day of the Dead and she was free to enjoy some peace and quiet and to contemplate, among other important things, the peculiar circumstance of Jhonny Pretty and Astrid de las Nieves.

She burrowed back inside the shamefully decrepit niche to think. The name inscribed on the front was Mercedes de la Fuente and there was nothing remarkable about it other than a haggard, plaster statue of the Virgin Mary planted in bird shit. Luisa Rocio Suarez didn't like the statue. She considered it not only ancient and filthy, but a disgustingly crass likeness. However, it seemed to be beyond her power to remove it or cause it to fall to the ground. She assumed this was because she was not Mercedes de la Fuente. She took over the niche because not one living soul ever visited it. The only exception was Señora Ruby, the old caretaker, and Luisa Rocio did her best to keep Señora Ruby at a safe distance. She did not want her to spruce it up in any way because she was afraid that this kind of attention might draw back the spirit of Mercedes de la Fuente and she would be forced to fight for the niche. Although Luisa Rocio Suarez could hold her own in a fight, she wasn't in the mood and didn't want to explain why she had rearranged the bones of de la Fuente, reducing them to a compact pile that she shoved to one side, without so much as a "Do you mind? Would you please...?"

Luisa Rocio Suarez died about 100 years ago at the age of 58, having married but never having born children. Her husband had been a local magistrate and his status permitted them both to be buried in an affluent sector of the cemetery. However, the constant bickering with her dead husband left her unable to rest. One day she realised that being dead, he could no longer batter her, which meant she was free to up and leave without any threat of reprisal. She thumbed her nose at him and left the upscale crypt in search of something more peaceful.

Mercedes de la Fuente's uninhabited niche was the first one she came across and, derelict as it was, she was happy with it because it left her free as a bird to mix and mingle and do whatever she desired. Her dead husband would never stoop to enter the lower echelons of the cemetery so she had no fear of encountering him there.

Luisa Rocio Suarez was, in death, as she had been in life, nothing more than a busybody. She died before she discovered why God had put her on earth in the first place. In the grand scheme of things, she had been nothing more than a waste of skin. Now, in death, she wandered about aimlessly, eavesdropping, picking flowers, chewing on mint leaves, eating jasmine blossoms and often leaving a trail of farts that had no smell.

In truth, she was quite bored. This boredom was the sole reason for her unnecessary meddling in the lives of others (most recently, that of Astrid de las Nieves). She longed to be important. As a result, Luisa Rocio set about to become a spirit of notable presence. Since it had not happened in life, she reasoned that it must be destined to happen in death. She would make a difference.

CHAPTER 15

Jhonny's Windfall

From amidst the shadows of his mausoleum, Jhonny Pretty was humming one of Astrid's favourite songs. She stood like a schoolgirl on the other side of the gate, brown leather loafers firmly on the bottom step, and a safe distance from the king of croon. Her hands were clasped loosely behind her back, her face flushed with shy emotion. She twisted slightly from her waist, her shoulders swaying from side to side in time to the rhythm that Jhonny was tapping out with his fingers.

She had no way of knowing that her sighs aggravated him, resulting him bringing the song to an abrupt end. In her state of delirium, she continued to sway in the sudden silence. Jhonny regarded her with disguised derision, wishing she'd just hurry up and pass him a cigarette. Had he not sung enough for his supper? Speaking of that, maybe she brought rice pudding this afternoon. She liked to hide things in her cart and pull them out like a magician pulling a rabbit out of a hat. He always responded as she predicted. "Marvellous, mi amor. You are the light of my life." Or, "Gracias. Only you, my most precious gem, would think of this." Or, "My queen. You have stolen my soul. Have mercy on me, mi vida." Or, "It looks exquisite. Only your rice pudding knows the way to my heart." Well, in this case, it wasn't a lie. He had to admit that her rice pudding was superb. But alas, he, Jhonny Pretty, the writer of some of Chile's most popular love songs, was running out of unique romantic phrases to shower on this woman.

Astrid didn't notice. As far as she was concerned, as long as he addressed himself to her, Jhonny could repeat the same five words all day long and she'd still be ecstatic, the genius of those five words would never be understated. There was no cure for the love that Astrid felt for Jhonny. And to have it reciprocated was more than she could have ever dreamed. Astrid decided that her life was complete; Jhonny had fulfilled her dreams for an almost perfect relationship. And what other reason was there to live? It occurred to her that if she died now, it would be with a smile on her face. However, when she allowed herself to think about it more deeply, she admitted that her relationship with Jhonny lacked just one tiny, unmentionable detail. Although she had agreed to forfeit the pleasure of the flesh for Jhonny's otherworldly attentions, it did sometimes niggle at her.

His ghostly apparitions at bedtime were not really the same as having a living, breathing man by her side. But she rationalised that it was still the best of all possible situations given that she didn't have to worry about her man being unfaithful. "Bless your soul, Jhonny. You are the best thing that has ever happened to me." She would wrap her own arms around her shoulders and slide them down her torso to experience what Jhonny would feel were he able to hold her. "I'll do it all for us both, Jhonny, so you don't have to regret anything."

As Astrid stood giddily before Jhonny that early December day she knew that all was right with the world. He expressed his love through beautiful songs and he addressed her so tenderly. In return, she brought him two loose Derby cigarettes and a loaf of freshly baked Christmas bread wrapped in cellophane and red ribbon. "I was so busy baking this for you Jhonny that I didn't have a spare moment to look for new treasure among the tombs. But don't worry. There are more. I'll find them for you. And when I do, I'll be back."

Juan's mind was elsewhere. Recently he felt a renewed passion for life at Slaughterhouse Square. Perhaps it was the pre-fiesta atmosphere. Vendors were beginning to talk about Christmas and New Year's Eve. Their increased sales spawned jovial marketplace fellowship and a more generous attitude towards the market's regulars, of which Juan was one. Mario had offered him a free beer the other night and the owner of one of the soup stands uncharacteristically waved off his payment as he cleared away his bowl. "Not this time, Jhonny. Consider it a favour that I will ask you to return one day." But besides this, he felt an injection of good luck that had manifested itself in at least one fruitful encounter with a beautiful woman. He could feel the momentum building; it was time to apply himself again, to spend more time with the living, to become more available. And to start with, he would let this woman catch him.

He brought himself back into the moment and looking down at the caretaker, he tried not to let his words sound mechanical. "Thank you, my dearest. You know I'll wait. For you, my love, I'm here." Even as the words rolled off his tongue, Juan was aware that he needed an excuse to explain his planned absences in the near future, something that she would not feel threatened by, something to keep her returning with her gifts. It was necessary to ease her into the fact that he may not be waiting in the shadows as often as usual. He hummed a few bars of "Waiting in the Shadows" to buy some time for him to develop just the right phrasing.

"Mi amor, I'll savour each bite of this bread. I'll ration it so that I can extend the taste of you, and in doing so, I will picture your lovely expression of concentration and the softness of your hands as you kneaded this dough." The woman glanced at her rough fingers. He added, "I wish I could caress your skin, my angel."

"Oh, no Jhonny..." she blurted as she shoved her hands into her pockets to the jingling sound of an increasing number of San Expedito trinkets. "I know it's too much to expect. Although it is something I, too, dream about, I've told you how satisfied I am with your presence and with the situation as we have it." She looked down at her feet and then up again coyly. "Besides, Jhonny, please don't taunt me with such impossible dreams. I don't ask for more than what is practical. I'm a simple woman with simple needs. My greatest pleasure is in coming to hear your voice, here, on these steps." She lowered her eyes.

"Yes, well, my dear, like you these are indeed my most treasured moments. I will continue to be here for you." He waited for an appropriate number of seconds to pass before he cleared his throat to being spinning his excuse. "As a person of your position knows very well, there's been a lot of commotion here since the earthquake. I've overheard many people – both dead and alive – who are still trying to find their way to loved ones, having had to abandon the usual meeting places."

"Claro," she nodded. "Oh yes, I know."

"Well, there are some of us who – thanks be to God – were not disturbed after the quake and we still have our bearings and feel secure in the usual habitat. But others have not been so lucky. As a result, several of us more experienced spirits have decided to act as volunteer guides for the lost souls, in an effort to reunite them with family."

"A valiant idea. Oh, Jhonny, you're so kind and considerate. I have to say I'm not surprised."

He retreated further back into the shadows to better conceal his lie and, because of its obvious success, his involuntary gloating. "Thank you. Yes, well, I mean, it's just a practical thing, isn't it? It'll help restore order. And not only for those who are lost… it will bring peace back to those of us who are not accustomed to the disturbance caused by wandering souls. Surely you know how disruptive a lost soul can be."

"Oh yes, no doubt about it." She was shaking her head vigorously.

Juan looked out at the woman, once again willing in vain for her name to rise to the tip of his tongue so that he could pronounce it. It seemed like a fitting time. But he still couldn't remember it. "My dear heart, since you understand this, then you will also understand the possibility of my more frequent absences. Helping others requires sacrifice, as you well know. It won't be for long, though, perhaps just a few months. We calculate that between the restoration and relocation of tombs and our own efforts, we should be able to reunite most families by the beginning of the spring, if not before." Juan made it sound like he was the brains behind a new social movement.

Astrid felt her heart drop. A cold wind blew in. She suddenly felt empty and wanted to go home and lie down. She raised her eyes to meet Jhonny's, willing to allow him to see the disappointment but she noticed that tears appeared to glisten in his eyes too. He must truly feel a responsibility towards family reunification. In light of his dedication, surely she could see her way to making a small sacrifice. She searched for a moment for words that would at once sound encouraging but that would still demonstrate her sadness at his pending absence. She was not successful and simply blurted out, "I wonder how often I will be able to see you then?"

"Well, it may be that we don't miss each other at all. It depends on who I am assigned to help and when. But if I'm not here, then you will know the reason why. I just thought you should know. I wanted to tell you."

She brightened visibly. "Bueno. I understand. And it's no problem at all, Jhonny. I'll be dropping by and hopefully our visits will be as regular as they are now. But if not, I will leave something in our private vault as a sign that I've been here. I don't want to ever give you reason to believe that I would forget about you."

Juan exhaled. She had called it 'our' private vault, like she was investing in their love. This was even better than expected. Now she would leave something without it even being necessary for him to appear and sing for his supper. Why hadn't he thought of it before? Another gust of wind blew in, making his eyes water again, enhancing what she saw as sympathetic tears.

"I'm sure we'll still see each other often. In any case, you know that you're always in my heart." He raised his right hand to his chest, posing with a sickly sweet expression, as though he was about to sing the national anthem.

Astrid blew him a kiss. "Yes, my love. Until next time, then." She backed down the stairs, waving a silly little royal wave. She tucked loose hairs behind her ear and then looked up into the shadows once more to blow a kiss. She watched as Jhonny caught it and brought it to his lips. Astrid levitated all the way home.

This afternoon had been a windfall for Juan Bonifacio. It was almost as satisfying as cutting a record and then just watching the money roll in from subsequent sales – just the initial effort required, thank-you very much – job well done – mission accomplished. He had just paved the way to spend less time for more donations. What luck. He began to whistle – a man's natural sign of satisfaction after success of any kind.

Then he remembered the lost lucky blue eye. It occurred to him that without being aware of it, he must be in possession of a new talisman, perhaps one of the small treasures from the caretaker that had never gone to market, so to speak. That the reason for his positive turn of fortune was the mere absence of his old blue stone would never have occurred to him. Such heresy would challenge more than 20 years of self-affirmed doctrine, not to mention the caring and rubbing of the stone itself. If there was any truth to be found in the idea that his lucky blue eye was, in reality, his nemesis, his world would have fallen on its ear and, were he really dead, he would have turned over in his grave.

Juan took a leisurely toke on one of the Derby singles that the woman had placed into the private vault. Then he went down into his family dungeon to rifle through the trinkets in search of the mysterious lucky item. Whatever it was had suddenly become very valuable and therefore, it was important to identify and protect it. Among the objects thrown into the corner: one small alabaster virgin, a four-inch bronze cross with Jesus figure intact, a glass turtle, a turquoise cat with two small chips where its ears once were, a miniature stained glass pinwheel, a small porcelain vase with red roses, a marble penguin, a tarnished, cup-sized pewter vase, a set of wooden spoons, a heavy silver keychain engraved with the sun and the moon, and a small copper bowl with turquoise inset around the entire rim. He sighed. Unlike his lucky blue eye, none of these things would fit comfortably into his pocket. None of them could be transported conveniently. Yet, he realised with some relief that this new luck he had obtained (undoubtedly by virtue of something here) did not require that he carry the object; the luck was just with him where ever he went. The question was, which of these items was responsible? It was not possible to discern. He had received all of them within the space of the last couple of weeks, the same period of time during which he was showered with good luck.

He concluded he would have to guard each and every item, treat them all with the dignity and respect a proper talisman deserved. His conscience tugged at him as he perused the inventory, which was scattered all over the cold cement floor. He had not treated any of these things with due care and attention. Well, that was about to change. He felt a sudden sense of responsibility towards the assorted objects.

Something in this corner had been extremely good to him recently and he must safeguard it. He sat cross-legged on his mattress, leaned back into the cold marble wall with his mother's name on it and closed his eyes so he could think. More than a few interesting events had transpired over the past two weeks. It wasn't clear yet where they would lead, but he could see they had potential. In the twenty-plus years since the band's accident, Juan hadn't developed a program for his life, and because of his damaged brain, he no longer had the ability to plan more than a few days ahead. A week in advance was a stretch, and a month into the future could almost be considered a miracle. All those years of wandering aimlessly with the wind pelting senseless thoughts into his soft brain and the devil – who else could it have been? – whispering in his ear, had made it impossible to concentrate. He had slugged onward in his mindless vacuum, giving himself up as a lost soul, a zombie, open to suggestion and impulse. All he knew how to do was sing. Drink helped him to get on with it. But inexplicably, today, as he rolled back into his mother's smooth marble exterior, he was able to envision something like hope, something that felt remotely like real opportunity. Unaware of the tears that rolled down his cheeks, he offered a prayer, "I ask someone, somewhere to guide and support me in honest efforts to be a better man. And I thank you for giving me a chance. And I mean it." He felt the Virgin Mary statue on the upstairs altar tremble and saw her ceramic expression soften into a smile. A voice that sounded remarkably like his own mother's said something that he had never actually heard her say when she was alive, "That's my boy. You see. It'll be alright now." He felt a soft kiss on his forehead and raised his hand to touch the spot.

To Juan, as with most other people, answered prayers and good luck were one and the same. He did not distinguish between superstition and religious beliefs. God, the Virgin and saints on high responded to superstitious practices. He negotiated with them in the same way as he spit and shone his lucky blue eye – with promises and whispered poems. It was always one thing in exchange for another; you scratch my back, I'll scratch yours. God and saints certainly didn't work for nothing. At the very least, they demanded attention and compromise, and at the most, adoration and your life. People were no different. It was the universal rule of thumb, the way of heaven and earth. God himself provided the true test of the axiom; he did not forgive sins freely. His forgiveness came at the highest price, the sacrifice of his own son.

Juan was accustomed to blessings that came about as a result of negotiations with the Virgin. He reflected on a couple of recent events, things that felt real, that seemed to validate his newfound luck. Since he was unable to pin the source of recent good fortune on the lucky blue eye and he had not yet considered the good luck to have been an item from the caretaker's grave-robbing efforts, he had supposed during a brief period, that it came from the Virgin, with whom he had had a few words lately.

He vaguely remembered bargaining with her to keep himself afloat. He gazed upon the stalwart statue that had stood patiently for years on his family altar, and decided she was worth dealing with. Although she did not approve of his unholy entrances after a night of carousing, she was obviously loyal to the family. He could see that she was disappointed, but she hung onto the hope that he would make an effort. He recalled one of his teachers in his last year of school, "Juan Bonifacio, if only you directed your efforts towards what was asked of you, we would all be happier." Perhaps if he promised to do so, she would grant him small victories, and together they would progress to brighter days, less of her frowning upon him and less of him avoiding her. So he promised to make such an effort and the result was basically that he felt more comfortable entering his home, less like a thief in the night. Nothing more, nothing less, but something.

Then there were minor incidents that raised Juan's hopes and pulled him out of an otherwise bleak future, like the call from a family of more than modest means requesting Jhonny Pretty for their daughter's 'quinceañera' (15-year-old coming out party). In addition to her own choice of live music for the fiesta, her mother insisted on including 'something for old time's sake.' The money was more than he would earn in three weekends at Slaughterhouse Square. He counted himself fortunate but didn't know whom he should thank. He couldn't quite reconcile the idea of the stern-faced virgin statue as the benefactor of so much, especially considering that his efforts, although in earnest, were minimal.

He became convinced that there was something else at play when, following on the heels of the unlikely quinceañera gig, for the first time in more than 20 years, Juan won something – 50,000 pesos –from 'El Pollo' the national lottery. He wasted no time celebrating the win by buying rounds for the regulars at Slaughterhouse Square.

As if that wasn't enough, the luck then engaged his sentimental side. Two weeks ago on Saturday night Juan noticed a new face among the usuals who lollygagged across the benches and stood leaning on one another around Slaughterhouse Square. He was into the third song of his set when he saw a wide smile stretch across a beautiful face. The face was that of a tanned, bleached-blonde. Her white teeth shone like fluorescent pearls into the dark and he half-expected her to float up into the midnight sky and disappear like an elusive angel in a trail of blonde essence of coconut. He allowed his gaze to return to her several times during the first two verses. The flirting commenced in earnest during the third verse when Jhonny, in his navy blue military-cut suit, swaggered towards her, the velvet in his voice spreading like cream over coffee. She drank it all in, sipping slowly, dropping her head back to reveal a long, white neck. Her red-tipped, manicured fingers played coyly across the edges of her low-cut blouse. Jhonny Pretty closed in. He leaned down and slowly wrapped one arm around her waist and as an invitation he raised one eyebrow. She acquiesced with a discreet nod and the crowd went wild as he swept her into the centre of the plaza. He twirled her around and held her when she dipped back – an elegant ballerina in the arms of a legend. He would be the talk of the Square for weeks to come.

He leaned over her, his smooth voice flowing from the speakers in the corner. But his attention was there, in the centre of the plaza. They smiled into each other's eyes. Jhonny Pretty was back with a vengeance. He felt the heat and vitality of his youth and knew that his luck had indeed changed for the better. However, the woman was elusive and in the course of the show, she eventually dissolved into the crystal dew of the early morning air. By the time the remains of other human life had staggered out of Slaughterhouse Square, he saw that she was definitely gone.

The following Saturday she decided to go slumming again. She returned to the Square and he swept her away from the music and lights before she could disappear. She drove him to her apartment in the east end of town. They cruised through the city in her white convertible, leather roof folded back, stars twinkling down onto the tops of their giddy heads. She pulled into a luxury complex where purple and green lights lit up palm trees from below. Security cameras buzzed and robotically shifted angles to follow them with their beady-eyed lenses from strategic positions along the fence. She warned Juan that this was just a one-night-stand, "I love my boyfriend but he's been away a few weeks. You know how it can get." Juan was in perfect agreement. He didn't want a commitment, only a taste of the honey that seeped from this woman's pores.

He never did get her name. And he hadn't seen her since, although three days later, he noticed her car parked near a cafe behind Cerro Santa Lucia and he allowed his instincts to abruptly turn him around and walk him in the opposite direction.

The next night as he stood in the shadows at Slaughterhouse Square, Jesica flounced across the plaza wearing a new outlandish outfit. In response to his gaze, she said, "Isn't it nice, Jhonny? It makes me feel especially luscious." She hesitated long enough to pucker her lips in collagen fashion. "As a performer, you understand it's essential to feel right in your skin." He thought to himself, as he ran his hand down the length of his refurbished Salvation Army suit, "She's talking to Jhonny Pretty. Who does she think she's trying to teach about the right outfit?" His eyes gave her the once up-and-down.

Starting with her purple lipstick and the purple sparkles on mauve fingernails, Jesica's resemblance to a female vampire was uncanny. Her straight black hair now included a long bleached strand that hung down from just in front of her right ear. And she had definitely done something with those lips. He tried to turn away but their sheer volume, not to mention their deep bruising purple drew his eyes in like a magnet clinging to its opposite pole. It was painful. The swollen lips began to speak, "Do you like them?" Jesica batted her vampire eyelashes. He glanced up at her eyes for a split second but was compelled to return to the lips. He watched as her purple fleshy rims slid open to reveal nicotine-stained teeth. It was the best smile she could offer. "I just had them done." Juan stared. They were uncooked sausages stuffed to the point of explosion. She touched them together, attempting to throw kisses, but they made rude bubble sounds and Juan envisioned the purple bottom-feeder fish that he'd seen in a bowl of soup at the central market.

"Never mind," she said. "I can see you're smitten. But as you know, I am spoken for and have been for weeks now." She tapped his elbow and winked. "He works in tourism, you know. But hey, you don't have to feel left out. I met him through his sister, and when I told this girl about you, she said she would die to meet you."

Juan straightened, making himself taller as he inflated his chest and shifted gears. "Well then, let's set something up, shall we?"

"Don't you want to know something about her?"

"Well, only that she's good looking."

"But of course. I have no ugly friends. And what's more, she's involved in fashion, Juan. She sold me this outfit."

Juan examined the tall, laced boots and the black blouse (which was a little too low-cut) and the short blood red leather skirt (which was a little too high-cut). "The gloves are a nice touch," he offered. Jesica had accessorised with a pair of black fingerless gloves made of stretch net. She also wore a heavy chain like he was sure he'd seen on more than one bull dog, and she had stabbed one silver cross earring upside down into her left lobe.

She felt she had to explain. "It's Gothic. My friend has just made an agreement with a couple of men who are up-and-coming designers. They're promoting this. It's their first fashion line."

Juan stepped back. "Turn around. Give me the 360."

Jesica enthusiastically took a step away and stretching her arms above her shoulders, she turned, amplifying the sway of her hips. Juan felt a pang of something indescribable; he didn't even know if it was good or bad, but he decided that a unique woman might be just what the doctor ordered – not Jesica, of course, but her friend.

Jesica read his mind. "She's dying to meet you, Juan. I plan to go back to her shop in the next couple of days. I'll set it up. I'll bring her brother and we'll make it a foursome."

Bingo. Another interesting woman in less than a week. He looked up to thank his lucky stars... or whatever it was that was bringing him the good fortune. During those few days, Juan had killed a few more grey cells, not only on drink but because at that time he was still making an extraordinary effort to locate his lucky blue eye. He had been half-convinced that his recent stroke of luck meant that the lucky blue eye was actually still somewhere in his midst.

Today, though, lying around in the family crypt, as he leaned onto his mother's marble bed and looked over the items in the corner of his dungeon he decided, with unusual nostalgia, that he had to say goodbye to the lucky blue eye and that one of these was its replacement. Therefore, until that item somehow made itself known, it was not only right and fitting, it was imperative, that the entire inventory be appropriately safeguarded. This hodgepodge of items scattered willy-nilly would not do. A worthy vessel was required.

Juan climbed the stairs to peer through the evening's semidarkness towards the niches across the way. From the first week he took up residence here, he had noticed a small leather box on the open shelf of one of the niches. It was an antique Spanish-style leather trunk. It had never been moved. He remembered noticing its artistic tooling and wondered why no one had stolen it yet. Perhaps there was something ghostly and intimidating inside. Until now, that thought would have been threat enough to prevent him investigating. But today he had good reason; he had a real need. So he braved himself for the short trip across the path, hoping his luck would be constant and that this old trunk would prove to be the perfect receptacle for his talismans.

It was at this moment that Juan Maluenda-Valdéz (aka Jhonny Pretty) came face to face with Luisa Rocio Suarez (aka the woman of Santa María Street).

CHAPTER 16

Dead versus Alive

Juan had never before encountered a woman of 158 years. The figure that stood before him – arms akimbo, legs spread apart so wide that he thought she might tear vertically from her crotch to the top of her head – was threatening him with a cold stare that she had summoned from the mysterious world beyond. Her leathery skin hung on a skeleton frame and when she jerked her elbows, he could hear the withered skin crack, just like the wind moving a brittle branch. The old lady was wearing a younger woman's clothes. The pink Adidas shoes were far too big, the brightly flowered skirt, although long, was very youthful for a woman as wrinkled as this old raisin.

He noted her heavy rouge and her thick lipstick. She must have applied it with her own shaky hand. Smudges rose from the corner of her red lips and disappeared under her nose. Circles of rouge on the saggy skin of her cheeks gave the impression that she was wilting.

This painted bag of wrinkles stopped Juan in his tracks. She pointed a bony forefinger at him and half a dozen silver bracelets slipped down her wrist to clank into the crevice of her elbow, causing her to lose her balance. She wobbled slightly, but pretended not to notice. "I'm watching you, young man." Her voice was as dry as sand.

"And good afternoon to you, Señora." Juan attempted to circumvent the impending conversation by tipping a make-believe hat and stepping widely around her. She spun on her heel, her old skin slithering over her bones. The motion triggered the release of a jasmine fragrance. From the dry old skin? Its incongruity halted him mid-step.

"I know you for what you are, you two-timing Don Juan!"

It was an unprovoked attack and understandably, he was unable to respond immediately. He stood there looking at her, mouth gaping, trying to overcome the shock of her appearance, to say nothing of her offensive attitude. He attempted to gather his wits and she continued.

"I've been watching you from over there," she half-turned to indicate the wall of niches and the motion made her neck resemble a twisted old sock. "And I've heard you sing to that woman and I've seen you take the gifts she leaves for you. Don't think I don't know what you're up to. You're nothing but a singing thief. And worse..."

Juan snapped out of the shock in time to interrupt her. He didn't like this old girl. She was ugly and assuming. "What business is it of yours? You don't know who I am or what I'm about."

"Well, you're certainly not a spirit guide." She guffawed with such force that her top dentures slipped out of place and suddenly there was a set of teeth resting on her lower lip. She sputtered before sucking and pushing them back in with a shaky hand. "What's this about guiding lost souls back to their graves? You charlatan! Do you think I'll let you get away with this?"

"What's it to you? It's none of your business."

"I have been protecting that woman for months now and that makes it my business. I am her angel."

Incredulous, "You?" he pointed. "An angel?" He laughed in her face. "Is this what the heaven stoops to nowadays? What happened to the beautiful blondes?"

"Don't make this about me, mister! This is about you. That woman is dedicated to you and you're making a fool of her. I will not allow it."

Worse than her accusation was the idea that this dried up prune of a woman could be a menace to his newly found luck or that she could possibly have some influence over it. He couldn't allow that. He twirled around to grab her bony wrist. "Listen, you ugly..."

But he was unable to make contact. She was nothing but air.

Luisa Rocio surprised herself by inadvertently mastering the ghostly art of being seen but intangible. She assumed a karate stance and dared him to try again. "Come on, you useless song bag. Let's see what you've got." Luisa was pumped, inspired by her own skill and daring.

Juan froze in his tracks. "Who are you?" He leaned into her, squinting, "What are you?"

In her most menacing voice, "I am the dead, come to eat you alive. Do you hear the grinding and gnashing of teeth?"

It didn't matter who or what she claimed to be, or even that she was an ancient woman. He would challenge this ugly wretch from hell. Juan rolled up his sleeves. "I hear nothing and I see only an old woman gumming the air with toothless threats. If you really are a ghost, then you are helpless to interfere in earthly affairs. Whatever you are, let's see what you're made of. Let's go!"

"Just watch me." Now it was her turn to lunge at him. But Juan stepped aside and she whizzed by him, empty air in her hands. She twisted around like a snake and tried to grab him by the throat. But when she closed her fingers, they went through him as though he wasn't there. Neither of them could grab hold of the other.

She screeched in frustration. Her mastery of ghostly intangibility did not include knowing how to reverse it. Juan stepped forward onto one of her long shoelaces. She moved back, losing the trapped Adidas running shoe on the spot. The apparel was real. She flew backwards, her long, blackened toenails on dirty bare feet releasing an odour very unlike the sweet fragrance of jasmine. Juan plugged his nose with his thumb and forefinger and stepped past her.

"You mind your own business, you meddling old hag. I don't want to see you or your shoes or those flowers that are hanging from your hair coming close to me ever again. You just keep to yourself. Do you hear me? Disappear. Hazte humo." He waved her off with a wide sweep of his arm.

That would be the day she would disappear into smoke for him. He didn't know who he was messing with. But it was obvious she'd have to hone her skills because she had fully expected him to flee in terror. Perhaps she was, after all, just too kindly a soul to be formidable. But he would never discover the soft side of her. She huffed. "Don't underestimate me, Don Juan de Ridiculo. I will make my presence felt. You will know my heat and experience my burning. You have been warned."

Juan strode over to where the leather trunk sat on the niche. Grabbing it, he cradled it in his arms and then marched back across the path where the old woman had confronted him. She was gone. And so was the pink Adidas shoe.

He pushed open the gate to his mausoleum and backed inside, standing absolutely still, moving only his eyeballs as he scrutinised the path before him. Now he was being stalked and haunted by a ghost. Well, what can you expect when you live in a cemetery? It was part and parcel of the real estate. He would have to think about moving on, but it was still too soon. And besides, the situation with the cemetery caretaker was a gift from heaven.

Once underground, he set about arranging each of the talismans in the small leather trunk. There had been nothing in it after all, and he could see no reason why it hadn't been stolen much sooner. He shrugged it off to simple oversight on the part of passersby. The little trunk was almost perfect. Except for the set of wooden salad spoons, everything fit. He considered 'reducing' the spoons and laughed at his own wit as he reflected on the traditional burial practice of 'reducción,' which enabled families to bury more than one relative in the same small crypt. It was common to 'reduce' a body several decades after it had been dead and buried. At a family's request, a grave could be re-opened, and the bones of the resident skeleton were then bent and compacted in order to make space for another body in the same tomb. Of course sometimes it happened that the next person died before the first body had decomposed sufficiently. But with no other choice, and unpleasant as it was, the 'reduction' was carried out, the least of the revolting sights and smells being long hair and fingernails on a partially decayed corpse.

Juan couldn't bring himself to break the wooden spoons in case they were the lucky items. So he balanced them carefully on top of the leather case, in the form of an X and assigned them the added responsibility of being the guardian of the trunk full of good luck charms.

Meanwhile, across the way, from the dank hollow of the niche in which she had become a squatter, Luisa Rocio kept vigil on Juan's mausoleum. Having been close enough to touch him, she grumbled to herself, "It's just as I thought. He has a dark aura around him and he reeks of cigarettes, liquor and lechery. I will save Astrid from this scoundrel." The old woman wracked her brain. "Sorcery. I need to learn something about sorcery."

CHAPTER 17

The Gothic Nightmare

Astrid de las Nieves wrapped an emerald green scarf around her head in a loose turban, movie-star-style, and surveyed her otherwise naked reflection in the mirror. The glass was cracked diagonally from top to bottom and spider cracks ran to the edges like rivers out to the sea. She stood, arms raised above her head, a naked, albeit somewhat cracked Aphrodite wearing nothing but a polyester turban at the top and a pair of pink and yellow puffy socks that were folded down to her leather loafers at the bottom.

She posed, one foot in front of the other, knee bent out slightly, hands on hips. Maybe she should consider a new pair of shoes. No, it wouldn't help. She would put some clothes on because taking the loafers off was not an option. She could see no reason to expose her virgin toes for the sake of what she knew deep-down was a trifle, a vain little play that she would indulge herself in for the moment.

She slipped a comfortable Hawaiian flower shift over her head and let it float down to settle around her shoulders. She turned once more to Jhonny, whose paper face was framed, waiting patiently for her to come back to him. The candlelight flickered and his eyes glistened as she glided forward in her stealthy, leather loafers (despite how ugly and unsexy they were, she loved absolutely loved the old shoes). The Gypsy Kings were singing, "Quédate aquí. I will be happy if you stay with me," the rhythm rolling sadly from her old CD player into the orange air of her bedroom.

"Listen to this song, Jhonny. I want you to stay here with me, Jhonny, mi amor. Don't leave. Don't go back to your mausoleum where it's cold and damp. Stay here in my bedroom where it's warm and dry... and full of love. I'll give you anything you want, Jhonny."

She was addressing herself to the centrespread of a 1976 El Ritmo that was scotch-taped onto a card and propped inside an ornate, gold-painted frame. The frame was gorgeous. It made Jhonny look like a religious figure, perhaps the god of love and compassion. The photographer had zoomed in, cropping Jhonny's face just above his hairline and just below his chin. He was so close you could see the pores on his nose. His eyes followed her around the room. She found the magazine quite by chance at a street seller on her way home from work only a few days ago.

Astrid had arranged several candles around Jhonny's face. Some sat on risers behind the photo and others sat in low glass cups on either side, a variety of colours, some tall and others squat. She had ceremoniously scattered dried rose petals and some baby's breath, intermingling them with brilliant violets at the front of the altar, and she had cleverly placed half a dozen San Expedito charms so they appeared to have simply fallen into place amidst the petals. A few folded San Expedito prayer cards were balanced discreetly in the background. A love potion of rose, lavender and orange blossom oils floated in a delicate glass receptacle to the left of Jhonny's face. She dipped her ring finger into it and seductively made the sign of the cross over her torso, briefly sucking her fingertip before dragging it in the prescribed order and direction – beginning at her forehead, she drew an oily trail down, between her breasts, over her abdomen until she touched her pubic hair. Then she lifted her hand ever so slightly, brushing her skin on the way back up to touch her left shoulder, then across to the right. She shifted her knees in turn, her hips gently swivelling and she watched as the candle flames grew strong and tall. She sighed and fell back on her bed. She had stirred his inner being, she could tell.

"Take me, Jhonny. I'm yours." She said breathlessly as she threw out her arms and kicked one of her loafers into the air. It went flying, tracing a wide arc across the room before falling on the altar and snuffing out two candles right before Jhonny's eyes.

"Look away, Jhonny." she struggled clumsily to her feet and ran over, tossed the loafer to the floor and, using the flame from a black candle to light the two that had been so rudely snuffed out, she begged his pardon. She hopped on one foot and slipped the guilty shoe back over her heel.

"Where were we?"

"Sorry, my love," she heard Jhonny say, "That sort of killed the mood." She watched as the tall flames shrank to less than half an inch, flickering weakly and threatening to disappear.

"Oh, no." she moaned. "That's too bad. I was going to show you such a good time." But Astrid was capable of shifting gears too. To save face and keep with the program, which had unfortunately converted to something much more practical, she grabbed an emery board and settled on the corner of the bed to face Jhonny as she filed her nails. "Then tell me, my dear heart, what are your plans for the New Year?" She waited in silence for his response.

In fact, Juan was five kilometres away in Slaughterhouse Square, about to begin his second set. 'Let's Play the Fool' was first on this evening's repertoire. When Jhonny belted out the tune, the cemetery caretaker was the furthest thing from his mind. He was conscious of Jesica's friend somewhere in the crowd and he surveyed it for the pretty little thing who was excited to meet 'the legend.'

His eyes settled briefly on a woman in her late twenties. He would have passed her by but he noticed that she was dressed in the same Gothic fashion that Jesica had adopted recently. Please, dear Lord, this must not be her. Fearful of demonstrating premature interest, he forced his eyes to move along. Several of the usuals were there; most of them middle-aged couples or older, sharing sips from deflated bottles of Gato Negro or Medallion 120. A bearded man was pushing his tongue inside the lip of a bottle after tilting it upside down for so long that his companion finally grabbed it and hid it behind her back. She grabbed him by the hair and forced his face into her bosom, causing him to lose his balance and a small ruckus ensued, other patrons yelling at them to settle down so they could watch the show they came to see, not some uncoordinated lovers' free-for-all. The man in question regained his composure, feigning innocence as he frowned and whistled at Jhonny, leading shouts of "Bravo" that scattered throughout the air and over their heads as Jhonny's voice faded off into the final note. He made a discreet bow and turned to point to Jesica, who was working the karaoke machine, instructing her to continue with 'Tonight's the Night.'

He broke into song, this time looking directly at the Gothic woman. Her eyes were bright with excitement. He saw something familiar. "A star gazer, a typical groupie." It brought back old emotions – both thrill and trepidation. "So what if she's a few decades younger than me? She loves me. I'm Jhonny Pretty." But there was something more. He looked at the protruding lips, their chemical fullness enhanced with dark lipstick – confirmation that this was the woman Jesica told him about. She and Jesica must have gone to the same cheap surgeon. Her lips had the trademark algae-sucking fish characteristic – plump purple, about ready to explode. He blinked hard at the semi-rigid, half-smile that was reminiscent of a mannequin from a shop window in El Patronato, and he found it hard to disguise his horror. Although it was impossible to avoid the lips, they were not the woman's only familiar feature. There was something else... but he couldn't quite put his finger on it.

He carried on mechanically with the lyrics. "We'll hold each other and it will be forever." He strived to concentrate, to perform above and beyond expectations, as had been his plan for the night, but his attention was involuntarily drawn in the direction of the eager eyes of the female Goth. He wasn't in quest of a long-term relationship. He'd only ever been a thrill-seeker. A one-night stand, maybe two or three at the most. "And we'll be in heaven, our love blessed as the stars," he crooned to end the song. As he bent into a sweeping bow, thanking his gracious public, he knew this night was not going to be the thrill that Jesica had promised him. He would, at all costs, avoid potential contact with the dreaded purple lips.

Jesica was waiting at the karaoke machine, her own fleshy mouth forming an unnatural pucker. "The night is still young, my pet. Just a few more sets and the whole city – no, make that the whole world – is ours. For now though, I need to stay at my post. Why don't you wander down into the crowd and dish out some famous Jhonny Pretty charm?" She pointed to the corner where the identical set of swollen purple lips was sitting, and she winked. "I think there's a young woman who has a special interest in meeting you."

"Yeah, but first I need to quench my thirst. I'm going to Mario's for a beer and I'll be right back."

Indulging the overwhelming urge to flee, Juan turned on his heel and rushed to Mario's cafe. It was overflowing with a random assortment of misfits and merry makers. Three figures were asleep in a heap in the corner under a table. In an overt show of disgust, the polished shoe belonging to another familiar face was pushing and compacting the heap, shoving them further away from the body that belonged to the shoe. Juan couldn't place where he had seen that face before, but it evoked his internal warning mechanism, and he put a rush on to go and stand at the opposite end of the counter. Two familiar faces in one night. Too much to think about. He no sooner signalled Mario for a beer, than a wrinkled prune of a figure flounced in and sidled up to him, her bones creaking from the effort. She huffed loudly, nose in the air, looking at him sideways. Flowers that looked half dead hung limply from the bun at the nape of her neck. Bright lipstick smeared around wrinkled lips that sneered up at him. She wore large pink Adidas shoes and smelled of jasmine.

How did she get in here? Juan swigged his beer and couldn't escape fast enough. He was gone before the old lady could finish yelling "Make yourself into smoke, hey? Be gone! Disappear, hey?" Mario raised his fist and yelled after him, "Hey, Jhonny, that'll be 900 pesos. You owe me 900 pesos, man! That's it this time. I mean it. No more beer until it's paid."

CHAPTER 18

The Good Doctor

Constancia's full lips were pouting.

"Never mind, Constancia. I see Jhonny Pretty almost every day. I'll find out what happened and we'll set it up so there is no misunderstanding next time." Jesica was puckered, poised to kiss the air beside Constancia's cheek in a bid to rush out the door with an armful of black stockings and a leather whip. "I must go, darling. I have errands to run before the gig tonight. Thank you for the tip on the outfit. It'll be a smash."

Constancia had only just opened the shop, but she pushed past Jesica to lock the door and flip the sign to 'Closed'. Turning to face her, Constancia made an anguished plea, "No, don't go yet Jesica. I need to show you this. Look!" She tilted her face upwards, the deep red polished nail of her pinky finger drawing a line from the centre of her top lip to the corner of her mouth. "Look," she repeated. "It's going back to its normal self. The fullness is disappearing." Constancia's morning had already been fraught with disappointment and inconvenience and she couldn't bear one more thing, especially something like this. Her eyes were teary. She whined, "And not only that, it's worse. Now I have little wrinkles around this edge. And they weren't there before! My lips are wilting!" The half normal lips turned down in a pout.

Jesica leaned in to examine them more closely. If there was any transformation, it meant that she too, had reason for concern. She had taken Constancia to an Argentinean doctor that she met one afternoon at Slaughterhouse Square. He was in Santiago only for two months, he said, to fulfil appointments made with local clientele. He quickly pointed out that he was not one of the three Argentinean plastic surgeons who had recently been sent packing by the Chilean health authorities. "No Señorita, my medical education and competence are held in high regard. It's a travesty that such charlatans can tarnish a reputation as impeccable as my own, not to mention that of other perfectly competent compatriots. But no need to go into all of that. My results speak for themselves." He handed her a card, on the back of which he had scribbled two phone numbers of women who would be happy to recommend him. And he invited her to his Santiago apartment-surgery so that she could see for herself the overall hygiene and view photographs (before and after, of course) of entirely satisfied clients. He winked, "I hope to see you there in the near future. After all, my dear, with just a discreet touch here and there, your lovely features can be enhanced beyond belief. And of course, being from across the Andes where the economy is a different story, my fees are much lower than those of my Chilean colleagues. You really must pay me a visit, my dear. And don't wait too long because my clients in Rosario are crying for my return. I have to be back there in three weeks."

Within a week, Jesica turned up at the good doctor's apartment, which was just off Plaza Brazil in the centre of the old university district. First she had called each of the two numbers on the back of his card and as he promised, she heard nothing but praise and the highest recommendations. "He is fantastic, sister. I can tell you that I am more than satisfied with his work. I started with a lip enhancement and then I returned twice more – once for some work around my eyes, and then for a chin tuck. It was all performed to perfection. You can't ask for a more skilled plastic surgeon. And his prices. Well, his prices are entirely reasonable. I plan to follow him back to Rosario for more work as soon as I can arrange it." The second reference, by a woman with an Argentinean accent, was just as glowing. The references seemed to be proof beyond a doubt. Jesica was excited at the prospect and was almost sure she would ask for at least one shot of collagen and maybe a chin tuck. She found the apartment without any trouble. Two middle-aged women were walking out the door and chatting excitedly about how bright their futures looked. They both wore oversized dark glasses so Jesica deduced the doctor had just transformed their eyes into the seductive orbs of their dreams. She was feeling very positive when she buzzed the number that was printed on his card. Making her way beyond the mezzanine to the second floor, she encountered the good doctor smiling broadly as he held open the door to his apartment. It was sparser than she had expected, but the man himself was even more gracious than she remembered. "Please excuse the lack of decor, my lovely, but you understand that I'm here only for the short-term and in order to offer my services for such a low fee, it makes sense to be frugal." He led her to the dining room where a set of yellowed sheets were spread, one across the table and the other over an old reclining chair. Instruments, all sparkling, set on silver trays, glass canisters with cotton swabs and others that were filled with yellow and pink liquids were arranged on the polished marble-topped sideboard. A pile of unwashed plates and teacups filled the sink. He saw her frown. "My maid called in sick today. My apologies if you find the place in a bit of disarray."

"Well, you come highly recommended, but I wonder if you can show me some examples. Do you have before-and-after photos? Would you mind?"

"But of course. If you hadn't asked, I was going to offer. This way." He glided across the floor, tall, shoulders back, careful steps, and led her across the parquet towards the bookshelf at the corner of a wide, barren living room window. The room was so empty it echoed. He pulled out one of two matching photo albums, both covered in quilted pink plastic, recently cleaned with a damp cloth that left curved traces of soap on the surface. A framed image of Jesus was propped beside the books, his hands outstretched, as if to say 'It's none of my doing, darling; this man is totally responsible for the outcomes. But I am here to oversee the process. Bless him and his touch that results in miracles.'

The doctor's impeccably manicured index finger pointed to Maria, one of the women she had spoken with only the day before. "See here," he said. "Notice how thin and pale she looks. Lacking fullness in her lips. And see the puffiness around her eyes. Also the bit of skin beginning to sag on either side of her chin. Quite a beautiful bone structure though, and a treat to work with. For only 150,000 pesos, I was able to transform her." The after photos, taken from various angles, showed a beautiful woman, lips puckered as though throwing a kiss to the camera, eyes bright, a sheer long neck leading up to a clean, well-defined jawbone.

Jesica hadn't expected such convincing evidence. The doctor turned the page and continued with a second set of before-and-after shots. "This lady is much older than you are and she asked for more work yet. As you can see, some of the lines on her forehead are too pronounced, to say nothing of the deepening crow's feet. And of course, although her lips are not as thin as Maria's, she asked for them to be slightly enhanced since we were going to do some work anyway." He thrust out his chest, " I recommended a chin tuck for her too." As Jesica looked over the after-photos, a sensation of warmth and trust settled over her. Yes, she had a good feeling about this doctor. She would definitely come back. And she would bring Constancia.

Thus it was that the two of them visited Dr Emilio Montalvo-S. in his apartment-surgery only days after Jesica's initial investigation. Jesica was able to negotiate a good two-for-one price for a collagen lip job for herself and Constancia. They left arm in arm, feeling like two potential beauty queens. When Jesica snuck back two days later to arrange a bit of work around her eyes, the apartment doorman told her that the good doctor no longer lived there. She walked away berating herself for not having had all the work done at once. He had, after all, warned her that his time in Santiago was short.

Now, less than four weeks later, standing inside the shop door that Constancia refused to let her walk out of, she was studying Constancia's lips, and tiny doubts were poking holes in her inflated confidence. There were some small lines there. No doubt about it. And yes, the right side of Constancia's lip looked like someone had let the air out of a balloon, but the other side was still inflated.

Constancia was agitated. She stamped a studded orange high heel on the floor so violently that the purple bow on the toe almost fell off. "You see... it's coming undone. And not even all at once, but one side at a time. I'm unbalanced. When I look at myself in the mirror, I lean to the right to try to make up for it. I was bumping into small children this morning on the way to work. They all looked up at me and laughed." Constancia was crying real tears now. She whimpered. "Even small children notice, Jesica. What am I to do?"

"No, no, it's not really noticeable." She lied as she leaned to her left for a closer examination.

"Well, and what about yours? They're not exactly beautiful anymore."

"What are you talking about? My lips were beautiful this morning. I used this new flaming red lipstick and they looked fabulous."

"Well, look at yourself now." Constancia clipped over to the counter as fast as her pumps would allow and picked up a hand mirror. She suddenly felt righteous. "I told you his apartment looked too dingy for him to be a bona fide plastic surgeon. I don't care if it was just a temporary living situation. Real doctors wouldn't suffer that; they insist on very posh surroundings, you know." Suddenly Constancia was expert on surgeons.

Jesica scratched Constancia's wrist in her panic to wrestle the mirror from her hand and check for herself. She looked, shrieked and slammed the mirror onto her thigh before raising it again, hand now trembling, for another look. "Oh Diós Mio, what is this?"

Her bottom lip was flat and her top lip was a flaming red overhang. It looked like an awning.

"This shitty doctor. This shitty non-doctor! Look what he's done. Look at us. We're freaks! We will denounce him, Constancia. He's not getting away with this. We'll charge him with malpractice."

Constancia stiffened with satisfaction, and without hesitation she officiously selected a wide-brimmed hat for each of them, which they donned, fussing a bit with the angle to ensure it cast a discreet but handsome shadow over their deformed lips. Then she hustled Jesica out of the shop and locked the door. They pounded towards to the Office of Consumer Affairs, which was located a few blocks from the bridge on the other side of the river. Indignant, they defamed the good doctor. "He won't get away with this. The imposter! He turned us into the Adams Family, Jesica! We look like we belong in the cemetery." Constancia whined, "He made us ugly and he took our money to do it. He'll pay for this. How dare he come into our country with his foreign tales and think he can get away with it? He doesn't know who he's dealing with." They spit and hissed from behind their hands to shield the public at large from their unsightly lips.

Although Jescia would have been an easy target for venomous words, Constancia refrained from blaming her. Jesica was her friend after all, and Constancia had agreed to the procedure. She had to admit that she had been just as excited about the newly found beauty, if not more so, than Jesica. She had dreamed of collagen treatments for years. Now she could only hope that the damage was not severe and long lasting. She blinked back tears. "Jesica, we'll get revenge for this. Don't you worry," she said, more to convince herself and to transform bitter disappointment into useful anger.

When Jesica and Constancia entered the building, the elevator operator couldn't look away and found it impossible to suppress a comment. He chortled, "Were you in a fight with a one-handed lightweight? He must have been quite a marksman." The two women speared him with dark looks. Jesica moved her hand close to her lips and retorted through her fingers, "You, you nasty little man, will find yourself without a job tomorrow. You don't know who you're talking to!" He didn't, so he wiped the smirk off of his face and thought about what his job meant to his family. Maybe she was one of the disfigured top models. He had seen at least a dozen of them here lately. Until two weeks ago, they all looked good. He knew because he'd seen them on TV gossip shows and in the sensational daily rags that people left behind. But by the time they reached this building most of these beauties were inconsolable – no longer beautiful. Their anger at the doctor's handiwork had bounced around these elevator walls until he knew each circumstance first-hand. In reality the circumstances were all identical. It was easy to conclude that these two were among the group of unfortunate patients of the good doctor from Argentina.

Jesica and Constancia reached the smoky glass doors marked 'Office of Consumer Affairs' and strode through like a couple of conquistadoras. But they stopped in their tracks as they surveyed what lay before them. Dozens of mutant faces turned in unison to look over at the newcomers. There was a woman with a deformed face or abnormal upper body in each and every chair. Several of them had one fat lip above a thin, wrinkled one. Others had swollen eyes and yet others had faces that were distorted by strings of taut, dry skin pulling their jaws down into their collarbones. These poor creatures sat crookedly with their mouths permanently hanging open, as if someone kept surprising them and they were gasping for a little understanding, a little tolerance. Please. And then there were the discoloured faces. Complexions varied from white to red to blue, an ugly patriotic presentation of the Chilean female gone wrong. One of the women must have gone all out to improve her natural beauty. The right side of her chest had caved in and the skin on the left of her neck pulled her head down so that she was frozen into this cocked position. One eye was half-closed, the upper lid swollen like a plum. Deep wrinkles exploded all round her dry lips and veins trailed across her transparent yellow cheeks. She was like a decaying corpse.

Constancia and Jesica, sickened by the unsightly flesh before their eyes, took a number and leaned against the wall in black silence. These women were, until recently, attractive – if not beautiful – until vanity stepped up and made fools of them all.

There was a brief but intense commotion in the back office before a bureaucrat was pushed into the reception area. He straightened his tie, tugged at his suit and stood protected behind the counter, trying to prepare for whatever might come, surveying the group before averting his face momentarily to choke into a handkerchief. They waited until he tucked it safely back into his jacket pocket and turned his attention to the matter at hand, mustering a professional exterior. All eyes were on him, expectant, as he drew in a deep breath and began, "It would appear that all of you are here," he performed a very rapid 180 degree rotation on his toes so that he could address everyone in the room without actually looking at anyone in particular lest his horror make itself evident once more, "to lodge a complaint against a Dr Emilio Montalvo-Suarez from Argentina." He turned sideways and coughed lightly into his hand before continuing. "I must advise all of you that after our first three complaints last week, we instructed the Policía Chilena Internacional to investigate this man. Unfortunately, he does not exist, at least not under the name given." Several women stood up to interject but he held up his hand and continued, raising his voice above their protests. "This is not to say that this man, whoever he is, did not commit terrible atrocities. Unfortunately you are all evidence of that."

Again he made a small fist and coughed into it. "We have more than enough to proceed with criminal charges and will, with your permission, take several detailed photographs of each of you to enter as evidence along with the details you will describe in each of your written reports. When we find this man, he will be punished to the full extent of the law." He cleared his throat and added with authority, "Now, having put our brightest associates to work on this project, we are, at this time, also able to advise you where to go for corrective surgery, should it be necessary. After each of you in turn comes forward to submit your report, we will then direct you down the hall to a plastic surgeon intern from our own Hospital Universidad Católica. He will examine your scars and current condition and send you to the appropriate clinic for further exams and advice. If you are among the lucky ones, and the surgery performed on you was minor, you may leave today with advice and a prescription, and nothing else. Others of you," he involuntarily averted his eyes, "who are not so fortunate, will have to start with our advice and move forward from there. The Government of Chile is not responsible for your choice of surgeon and we cannot, therefore, be responsible for the damages incurred by this butcher, nor for the cost of repair. We are authorised only to advise you." This caused a major uproar and several women burst into tears. The bureaucrat sought to put them at ease. Tempted to chastise them for their misplaced vanity, he chose instead to satisfy them with a taste of revenge for the scars on their delicate bodies. "And of course, we will make this man pay through his nose once we catch him."

Jesica and Constancia spent five hours in the Office of Consumer Affairs, completing their reports, tasting the tears that rolled unnoticed down their cheeks and opening their mouths to allow the intern to probe and pinch their once sensuous Gothic lips. Dreams of further beauty treatments were sucked into the abyss of misery that surrounded them.

Finally, they were given some news of hope. "You are among the lucky ones. I don't know why you stopped at lip enlargements, but it's lucky you did. And..." he checked his notes, "You say you had only one treatment each. Count yourselves fortunate indeed. The good Dr Montalvo seems to have used cooking oil in place of collagen, but because you had only the one treatment, you will come out virtually unscathed. Just give yourselves another two or three days and you will be back to normal. You may feel a little tender and you might feel some pulling on the skin surrounding your lips, but simply apply your usual moisturizing cream and nothing more. Nothing more! Just do as I say, and you'll be fine. Now, at this time, I am obliged to ask if you would like to add your names to the class action suit that has been initiated by a another of the unfortunate victims of Dr Montalvo who also happens to be a lawyer. Although she has, up to this point, worked exclusively on real estate cases, she is confident she will be able to litigate in this instance to ensure that all of you get your money back as well as a healthy chunk of damages. That, of course, will have to wait until she has undergone corrective surgery." He nodded in the direction of a young bleached-blonde woman in a tight-fitting business suit. She looked up and smiled a grotesque smile, the skin under her left eye sagging heavily towards the bottom of her nostril, which was inflamed and enlarged. "Looks like she was going for a nose job." Jesica whispered behind her hand to Constancia." Then she turned to the young intern, "Add our names to the list, please. Where do we sign?"

Both women eagerly added their names to the list and left out the back door. When they passed the main entrance, they saw teams of television reporters panning a line of deformed females unlike anything seen even during the Fright Night Film Festival. The reporters were rendered practically speechless. "A picture is worth a thousand words," they heard one of them say. Constancia shivered and grabbed Jesica's elbow. "Let's get out of here!" They ran hand-in-hand down the sidewalk, across the bridge and into Constancia's shop, where they locked the door behind themselves and rushed to look in the mirror. Constancia moaned breathlessly, "I want my skinny lips back, Jesica. Did you see some of those women? They were absolute monsters."

Jesica was leaning very close to the mirror, examining her lips, pushing the flesh with the tip of her baby finger and watching to see if the dent filled itself in. She murmured, "This is a travesty, Constancia. But we will be rewarded for our pain. Mark my words. We won't let go of this thing. That butcher will pay." Constancia nodded, "But at least we didn't go for the full treatment." "Thank the Virgin that we didn't have enough money. Can you imagine...?" she let the thought trail off.

Constancia leaned into Jesica's shoulder as she peered at her own reflection. They remained gazing into the mirror for a good hour, alternately squeezing their lips into hard puckers, then sucking them in, fingers poking and prodding, the odd sigh and whimper escaping into the otherwise heavy silence as they smoothed moisturising cream round the edges of their deformed mouths.

That afternoon they decided to turn their backs on Gothic fashion because it was a painful reminder of the cooking oil injections. Thus, the amalgamation of black leather and lace that flew artistically around the windows of Constancia's shop was immediately replaced with childish yellow daisy prints and pink leotards. Bald mannequin heads were topped with short blonde curly wigs and accented with outrageous purple ribbons. Huge cardboard lollipops, some creased and tattered, hung limply on thick threads in the background. The up and coming gay clothing designers haughtily turned their noses at the display. They made rude hand gestures and leaned into the window yelling curses. They vowed to tear this frivolous garb off the back of any compadre who dared replace their gorgeous garments with the tarty bits of wanna-be fairytale tatter. So it was that Constancia lost a good share of the gay market. But she was confident in her ability to drag a percentage back in with the feather boas, tangas and high boots that she had on order in time for the annual gay parade.

CHAPTER 19

Seasonal Nostalgia

It was a warm evening, just a week before Christmas. A light breeze cooled the summer air and carried a mixed aroma of fried food and stale beer across Slaughterhouse Square. Juan was content, having just devoured the white fish, salty rice and mixed salad at Mario's and was ready to entertain the local masses. He spied a woman flitting around Jesica's karaoke equipment. She was as bright as the breeze itself, huge flowers dancing on her full skirt and one pink pom-pom hanging from behind each ear. Like a bee to a daisy, he was attracted to the skirt and what was under it.

"Hello there. Are you ready for an incredible evening of entertainment?" he asked in his velvet voice, dragging his fingers through his hair and tossing his head back. Was she ready for Jhonny Pretty?

The woman straightened and turned to look at him. "Who are you kidding, Jhonny? It's going to be more of the same old, same old. But let's do our best to make it festive, shall we?" Her shocking pink lipstick revealed her best efforts at being happy.

Juan stepped back, astonished by Jesica's sudden transformation. Last time he saw her, she was Morticia Adams in the dead of winter and suddenly she had become an innocent Heidi flouncing around a Swiss meadow in springtime, her lips painted the loudest pink he had ever seen.

"What happened to you?"

"Whatever do you mean?" She blinked heavily, feigning ignorance.

"Well, what happened to the dark look of death? Suddenly you've become a child floating around the heavens." He stepped closer, looked down into her face, and touched the tip of his finger lightly to her top lip. "And I see your lips have been reduced to their normal voluptuous selves? What did you pump them up for in the first place? Do you have any idea how scary you looked?"

"Don't bother me with these questions. I follow fashions as I see fit. And recently I found something more to my liking."

"Well, it's more to my liking too, if you don't mind me saying so. You were enough to scare the ears off a bat for a couple of weeks there, Jesica. You scared the shit out of me."

"Well, I'm happy you approve of my latest choice but it doesn't really matter what you approve of." She went on the attack. "And hey, what happened to you last week? You were supposed to meet my new boyfriend and me. We waited for about an hour, but you were gone. What kind of treatment is that for an old friend?" She looked up at him accusingly, hands on hips. "To say nothing of my boyfriend's beautiful young sister who was ready to fall at your feet. I thought she was going to die of disappointment. You're shameful."

"Oh, yeah... uh, well, I'm really sorry about that, Jesica. It was out of my control." She glared at him, waiting for something better than that. "Someone showed up at Mario's. Someone I didn't want to see. And I had to leave the Square." He held up his hand. "Don't ask." He was not about to admit that Jesica's Gothic look-alike put the scare into him and then he was doubly frightened when the old bag of bones from the cemetery rattled up to him at Mario's counter. Now he was reminded that he'd have to think of a new excuse to escape Jesica's attempt at matchmaking. The memory of that pair of Gothic lips under the puppy eyes caused a chill to run up and down his spine.

He changed the subject. "Okay, tonight I'm going to light up the place with a little rock 'n roll, okay? I feel like doing some faster tunes, get some people moving here." He clapped his hands, in an attempt to believe his own enthusiasm. In the first place, he was disappointed that the bright young thing with big flowers on her ass turned out to be Jesica.

In the second place, he didn't really feel like working tonight. And in the third place, he was angry with himself for not escaping the cemetery soon enough that day, and for allowing the caretaker to drag him down with her sentimental crap about how this was the season for family and how important it was to be with loved ones.

Juan had hoped to have been long gone from his hard bed in the family residence before the caretaker showed up at his stairs that afternoon. But he overslept. He was dreaming about a road trip with the band in the days before the accident. Pato and Gringo were their old selves, playing cards with their favourite deck; the one with the naked woman poised mystically and permanently in mid-air, legs folded coyly over one another, hands flipping her long blonde hair around her shoulders. When Gringo shuffled the deck, the cards suddenly flew out and gravity had no effect on them. They floated about the bus and the guys started chasing them. Pato jumped over a seat when he tried to grab the queen of hearts, and instead of landing on the seat behind, he began to float too. Then all at once, everyone was floating like astronauts in a space ship. It was marvellous. Juan floated feet-first right down the centre of the aisle towards the front of the bus and he came to a stop when his shoes collided with the windscreen. So he tiptoed across the glass, past the driver's seat (there was no driver on this bus), turned himself around and started swimming leisurely through the air towards the back. "Make way, I'm coming through." he said, and his voice was in a bubble. He slowed, treading the air beside Gringo, who had gathered a hand of cards and was about to throw one away. "Here," he said to Juan, "Take this one. I don't need it." It was the ace of hearts. Juan smiled and accepted the card. Then he turned the card over and the naked woman with the long blonde hair was replaced by the Jesica look-alike, wearing black leather, her thick purple lips puckering up for a kiss. Juan yelled and dropped the card. That's when he woke up. His heart pounding, he blinked into the darkness, hoping the good news was that he really was sleeping with the dead. He fumbled for the flashlight and focused it on the wall where his mother and sister lay in their tombs.

Yes, thank God he was home. He glanced at his watch. He needed to rush over to the nearest public toilet and get ready for the day.

Too late. He had just climbed up into the daylight and closed the hatch behind himself when he heard the woman humming as she approached. There was no time to crawl back downstairs; he would have to face her. He quickly shoved his shaving kit onto the altar and sat down in front of it, posing, nonchalant, as though he had been waiting for her for hours.

"Hola, Jhonny, mi amor. How lovely to see you. I was afraid I'd miss you." She bounced towards the entrance in a carefree morning mood and pulled a small irregular-shaped package out of her skirt pocket. It was in a purple handkerchief wrapped with a narrow yellow ribbon. "Look, I brought a gift." She carefully unfolded the cloth to reveal a miniature clay crèche, complete with baby Jesus, Mary and Joseph, an angel, a couple of sheep and a cow, all roughly shaped and daubed with bold colour.

Astrid blushed. "Jhonny, I made it myself. Can you believe it? It's been years since I took lessons, but I must say that I haven't forgotten the tricks." She held it up and displayed it before her own eyes, which shone with pride. "It was created with love, Jhonny." She bent forward and gently reached in between the wrought iron rungs and placed it on the floor. "I was hoping you'd be here so that I didn't have to put it into the box, which can sometimes be too impersonal." Not meaning to complain, her blush deepened.

Juan remained in the shelter of the shadows, but he projected his voice, careful to maintain his trademark toffee softness in spite of needing desperately to run to the toilet. "Muchas gracias, mi corazón. You've outdone yourself. This is my first and only Christmas ornament. I'll place it here so that anyone who passes by can admire your handiwork." He gestured towards a space on the opposite end of the altar. "Or perhaps I should leave it closer to the door so that the details are more easily visible. Yes, I think I'll do that. But out of reach, of course, of anyone who might like to steal it away for themselves." Juan was impressed with his own impromptu grace.

"Si, mi ángel, I think you are right to keep it within view but safely away from jealous hands. I'm happy that you like it, Jhonny. It did take me a long time to complete it, but every touch, every bit of paint, every single second I worked on it, was done with you in mind. The meaning is that it will bring us closer to one another, even if we are heaven and earth apart. This time of year it's so important to be close to loved ones. Don't you agree?" She didn't give him time to respond. "I'm very lucky to have my children and now, this year, to also have you, my love, my one and only."

Astrid gazed towards Jhonny adoringly. So moved was he by her surprise that he appeared to be grimacing, a visible effort to hide the emotional impact of her gift. Maybe if she just kept her eyes lowered as she spoke, he would regain control and they could enjoy a relaxing visit. "Everyone in the world is preparing for Christmas. You should see the shops. Only a few years ago, it seemed to be a last-minute thing. I imagine your last Christmas was like that. But nowadays preparations for the holidays begin much earlier. Stores have been full of decorations and they've been playing Christmas music since just after The Day of the Dead and children are excited, people are planning their vacations and paseos at the beach. Families are arranging to be together. You would be surprised how things are now, Jhonny. The bus companies raise their prices and people pay double and triple the normal rate, just to be together during this season of love. And of course, the cemetery is also bustling. Have you noticed all of the Christmas ornaments and musical cards that we've added to the tombs? I just love this season. Of course this year is going to be fabulous. And all because we have each other, Jhonny. I have to admit you're still my best-kept secret and I don't plan to introduce you to my children, but no matter. We have the best of both worlds, you and I."

She had planned to while away much of the afternoon with Jhonny, but sensitive to the fact that he was fighting off emotions (this season effects everyone), she decided it was best not to embarrass him. Obviously Jhonny didn't like to cry in front of women. She reached into her pocket and pulled out two loose Derbys. She was going to light one and smoke it here with him, but she could see it was going to be awkward. He was unable to speak and was biting his lips.

"Jhonny, I'm sorry. I appreciate how you feel and I didn't mean for this to be an awkward moment." Perhaps he was also remembering the warmth of his own family Christmases.

Little did she know that during his childhood, the most important thing about this time of year was the decor. His mother stressed out about the details to the point of a nervous breakdown, searching for the final touch that would elevate her Christmas genius to new heights. The rest of the family avoided her until Christmas morning. Astrid put one of the Derbys back into her pocket and reached forward to slip the other one into the private vault. "Here, Jhonny, maybe you can smoke this and it will calm everything down. I think it's best if I go on my way now."

"Do you happen to have a light?" He managed to squeeze out the question, his voice breaking. "Can you please leave a match too?"

"Of course, Jhonny. My pleasure." Astrid winked up at him and dropped a single wooden match into the box. "I'll be back on Christmas Eve... and probably even before. By the way, I hope your guided tours are going well."

Jhonny managed a nod.

"Bueno. My love, I'm going to leave you for now. But of course you remain always in my heart." She raised her palm to her bosom.

"Thank you, my sweetness. I will be thinking of you too." He managed a tight schoolboy wave, barely able to lift his arms, his legs now tied in knots.

Juan waited until her footsteps faded away and he sprang off the altar. Careful not to disturb the crèche, he reached into the vault and grabbed the cigarette and match. He fumbled with the lock on the door, let himself out, and with one leg wrapped around the other, he bent over and locked the gate, forcing himself to concentrate on anything other than how much he needed to get to the toilet.

Unable to discern which was more urgent, he alternately held the front of his crotch and whipped his hand round to his backside as he crouched and hopped his way to the public toilet. He reached it in record time, slammed the thin wooden door and sat on the toilet with a huge sigh as he let it all go. Only then did the muscles on his face also relax, his expression of pain turning to one of ecstasy. He lit the cigarette and leaned forward, elbows on his knees, the filtered Derby playing an important role as he lounged on the toilet and listened to the birds chirping from the other side of the metal net window.

He sat back and considered what the woman said about Christmas and family. The past several years – he couldn't remember exactly how many – he'd done his best to forget Christmas day by getting blitzed the night before. Some years he had managed to sleep away the entire day. And when he awoke, it was in anticipation of the inevitable New Year's Eve party. This year would probably be the same. So he was surprised when the thought of poor people scraping together coins to pay two or three times the normal bus fare to reach their families, stuck in his mind. He had nowhere to be. His family had all passed on. At least the ones he knew about. He'd cut off contact with his cousins when his band started to make it big because they had constantly pestered him for money and favours. After the accident, they turned him away. Their excuse was that they were paying him back in kind, but he figured he had been right all along; they had never offered him true friendship. The bottom line was that he had no one.

Normally he was elated by the knowledge that he had no one to answer to, no commitments but this year, because of the caretaker, he had to run from the fact that he was all alone at Christmas. The thoughts she expressed reminded him of what he usually worked hard to obliterate. He finished his cigarette and flushed the butt down the toilet along with the sentimental thoughts he had foolishly allowed to clutter his brain. He pulled up his trousers, telling himself that he would just have to get back on track. There were opportunities out there and no time to waste, so he turned to more important matters. Determined to make himself beautiful for tonight's performance, he stood in front of the streaked mirror, looking into those blue eyes of his, and convinced himself of his reason for being. "Jhonny Pretty, you heartthrob, you. Let's go out there and charm the pants off a few young things."

It was in this mood that he had sauntered up to the bright, flowered skirt in Slaughterhouse Square. Now, as he watched Jesica set up for tonight's gig, he was once more disconcerted by the inadvertent intrusion of seasonal nostalgia. Unwelcome, it was insisting for the second time that day.

CHAPTER 20

Age with Grace

Astrid and Señora Ruby were enjoying the last of the sun's rays on Christmas Eve. Amazingly, Señora Ruby, in the autumn of her life, appeared as golden as the afternoon light itself. Less than two months ago, Astrid was certain Señora Ruby had reached the last hours of her winter years. And with no season beyond that, the natural progression was that she would wither away and die. But miraculously, Señora Ruby had turned the seasons inside out and was moving backwards through them. As they unwound, she gracefully regressed towards her youth. Astrid marvelled at the thickness and shine that had returned to Señora Ruby's black hair.

"Don't believe those balsam shampoo advertisements and their proven formulas. They have nothing to do with it." Señora Ruby smiled the Mona Lisa smile she had recently adopted. She ran her fingers through her hair like a young maiden combing her tresses before falling asleep for the next 100 years. Lately her eyes sparkled and the corners of her lips curled up. The creases on her forehead had become less pronounced. In fact, some of them had actually disappeared. The fine wrinkles around her eyes and upper lip were delicate now and her rosy complexion was natural, no more rouge. Smoggy soot no longer took refuge in the furrows of her once absent expression. Señora Ruby had been transformed, or to be more exact, was in the constant process of transformation. She was like a young woman in love. Each day, Astrid noticed a little more spring in Señora Ruby's step and a little more light in her eyes.

Having completed the day's work, they leaned back – Señora Ruby in the wooden chair over which heavy canvas had been stretched, and

Astrid in the plastic one with the cracks on the bottom that pinched when she shifted to the right.

"Por Diós, Señora Ruby, you've shaved your legs! What's come over you?"

Señora Ruby shrugged, head still leaning back, eyes closed, basking in the sun like a goddess rather than like the old lizard she used to be. She smiled a wicked little smile, and tapped her fingers on the wooden arms of the chair.

"And look at your fingernails. Querida Madre de Diós! You've painted them. Why, Señora Ruby, you've had a manicure. You've become positively elegant." Self conscious, Astrid curled her own stained, bitten fingernails towards her palms and, using her two fists she tugged at her skirt, trying to pull it down to her ankles to cover up the unshaven calves. She looked at her leather loafers. Outwardly, she was not much of a catch. But she was secretly pleased in the knowledge that her toenails had been carefully painted, her feet softened with cream and protected by her thick socks. It reminded her of what she'd do for Jhonny. She blushed and busied herself by ironing the creases on her skirt with her fists.

"Let me tell you something, mi niña," Señora Ruby adjusted her posture to sit tall in her chair, her hands grasping the ends of the wooden arms. She looked straight across at Astrid, who was still hunched and busying herself with her skirt. Why did she suddenly feel nervous in front of Señora Ruby? Perhaps she was intimidated by old beauty, or maybe it was a fear that this re-tooled matriarch could see past her brown shoes and into the red heat of her secret passion.

Señora Ruby's eyes were piercing and Astrid felt her cheeks heating up. She shrank lower into her chair, but was forced by Señora Ruby's intensity to raise her face and meet her eyes.

"Mira, Astrid... I am an old woman and I've been through more than you can imagine. I haven't told you half of it. Not because I keep things from you, but because there were so many things to recall and I don't think of them at the right moment, or we're busy, or we're not together when they do occur to me." She rolled back into the chair and the canvas accepted her weight soundlessly. Astrid remained bent over her own thighs, head up, eyes on Señora Ruby's face.

"I am not going to ramble on about my life experiences now. I just want you to know that I have been around long enough to see that you have fallen in love. I don't know why you keep it such a secret, but I don't want to intrude. I respect your privacy and I'm very happy that you are once again enjoying a relationship after all of these years. That's all, my dear. We don't have to talk about it. I'm not like other friends who would be demanding details. I just wanted to tell you that as your old friend, I'm very happy for you and I wish you all the best."

The golden light extended outwards from Señora Ruby's body and it become so extraordinarily brilliant that Astrid thought it might lift her like a hallowed figure into the heavens. That Astrid might be in the presence of a saint at the moment of her ascension filled her with awe. She loved Señora Ruby as she loved her own mother, bless her dear, departed soul. She wanted to share the secret of Jhonny Pretty and more than once she had almost given in and blurted out some of the crazy events of her unusual arrangement or her aspirations for Jhonny Pretty. But in the back of her mind, she knew that people – Señora Ruby included – would tell her to stop the silliness, demand that she scrap the altar in her bedroom and stop dropping by the mausoleum to leave gifts. They would tell her that her energy was much better spent on a living man, a mortal soul with whom she could properly share her bed and who would help her with daily challenges. They would say that being in love with a ghost was like loving a fantasy. They would tell her it was not real, and accuse her of stubbornly clinging to absurdities that would, in the end, destroy her. Astrid searched for a way to excuse herself from this conversation without excluding Señora Ruby from her personal affairs and without giving up the true nature of her love affair with Jhonny Pretty. More than anyone, Señora Ruby deserved to be entrusted with intimate details of her life.

Astrid floundered for the right words. Finally, she came up with, "Señora Ruby, you are without question, my most dear and trusted friend. I'm ashamed to exclude you from my affairs, and you guessed correctly... I am in love, and he is just the perfect man. But the situation isn't quite right yet. I mean I can't introduce you to him yet. Don't worry. It's not what you might imagine – that he's a married man, or otherwise tied to someone else. No, it's not that at all. But let me think. Just let me think... I feel that it might be possible to introduce you to him in the New Year."

Señora Ruby was intent and remained silent so as not to interrupt Astrid's confession. She waited for more.

Astrid wasn't sure why she made such a promise. Perhaps it would be a good idea to 'out' Jhonny Pretty, but she knew deep down that it probably wasn't. She regretted that she was lying to Señora Ruby, but she couldn't bring herself to stop. She would find a way around this later. The lie would buy her some time. She forced a bright smile and prayed with a brief glance to heaven, for the right words, something to divert the flow of this conversation without more fabrication. She would find something truthful, but safe.

She was struck with the bright idea to start at the beginning and also end there. "Señora Ruby, do you remember the day in October when it rained without warning? Do you remember we sat and watched it for hours, and still it didn't stop?"

Señora Ruby nodded. "Yes, a most unusual day."

"It was." Astrid agreed, nodding herself silly, relieved to have found some common ground, a launching pad that offered some truth from which this lie would spring. She swallowed hard. "Well, after you went home that day, I met a man in the cemetery. He was rushing to get out of the rain too." Here she stretched the truth, "We bumped into each other, and he apologised and we had to run for cover. We ran to the steps of the great pyramid mausoleum. You know the one. Yes, and we stayed and talked well into the night, until long after it stopped raining. And we agreed to meet again. Things just continued from there. He's from a good family. More than that I can't tell you yet. Well, except to say that he is a very famous man and he is extremely jealous of his privacy. But let me talk to him about it. Although it has proven really awkward to arrange, we have plans for the holidays, so I'll see how it goes."

"Please, Astrid, my dear, don't compromise your relationship on my account. I'm not that curious and you don't need my approval anyway. I just wanted to tell you that I know you're happier than you have been in years and that it makes me very happy. Your mother, may she rest in peace, must be as pleased as I am."

Astrid looked up to the sky and prayed, "Mamá, please forgive me these white lies." Aloud, she said, "Yes, of course. I know. And I appreciate that you're happy for me. You're a good friend, Señora Ruby."

Not to get bogged down in something awkward, Señora Ruby abruptly changed the subject. "Tonight is Christmas Eve, Astrid. Have you arranged a chocolate party with your children?"

"Yes. But I plan to come back here later this evening because some of the patrons will visit and, as you know, they'll be in generous moods. I thought I might be able to collect some extra tips for both of us. Constancia and Hector have agreed to an early chocolate spread tonight. In fact, it was Constancia's idea... it works out better with their plans too, so we'll all be full of hot chocolate and cakes before the sun sets. We agreed to exchange our gifts early too, so after a few hours I can come back here and they'll go and meet their friends. I bought some mussels and managed some artichoke, not very traditional, but it'll be nice for tomorrow's dinner. We'll probably have some of my rice pudding. What about you, Señora Ruby? What are your plans?"

"Bueno. It's a funny thing... remember the brother of Señor Rodriguez-Rodriguez?"

Astrid nodded and shivered, remembering the sound of his brother's cell phone the day of the quake and how she spent the 3,000 pesos he had pushed into her hand.

"Well, he and his father were looking for the crematorium a few days after the quake and, well, I didn't know at the time that they were meant to be your patrons, but anyway, they were looking for directions. Remember how everything was blocked off at first? I wasn't much help because I wasn't sure what was going on then, everything being so disorganised. But the point is that the old man was even more distraught than the brother. Plus he couldn't walk. He was in a wheelchair. So I went with them to find the crematorium and I was doing my best, you know, to comfort them. A few weeks ago, they found me again, in that path over there," she pointed and her fingernails shone in the sunlight, reminding Astrid of what a young spirit her old friend really was. "I was playing with this," she lifted the silver chain that was around her neck and pointed at the lapiz lázuli. "I mean, the stone not the necklace. It wasn't a necklace then."

Astrid interrupted her, "You should be careful with that here, Señora Ruby. You don't want to lose it again."

"Why do you think I put it onto such a long chain? It's well protected here." She patted her bosom. "Anyway, at the time I was holding the stone in my hand. I know you warned me not to carry it around in my pocket and take it out to play with it. But I did anyway. The old man and the son came upon me by surprise and I dropped the stone right there on the ground and the old man nearly rolled over it with his chair. I had to put my foot over it, and then he ran over my toes. The long and short of it is that he was sorry for running over my foot and he told me that he was a retired jeweller. So he offered to set it into this pendant for me. And now, well, now it's really quite a curious thing..." Señora Ruby flushed from her neck to her forehead. "Now, he has invited me to join him for dinner on Christmas Eve. I would imagine that if all goes well, we'll arrange to spend New Year's together too. I could be jumping the gun, but I have a feeling..."

Astrid surveyed Señora Ruby, seeing her for the first time as a woman with romantic possibilities. Never, in all the years she had known Señora Ruby, had she ever thought of her with a man. She had always been a soul satisfied within her own solitude. This new side of her was where the shaved legs and manicured nails belonged. Surprisingly Astrid didn't find Señora Ruby's distinct sides at odds. Señora Ruby also, it seemed, had a rare skill for making odd things fit together. Astrid glanced down at Señora Ruby's heavy shoes and guessed that her toes were probably as bright as her own. The sly old girl. "Well, aren't we two peas in a pod?"

Señora Ruby lifted herself slowly out of her chair, a process that Astrid noticed had also become somehow more graceful over the past weeks.

"You have become a spring flower, Señora Ruby."

"And you don't know the half of it." she said as she walked away.

CHAPTER 21

Happiness After All

It was Christmas afternoon and Astrid presented each bowl of Spanish-style rice pudding with the flourish of a young French pastry chef. She sprinkled the surface with ground cinnamon, scattering scant raisins over the top and slotting an orange ring into the side. Then she inserted a cinnamon stick at an angle and gently pushed a single red cinnamon heart onto the surface of the pudding. The final touch was the placement of a miniature daisy on a very short stem. She centred the bowls on white china plates, adding small stainless steel spoons on the side of each one.

"Mamá, you have outdone yourself once again." Hector's spoon was in the bowl before she had a chance to remove her hand. He was speaking with his mouth full, omitting the part where he should offer a compliment. He even inhaled the daisy.

Constancia daintily introduced her spoon and sucked a portion from its tip before closing her eyes. "Exquisito, Mamá. I wasn't expecting more after last night's chocolate and dessert." Suffering from a hangover, she kept her head down.

"Gracias, mis niños. Well, I had a good night and had energy to do a little extra today. I knew you would enjoy it." Her voice was full of youthful vitality and she bounced back to the kitchen to serve herself.

Last night was Christmas Eve and, in the most unexpected way, it had been a huge success at the cemetery. Astrid was so satisfied and encouraged that she rose early this morning, pecked Jhonny's paper cheek, ignored her sore back, dropped the needle onto the vinyl copy of Jhonny's "Not One More Day Without You," and danced about in front of him before wrapping herself into her dressing gown. As had become her habit, she kissed the tips of her fingers and touched them softly to his paper lips before backing her way to the door, one slow step at a time, never turning away from him, blowing kisses all the while, then finally locking him in the bedroom, dropping the key into her pocket and going about her day.

This morning Astrid was inspired to the point of violent creativity. With tropical music blaring from the radio, pans clanging and cupboard doors slamming, she swung a wooden spoon above her head and pranced about the kitchen, a maniac in a fit of baking hysteria. She added a touch of this, a daub of that, an ounce or two of rum here, and an extra one or two there, swallowing several swigs in between. A toss of sugar, and why not some rum with milk? When she finally wound to a halt, she found herself with 20 bowls of rice pudding, all lined up along the counter, fully bedecked and ready to serve. She stood back in her intoxicated glee and beamed at the creations. It was undoubtedly the most eccentric thing she could remember doing. But it was beautiful. Too bad Jhonny couldn't be here to see it; he'd be in awe.

The idea of Jhonny enjoying her pudding incited yet more lunacy. She ran off into the bedroom and draped herself in several layers of skirts so that she could dance with more flounce. She decided on a chiffon blouse with ruffles running vertically down the front and at the bottom edges of the three-quarter length sleeves. She attached extra baubles to her long feather earrings, poked three paper roses into the bun on top of her head and slid a couple of San Expedito rings onto her fingers. Then she made up her face, which included lining her top and bottom eyelids with heavy black eyeliner and shimmering blue eye shadow that somehow got smudged well beyond the corners of her eyes.

She was entirely satisfied, but had Hector and Constancia been in the condition to pay even the least attention to detail, they would have been horrified with what was going on with their mother. Had they known that she had spent several hours at the Maluenda-Valdéz mausoleum last night after midnight, smoking, talking and gesturing to an empty space, they would have restrained her in Hector's sweater, tied her up with the long sleeves and belt, straight-jacket-style and dragged her to the public hospital, or at the very least, insisted she remain under house arrest and under their constant supervision.

As Astrid had predicted to Señora Ruby, several patrons had shown up last night to pay respects to their relatives. Most of them were in jovial holiday moods and settled down on benches in front of the relatives' niches to socialise, updating them on the news and events since they had last visited. Healthy sips of wine encouraged them to amplify their satisfaction with Astrid's work. "My dear woman, you have been an excellent caretaker. Look at the impeccable state of my father's (may God bless his soul) window. The arrangements are beautiful. A toast to you my dear." And they tipped Astrid generously for her hard work and dedication. She mingled with families, making small talk, during which she detailed things like the groans and greetings that had been emitted from behind these concrete walls. The living liked to be made aware of what their dead were up to, and they were particularly interested to know if they had communicated in any manner via Astrid. Every so often Astrid saw fit to create memorable events, such as a repeated cough from a coffin or some unusual banging on wood from inside the wall. Sometimes she even recalled some writing scratched in the ground, most likely a coded message from the dead. She intuited the dates for these events as best she could, hoping to make them coincide with a birthday or something the living had actually experienced at home. She did so in the best interest of her client-patron, when it was obvious they were hungry for some news of their deceased, when they yearned for some sign of their wellbeing. The most common result of her stories were even more bountiful tips, and although she preferred not to focus on that, it did influence how much she embellished the story.

Last night, Christmas Eve was full of the usual merriment and communication from beyond the grave, but for Astrid the night held an extra component as she anticipated her private visit with Jhonny after the satisfied visitors had all gone home.

Approaching his mausoleum, she went cold with apprehension on the off chance that he wouldn't be here, that perhaps he would be out giving one of his guided tours of life beyond. She shivered and pulled her new purple sweater tighter around her chest and shoved her hand into her pocket to finger and pray on all seven San Expedito pendants that she now habitually carried. "Please San Expedito, let him be here tonight, of all nights. I long to hear his voice." She didn't forget her part of the bargain. "I promise to go and visit your chapel during the next annual pilgrimage and I'll bring gifts. Gracias, San Expedito." A canvas bag was slung across her shoulder and she patted the shape that protruded through it.

The sidewalk narrowed and snaked around the corner leading to Jhonny's place. Out of childish superstition she was careful not to step on any cracks. She reached the steps of the chapel-style mausoleum, breathless from excitement, her face flushed, and inhaled deeply before she peered into the dark interior. There was no sign of him. Disappointed, she lowered the bag and sank onto the top step, hands folded limply on her lap, shoulders hunched, squinting up into the deep shadows above the altar. She whispered. "San Expedito, let him know I've arrived. Tell him to come out now." She leaned in, craning her neck and summoned all of her energy to focus on her simple request. "Make him come out. Make him be here. Make him come out and talk to me. Let him be home. Let him feel my presence."

Nothing.

She prepared to wait, picked herself up enough to slide down one step and she leaned an elbow on the landing. A cigarette would be nice. She pulled the leather case out of her skirt pocket and extracted one of two Derby filters. She lit it, inhaled, relaxed and eventually leaned over to pat the contents of the canvas bag.

"I brought something for you, Jhonny." She waited for a sign. Nothing. She would be patient because the gift was not something she could just drop into the box and walk away from. No, she sought spontaneous approval on this. More than that, she was hoping for enthusiasm and response that would feel something like a real touch on her skin, a breath on her cheek perhaps, or a feathery caress beginning at her fingers, running along the back of her hand and extending up her arm before finally terminating with a light fondling of her earlobe. She shivered at the imagined pleasure of it and dragged on her smoke. Maybe by the time she finished it, he will have returned. She looked down her nose at the burning Derby cigarette, willing the tobacco-filled paper roll grow longer, giving Jhonny the time he needed to come back to her. She prolonged it, head lowered, hoping against hope that when she looked up, it would be into his striking blue eyes. She let the cigarette burn to her fingers and finally had no choice but to put it out. She ground and rolled the butt into the marble, watching as she mashed it into fragments of foamy filter scattered amongst flakes of tobacco. When she finally dared raise her eyes, she felt the wet sting of disappointment. Jhonny was not there. Grey sadness weighed her down and she sank into the frigid marble stairway.

She tried to remain hopeful, fingers fondling her canvas bag. Perhaps he was behind her, watching and waiting, curious to see what she carried. Or maybe he was in another patio, he could sense her presence and was rushing the newly deceased along, trying to finish his guide duties so he could leave the newly dead to their own devices and join her at his steps. "And you've seen this already," he would be saying to the freshman souls, perhaps gesturing towards the chapel near the main entrance, "But we will re-visit it tomorrow or the day after. Don't worry you have lots of time. Nothing but time. For me, it's different, though. I have an urgent engagement. So before I bid you good night and Merry Christmas, I will just suggest that you avoid the crematorium, mainly because it's a harsh, immediate and burning reality in more ways than one. We recommend not venturing over there, especially if you have recent memories of the place and, in general, just avoid it if you want peace of mind as you settle in."

She played with the edges of her bag, vacillating between opening it and going home. But she really didn't want to leave. She wanted to wait for Jhonny. She procrastinated. Then finally, reaching into the bag, she took her time to extract a heavy rectangular package and rested it on her lap. The package was wrapped in red paper imprinted with green holly leaves. A wide golden ribbon ran up one side and criss-crossed at the back, coming together again on the front under a generous red velvet bow. A fresh twig of mistletoe had been carefully tied to its centre, its sad stem drooping with the weight of the berries. Astrid sucked in a long breath as she gazed at the gift. She had to admit that the wrapping was impressive. It had taken a full hour to do it, unwrapping and re-wrapping until it was perfect. She never ever thought she'd actually use this paper. It was her mother's and, in fact, her mother had saved it from an anniversary gift from her father. "So fitting," Astrid thought, "That I'm using it for Jhonny, the light of my life."

The package contained a scrapbook, designed and compiled by Astrid herself during rapturous moments alone in her bedroom. Mostly it contained old photos of Jhonny from El Ritmo magazines, with the piece de resistance being a 5x7 glossy that she had convinced Susana to relinquish in exchange for her Spanish rice pudding recipe. Susana had approached her only two weeks ago, animated and beside her plump self with excitement, "Listen Astrid, you know your rice pudding… well, I know it's your secret recipe, but I could really use it." She anxiously redistributed her weight across her wide bottom. "Siete Pelos is at the point of asking me to marry him, but I can see him stalling." Her bright eyes drilled into Astrid. "I guess he's just been a bachelor for so long that he's scared. But I know what's good for him, and I know that if I give him something for his stomach, it'll push him over the edge. I thought of your rice pudding. And, well, what do you think? Can you help me out?"

Astrid pondered the request. She did enjoy the reputation she had created with her rice pudding, and it was rather exclusive. Therefore, she couldn't let it go just like that. It was worth something. She ventured, "Susana, you know I would love to share it with you, but it's a big favour you're asking. I mean everyone knows that once you know it, then the whole world will know."

Not offended, Susana replied, "Yes, I admit that, but this is really important, Astrid. I mean it's the best idea I've had in a long time. You don't know how I've wracked my brain for something that'll do the trick. Well... for ages! Then I thought of your pudding and I just knew it was right. It's exactly what I need. What can I give you in exchange? I mean I'll give you whatever I can. Anything. Really!"

Astrid rolled the request around in her head for a minute to see if it hit upon anything useful. Like an arrow, the request went whizzing through her brain and hit a target with Jhonny's face on it. She formulated a white lie. "Well, yeah, maybe there is something we can do. I've been thinking lately about one of my patrons. She's a huge Jhonny Pretty fan. And I know that you have a whole collection of stuff hidden away. Remember, you said you had loads more but couldn't be bothered to look for it? Anyway, I think if I could give this patron some pieces from your collection, then she'd be really grateful. I mean, you know how it is this time of year... one gift breeds another. If I can find something for her, then she'll be generous with me for the whole of next year, to say nothing of the tip she'll give me on the spot."

Susana leapt at the idea. "Come over to my place, Astrid. It's true, I have a bunch of stuff in a box. I can't even remember what's there. I mean, who cares about Jhonny Pretty anymore?"

Susana's cardboard box turned out to be a treasure chest. Astrid found duplicate copies of several El Ritmo magazines with images of Jhonny in his better days. Her heart still skipped a beat when she looked into the eyes that looked back out at her from the pages. She was like a teenage groupie, unable to control the impulse to kiss his face at every opportunity. The glossy photo was found inserted in a September 1979 edition. "Oh," Susana waved dismissively. "Oh, that. Yes, I totally forgot about it. One of my friends went to a concert. Actually saw the band live. Can you imagine? My parents never let me out of the house. She gave me this photo because when they tossed out photos at the end of the show, she was lucky and caught two of them."

Susana continued to buzz around, chattering incessantly as she pulled out one thing after another. In the end, Astrid wound up taking the entire cardboard box in exchange not only her recipe but for several servings of the pudding that Susana would serve to Siete Pelos that very afternoon. "The big day," she said, so sure of her plan.

Astrid had been so sure of hers too. But now look... here she was, alone with the gift late on Christmas Eve, with no one to give it to.

Then she became aware of a familiar jasmine scent. It edged in on her and she felt comforted to know she wasn't alone. She heard the rustle of bushes from behind the Maluenda-Valdéz mausoleum. Then a strange whisper, nothing like the sound of Jhonny's voice. "I'm here for you mi querida, my dearest."

Astrid jumped.

The voice whispered again, "Don't come near. Stay where you are."

"Is that you, Jhonny?" Astrid asked, allowing herself to fill with hope, even though instinctively, she knew it was false. As if in response, the darkness around the Maluenda-Valdéz mausoleum steadily began to fill with a strange light until it was totally illuminated with a clear yellow aura. She blinked up into the heavens and saw a low-hanging star beaming directly from deep in the darkness to land inside the iron entrance and splay across the little clay crèche she had created. Like a beam from the roof of a disco, it was inviting the whole city to pay attention.

Astrid brought her hands to her face, folded as in prayer, covering her nose, and closing her eyes in disbelief. She was in awe of the power of Jhonny's spirit, suddenly so mature and controlled. "That you can hurl this beam through the heavens with such precision is truly amazing, Jhonny. I... I'm, well, I'm speechless." Then motioning to the crèche, "Your light has glorified this place just like God shone his face on Jesus' manger."

"It's just a little trick I learned." whispered the voice.

The voice was not right. "Jhonny, is this really you? Why won't you show your face? Is something wrong?"

"No, my dear. All is as it should be."

"But something isn't right here. Please don't play tricks. I've already been through enough disappointment for one night."

The voice sighed. But it wasn't a Jhonny sigh. For the first time in her life, Astrid was afraid of the graveyard. She insisted, "Who are you?" Maybe ghosts suffer from head colds too and Jhonny just lost his voice. Hoping against hope, "Is that really you Jhonny?"

"No," the voice sighed as if in defeat. "I am his mother."

"What?"

"I am his mother, my dear." The voice repeated in its odd whisper.

"And do you know about me?" Astrid was suddenly feeling self conscious and very foolish. What exactly did Jhonny's mother know about her? Did she listen to their conversations? Did Jhonny confide in her? She didn't know if it was good or bad.

"Yes, of course. You are important to my son. I know about everything that is of importance to him."

Astrid shifted and brightened. "Oh."

There was an extended silence. The mother said, "What are you doing here, my dear?"

"Well, it's Christmas Eve and I wanted to give Jhonny his gift. I waited, but he must be out guiding some of the newly dead around the cemetery."

The voice groaned.

"What's wrong? Did something happen to Jhonny? Do you know if he encountered a nasty spirit? Everyone knows there are some terrible ones around. In death as in life. I hope he knows who he can trust and who to stay away from."

"Oh, he knows all right."

"Well, I'm relieved to hear it."

Jhonny's mother –a shadow without matter – remained hidden in the behind the bushes. Astrid imagined her peering around the corner, trying to stay out of sight, perhaps shy, perhaps not wanting to frighten Astrid, as though Astrid was not already accustomed to dealing with spirits.

"Do you know if he will be back any time soon? I mean is he coming back tonight?"

"You know, my dear, from the way things look, I think he will be gone until well into the night, and might not even return until the morning."

Astrid tried to digest the bad news gracefully. Since this was Jhonny's mother, it was important to present a well-educated face, something she could not complain about in the future. Mothers-in-law could be notoriously difficult. She cleared her throat and attempted to sound caring but not overly possessive. "Oh, I'm really disappointed that Jhonny's not with us, but now that you're here in his place, maybe you can pass a message and this gift to him for me." Astrid was sorry she blurted it out the moment she said it. She preferred to linger in hope. Just knowing that Jhonny would return in the future was a comfort. She could wait. But at the same time, she didn't want to stand here making conversation with his mother, who she felt distanced from. Was the mother judging her? Obviously Jhonny Pretty's family was a wealthy one, and most likely a snobby wealthy one. Would his mother force Jhonny to end their relationship out of predictable class resentment?

But the mother was already answering, "Yes, of course, my dear. But I also have a message for you."

"Thank you, Señora. First let me say that I just wanted to tell Jhonny that I made this gift for him out of love. Every second I spent putting it together were with thoughts of your son, your kind, loving son, Señora, who has been so good to me since I met him a couple of months ago." She looked tenderly down at the package. "And I wrapped it in special paper, paper that was once used for a gift that my father gave to my mother. I never thought I'd use it." Tears filled her eyes and she surprised herself by admitting even more. "Señora, I have not had a man in my life for many,

many years because I was afraid of how much it would hurt. I have longed for someone, someone like myself, another gentle romantic, someone who understands what it is to truly care and knows just the right words, who can make my heart sing. And you know, Jhonny does that Señora. When he opens his mouth to speak to me, or sing to me, I am filled with a joy that defies description. I am so grateful for his companionship and dedication. I cannot express how important it is."

"Yes, my dear, I understand and I was going to say..."

Astrid continued, paying no attention to what the other woman had to say, "I am devoted to him, too and this gift is just one of many that prove it. Sadly, I can't give myself to him as I dream of doing, and only because we exist on opposite sides of the veil. But when I die, my hope is to be with him and our relationship will be complete. At present, this hope is what brightens my days and it will continue to do so until I die. Your son, no matter if he exists in death or in life, is my happiness."

Astrid could hear the woman's spirit rustling behind the mausoleum. She was fussing and fidgeting with something, the sound of her feet hitting the ground repeatedly. Perhaps she was preparing to show herself. Jhonny's mother muttered something under her breath and then she spoke in a whisper, "Astrid, my dear, you have brought a world of light back into Jhonny's life too. My son lives to see you here at his front steps. He loves your visits and talks of you often. He has shown me the many gifts you've so generously given and he takes pleasure in them. Leave this one here with me now, and I will deliver it into his hands."

"May I see you, Señora?"

"No, my dear. My features are no longer youthful and I'm self-conscious about appearing to anyone... living or dead for that matter. But don't take this as an affront. I'm enchanted to know you. I understand why my Jhonny is smitten with you. I promise I'm a good mother-in-law and will not interfere in your relationship. I will pass him your message. Go in peace, my little heart. Don't look back and I will see that no harm comes to you as you leave this place at such a late hour."

Astrid placed the gift just inside the entrance grate and backed away slowly. The light that was shining around the mausoleum short-circuited and went out. Then she turned and walked away, obediently fighting off the temptation to look back.

But she felt the older woman's presence as she approached the gate. Once or twice as the breeze drifted past, she smelled the familiar jasmine fragrance and the third time she smelled it, she stopped suddenly in her tracks. She recognised the scent. It belonged to the old woman from Santa María Street. Disregarding the old woman's request, Astrid turned on her heels but the old spirit was fast. Astrid succeeded only in catching a glimpse of a foot as the ghost disappeared behind thick bougainvillea. But that was enough. In the moonlight, she saw the hem of the familiar cotton skirt and the oversized bright pink Adidas shoe, and, in addition, as the old woman hastened away, her sweater caught on a vine and when she paused to unhook it Astrid positively identified the bright red nail polish. She had identified the woman of Santa María Street. She was elated. The question of the woman's identity was answered. It was Jhonny's mother.

CHAPTER 22

Discombobulating

On Christmas Eve, Astrid floated home from the cemetery in a mauve jasmine mist. With the revelation that Jhonny's mother and the old woman of Santa María Street were one and the same, things suddenly made sense. She deduced that even as far back as the earthquake, the old woman had wanted to save her for her son because she knew that Astrid was Jhonny's chosen one. Astrid was beside herself with joy. There could be no doubt of her and Jhonny's shared destiny.

She dared to speculate further. Perhaps it was the old woman who had produced the freak rainstorm that day, chasing everyone out of the cemetery so that Jhonny could present himself to her alone. She remembered how he seemed to sparkle through the sheets of rain. It was the most magical day of her life. If the old lady was capable of making a star shine directly on Jhonny's resting place as she had done tonight, surely the rainstorm had been well within her power.

She concluded that if in fact, Jhonny's mother had planned their chance meeting then she, Astrid, occupied an unusually honourable position. It was very rare indeed that a mother would want to share her son, let alone arrange for such an unconventional love affair. Therefore, Astrid understood the importance and accompanying responsibility Jhonny's mother had bestowed upon her. Now she was not only taking care of him for herself, but was also entrusted as Jhonny's caretaker by none other than his own mother. Astrid unreservedly accepted the task.

The affirmation of her role in Jhonny's life made her drunk when she awoke on Christmas morning. It was the source of her rare, youthful energy. It was the fountain of her rice pudding creativity, and it was what filled her little kitchen with such delight.

Unfortunately Luisa Rocio did not share this positive feeling. She, the old woman of Santa María Street, aka Jhonny Pretty's mother, was weighed down by a growing feeling of doom. She had been in her ugly niche across from the Maluenda-Valdéz mausoleum on Christmas Eve, spying from behind the old virgin statue, ready to light into Juan Bonifacio for his cold-hearted treatment of the caretaker when she saw Astrid approaching, carrying her neatly wrapped gift. She observed with a sour expression as Astrid extracted it and waited for Juan on his front steps.

Looking on, she felt her own heart beat sadly in her cold chest. The lovesick caretaker was sitting, shoulders slumped forward, head down, inhaling the miserable smoke from her cigarette, disappointment emanating from her every pore as she waited in vain for her loved one to appear.

Luisa Rocio wanted to ruin the scoundrel who was Juan Bonifacio, aka Jhonny Pretty. She wanted to expose him for what he was. She wanted to rescue this poor, misguided caretaker from her heartache. It would be difficult to break the news, but Luisa Rocio had experience in meddling and was confident she could reveal the truth as painlessly as possible. So, keeping her eyes trained on Astrid she flowed like slimy liquid from between the concrete cracks of the niche, careful not to disturb the virgin on the ledge and, like a shadow, she glided down the front of the wall. She slid over the path to take her position behind the Maluenda-Valdéz mausoleum. There she assumed her customary ghostly form and discreetly introduced her presence by rustling some leaves. It was going to be straightforward. She intended to intervene and put a stop to this abusive relationship once and for all. She would make Astrid see Jhonny for what he was – not a gentle ghost but a living, drinking, cheating liar who was nothing but a waste of skin and bone. She would help dull Astrid's pain by offering her a hand, reminding her of the warning about the earthquake, how this was proof that she had Astrid's best interests at heart. She would coddle and comfort her.

But she blew it. And now she was kicking herself with her extra-large pink Adidas. Whatever possessed her to pretend to be Jhonny's mother? It happened spontaneously, totally out of her control. It was innocent. The words escaped her. If she wasn't so clever, it could have been a fatal error, but she quickly realised how, in the future, she would turn it to her advantage. This role would actually give her more credibility. Since a mother being honest about her son's unacceptable behaviour was something quite rare, Astrid would sit up and pay attention to anything she said. It was a brilliant idea. If only she hadn't lied out of pity. It was her instinctively kind nature that had prevented her from revealing Jhonny for the scoundrel he really was. But after the first lie was out of her mouth, it was impossible to retract it. So she prevaricated again and again, validating all the feelings that Astrid attributed to Juan Bonifacio, the man Luisa Rocio had come to hate more than her own dead husband. She had stupidly, and against every fibre of her being, carried on to make the slimiest woman's-man in the history of Santiago look like a faithful lover and hero of all women. What a crock. But it was too late. Now poor Astrid fervently believed that Jhonny truly loved her. And worse, because the words had supposedly come from the mouth of his mother, it would never be challenged.

Luisa Rocio would have to rectify this problem. She thought about how things had progressed from the outset, since the day of the quake. She rationalised that maybe it wasn't all that bad. She was pleased to see improvement in her fine art of 'ghosting' – mastering how and when to appear and disappear at will. With this skill she dared to wander beyond the perimeter of the cemetery more often. The day of the earthquake was the first day she had successfully controlled her appearance and tactility. Since then she had slowly, and with growing confidence, made use of her 'magic' to play meaningless games. Granted she wasn't always successful and often made mistakes, such as on the day she wanted to beat the daylights out of Juan Bonifacio on the path. But she was getting better and her powers were more predictable. She had had to gather all of her courage to follow him to Slaughterhouse Square (the unholiest of unholy places) a few weeks ago, but now she laughed to herself when she recalled how the very sight of her had caused him to bolt from Mario's restaurant like a fugitive. She was successful on that occasion.

Encouraged, she dreamed of one day travelling further and further afield, both for her own pleasure and in her role as Astrid's guardian angel. Having donned the mantle of this heavenly office, albeit self-assigned, she determined to follow and protect Astrid where and when necessary. Given her newly found confidence, an open mind and a bit of transcendental ingenuity, she was certain she would be able to correct Astrid's situation. Luisa Rocio's own aspirations included a trip up to the long, white beaches of Iquique in northern Chile. Although her deceased husband had promised to take her there, they had never gone. She wondered how she might entice Astrid to join her for a holiday, thereby satisfying her own dream while fulfilling her stewardship. If she could find a way to sort this mess out, the holiday would not only be long overdue, it would be well deserved.

CHAPTER 23

The Date

Jesica finally managed to bring the four of them together on Christmas Eve – her new boyfriend Hector, who ran a successful tourism business in the heart of Santiago, his sister Constancia who, God willing, would one day open her own little fashion boutique in El Patronato, and her dear old friend, Juan Bonifacio, aka Jhonny Pretty, who really needed to settle down with someone just like Constancia.

The timing worked out perfectly. Hector and Constancia were sharing the traditional hot chocolate and treats at home earlier in the evening and they agreed to meet at Slaughterhouse Square just before Juan's last set. As Jesica predicted, it was a quiet evening, even the most loyal of patrons deciding to try to find family with whom to spend the night. Unable to contain her excitement, Jesica packed up early and as they drove down to Plaza Ñuñoa for a few drinks and some pizza, she and Hector provided animated conversation, entertaining Juan and Constancia, who both sat demurely in the back seat.

"This is the night chickies, it's time to party!" Jesica bounced behind the wheel of the old Amazon as she turned sharply onto Avenue Pedro de Valdivia and sent them all flying to their right.

"Are you up for it, Con?" Hector held onto the dashboard as he turned around. "Why so quiet? It's Christmas Eve. We'll all get presents tonight." He winked at Juan. "But you behave yourself, Con. Your big brother is watching."

"Right, Hector. I know you have better things to do than keep your eyes on me all night."

"You should have seen the plaza today." Hector changed the subject. "Just swimming with tourists, fanning themselves because of the heat and to ward off the smell from the old farts dressed up like Santa. I tell you those Santas smell worse every year. I don't know which is more rank, their body odour under the stale old suits that get washed once a year, or the shit from their burros dressed up with antlers."

"I was down there the other day," Jesica chimed in. "Half of them were still drunk from the night before. I think they lose customers because of bad breath, to say nothing of B O, especially if you let them get close to you."

"Yeah, but maybe it's worth it for the tourists just to be able to go home laughing with a photo of our Chilean-style Santa, his sweaty armpits resting on their shoulders. Most of them are holding their breath. I imagine they brag about how they survived the contaminated Christmas air of Central Santiago – and it has nothing to do with the smog."

"I guess the greeting card sellers outside the post office are still selling pirated cards from Hallmark?"

"Yeah, I think so. But the sellers of the religious cards and statues are doing much better, and not just among the tourists. Maybe I should change my focus." Hector chuckled. It was a fake chuckle and Juan suspected it was his professional laugh, something like a hard smile with a practiced throaty sound that could start or stop on a dime.

The rest of the drive was filled with meaningless banter between Jesica and Hector, which gave Juan the opportunity to sit back and observe. He nodded politely and muttered single syllable responses but remained aloof. Normally he would have already had his arm around the girl's shoulders, hand dangling dangerously close to one breast, and he would be charming her with his crooked smile and a toss of his hair. But something about Constancia haunted him. Apprehensive, he tried in vain to identify it. For one thing, he knew her voice, but he couldn't for the life of him remember why or from when. They hadn't spoken before tonight; and before that he had only seen her from a distance in the crowd at Slaughterhouse Square, and even then he had flown the coop like a bat out of hell because she looked like a vampire's widow. He was relieved that she and Jesica had grown out of the Gothic period. Their fat purple lips and heavy dark eyes were worse than anything he could have imagined crawling out of a niche in the cemetery wall. By contrast, their new style was refreshing. Although neither of them would achieve the Barbie Doll look they sought, they were not unattractive in their bright flowered mini-skirts and clunky fabric-printed high-heeled shoes. Tonight they both wore the same vibrant pink lipstick. He suspected they had coordinated their outfits at Jesica's house, giggling like a couple of schoolgirls.

Constancia's thick black hair was attractive on its own; the way she wore it tonight, for example, with a single fabric rose at the nape of her neck, where the tress was tied back into a long ponytail. Two small ceramic rose earrings matched her lipstick. Her big, dark eyes were glittering with expectation. He had seen that look before and normally he took advantage of it. But tonight he was disturbed by the mystery of her familiarity and his automatic defence system put him on alert, making him less eager to dive right in. On top of that, he had identified her brother Hector as the slippery man he had seen at Mario's on a few occasions. And, surprisingly he had managed to dig out of his memory the warning he had issued to himself to avoid this guy.

Largely because of the disapproving looks Jesica shot him through the rear view mirror, he was aware that he was acting too aloof and that if he didn't snap out of it, he would spoil a perfectly festive evening, and if that happened Jesica would be quick and merciless in reminding him that she had sacrificed and slaved to finally bring them together. He owed it to her to loosen up. On the bright side, he admitted that at least on the ride over, Hector had been very amusing and they had already enjoyed more than a few good laughs. The guy had an excellent sense of humour. Besides, Jesica was obviously happy to be with him. No doubt the relationship would be short-lived, Jesica's affairs normally were. But for now, she was content. And Constancia, although transparent, was not overbearing and could even be described as sweet. By the time they arrived at the plaza, Juan had relaxed a bit and prepared himself for an evening of food, beer and good times.

Constancia was aware, as she sat in the back seat looking up at Juan, that she had a permanent smile on her face. But she couldn't help it. She was so tickled to be here with him. She loved his haircut. Old-fashioned as it was, it suited him. His blue eyes were almost as dazzling as in the pictures she had seen on her mother's old album covers. (They had recently disappeared from the living room shelf and she reminded herself that she would have to ask about that.) But she knew that even 'back in the old days,' they photo-enhanced eye colour, particularly blue eyes, for marketing purposes. In spite of his age, (she estimated that he was at least 25 years older than her), there were very few, if any grey hairs on his head. She was drawn to his rugged handsomeness. The dented nose and laugh lines around his eyes were evidence of his adventuresome, fun-loving character. During the ride to Ñuñoa, he chuckled now and then but didn't utter more than a few short phrases. She wondered if he was preoccupied or if he was just a little shy. The latter endeared him to her even more.

When Jesica pulled up to the curb, Hector rushed over, wrapped one arm around her waist, pulled her into him and gave her a bold, open-mouthed kiss. They both looked up and laughed self-consciously, as though this small gesture of affection was a circus spectacle. Juan suspected it was rehearsed but Jesica's youthful flush told him he was wrong, and for a moment he thought she might actually be in love. Juan ran his eyes over the threadbare coat that was stretched across Hector's expansive belly, the fabric of which was almost as shiny as his heavily greased hair. Against his better judgment, a rare and probably undeserving sympathy towards the man crept over Juan. He didn't exactly feel sorry for him, but he saw his joviality in a different light, and he softened.

Plaza Ñuñoa was in fine festive form, lights strung across awnings and wound around tree trunks, triangular red and green flags flapping on heavy strings that were tacked between poles and building façades. Latin techno dance music blasted from each locale and several drunken couples with blue and orange hair pranced and jumped past them on the sidewalk. The crowd here was young. Most of them had not been born when Juan headlined as Jhonny Pretty y los Rockeros. Not that he was beholden to a reputation anymore, but still after all these years, he was conscious of his idol status and usually felt he had to play the role. Tonight, though, as part of this anonymous foursome, he was free to act the fool as he pleased. He relaxed and mentally turned to the young woman who had just snuck her hand into the crook of his elbow. She was exuberant without demanding centre stage. From time to time, she threw a little skip into her walk, either to get into step with Juan or just because she was feeling light. Continuing to be haunted by her voice, he was attracted not only to its tone, but also to what she was saying and he surprised himself by retaining most of the details of her chatter.

She was laughing and saying something about mannequins. Oh yes, of course, she managed a clothing shop in El Patronato. "...and the first time I met Jesica, she practically destroyed my shop by dancing around like a crazy fool in the fringed outfit. Surely you've seen the outfit that I mean?"

"Yes, I've seen it." He didn't want to crowd his thin brain with that broad vision again. It had almost given him a heart attack the first time.

"She's lovely, though, isn't she? She's been such a good friend since that very first encounter."

"Yup, that's Jesica. I've known her for years too." What else could he say? He wasn't going to tell Constancia they had been lovers. It would, without a doubt, set off premature fireworks between them and maybe even break off Constancia's friendship with Jesica. The true extent of his relationship with Jesica was safely locked into his thick vault.

The foursome roamed the perimeter of the plaza, avoiding clusters of merrymakers who spilled out to the tables, which had been hastily placed on sidewalks at the entrance of each restaurant. They pushed and stumbled into each other in jest. Newcomers greeted friends, a jumble of arms thrown about each other's necks, kisses sent into mid-air beside lifted cheeks and heavy back-patting between men who then turned and picked up small women, twirled them around on the sidewalk, a flutter of feet clipping passersby. Waiters wound their way between groups, taking orders on the fly. It was noisy. Bursts of laughter mixed with screams of delight and spontaneous shouts of hilarity punctuated the steady loud roar of people having fun.

Hector spied an empty table at a rustic looking locale called La Cueva. "This place looks good." The crowd was boisterous; couples were dancing to a tropical band, drinks sloshing out of their glasses. They pushed their way to the table, laughing at the sheer craziness of the place.

Hector ordered a round of beer for everyone and then disappeared into the washroom. When he returned he slapped 5000 pesos on the table, "The drinks are on me." He raised his arm to ask for two more rounds and the waiter returned to cover the top of the small table with pint glasses full of beer. Hector slapped down another 10,000 pesos. He winked at Jesica. "I had a good week."

Juan indulged in the free beer and paid no attention to the young man with blue hair who came running out of the washroom claiming to have been robbed. He was expelled from the bar for imposing his suspicious energy on an otherwise great party.

The revelling carried on well into the early morning, by which time Juan, Constancia, Jesica and Hector had formed a tripod on the go. Arms wrapped around one another, as at any given time, three of them dragged the fourth and they drifted happily across the floor, bouncing off the walls and back into the centre of the now sparsely populated restaurant. The bartender was drunk, the waiters were sprawled on chairs around the exterior walls and the owner was counting cash in the back room. Hector had been in to congratulate the owner on two occasions, returning each time with a grin and a pocket full of bills. Upon his first return he ordered a generous amount of Mexican beer and the second time he asked for a table full of tapas, both times pressing extra pesos into the palms of the grateful waiters. Before they left, they made a reservation for New Year's Eve.

Juan's capacity to relax and enjoy himself grew proportionately with Hector's capacity to keep the beer flowing. In Juan's eyes, Constancia grew increasingly attractive and by the end of the night, he was very fond of her. In spite of Hector teasing her about being a whiner, Juan found her to be amusing and a willing dance partner. "You don't have to live with her, man. You haven't seen her in the morning, or in a crisis, which, for Constancia are one and the same thing." Constancia retorted with a swipe in the air, "And you, Hector, what would you do without me? How would you solve your fashion problems?" She pointed at his suit jacket, which he had removed and that was now half hanging onto the floor. "Take care of that, brother. It's a labour of love." Jesica leaned over and inserted her fingers inside Hector's shirt, inadvertently popping a button. "But he can't help it. He's got a lot to work with, my dear." She lifted her face, grinning lustfully up at Hector who smiled stupidly and let his head fall back, enjoying the attention.

Juan chimed in to validate whatever Constancia had said. He had already forgotten, but no matter. "I second that. She knows what she's talking about, man." He put his arm around Constancia, reaching down to fondle a willing breast. "She's very cute. And I like her. That's all that matters."

They had all consumed a record amount of alcohol and by the time they reached Jesica's place, they were helpless to execute the intimate Christmas greetings that were meant to be the piece de resistance. Hector and Jesica trundled down the hall and soon fell silent while Juan sunk limply onto the sofa beside Constancia who, after a couple of failed attempts to revive him by brushing her bare breasts against his cheeks, passed out on the floor at his feet.

Plaza Ñuñoa, now wrapped in Christmas morning sunlight had also only just fallen asleep. The restaurants were quiet – flyers, paper receipts and empty paper cups blew around and a few wine bottles rolled down and clanked into the curbs. The triangular pendants flapped in the breeze, some of their strings having been torn away and left to hang down the side of a tree. Last night the plaza played host to several people who, seated just around the corner and out of sight of one another, would have been curious about their various reasons for celebrating.

Señora Ruby was first among them. Wearing a dress that was too low-cut for a woman of her advanced years, revealed not just her wrinkled cleavage but a freshly polished silver chain with a lapis lázuli pendant. A certain elderly gentleman in a wheelchair by the name of Señor Rodriguez-Gomez was unabashedly gazing at it. He slowly glided his age-spotted hand across the table towards Señora Ruby's twitching fingers. She reached over to touch his hand with her own and their eyes met. Both of them smiled their secret smiles – he was thinking about her cleavage and she was thinking about romance and money.

Around the corner, in a restaurant on a side street, Susana was smiling broadly across the table at Siete Pelos, who had just opened a velvet-lined box containing a pear-shape diamond in a setting vaguely emblematic of a Roman shield. She flapped her hands in the air like a fat duck and whispered not so discreetly, "Oh yes, Siete Pelos, yes." He carefully extracted the ring from its velvet bed and slid it up to the knuckle of her ring finger. Several attempts to push it beyond that failed. Undaunted, he said, "Never mind, we'll have it resized next week so that it goes all the way on and then never comes off."

"No matter, Siete. I'm so happy. You've made me the happiest woman in Santiago." She jumped up from her chair with such force that it fell crashing down behind her. Everyone in the restaurant turned to look and, ignoring the clamour, she announced. "We've just become engaged." She broke into happy tears, her bright cheeks illuminating the dimly lit locale. Everyone in the restaurant broke into spontaneous applause and whistles, and one generous customer even ordered them a bottle of champagne. Siete Pelos beamed and stood up to bow properly, bending low from his waist. His single strand of hair loosened and was in danger of escaping the extra pomade he had thoughtfully applied that evening, at which point he abruptly straightened but continued to beam at his admiring public. "I am

Siete Pelos, and I own a kiosk on the corner of Santa María Street. If you want to have the same good luck that I have had with a woman, just come and ask me about San Expedito."

More applause as he bowed again, less energetically this time, and took his seat.

"It was the rice pudding, wasn't it, Siete? I knew you'd love it. I promise to make it for you at least once a week after we are married."

It was about this same hour that Astrid had returned home from the cemetery, having solved the mystery of the woman of Santa María Street and possessing a deeper understanding of the roles both she and the old woman played in Jhonny's life. She fell asleep, content in the knowledge that Jhonny Pretty had confided in his mother the romantic feelings he had for her.

For those whose grey matter had not been killed off during the festivities, Christmas Eve 2004 was a memorable night, not only because it was the first Christmas after the big earthquake but because it carried so much promise for so many. And even for those with less grey matter, destiny was closing in on them.

CHAPTER 24

Anti-Climax

Juan disentangled himself from Constancia's flowered dress. The fabric print was so bright it hurt his eyes. She was nowhere in sight, which led him to believe that she was running naked somewhere in Jesica's house. His head was pounding, his mouth was extremely furry and he was desperate to swallow something. He didn't care who was naked. Now was not the time. Testing his capacity, his brain ordered his fingers to wriggle. He saw them move. A good sign. Aware that it presented an almost impossible challenge, he slowly bent his elbows, and supporting his head with one hand, he used the other to push up from the sofa. He took his time, gingerly straightening his limbs until he eventually found himself on his feet.

He stood there, motionless, hunched and leaning to one side, both hands now on his head. Dogs barked and children were screaming and running around on the street just outside the door. He needed the sensory protection and solitude offered by his cold, dark basement abode. The challenge was how to get there. There was no movement inside the house. Jesica and Hector must still be sleeping and maybe Constancia had passed out in the bathroom. He had no energy to be curious. He tiptoed to the front door, and then remembering the sunglasses in his jacket pocket, he slowly extracted them, found his nose and hung them over his ears. As luck would have it the neighbour, a taxi driver and also, at least for today, a saviour, was just leaving in search of his first fare. He unwittingly saved Juan from burning in hell.

The mausoleum was a refuge from the noisy streets, the sun and life as we know it. He'd never been so happy to call it home. He patted the engraved name on his mother's tomb. "Gracias Mamá, the best home is still wherever you are." He collapsed onto his mattress and the rest of the day passed him by.

Luisa Rocio ruminated in the niche across the way. She turned and whirled inside the hollow wall, fuming, her heavy energy degrading the old concrete so that it smelled even more putrid. Since ghosts don't have a sense of smell she could be aware only of the growing rot. But even that didn't bother her in the least.

That morning she watched Juan stagger up the stairs in his wrinkled suit, the one he brazenly stole from the Salvation Army, one of the country's most charitable organisations. It was sinful – both the staggering and the stolen suit – and worse yet, the abomination of staggering while in the stolen suit. She saw how he returned home drunk in the early morning hours, as though it was just any other day. No consideration for the fact that not only was it the morn of the celebration of little baby Jesus' birth, it was a special day for the generous, love-struck woman who dedicated her life to this deceitful, washed up, drunken, womanising party hound. She didn't want to pass judgment on Astrid because Astrid was her chosen one, and could do no wrong. No, her focus was to exact retribution from the reprobate who made his home in the Maluenda-Valdéz family mausoleum.

Luisa Rocio never imagined that she would step in and save the skin of this despicable excuse for a human being. But in trying to spare poor, innocent Astrid, that was exactly what she had done. She kicked herself now, but it was too late. The surprising position she found herself in – granted it had been of her own making, but only because, in spite of her own naturally cold heart, she couldn't bear to hurt Astrid – made her resent him more deeply. She drew comparisons to her late husband and had to admit that even during his worst periods, God rest his soul, he did not come close to committing the moral crimes that the scum across the path was guilty of.

If Luisa Rocio had a heart, she would have used it to feel Astrid's sorrow, and tears would have rolled down her own cheeks when she remembered Astrid's misplaced, transparent demonstrations of love and devotion for Jhonny Pretty. But since there could be no certainty that her heart beat with any mercy when she was alive, there was much less likelihood that she would find tenderness there now that she was dead. No, Luisa Rocio's motivation to concoct a successful plan was, as always, to rely on her lifelong practice of revenge and cunning. This is also why it was easier to focus on Juan Bonifacio than on his victim. The fact that his victim had chosen him and not the other way round was beside the point.

Since stumbling upon the relationship that Astrid had invented with Jhonny Pretty, Luisa Rocio had, to a large degree, forgotten that she had assigned herself the exclusive role as Astrid's guardian. She was perhaps too much of a busybody to limit herself to one project at a time. At her core, Luisa Rocio was more of a bully than a protector and in her zest to prey on another person, the woman she had vowed to protect was cast into the shadows – at least for the time being. She had not made a single effort to encounter Astrid beyond the cemetery gates since the day she warned her of the earthquake. She herself had been shaken up in the disaster and it took awhile to find her bearings again. When she finally did, Juan Bonifacio had appeared on the scene in all his Jhonny Pretty glory and she was eager to become involved in his life. Just a lucky coincidence that his life juxtaposed with Astrid's and she could possibly kill two birds with one stone, as it were. Or at the very least, kill one.

So it was that while all Juan Bonifacio Maluenda-Valdéz desired was to be left in peace, the women who made contact with him, for good or for bad, still just wanted a piece of him.

Back at Astrid's house, as Juan slept off his hangover, Astrid was getting drunk on the rum that was meant for the Spanish rice pudding she planned to deliver to him that night.

Late that morning, Constancia and Hector opened the door of Jesica's Volvo Amazon and rolled out onto the sidewalk in front of their house. Jesica tried to appear sober behind the wheel as she waved goodbye, reminding them they all had plans again very soon. Both Constancia and Hector managed to hold it together long enough to sample Astrid's magnificent rice pudding before trundling down to their rooms to sleep it off.

Before she passed out on top of her bed, Constancia speculated about what had really happened with Jhonny Pretty last night. Whatever it was, she found herself naked in the bathroom and could only assume it had been lots of fun and, falling asleep with a silly smile on her face, she anticipated the joy of what was to come on New Year's Eve. Jesica had told Hector that she thought Constancia was just the right woman to turn Jhonny Pretty around.

Luisa Rocio stood vigil, breathing fire as she awaited signs of life in the Maluenda-Valdéz mausoleum, and invented new ways to attack him. Deciding that his real mother had long since given up, Luisa Rocio wouldn't turn down an opportunity to play the role again. She would wager that she was just the woman to guide him back onto the straight and narrow.

CHAPTER 25

Jesus' Birthday

Although Christmas Day was a write-off because of the hangover, Juan roused himself by 5 p.m. and was perched in the shadows of the altar, as had become his custom, waiting for the cemetery caretaker to show up with a cigarette. As it happened, she brought him three bowls of fresh Spanish-style rice pudding and had outdone herself with added candy and fruit, not to mention rum. The woman's face was flushed and he could see immediately by the way she stumbled and faltered that she had tipped back quite a few ounces herself.

"Merry Christmas, Jhonny." she greeted him as she extracted a cigarette from her leather pouch and inserted it into the private vault, as had become her habit.

"Merry Christmas to you, my dearest." He whispered the response, trying to disguise the sound of liquor-worn vocal chords.

She uncovered a basket with the pudding, pulled out the bowls, set them on the top step, and slid them one by one, just inside the wrought iron gate. "My specialty. Just for you."

"Ooh, I can smell how delicious they are from here. I will enjoy them. Thank you."

"Sing me something, Jhonny." This time without her usual apprehension, the request was more of a demand. The rum had emboldened her.

Feeling something was afoot, he complied immediately with "Bésame mucho" just because it was floating around the top of his brain.

Satisfied with his choice, she sank down on the steps, turned her face up to him, closed her eyes and swayed side to side, humming along. She waited until his voice trailed off and then she asked, "How did guide duty go last night?"

He sat in silence for a moment trying to remember what she might be referring to.

She prompted him. "Your mother said you were guiding some of the newly departed, which I knew you would be anyway."

"My mother?"

"Yes," Astrid repeated, "She said you would be gone for most of the evening, trying to help new residents find their way around."

"Oh, yes, that, yes. It went very well." He struggled to keep a steady tone. "But my mother. How is it that you spoke to my mother?" Juan felt shivers run up and down his spine. She spoke to his mother? What if his mother's spirit had been following him day in and day out since he got here? He hadn't foreseen such an awkward or unpleasant situation and couldn't imagine a worse one; to have his mother be privy to his games and tactics. If that were true, she would have been nagging him incessantly since he got here. "Juan Bonifacio, you must look and act like a Maluenda-Valdéz. Where is your self-control? Your sense of propriety? Really Juan Bonifacio, if your father was around, he would cut you down with a lick of his tongue." Never mind his father's tongue, Juan thought. It all came back to him. So far, his mother hadn't successfully made herself heard from beyond the grave, at least not yet. If she was, in fact, speaking to him, he was deaf to it. There was a positive side to oblivion, no matter if it was the result of brain damage, too much wine, or simply sufficient insensitivity that you don't notice the ghost of your own mother when you are in her house.

He suppressed a smile. Let the woman explain. What else could she possibly tell him? She'd already proven herself to be crazy. Well, either that or a complete fool. But he had benefitted – and continued to do so – from her insanity or foolishness, and there was no reason to stop her now. In fact, it might be more to his advantage if he encouraged her. So he added, "And how did she look? Did she look well?"

"Oh," said Astrid, "Well, I didn't actually see her. I don't know why... maybe you do. But for some reason she chose to remain hidden behind your back wall. Even so, she kindly offered to accept the gift on your behalf. The one I brought last night, that is. Did she tell you that I made it myself? Well, you could probably tell. I was really pleased with how it turned out, Jhonny. I think I captured the essence of your career and I bet there were some photos that you haven't seen for years, if you ever saw them at all. My friend Susana has a collection of old magazines and we traded valuables." Astrid was on a roll. He let her ramble on and did his utmost to understand what had happened here last night. What gift? What photos? What mother? He had been too drunk to see anything when he returned at dawn and too ill to notice it later. He returned his gaze to the caretaker.

She was running out of breath, "...and so I collected the centrefolds and decided to build on those. After that, the rest of the album came easily. I hope you noticed the antique wrapping paper. Well, at least I think it must be antique by now. My father gave it to my mother years ago. It's a miracle it held up as well as it did, but I bet it was well-preserved so it could be used for this very purpose." Then she paused and seemed to lose her train of thought. "Why don't we have a smoke, Jhonny? I put one in your box and I still have one for myself."

Since she was obviously drunk, there could be no harm in it. So he slid off the altar and cautiously approached the entrance, allowing himself to be the closest he had ever been to the woman. There was nothing particularly threatening from this proximity, but he quickly grabbed the cigarette and retreated on the off-chance he missed a detail, like the fact that she had extra long arms and would grab at him, or maybe she was extremely quick and would lunge and try to kiss him, or perhaps something more mundane but equally as damning, like a camera or a recorder or something else that might give him away in the future.

"Here, Jhonny. Catch." She threw her lighter. It had an image of San Expedito on it. "I have more of those, so you can keep that one. A gift from me to you." She smiled a crooked smile and winked at him.

"You're too generous, my little angel."

"Not at all. San Expedito should be in your pocket too. Maybe you can ask to see him in person. Ooh, I never thought of that before." She slurred her words. "Can you make an appointment with a saint? You might be able to pass on my messages directly. If my messages are something you should know too (and, why not?) then maybe you can talk to him for me?" She hiccupped, wobbled sideways, laughed at herself and then straightened to face him more seriously.

She waited for Juan to light his cigarette before following suit with her own look-alike San Expedito lighter, holding it up afterwards and giggling. "Two peas in a pod, Jhonny, that's what we are. Two peas in a pod."

"About my mother…"

"Bueno. Sí, a lovely woman. And you know, it's a funny thing… I know I've met her before. Did I mention that? She's the woman from Santa María Street who warned me about the earthquake. Did you know that Jhonny? Did she tell you? Did I ever tell you? She wanted to save me for you. Sweet woman."

His mother disguised herself as someone called 'the woman from Santa María Street?' He couldn't imagine his mother being anything but straight-laced and serious, and certainly not dressing up as someone else. "So tell me how she was dressed last night. Was she wearing something fancy?" Juan recalled the formal traditions of Christmas Eve, with everyone forced to wear suit and tie, or semi-formal gown, as it were. They would eat a big seafood meal and finish it with hot chocolate and dessert. Then everyone was expected to make an appearance at midnight mass, at best a ploy to display emerald necklaces and diamond rings under fur coats, even though the temperatures were still sweltering at that time of night, and at worst flashy hypocrisy.

"Well, no, as I told you, I didn't actually see her. But you know what?

It was her jasmine perfume that gave her away. And, actually yes, I did catch a glimpse as she ran off. And no, nothing formal. She wore the same Adidas shoes and cotton skirt that she wore on the day of the earthquake, and I saw her painted fingernails."

Juan wouldn't expect someone like the cemetery caretaker to find it odd that his mother would dress in such a style. But the garb she described was totally out of the character for a socialite such as his mother. She must be turning in her grave as they spoke. He laughed, trying to picture her in such attire but it was impossible. "Oh yes, the manicured fingernails are one of her trademarks." That was not a lie.

The jasmine, the manicured nails and the Adidas pointed not to his mother but to the old woman across the path, the calcified specimen draped in wrinkled leather who had threatened him. And she had the audacity to pretend to be his mother. This bold interference was going to take a toll, and he would see that it wouldn't be served on him. Although he had never in his whole life been inclined to defend his mother – her own credence and actions being so contrary to his own– he would not stand for some bony, distasteful, ill-spirited, busy-body crucifying his mother's good reputation. He could feel his mother smiling down on him and he looked up at the sky, "You're welcome, Mother, it's the least I can do."

"What did you say, Jhonny?" Astrid blinked out of her rum haze.

"Nothing, nothing at all, just enjoying the cigarette."

Astrid moved on to the subject of New Year's Eve and Juan's attention caught up with her as she was making some practical arrangements. "...and so, Jhonny, I'm leaving you my address, and all you have to do is fly by at about 3 a.m. and I'll be there waiting for you. Just an informal thing but the house will be lit up. Don't be shy about coming in through whatever entrance is most comfortable for your festive soul on the first day of the New Year. If you find other activity in the house, then just come through to my bedroom. The house is small and mine is the only bedroom with the bed that will have me in it." She laughed, not timid at all now. "I don't know what's possible between a ghost and a live woman like me, but let's try, shall we? It's a New Year after all, and there might be magic in the air, and if not, them we'll make our own magic." She giggled.

Juan should have been prepared for such an invitation. After all, he wasn't oblivious to this crazy bird's feelings about him. But it took him by surprise, being that part of his hung-over brain was still preoccupied with how the old bag of transparent bones across the path fit into the picture. And the other side of his brain was gathering fragments of memories from last night, when he was sure he had made other plans for New Year's Eve.

Luisa Rocio, aka the woman of Santa María Street, aka the mother of Jhonny Pretty, did not immediately pay attention to what was happening across the path at the Maluenda-Valdéz mausoleum. Having kicked aside the brittle bones of Mercedes de la Fuente, she stretched out on her stomach in the cement hollow, daintily licking the tips of her fingers as she flipped through the pages of the Christmas gift Astrid had made for Jhonny. "Well, done, Astrid. You really pulled it together. This is very impressive." She had succeeded in unearthing a colossal amount of history about this evil man. Unfortunately, it was all propaganda. Even from the photos, she could see right through his beautiful steel blue eyes; she was immune to their charm. Nonetheless, because she was a woman, it was with great difficulty that she finally managed to disengage herself from the handsome images. "El Diablo. Contemptuous." She finally slammed the book shut. No one, living or dead, would be suggest she was interested in this specimen for anything other than revenge. No Señor, she would never be hypnotised by this piece of longhaired clutter who called himself Jhonny Pretty.

Luisa Rocio nudged the bones of Mercedes de la Fuente a couple of times so she could scratch her way past, to the front of the hollow. Her brown eyes peered out beyond the plaster virgin towards Jhonny's hangout where she spied several layers of flowery fabric that swayed on the hips of none other than Astrid de las Nieves. She scrambled closer to the edge and swore under her breath, "Son of a bitch."

She called herself into action, ghostly attack underway without a plan. Well, at the very least, some afternoon eavesdropping. If she had any saliva, she would have been licking her lips at this opportunity to be a fly on the wall. She escaped the niche in the breeze of the afternoon and floated over to the back to Jhonny's crypt, craning her neck around the corner as only a ghost can do. She held her hand over her mouth, eyes popping out of her cranium. She couldn't believe her ears. An invitation to Astrid's home? She held steady for the details. If ever there was a moment to summon all of her ghostly tricks and save this poor woman from herself, this was it. She manoeuvred into position behind the stained glass window and glared at the back of Jhonny's head, silently promising serious consequences if he so much as approached Astrid's own home. She, Luisa Rocio, would launch herself into the situation to shield her innocent angel from his evil spell and ensure that he would burn in hell.

CHAPTER 26

Anticipation

Hailing in the New Year is like beginning a fairy tale. Once upon a time... starting with the same characters in the same place, doing the same thing but with hopes that it will all somehow magically reshape itself into the best year of your lives.

The sky over Santiago was prepared for the big night. Of course it would dress in its standard glittering attire, and given the festive date, it might set free a meteor shower for those lucky enough to appreciate it, or perhaps allow a glimpse of a far away galaxy or a new star, causing one of the scientists in a local observatory to rub his eyes and blink several times, and finally give up as if it had been a dream, the sky flirting with him once more.

No one, not even through their most creative inspirations and earnest efforts, would ever be able to hold a candle to Santiago's intense blue sky as it sinks into the velvet depths of the universe, tastefully, and for a limited time only, presenting an unlimited array of low-hanging stars, designed to explode without pause and perhaps to highlight the Milky Way. Local designers attempted to mimic the grand effect of the stars, but the best they could do was set diamonds into rows along gold and silver chains that clasped behind someone's neck. These wanna-be star chains that accessorised finely-stitched silk or velvet dresses could only blink into the depths of fleshy cleavage and maybe feel the beating of a heart.

In the case of Constancia's shop, fashion did not have the means to imitate the sky beyond cheap plastic sequins on lightweight stretchy t-shirts and leggings or imitation silk skirts that were sewn together so quickly that they clumped at the hips. During the week between Christmas and New Year's Eve her windows were decorated with tinsel and shiny plastic bobbles that hung from various lengths of thin silver ribbon. This year she incorporated a dozen three-dimensional stars made of shiny yellow card and she installed a spotlight that shone up from the floor, attempting to achieve the effect of a low moon on a star lit night. Jesica clapped with childish glee when she saw the window dressing. "I couldn't have done better myself. But what you need are sound effects. Why don't you borrow my old tape deck and play some new age music?"

"New age music? Are you kidding? No! It has to be exciting. It has to be dance music. I'll take your tape deck but you have to give me some party sounds." Then her eyes lit up. "No, better yet, what about some Jhonny Pretty tunes? Then we can bring him by here... as though he just sort of casually wandered along. Don't tell him this is my shop. We can surprise him."

"Well, the thing is, Constancia, I don't think Jhonny ever did any super dance tunes. I mean, not anything that can compete with today's techno music. If the point of adding the music is to create a hot shopping ambience, then stop and think about it. If you didn't know Jhonny Pretty, would you actually choose his stuff for this purpose?"

Constancia crossed her arms, tapping her pink-tipped fingers into her elbows, the toe of one foot beating the floor, prepping her brain to meet the challenge, reaching out for the familiar sounds of Jhonny Pretty, begging them to be truly danceable. But Jesica was right, they were not up to today's competition; they were more sentimental and romantic, even with their catchy Latin rhythm. "Well, but maybe you can make me a compilation with just a few of his songs in between... I mean, mostly techno and then, boom, an old Jhonny Pretty number. Who knows? It might draw in a retro crowd." She turned to indicate a mini-length dress that was pinned around a headless mannequin. "I can even change this for a pair of capri pants." She looked around, her hands fluttering. "I don't know what else, but I'll find something. And, you know what? My mother has a whole stack of old Jhonny Pretty albums. I could bring you some."

"What? Who do you think you're talking to, Con? Among other artists, I'm the queen of Jhonny Pretty y los Rockeros collectors. Leave it to me. I'll combine the right songs with the right sounds and your shop will be the hit of the street... forget the street, what about all of El Patronato. Maybe we'll get you some free publicity on Chilevision."

But more often than not, even before the New Year begins, the best of intentions fade away behind immediate priorities. So it was that although the stretchy mini-dress was exchanged for the capri pants on the headless mannequin, and Constancia found just the right translucent cap-sleeved blouse with horizontal silver threads that glistened in the sun, no sound ever enhanced the display, and Jhonny Pretty was never casually led past the shop. At least, not before New Years.

Jesica immediately forgot about her promise to Constancia because her attention was focused on trying to make a decision about Hector. Hector was a fun guy and was more generous than man she'd been with. But occasionally there was something disquieting about his manner and it did not fall into a predictable pattern. Although his work took place in the mornings and usually early afternoons and she worked late into the evening, they found time to escape to her place to enjoy a few intimate hours. Besides the sex, which she found more satisfying and often delightfully playful, she was able to converse with him about almost anything. But he was unusually closed when she asked about the two most basic topics that describe someone to someone else – his family and his work.

Sometimes he went on at great lengths, describing the habits and expectations of English and French tourists, the eccentricities of Italians and assumptions made by Americans. But when she asked him about specific circumstances and scenarios that unfolded throughout the day, he became extremely vague and uncooperative, often to the point of agitation. As far as his familial situation, of course she knew Constancia was his only sister and that they both lived with their mother in the family house in the neighbourhood of Recoleta. But he refused to talk about his father, and he never elaborated on his mother's activities. Jesica took for granted that his mother was a homemaker and that Hector and Constancia had assumed the role of breadwinners since their father disappeared under circumstances that Hector refused to disclose.

Jesica was surprised to find that she was thinking more and more about settling down with Hector. She didn't mind his shiny suit and matching glossy hair. In fact, his style endeared him to her, partially because it was reminiscent of her father's look. Granted it was out of date, but no matter – everyone makes their fashion choices and decides how to represent themselves to the rest of the world. Constancia often chided Hector about his 'look', but he stubbornly refused to change anything about it, and he teased her back, pointing out how that she had no depth and lacked true style because hers changed with the wind. Aside from the imprecise information about family and work, Hector was as transparent a soul as any potential wife could wish for.

He didn't strike her as a lady's man – maybe in the past, but certainly not now. He was a stalwart individual who, although he enjoyed a night on the town, he never allowed it to interfere with responsibilities. And he led her to believe that she was at the top of his list of priorities. "You're important to me Jesica. I want to keep you around." She believed him. As she sifted through the information she had about Hector, her only serious misgiving were the mysteries surrounding his parents and the details of his job.

New Year's Eve was going to help her decide what to do about him. The four of them had made plans when piled into the Amazon en route to her house on Christmas Eve. They had decided to make their final toast to the New Year at Hector and Constancia's place. First they would party at La Cueva, and then, although it remained unspoken (it was anticipated with excitement), they would pair off to share a bit of coital joy to ring in the coming year.

Jesica failed to notice that Jhonny never made the slightest hint about inviting them to his place. All she knew of his domestic situation was that he was still single, and that's all that mattered. She never gave any thought to where he lived.

Constancia, on the other hand, had a very clear picture of Jhonny's home. She saw him wearing a smoking jacket and sipping from a large glass of pisco and cola in an overstuffed 1970s chair, his legs stretched out across an orange, leather ottoman. She imagined his maid fussing around him, fetching him the paper, rustling up steak and rice in the galley kitchen that was part of the luxury apartment. Jhonny would occasionally sit on the low leather stool in the corner and strum on his guitar, pausing to pull a pencil out from behind his ear to make notes about new songs and sipping thoughtfully from his crystal glass. Constancia was positive Jhonny must be on the verge of a new album. He was coming back, she could feel it in her bones. When he danced with her on Christmas Eve he hummed a melody into her ear and said it was a little something he was working on. She was so impressed that her knees buckled and he had to pick her up and carry her to their table. Constancia just knew that late in the afternoons his maid helped him slip into his now-famous navy blue jacket before heading out for an evening at Slaughterhouse Square where he would once again croon the songs he was most famous for, his irresistible Jhonny Pretty style drawing the crowds.

She had hoped to show up at Slaughterhouse Square every night this week, but Christmas sales proved to be sensational and she couldn't get away from the shop. Hordes of women (well, maybe a dozen so far) suddenly wanted to wear the capris that she dressed on the headless mannequin. Constancia, herself, found them very comfortable and stylish. To attract customers she pranced around out on the sidewalk near the shop entrance, wearing tight-fitting green capris with a gold sequinned halter top and a pair of high heels that had a big yellow daisy on the toes. If Jesica had come through on the music, it would have been impossible to contain the crowds. Imagine the madhouse. As it was, the first-hand promotion worked and she was run off her feet.

Constancia literally licked her lips as she anticipated New Years Eve with Jhonny Pretty. Whatever it was that had taken place at Jesica's on Christmas Eve, she was game for more. And no doubt Jhonny was dreaming about her too. She had already begun to re-arrange her room, replacing childish posters of kittens and puppies with near life-size images of Marilyn Munro and James Dean. And she covered her headboard with the bolt of deep blue velvet that had been used to dress the store window. Too bad she couldn't exchange her single bed for something a little more accommodating, but that was one thing that was not going to change, and anyway, for what she had planned, Jhonny Pretty's head would be in the clouds, and he wouldn't even notice the size of the bed. The back room of the shop was full of possibilities for decorating her room. She tried several types of fabric before finally settling on a loosely woven baby blue woollen blanket and several small cushions to cover her bed. She stood back and admired her handiwork. It looked like heaven with windows into her own soul. Maybe she had inherited her Mother's talent, but there was no doubt that her flair was for the living.

Astrid was busy cleaning and re-arranging the whole house. She said it was because she really wanted to start the New Year right, everything in its place, ring it in style. She was really upbeat, humming in and out of each room, dust cloth in hand. Pushing the heavy sofa to this side and then shoving it to that, she changed her mind several times before leaving it where it was. Her creativity was stifled by practical limitations created by the earthquake, such as unrepaired cracks and holes in the walls and boards that covered sinkholes in the floor. She was forced to tack the living room drapes to the wall well beyond the window to conceal a floor-to-ceiling crack. And photos, framed and unframed, hung from nails over large chips in the plaster. Missing and cracked ceramic floor tiles were hidden under throw rugs that Constancia had knitted from rags. But with several vases of flowers from the cemetery, the place would be fresh and welcoming.

Astrid was uncertain about how much to change her bedroom. Would Jhonny love the altar, or would he think she had gone overboard? There was so little time to decide. She exited the room and then re-entered, trying to be objective. First of all, the lighting was wrong. The bulb in the ceiling fixture was too bright. She threw a purple scarf over it and arranged it to look like it had drifted up there on a breeze. The small lamp beside the bed was okay but the atmosphere could be improved with a couple of the scented candles, which she removed from the altar and placed at the base of the lamp. Then she decided that this lamp, too, could use a bit of bohemian flair and she threw another thin scarf over top, painted irises coming to life over its yellow light.

She was pleased with the bedspread she'd had for years. No need to change this southern Chilean style for anything else. The altar was the only question. Finally she decided to leave everything in place, especially the San Expedito paraphernalia. She was afraid that if she removed any of it San Expedito would not only ignore her but attack with force. Although she trusted him for his favours, she didn't know if, once provoked, he would be a vengeful saint and she didn't want to risk it. As for the Jhonny Pretty photos on the altar – all seven of the large ones and twelve small ones – she would just turn them around or cover them with antique family photos from the pre-Jhonny era. She reasoned that this was discreet but not rude, that if Jhonny appeared disappointed by the lack of sentimental evidence of himself, she could simply, based on his reaction, reveal his photos, deciding then and there, which and how many of the images would be appropriate. She didn't want to appear obsessed and risk scaring him off. It would be entirely unnecessary to remove any of his old vinyls. In fact, she could set the mood by playing one or two of his records and he would be impressed and ask to scan her collection. She pictured him hovering over the old album covers, grinning, "Que bueno! You have them all. Do you know that we started to make this album two years after the coup d'état? And it took us a full year to record because we knew the secret police were keeping an eye on us."

She would raise an eyebrow. And he would continue, "But we were not a threat. We were innocuous. Our music was always about love. Nothing political." And he would wink and look at her meaningfully. He would select other albums, turning them over to read the notes, and run his finger down the list of the song titles. "Your collection is just about as big as mine. And everything in such good shape. I have to say I'm very impressed."

Smiling to herself, she turned her attention to other details. She had thought of everything, including the most important of all – her negligee. An odd gesture from a daughter to her mother, it was the first gift Constancia gave her after she started working at the shop. Constancia had been beaming with excitement when she handed her the pink box wrapped in a yellow and white polka-dotted bow. She had gone to such trouble. Perhaps it was because she knew Astrid would never dream of buying such a thing for herself, even if she did have a man around. Perhaps it was her way of encouraging her to find a boyfriend. She should have thrown it away years ago, but it was a special gift from her daughter, given in good faith and in spite of everything, there always remained an iota of hope that she would use it one day. But not even in her wildest imagination did she dream it would be for something as out of this world as what she was planning this week.

It was shortly after the rainy day in October that she remembered and lifted it out from between the layers of tissue at the bottom of her bureau drawer and began to dream Jhonny dreams. Several times over the past week she gave in to temptation and bent into the drawer to finger the fabric as it lay like the innocent virgin garment it was and her heart skipped a beat. It was more seductive than she remembered.

The negligee was a black, two-piece, translucent baby doll – a pair of bikini briefs and an open-front camisole with a silver ribbon that tied across the breasts. She tried it on. It reached mid-thigh and swung out lightly with each step, caressing her skin so that she felt like a large butterfly. When she attempted a few graceful leaps across the room to catch her reflection in the mirror, she tripped and fell backwards onto the edge of the bed, one hip weighing her over the side. She stretched her arms to the floor, pushing up on her fingertips, veins popping out and face red with the strain but she saved herself. After this small rehearsal, she decided that on the important night she wouldn't leap.

She planned to accessorise the negligee with a black choker that had one silver bead hanging by a thread at the centre. It pointed to her mostly-exposed breasts. To accent her virgin feet that had been hidden away for years in the clunky leather chambers that she called shoes, she had chosen a set of ankle bracelets. They were fine silver chains with miniature ceramic moulded San Expedito images. Both pendants dangled just below her outside ankle leaving San Expedito to stab into the air with his Roman lance, his centurion splendour limited only by his short leash.

Having discarded leaping from her repertoire as too extreme, she wanted to at least glide and lift her arms in order to exhibit the versatility of the garment and accent the sensuous curves of her body as she moved. The mirror must be inaccurate because it made her look slightly pudgy through the semi-transparent fabric. Keeping her eyes focused on her reflection, she twirled slowly and watched as the chiffon rippled around her. She raised one foot at a time, pointing her toes down and a little to the side, and pranced around the room like one of the extras in a ballet. She artfully parted the camisole to expose the tiny panties under her rolling belly, bowed gracefully and, with one arm artfully extended, she invited Jhonny to take her hand so that she could lead him to her bed. He would walk forward gazing steadily into her eyes as he did so. Then he would say, "Lie down, my angel. I want to make love to you."

She lowered herself onto the edge of the bed, arms stretched above her head, and rolled back until she lay flat, feet dangling at the fringe of the bedspread. She pinched the heavy cloth between her toes and pretended to tease Jhonny, who would be standing directly in front of her. But as she coyly twisted her feet to cover them with the bedspread, one of her big toes caught in the loose weave and she couldn't free it. She lay flat on her back, pumping her leg in the air to no avail. The threads around her toe only seemed to tighten. Her face reddened in frustration. "Por Diós, what is this mess?" She flailed her arms, rolling about on the rehearsal bed and in a husky whisper, so that she didn't alert Constancia or Hector, she complained into the room, "This is not the plan! Who made this blanket with big holes in it? Who taught them how to weave? How are you supposed to cover yourself with dignity?" She struggled to snatch her feet out the yarn trap, pausing to shake one fist at the roof. Her graceful tussle on the top of the bed ended in a clumsy floundering and waving of arms, exposing a less than elegant demeanour and expanses of dimpled skin and the extra rolls around her hips. Luckily she didn't observe any of this in her mirror but she was sure that there were certain types of men out there who would have loved to see her fail in this way, watching her body as she spun about helplessly in this woollen web, drooling over her nakedness, which she knew was seductive. She finally settled down and succeeded in sitting up. When she bent over to untangle her big toe, she was reminded of the beauty of her soft feet. Stroking them helped to calm herself, "Ah, so perfectly maintained. These are the feet of a movie star." Maybe she should get Jhonny into the dark room and somehow find a way to wave her feet about in front of his face. Maybe that should be the introduction, the welcome to her naked body, the way to hidden paradise. Or, no, perhaps they were better saved for last, like fine dessert, or the brandy after a satisfying meal. She imagined him gently holding a foot in his hand and then bending into it, kissing her ankle as San Expedito looked on (perhaps he would even pause to thank San Expedito – that would be acceptable), and then he would lay down a trail of kisses beginning under her ankle, across the top of her feet, all the way to her toes. He would take his time to kiss the end of each toe and suck on them as she squirmed with delight and her black baby dolls would part for Jhonny once more. "Oh, Jhonny, what a night we will have."

CHAPTER 27

Out of Destruction Comes Hope

"I told you there would be trouble here, didn't I? It happens every year at this time." Señora Ruby pointed in all directions, waving her index finger at nothing and everything. Astrid bent down to pick up broken glass and she tossed it into the cart as she proceeded slowly around the south corner of Patio 35.

"Well, I never had this sort of trouble in Patio 62. I mean, of course, I knew about it, but never had to clean it up before..."

"It's only because Patio 62 is out of the way and the tombs there are not rich. But the wretched vandals are not after riches; they are just making a statement. They're ruining sentimental things, valuable or not. They call themselves anarchists and they rant about inequality and government. How does this destruction serve their purpose?" Señora Ruby was close to tears. She threw up her arms and let them flop back down to her sides. "These are just individual families trying to remember people they love. How does that harm the rest of the world?"

"Well, maybe it isn't really a political statement. Maybe they were just a bunch of drunken kids with what one of them thought was an original idea. And the others followed blindly along."

"No, Astrid, my dear. I've seen this year after year. Look at this graffiti." She pointed at red and black spray paint on the side of the grey marble Patiño-Blanco mausoleum. The patriarch of this family is the founder of the jewellery store chain... you know the ones. I can't think of the name, but it's something like La Joyería Preciosa. It's a crime, Astrid, it really is. These anarchists – I don't know who they are or why they call themselves that when really, they aren't following any ideology. They're just petty vandals. They come back every year, and no matter what precautions the families take, they succeed in causing at least some degree of destruction. And you know what? The living members of the family aren't even doing well with the jewellery stores. About 10 years ago, one of the sisters was sobbing here on the stairs and she told me they have lost so much over the years, a lot of it to thieves with sledgehammers who broke into their small shops. And then this... I felt so sorry for her. I offered to take care of the tomb but I can't be here all the time to protect it. They climb the walls at night."

"But how do you know they are anarchists?"

"Because of the graffiti. They leave an 'A' in a circle. I don't know what everything else means, but this their symbol. Just watch the news. The cemetery is only one of the targets. And you noticed that the Catholic Cemetery closed their catacombs to the public, right? Now people have to make an appointment to visit the dear beloveds who are buried there. Can you imagine being restricted from a spontaneous visit to your grandmother or your great-aunt? It's out of the question. It is unpardonable."

Astrid advanced along the path, bending down to pick up a broken Sleeping Beauty statue from a Disney movie. "And this?"

"That belongs to Señora Alvarez. She died about 6 years ago and one of her grandchildren gave her this statue because they used to watch the movie together."

"Oh." Astrid felt a deep despair and didn't know how to respond. When she looked over at Señora Ruby, she saw the tears running freely down her cheeks.

"This family's situation changed, just like the Patiño-Blancos. They also used to be well off, but the last generation has had bad luck. Now they'll have to find money to repair the broken glass. And how can they replace this little statue? I mean, they can't. It was such a precious gesture, a gift from an innocent child, and now look." Señora Ruby's face contorted in pain, imagining the granddaughter's disappointment. "How can I tell them that I couldn't protect this? You know that they'll have to send someone to beg for money for the repairs. I've known it to happen. Last year another patron had to give up two months' worth of heart medicine just so that he had enough money to fix what the vandals had done to his wife's tomb. And within six months, he was dead himself. This, this..." she waved an arm in despair, "is so senseless, this destruction and lack of respect for poor families. And on the same year as the earthquake. You'd think they could have given it a rest, at least for one year. People have suffered enough. They don't know the individuals they're harming. They don't care. For 'the greater good' or something...." her voice trailed off but Astrid heard her whispering, "Shameful, shameful."

"Sit down, Señora Ruby. Let's go back to the shack." She took her elbow and led her around the corner, pulled out the old chair and helped her sit down. "I can clean this up. Don't worry about it for now. Look, I'll pour us a cup of tea." She hurried inside to grab her thermos and their mugs.

"We don't want to look complacent in the middle of all this mess, Astrid. We can't sit here and drink tea. Los muertitos are calling for us."

"No, you stay. I'll go then."

"Wait." Señora Ruby's face changed. "Wait. I have some news. I don't want to let another day go without telling you. And I want to take my mind off this vandalism. There has to be some good in this day."

Astrid sat on the chair opposite and leaned forward.

"Astrid, you remember I told you about Señor Rodriguez-Gomez?"

Astrid nodded.

"Well, we had a wonderful dinner on Christmas Eve and I've seen him twice since then."

Astrid couldn't hide her surprise. "What's going on with you two? You only met him a few weeks ago."

"Well, it must be destiny, my dear." Señora Ruby smiled. She fondled the lapis lázuli that hung around her neck. It looked beautiful in

Señora Ruby's pendant. Astrid was mesmerised as Señora Ruby tilted it to and fro, altering its angle to catch the sun's rays, and when the lucky blue eye winked up at her, Astrid jumped back, shocked to be reminded of Jhonny's steel blue eyes. She blinked self-consciously and looked at Señora Ruby who seemed not to notice. The lucky blue eye dared to wink at her again, and embarrassed, Astrid turned away. Was Jhonny present here this morning? She looked around.

"What is it, mi querida?" Señora Ruby noticed Astrid's discomfort.

"Oh, oh, I think the sadness of the vandalism just hit me, Señora Ruby. You stay here and I'll go back and pick up where we left off." She stood up to leave.

"But I wanted to give you some happy news on this day that is otherwise be full of sadness."

Astrid sat back down again. "Oh, yes, of course. I'm sorry. Carry on."

"Astrid, you know that I'm not getting any younger."

"Well, you could have fooled me. Look at how you've transformed yourself over the past several weeks." It wasn't only the nail polish and shiny, healthier hair, or even the makeup; it was her complexion, the spring in her walk, the way that she stood so much taller, and lately how she bent down and was able to straighten immediately without groaning or leaning on a wall to help pull herself up. Astrid shook her head, "You have to give me your secret Señora Ruby. What have you been eating?"

"No, nothing. I don't know. I have to admit that I feel lighter and more agile but I honestly don't know what I've done to achieve it. I can't afford to change my diet; it's still bread and margarine and rice for me. Maybe I've managed to eat a bit more fish lately because my neighbour's son has been fishing. But, no... I don't know. Anyway, I'm not complaining. And why question it? I'll just carry on, enjoy it while it lasts." She shifted and said rather more sharply than she intended, "You've interrupted me. My news. I want to tell you my news."

"Yes, of course. Sorry." Astrid closed her mouth and waited.

Señora Ruby looked up to the sky and blinked into the distance. "It's

Señor Rodriguez-Gomez... well..." and when she turned to meet Astrid's eyes, her face was radiant. "He said he wants to marry me."

"What? What?" To say she was stunned was an understatement. Señora Ruby had never been married nor, as far as Astrid knew, had she ever had a long-term relationship. Oh, surely she must have had affairs and she knew her way around a live man as well as a dead one. But the truth was that she had never shown any interest.

Señora Ruby read her mind. "I know it's a surprise."

All Astrid could do was nod. She leaned back in her chair and waited.

"You know, mi corazón, there's a story that I don't know if your mother ever told you."

Now she really had her attention. Astrid remained silent.

"You remember that I told you I lived in an apartment in Santiago Centro and that the apartment burned down? Remember? I told you. It was years ago. But I lived there for fifteen years before that. I was a sort of Bohemian. I had this job at the cemetery, and I never dreamed of giving it up. But I was also a singer in a band. I sang in several, but the one that I ended my career with was called La Calma. Being a singer was a sort of secret desire but it never took me very far. Even with La Calma. Maybe the name of the band had a little bit to do with that, now that I think about it."

Astrid was still speechless. What? Although she had never underestimated Señora Ruby, she wasn't prepared for a singer in a band.

"I was quite a good singer, actually. I used to perform here in Santiago, and because of my day job, I never travelled, except for a couple of times when we went as far south as Curicó."

Suddenly Señora Ruby got to her feet and, fingering her pendant, she started to sing "Como una promesa, eres tú, eres tú, como una mañana, de verano..." It was an old love song by Juan Luis Calderón.

"Bravo! Señora Ruby, listen to you! I had no idea." Astrid couldn't contain her delight or her surprise. "Why don't I ever hear you singing?"

Señora Ruby just shrugged. "It was so long ago." She closed her eyes, clasped her hands modestly in front of her waist and bent in a timid little bow. "Thank you." She accepted the applause before sitting back down to resume her story. "Bueno. I guess I was an okay singer. The band broke up after I left, saying they were lost without my voice."

"Why did you leave the band then?"

"Well, you know I helped my mother here. It was my first responsibility and although she let me go and live on my own... and well, actually, I didn't live alone in that apartment; I lived with a man who was the drummer in the band and his son, who was the bass player. In those days, it was considered something terribly sinful to live with a man outside of marriage. My mother had a hard time with it. Sometimes I wonder if that was part of the reason she became so ill. But anyway, everything fell apart at the same time. My mother's illness became really serious and I couldn't leave her side. But I also had to carry on with her work here." She indicated the cemetery in general. "It was a really hard time for me. I started to skip rehearsals and then even missed performances and the other members of the band were forever angry with me. The drummer began to make my life hell. By this time, I was already well beyond the age of a young woman, Astrid. I was already past 50 years old. But you know, I had experience and a certain style and people liked to hear me sing. So I could never give it up. And anyway, I loved it.

"Then, only a week before my mother died, I was going to call it quits with the drummer. That's when the apartment building caught fire. It was a sign, Astrid, a signal. Everything was over. It was time to move on." She gazed a long way in front of her. "I moved into my mother's house to take care of her, you know, to be at her side during her final agony. It was all very unsettling. I remember, in all of that, feeling I had lost more than my life, because even my lapis lázuli pendant had disappeared. And I took that as a certain sign to forget about everything from that life and carry on only with the life that my mother offered me."

"But what has all of this got to do with Señor Rodriguez-Gomez?"

"Oh yes. Well, I only found out when we went for dinner on

Christmas Eve..."

"What? You spent Christmas Eve with him?"

"Well, who else? I have no family. And it was just dinner."

"Yeah, I guess so."

"Anyway, during dinner, we started talking about our younger years and he admitted to me that he had always had a crush on me when I was a singer for La Calma. Imagine that, Astrid. After all these years, he recognised me. And do you know how he positively identified me? Because after you gave me the lapis lázuli and I dropped it on the ground in front of his wheelchair, he said he remembered that I used to wear it around my neck, that every time he saw me perform (which was apparently quite often), I was wearing the pendant. He told me that once he spoke to me during a break at a club. I have no recollection of that. He said he remembers me playing with the pendant in my fingers when I spoke just as I did when I sang, like it was my lucky charm."

"This is an incredible story, Señora Ruby."

"Yes, isn't it? And what's even more incredible is that his wife died about ten years ago, and that even during their marriage, he often found himself thinking of me, wondering where I was. He's an old man, mind you, but he still has all of his important parts and he tells me he is in perfect working order."

Astrid blushed. "Señora, please..."

"Anyway, Astrid, he asked me to think about marrying him. He told me he's well off financially, but he doesn't enjoy his money by himself. He wants me to marry him. Just like that."

"Just like that?"

"Yes, just like that."

"So, what, then? I mean are you going to marry him?"

"Yes, Astrid." She was totally serious now. "You know, I thought about it and it didn't take long to decide. Look, I'm old, and I'm in the best shape I've been in for years. I've been working here my whole life, since I was a little girl at my mother's side, may God bless her soul. But Astrid, you know how it is, my dear. It's hand-to-mouth. And there are many weeks where my hand has nothing to put into my mouth. If I marry this man, I'll be able to retire. I'll be able to sit in the sun and listen to music day after day because he has enough money for both of us. I don't love him, but I like him enough. And at this stage, it's not even an issue. And I know we'll enjoy our last years together. It won't be a struggle. And you know what else? I will probably do a lot of singing."

Astrid sat with her mouth hanging open, unable to think of anything to say.

"My dear heart, I would like you to take over the whole patio. Maybe Constancia will agree to help you. But if not, I'm sure there is a list of willing apprentices at the front gate. I, my dear, am going to become a lady of leisure." She turned her hand palm up and bent her fingers inward so she could run her thumb over the fresh nail polish on each of the manicured nails. Astrid thought she already looked like she was trying to decide whether to eat beefsteak or lobster, fresh strawberries or mango, and should she wear the pink or the green silk dressing gown?

"When will you marry? And am I invited to the wedding?"

"Well, we have to set a date, but it will definitely be in the month of February. He wants us to go south to Frutillar for a honeymoon. Says there are some very comfortable cabins on the lakefront with a clear view of the Osorno Volcano."

"You sound like you're used to this already." Astrid's voice was accusing.

"No, of course not, but for him it's an easy fact of life, this travel and luxury accommodation. I plan to get used to it, at least for the years I have left. Are you not happy for me?"

"Oh yes, Señora Ruby. Yes. I'm sorry. Congratulations. A million congratulations. I'm just still so shocked. I want everything that you want for your life."

"Thank you, Astrid. Thank you."

"Okay, well, I better get back to the cleanup. And then I'll bring up the idea with Constancia. I can tell you right now that she won't be excited about it. She's doing very well in the shop and has no reason to change, so she probably won't even give it a second thought. But she's the first one I'll talk to. Let it sink in with me a bit. Leave it with me until after the New Year."

Meanwhile, in the neighbouring patio, around the corner and a long ways down the path from where Señora Ruby sat as Astrid brushed broken bits of statues into her dustpan, Juan was rousing himself on the mattress beside his mother's tomb. He lay still, watching the single ray of light jump back and forth as he alternately opened one eye and the other, remembering the week's events.

Predictably, Slaughterhouse Square benefitted from the holiday spirit. Business was brisk and the entertainers offered dynamic sets that drew boisterous response from the crowds. Tourists and shoppers mingled with the regulars at the plaza, throwing coins in the hat and buying copies of CDs that Jesica displayed beside the karaoke equipment, often asking for autographed ones and paying more for the added value. It had been a good week for money. And it had been a good week for parties too, beginning with the one on Christmas Eve. And in three days, after Juan drank in the applause and pisco and colas offered to him by happy fans at the Square, he would be joining the merry-makers at La Cueva, drinking all the wine that Hector could put on the table and dancing with Constancia, who had been in his thoughts more than once over the past few days. He sought to identify the familiarity of her voice, but the connections in his mind were foggy and it was too much effort to concentrate. So he decided that rather than being perturbed by it, he'd just relax into its evocative familiarity. He looked forward to New Year's Eve with more anticipation than usual. He surprised himself by thinking of his evening with Constancia as more than a one-night stand with a Barbie Doll. She had personality. She was innocent but not entirely naive. She seemed trustworthy and responsible, which, God only knew, was a quality he needed in his corner. She and Hector appeared to be from a good family, albeit noticeably one of limited resources. But he hadn't exactly been flying with the jet set over the last few decades either. "Sorry, Mother, but I've moved down in life," he shot her crypt a doleful glance. Squinting into the light as he mounted the ladder up to the main level, he listened for signs of life nearby. Except for the songs of birds and a distant rumble of a bus, it was quiet, so he moseyed over to the altar, hopped onto the edge and inched his way back to lean on the wall. He pulled out a Derby, lit it, blew three lazy smoke rings and watched them dissipate.

Perhaps it was just the season and nothing more, but Juan felt a heavy nostalgia and turned to the photo of the misbegotten members of los Rockeros. He wondered if any of their families had been stricken by this year's earthquake. How did they survive it themselves? Where were they when it happened? He looked at the crooked grins on their faces and smiled back at them. Maybe each of them had enough time to heal and were living full lives now. He should look them up. He could start with Traintracks, who probably still lived on one of the hills surrounding Valparaiso. Or maybe Fishface – whose ears, back in the days when he was normal, picked up so much news and static that he could have been hired by the university seismology department as an early-warning system -- still kept tabs on the whereabouts of the other guys.

Juan perked up as he realised he was sowing the seeds of a comeback. Jhonny Pretty y los Rockeros on the road again. Well, maybe not on the road. He hadn't left Santiago since the accident because he couldn't find the power to take that first step up onto an inter-city bus. Plus it would be a good idea to reduce his drinking to something acceptable – never quitting altogether, of course; that would be expecting too much, and he didn't want to set himself up to fail. He tossed the idea around. It was far-fetched, but if they were all healthier now... well, who knew? And maybe if the stars were all lined up, they could pull it off. The only member they would not recall would be Mauricio, but it would be easy to find another manager. And this time it would be someone with scruples. He intended to let the seeds of the idea germinate. Yes, this New Year would bring something different. He could feel it in his bones.

CHAPTER 28

What the Cat Dragged In

It was late afternoon on December 31st when Juan sauntered into Slaughterhouse Square carrying a bunch of yellow roses. He'd been wearing the same grin since he got up that morning. He first noticed it in the mirror of the men's washroom at the cemetery, where he had tried to wipe it off. But it wouldn't leave. It appeared he was not in control of the muscles on his face. It was very inconvenient to shave and the result was an uneven shadow of whiskers that emphasised the smile. His eyes were alight with humour. Something must be funny but he couldn't remember what. Mercifully, the expression in his eyes matched the grin so that it didn't look like a silly hard smile pasted on his face.

He approached Jesica who was organising several piles of CDs. Her hand-painted sign read, 'Buy one tonight and remember New Years Eve 2004 forever.' Without looking up, she said, "Jhonny, it's going to be very busy tonight so I want you on your best behaviour. And please sing the songs in the order we discussed, okay? Another thing... no beer until you finish your second set. We're partying after this gig and I want all of us to have a good time."

His silence finally caused her to look up. That's when he pushed the thick bunch of roses in front of her nose.

"What? For me?"

"Of course for you." He insisted, grinning and extending his arm so forcefully that she was almost forced to eat the flowers.

"What's come over you? Did you win La Polla lottery?"

He responded with his grin.

"Jhonny, what's wrong with you?"

"I don't know. I woke up in a good mood." He said through his teeth.

"A freaky mood, you mean." She looked the roses. "Well, these are beautiful, Jhonny. And so many... por Diós, it looks like you robbed a cemetery." They both laughed. The laughter seemed to break the spell over Juan's face, after which he found that he could close his mouth for the first time that day.

An ebullient atmosphere had already settled around the Square. Jesica was playing loud techno cumbia and people couldn't resist dancing as they passed by. The Square was the traditional location for Bio Bio's exclusive New Year's celebration. In this case, 'exclusive' meant that anyone outside of the Bio Bio community didn't know about it, or if they did, it wasn't their cup of tea. But the usuals attended, along with an insignificant scattering of tourists, who would be amused for a few minutes and then move on to an expensive east-end club where they had already booked a table for the night. People would start to straggle out after their dinner at Mario's and they'd fill the benches around the square, bottles of wine in hand. Jhonny was the main entertainment at Slaughterhouse that night but Jesica had also slotted in three others. "They twisted my arm, Jhonny. I had to give them at least a couple of songs each. You know they've been here for five years, begging to perform and you know what'll happen if I don't allow this."

She was surprised when Juan's grin re-appeared. "Yeah, I know and this time, your schedule better work. Make sure they don't steal into my time. I'm gonna follow the plan and do my whole set – without interruption." The grin disappeared and he shot her a stern glance. Every year it was the same thing; performers got drunk and pushed their way into the centre of the plaza, clawing for the microphone so they could sing along with Jhonny Pretty. When Jesica unplugged them, the pushing and shoving began. Mostly Juan was able to manoeuvre away from the centre of the brawl before members of the audience, who enjoyed the earthy texture of a good fight, roused themselves from the benches to throw indiscriminate punches in all directions.

All but the hardcore crowd would thin out by about 11.00 p.m. as most people made their way to the Entel Tower in the city centre to watch the fireworks from close range.

"Oh, Jhonny, before I forget... Hector said that he'd bring Constancia. They're both still working, but they'll be here before 11 because they want to catch your act."

Over on El Patronato, Constancia shooed last minute shoppers out of the store, tallied the day's earnings, shoved it all into a bag which, in her haste, she all but threw into the arms of the shop owner, saying, "It was a great day, busy day, profitable day. I have to go. Can you lock up?" The owner appeared daily at closing time to collect the cash, but never locked up and didn't even remember how to do it. Tonight Constancia left her no choice.

She hailed a taxi and rushed home to prepare for a night with Jhonny Pretty. She knew that her mother would already be at the cemetery as per usual on New Year's Eve. Astrid was disappointed that Constancia and Hector weren't going to visit their grandparents at midnight this year but they would all go on the second day of the New Year. It was within the acceptable time frame she said – but just barely.

"Hector, we can't let Mamá visit the grandparents alone. You know that." Hector was getting careless about these traditions and it bordered on disrespect. "So whatever your plans are for the day after tomorrow, change them! If not, it won't only be our grandparents that Mamá and I will be visiting at the cemetery." Hector frowned and promised he'd be there. Annoyed with pressure to comply with any plans that weren't of his own making, he said, "I'll get home when I get home. You know this is a crazy tourist time of year, Cona, so don't put pressure on me. But anyway, don't worry, and I know what Jesica has planned for tonight. I'll be there for too."

Astrid always put in extra time cleaning the windows and rearranging flowers before family visits at midnight and stayed only long enough to receive the extra tips and to wish her muertitos a Happy New Year. She was always invited to share a glass or two of champagne with generous patrons and to toast the dead ones along with the rest. But before any of that, she never failed to pay a leisurely visit to her own parents. They were buried in a patio at the far end, beyond the gypsy sector, where grave plots were the cheapest.

"Mamá and Papá, you know that I have to be here early because of my work tonight. But here, I brought some wine so that we can make an early toast. She pulled a box of Gato Negro and three plastic cups out of her bag. Pouring a small amount of wine and setting the cups on either side of the granite headstone that she had scrimped and saved for and finally installed ten years ago, she prepared a toast. The engraving on the tomb said, 'Hector Arnoldo Nieves-Villegas, 1930 - 1985 and Rosa Edith Sanchez de las Nieves, 1935-1986. Resting with the angels and dearly missed by their only daughter.' It had taken her a long time to compose that one sentence. She looked at it now and raised her cup. "I hope you and your angels have had a good year. I wonder if you know how things have changed for me recently? Have you been watching? I imagine you have." She paused. "Salud! May the New Year keep you safe and happy." She sipped her wine and sat down on the edge of the narrow board that ran around the perimeter of the plot, preparing, as was the custom, to recount events since her last visit. "It'll be a long time, maybe years, before things are back to normal here, but I thank God you were untouched during the quake. Well, I know you were shaken, as we all were. But I have to say again what a relief it was to see your tomb intact after how everything in so many sectors was ruined. " She patted the headstone and took another sip of wine. "You don't know how lucky you are." She glanced around. "And you don't know how lucky I am."

A light breeze blew across the open ground. This part of the cemetery, although in the open, was one of the most isolated and most barren. It was devoid of trees and grass and its tomb markers were low and flimsy, most of them being thin wooden crosses. Everything hugged the ground so that the wind didn't untie and steal away decorations and so the sun didn't burn them into dry rags and brittle, faded bits of paper that would be stepped on, their precious messages ground into the dust and lost. The quiet absence of colour and adornment gave the impression that this poor sector had an inferiority complex and wanted to retreat into the background to avoid being teased and heckled. "Just leave us to our poorly-dressed selves so we can rest in peace with kindred souls. It's been a life-long habit and there's no need to try to change us now, to glorify our status, make us something we have never been and never will be. Even in death, there is status. And we know we won't achieve recognition. But I wonder, who among you wealthy souls knows of the many true saints that are buried in our patch? And who among you, even if you can point your finger at a saint in your own elegant patio, would have enough money to pay the lawyer in Rome? We know of him – the Saint-Maker – who is really just an Italian public relations expert with Vatican connections. Who among you can raise sufficient funds to beatify one of yours? Not one of you. So leave us." But in spite of this, there existed a few exceptionally lively plots with an unusual number of plastic flowers, and pinwheels with ribbons that blew in the wind, and low metal fences that protected candles lit by believers who prayed for intercession to the saint they had, themselves, sanctified. To hell with the Saint Maker and the cardinals of Rome. The local people could recognise a miracle and heartfelt kindness and extraordinary humanity when they saw it. No need for lobbying, bribery or decrees from on high. No, these local saints were venerated because of their gestures of solidarity for public injustices, or perhaps because of their deeply tragic end, but most importantly because of their kindness, and because they belonged to this patio, to this social position.

There were no such special 'celebrity' plots in the vicinity of Astrid's parents so tourists were few and far between. "I'm happy you have each other for all eternity. I miss you both, but it's satisfying to know that you're together. There's not much activity in these patios and without each other's company you might be bored or lonely. But I would imagine that you can visit old friends. I wouldn't doubt if you have something special planned for tonight." She finished the wine in her glass and poured some more. "I do. I have something planned for tonight. It's rather unorthodox but the opportunity just sort of presented itself, so I'm taking advantage of it. Maybe you deserve credit for understanding things that you might not have been so willing to accept when you were alive. Still, though, I prefer to reserve more details until after the fact. Then I'll come back to visit and tell you all about it." Her cheeks were turning very pink. Astrid was intoxicated not only with wine but with the confidence that Jhonny would accept her invitation for tonight. The anticipation was almost unbearable. Time to go, the wind came up and pulled at her, mussing her hair, tangling her earrings and lifting her skirt, exposing her skimpy black and red San Expedito tanga for all the world to see. She heard her mother gasp. "Don't worry, Mamá. It's not what you think. Drink your wine and toast to the New Year." She quickly punched down the ballooning skirt and walked briskly back to Patio 35 to make small chat with the muertitos as they waited for family to arrive.

Back at Slaughterhouse Square things were jumping. One of the three singers to join Jhonny and the crew that evening turned out to be more of a comedian than a singer. The crowd was hot and extremely responsive. People were laughing uncontrollably and two or three actually rolled off the benches, but it was impossible to say if it was a result of the laughter or the wine. Jibes were thrown as the comedian targeted one poor soul after the other and encouraged the crowd to participate. Hector and Constancia arrived just as the banter intensified. A young man in the crowd who had consumed more than his share of wine, crouched close to the ground and waved his arms for balance as he staggered and hopped towards the centre of the plaza. He paused now and then to reach into his trouser pockets to grab handfuls of rice, which he threw into the air with bluster. The effect was diminished by his drunken efforts, which were too weak to toss it above shoulder height, so the breeze didn't pick it up and it fell flatly to the ground.

However, a skinny tabby cat found it exciting from where he was crouched between the feet of the observers and he lunged into the centre, darting after grains as they landed helter-skelter at the feet of the comedian and the drunken interloper. Not to be upstaged by a cat, much less the young wino, the comedian kicked the cat because it was smaller than the drunk and within reach. He fully expected the crowd to explode with laughter as the poor bony piece of fur went flying and came to rest at the edge of the square near a group of cat-lovers. How was he to know that the secretary of the local animal shelter would be there tonight?

All hell broke loose. The comedian tried in vain to shout out apologies above the din as the animal lovers lunged at him, and right there in front of so many sympathetic, inebriated, and therefore, not very reliable witnesses, they mercilessly beat him to a pulp. Then the whole crowd began to fight, fists flying in every direction. It was a case of hard-drinking animal lovers versus intoxicated human bashers.

After the cat screeched onto the ground at warp speed, causing his brain to rattle inside his small cranium, he came up against a nest of dark brown hair that had the characteristics of a large rat. He instinctively snared it with one paw. Although he was half-starved and lacked strength, when the adrenalin kicked in, the cat had the power of Atlas himself. And being a cat, he chose to play a little before releasing his full fury onto the rat, which didn't respond one iota to the brutal snatch. Disappointed, the cat pawed it again, this time darting in to take a bite out of it. He waited for a reaction. There was none. The cat was so wound up that he didn't care what kind of rat this was, nor was he fearful of the consequences. He grabbed it in his teeth and went running into the centre of the plaza, oblivious to the growing number of guerrilleros who were being punched to the ground all around him. He grappled for control over the rat and he knew he was winning, hands down. Never had his skills been more potent.

The cat dragged the rat to the edges of the skirmish and was settling to teach this cowardly piece of fur a lesson about how to take pride in the fight. That was when Juan, who had carefully sidestepped the activity in order not to muss his suit or fall victim to a loose punch or a coincidental gash on his face, looked down to see the cat at his feet. The cat threw the fur into the air and jumped to grab it. Juggling it with his front paws, he shook it, twisting it about with such fury that he lost control and the rat landed on Juan's polished shoes. Juan shrieked and jumped back, squishing the toes of a fat lady in pink ruffles who cowered behind him. She screamed and swatted him so hard across his cheek that her handprint burned into his skin and his eyes watered.

Constancia, who had only just arrived but who had spotted Jhonny Pretty at the edge of the turmoil, deserted Hector, who, entranced by the violence, was frozen. She ran to Jhonny's rescue, punching the fat pink lady directly in the mouth. It sent Big Pink backwards so abruptly that she lost her balance and knocked herself out on the pavement. Constancia grabbed Jhonny's hand to haul him away from the scene of the crime. But before they could escape, the cat flung the rat so high that it landed on Constancia's chest, hooking itself in the cleavage between her breasts.

Juan was absolutely paralysed with fear because this thing was larger and more repulsive than a mouse. He stood there, eyes glued on the creature that clung to Constancia's breasts and if he could have conjured up a thought, it would have been to question how he would ever bring himself to kiss them later that night.

Constancia outwardly demonstrated courage and valour, but in fact, she was so disgusted with the whole scene because it was not at all how she had envisioned this special evening, that it wasn't bravery but anger that motivated her to kick the cat again and grab the piece of fur that clung for its life to the soft, perfumed skin she had been saving for Jhonny Pretty. She lifted it into the air and was about to fling it with as much force as her feminine style could muster, when she noticed that it had no body and it weighed next to nothing.

She lowered the thing down to examine it more closely. It was a toupee. Clutching the wimpy hair rug to her chest, she scanned the crowd. She spotted a man who was passed out on a bench, his shiny head, which had two tell-tale splotches of cement in the centre, was hanging over the side and his arm dangled limply to the ground. By then, the five drunken machos with the most endurance were still wobbling in the centre of the plaza, but the rest had either drifted away from the action or were down for the count. With Jhonny Pretty in tow, Constancia stepped over the bodies that lay in the path between herself and the man with the glue spots on top of his head. With surprising gentleness she bent down and balanced the hair-rug half on his head and half over his eyes. It was not unlike dressing a mannequin. She patted it into place. "Happy New Year." She looked at her watch and spun on her toes to kiss Jhonny smack on the mouth. "Happy New Year," she repeated. It was two minutes past midnight. Juan wrapped his arms around her like the heroine she was and they locked in a lusty embrace for a solid minute.

Hector, who was no longer spellbound by the brawl, found his way over to Jesica and pulled her to him, as much to convince himself he was still among the living as to wish her a Happy New Year.

Fireworks lit up the downtown sky, casting shadows on the prone bodies littering the Square. Dogs wandered in, sniffed and laid down to sleep in the warm cruxes of elbows and knees.

The foursome broke up with laughter as they piled into the car to make their way to La Cueva. The night was still young.

CHAPTER 29

After the Fireworks

La Cueva did not disappoint. It was rowdy and Hector made frequent pit stops to the men's room because the constant flow of beer and wine led to the steady stream of wallets that slipped all too easily out of back pockets and into Hector's ready palms. He always chose the bars in Ñuñoa for New Years Eve because it was a popular, relatively safe sector and, although it could never be called upper class (such a label would be an insult to its residents), it attracted people with full pocketbooks. On festive occasions such as this, there was always more money than usual and less suspicion and vigilance. In addition, La Cueva didn't employ bathroom attendants, leaving him free to operate unrestricted.

Hector did not disappoint. He waved his hands over the top of the table like a magician and said to the waiter, "I don't want anyone here to see so much as one of the checkers on this table cloth. Do you understand? I want this surface covered at all times with beer and wine and platters of your seafood pizza." "Si, Señor," the young man clicked his heels and saluted with a grin, "Your desire is my command." And that's the way it was – nothing but food and drink and music and boisterous camaraderie. A live band was playing and after plying Jhonny with several glasses of wine, the lead singer cajoled him into jumping up on stage to do a number. The crowd went wild once they understood who had just agreed to croon out the decades-old tune. "Wait until I tell my mother," was whispered all round the room. "She'll start coming here every weekend. My God, I'll have to find a new hangout." Constancia stood at the foot of the stage, arms crossed, one foot tapping out the rhythm as she watched Jhonny perform. When he stepped down from the stage, Hector grabbed him before Constancia could. She shot Hector a glare but let it go. "Jhonny," Hector was excited. "Listen. You've still got it, man! You're still great up there. You should be up on stages much larger than this. The whole country would go wild if you made a comeback."

So it was that plans for Jhonny's renewed music career, with Hector as his manager, were laid during a semi-drunken conversation over a table full of beer at La Cueva.

"Enough. Enough of that, you two. Get your heads over here where they belong. I want you to myself, Jhonny." Constancia slid her arm through his she refused to let go all night. Possessive and appropriately pouty, she threw threatening looks in all directions to ward off flirtatious young autograph seekers, or worse yet... "Don't even think about it. This man is mine." She snuggled close to Jhonny's side at the table and danced around him scandalously so that many of the men in the crowd stopped mid-step to watch her, mouths hanging open only to have them clamped shut with the back of their girlfriends' hands. Jhonny grinned and let her dance. The truth was that most other young women were not interested in the slightest because although there was no doubt about his charm, it was a bit stale for them. Constancia overheard a conversation in the ladies' room. "No, that singer is definitely material for my mother." But not as far as Constancia was concerned. "Stuff your mothers. I would never dream of passing this man on to my mother, even if it was her dying wish."

Meanwhile, Astrid wrapped up her New Year's Eve at the cemetery with butterflies in her stomach. Not because at least drunken four patrons had cried at her feet, telling her how much she was appreciated and how much her work meant to their family; not because of all the extra cash she had crammed into her pocket and stashed in her sock; and not wasn't because she was worried about making it to the cemetery gate without someone with a balaclava jumping out from between the tombs and robbing her. And it certainly wasn't that she was worried about ghosts. It wasn't even about the prospect of the fresh New Year that was bubbling with exciting possibilities. It was for the immediate next three hours, during which time Jhonny Pretty would appear and make her dreams come true.

She missed him during the local fireworks display, which was pitiful compared to the ones downtown and in the east end. For Astrid, though, it was beautiful. She had managed to watch it from her post at Patio 35. It was a much better viewpoint than Patio 62, which is where she had stood every single New Year's Eve for as long as she could remember – another sign, she told herself, that this new year will be glorious. After the fabulous five minutes of exploding colour, which held her and her patrons captive, the glitter was over. However, the cemetery party was not, and she mingled dutifully among patrons as long as she could stand it and then she rushed to the exit.

By the time she reached the cemetery gate, she was out of breath. She asked the gatekeeper to hail a taxi, and it took more than 45 minutes to arrive because it was New Year's Eve and the taxis were busy. This made her more anxious and the butterflies in her stomach multiplied. She could feel them beating up to her throat and she had the urge to vomit. She paced the width of the cemetery entrance what seemed a million times back and forth, opening and closing her fists and then giving in to prayer. "San Expedito, this is a momentous night. Bring me a taxi and I'll be yours forever." Finally a taxi with an old driver who resembled a turtle stopped to let her in. She was too preoccupied to pay attention to the jasmine scent that clung to the interior of the cab, but the taxi driver noticed, "You smell lovely tonight, Señora. Must be a lot of fresh flowers on the grounds tonight."

As the taxi whisked her home, she watched the couples who straggled along the sidewalk arm in arm, the young revellers who wove their way down the side of the road. People poured out onto the streets to party in the open air, traffic be damned. The taxi driver swore under his breath, raised his fist and honked his horn, but they ignored him and he was forced to drive at the breakneck speed of about 25 kilometres per hour. She feared it would be dawn before they arrived and the butterflies in her stomach turned to moths, eating away at her. "I could have walked home faster."

"Do you want to get out right now then? Doesn't matter to me. I've got plenty of other customers tonight. So either stop complaining, or get out now and pay me the full fare."

"Never mind. It's just that I'm in a hurry."

They finally rolled onto her street and the taxi driver slowed down, accepted her money with a growl and was accelerating again before she had even climbed out. "Hurry up lady, this is a busy night." "And Happy New Year to you, too!" She yelled at the back of the taxi. But she refused to let him destroy the mood.

She stood in one spot for a minute surveying the house, trying to see it as a stranger might. But it was too dark to pass judgment.

Hector and Constancia were, without a doubt still at their party that meant she and Jhonny would have the house to themselves. She was positive the directions she had given Jhonny were absolutely clear, but as a last-minute contingency, she had hand-painted a nice little sign with an image of a bowl and the words, 'Rice Pudding Central.' She thought it was genius – positive identification without giving away anything else. Even Constancia and Hector would chuckle when they saw it. True to her word, she flicked on some lights for Jhonny's convenience.

The interior of the house was just as she had left it, her last-minute adjustments producing an attractive ambience for Jhonny's sake.

Although she fully expected a ghost could easily stride into any secure room, out of courtesy, and as a signal, she unlocked and removed the padlock from her bedroom door. She adjusted the silk scarf over the lampshade and ran her hands over the bedspread before quickly undressing and kicking her work clothes under the bed. Now barefoot she tiptoed to the bureau and lifted a corner of the tissue that covered the black negligee. Merely touching it caused lightning to streak through her arm to her heart. Wait until Jhonny sees this. Wriggling into the skimpy panties, she cavorted about the room as she slipped her arms through the translucent jacket and tied it loosely at her breasts. She leaned and posed, triumphant into the mirror, one hip pushed out, arms in the air, palms up. Then keeping her eyes on her smiling reflection, she drew graceful flourishes through the air, bending forward into a bow and then leaning in to kiss the mirror.

She untied her hair and brushed the thick tresses that hung beyond her shoulders. She touched up her lipstick and anointed her throat and chest with the last of her mother's aged Estée Lauder perfume.

The altar was as she had left it, photos draped with scarves. Before walking back to her bedroom door to re-enter and experience the full effect as though for the first time, she lit three of the candles on the altar, arranging one of the scarves so that it partially exposed one of Jhonny's paper faces. She decided at the last minute to turn off her bedside lamp so that the soft yellow candlelight was the only source of illumination. The candles themselves seemed to breath, casting dancing shadows over the wall and photos. Everything was perfect. Now she would simply have to wait patiently for Jhonny's arrival.

She was just about to settle on top of the bed when she remembered one last detail – her ankle bracelets and the foot cream. She massaged the cream around her toes, around her heels and up her calf, enjoying her own touch, gentle fingers against silky feet. Then she kissed each of the San Expedito images before clasping the bracelets and adjusting the pendants. She spread out her toes and her fingers on the bedspread to admire the sultry red polish. Trying not to compare the smooth skin of her pampered feet with the rough knuckles on her hands, she smiled at the overall effect. Finally she lay back on the bed, preparing to surrender herself to Jhonny. She positioned her head on the pillow, face tilted up and slightly sideways, loose hair arranged so that wisps of it ran across her face, adding mystery like a mask at a ball, while most of the tresses radiated out from her head like beams from the sun or the halo in a renaissance painting of the Virgin. Her hips were twisted in an exaggerated curve and at first glance someone might assume her back was broken, her legs together at the ankles, one foot slightly higher than the other, both San Expedito pendants facing out. With one arm curved coyly around the top of her head and the other flat on her belly, she resembled a crooked flamenco dancer who had died then and there on the bed. She laid still, listening, her heart beating and her chest heaving with anticipation. It was shortly before 3 a.m. when she eventually drifted off, but she managed to maintain her orchestrated posture in her semi-sleep state.

The festive foursome abandoned La Cueva at about 3 a.m. and Jesica slid in behind the wheel of the Volvo Amazon. She snuck along streets less travelled to avoid police traffic patrols, who half-enforced recently implemented laws against drunk driving. It was one of the country's efforts to bring themselves in line with more developed nations. But one of the popular spin-offs of the impaired-driving law was a booming business for drunken men who also owned donkey carts. Since they could not be pulled over for driving donkey carts while intoxicated, they were free to enjoy a full night out themselves. On top of that they proceeded to pile fellow drunks into their carts and delivered them to their front doors for a fee. The scene was reminiscent of bringing out the dead during the plague of the Dark Ages except that in this case, angry wives met the donkey cart and dragged the bodies back inside. It was not always an easy job for the operator of this business because he was the only semi-conscious man at the scene and had to take the brunt of the wife's anger. In extreme cases, he charged a higher fee to the men whose wives had a reputation for being particularly violent. For verbal abuse the charge was an extra 500 pesos up front, but if the wife habitually met him at the door with a stick, an additional fee of 1000 pesos was the minimum up-front charge. Jesica swerved to avoid collisions with two different donkey cart drivers on their journey through the side streets of Recoleta. Considering her own inebriated state and the mumbled directions to Hector's house, she congratulated herself for arriving at all, let alone without mishap.

The four of them tumbled out of the car and swaggered into the front door, all whispering and trying to suppress their giggles so that they wouldn't disturb Astrid, who, if she wasn't still out partying with her old friends at the cemetery, which was unlikely, she would already be in bed, exhausted from a long night's work. Upon entry, Hector's bulky shoulder knocked down Astrid's clever rice pudding sign, making it invalid. The house was as quiet as a tomb, and Hector signalled to Constancia when he spied Astrid's purse on the shelf near the door. Best not to disturb her; they'd wish her a Happy New Year in the morning. Hector led them in, silently shushing the others with his finger as they tiptoed into the living room.

Earlier, when the taxi had pulled up with Astrid, Luisa Rocio slinked undetected, out of the back seat, and stood beside the house, ghostly and transparent, the breeze carrying her tell-tale scent upwind. She gazed around the dark street. Not sure what to make of the strange surroundings nor how she would use her presence to protect Astrid, she decided to scout around the neighbourhood for signs of danger and/or Jhonny Pretty. She was out on her reconnaissance mission and was lost in the local maze when the merry foursome arrived.

"Well, Happy New Year." Hector whispered coarsely as he saluted to Jhonny and Constancia. "Que les vaya bien." He was grinning a silly, drunken grin as he pulled Jesica down the hall.

"And may it go well with you too, brother." Constancia held Jhonny firmly by the hand and they waited for Hector and Jesica to disappear behind his bedroom door. She turned to Jhonny and gave him a long, open-mouthed kiss, to which he responded enthusiastically. However, for no apparent reason, upon entering the little house he had begun to feel uneasy. Maybe another drink would soothe the apprehension. "Let's have one more drink to the New Year."

"Okay, sit here and I'll be right back." She directed him to the sofa.

She returned with a bottle of Casillero del Diablo cabernet sauvignon and two glasses. "I stashed this away a few months ago. Something one of my clients gave me. I was saving it for a special occasion." She smiled sweetly and poured them each a full glass. "And this is it. To us, Jhonny."

"To us." He allowed himself to look her fully in the eyes as they clinked their glasses, something so simple, but he couldn't remember ever doing it before, really looking straight into her eyes. He had never in his life had a serious, long-term relationship. Therefore, something must be affecting him; perhaps it was old age creeping up, or maybe it was because he was sleeping with death every night. Be that as it may, he wanted to concentrate fully on Constancia.

Even though she complied with his request for a drink, knowing it would delay the inevitable lovemaking, he could see that the late hour and the amount of alcohol she had consumed – although it didn't diminish her desire – had depleted her stamina. She was trying to keep up and he admired her for it. The power and confidence he felt from the Viagra that Hector had slipped him at La Cueva was an unfair advantage. What was he going to say to her in the morning? He fully planned to sleep the whole night with this woman and not run away before dawn, as was his habit. He took pity on her for the late hour and was making an effort to push aside the grey shadows that had haunted him since he entered the house. She was wilting and she lost the grip on her glass, but Juan gently pulled it away and set it on the table before it crashed to the floor.

"Let's make our own fireworks, shall we? Why don't we bring in the New Year with a proper bang?"

By now, her eyes were closed, but she laughed. "Okay, Jhonny. Just give me a few minutes to wash and get ready. I have something special for you." She struggled to open her eyes but managed only a squint. She bumped into the walls on the way to the bathroom and he heard her fumble and swear at the door handle before finally entering one of the rooms somewhere towards the back of the house. She managed, "I'll call you when I'm ready." Juan helped himself to a glass of water from the kitchen sink and splashed his face to freshen up a bit before his important performance and then drew out his last cigarette. Constancia was taking forever and he began to wonder if she had passed out. But he would be patient. He sank down into the sofa to smoke as he waited and began to hum a few bars "Fumar es un placer, genial, sensual. Fumando espero la mujer que quiero..."

As if on cue, Astrid woke up. Jhonny was here! Her heart skipped a beat. Excited, she clutched the bed covers but maintained her choreographed posture.

"Jhonny, I'm in here. Come to me now."

It was the signal he had been waiting for. He walked to the far end of the hall and entered the dimly lit room that smelled of candle wax and an identifiable musky perfume. He could see the shapely body under the transparent negligee, the invitation he'd been waiting for all night. No need to waste time.

Juan hummed as he undressed, casually at first, as the female shape on the bed teased him with her silent observation and an occasional throaty moan. He dropped his jacket on the floor and threw his shirt into the air, vaguely aware that it landed somewhere near the candles on the bureau. He dropped his trousers, kicked off his shoes and scrambled less than heroically onto the bed beside her. She rolled to one side, showing him her back and said, "Jhonny, hold me." Still wearing his socks and reeking of wine, he lay down to spoon her, and then he pulled her around and kissed her throat. She threw her arms around him, and pulled him down so she could feel the weight of him on top of her. "Oh, Jhonny, you feel so alive."

"You make me that way. I've never felt this way about anyone before."

Astrid was so excited she was delirious. "You are exquisite, mi amor," was all she could say. After that, she closed her eyes and her mind went blank.

Juan was unable to contain his own excitement and the whole thing lasted about three minutes. Viagra at its best. But in that time, Astrid's heart was pounding like it hadn't pounded in years. Could she be dreaming all of this? She ran her fingers across Jhonny's naked back and down to his buttocks, feeling the muscles tighten as he rose up and down on top of her own eager body. She could smell his sweat, the wine and the cigarettes. He was as real as any man could be.

She had fantasized about this moment for months and just as she felt herself reaching a climax, the blood rushing through never land, her pulse pounding hard in her ears, there was an excruciating pain stabbing into her chest. And simultaneously, she became conscious of the physical incongruity that she knew about ghosts – Jhonny shouldn't have been able to do this. It was a miracle. She reached far into her mind looking for San Expedito. She needed to thank him but instead, her thoughts ran back to Jhonny singing just for her, "This Moment is Forever."

She opened her eyes, just as Jhonny, his taut muscles suddenly relaxing as he released a long, throaty groan, was satisfied beyond words with his own intense orgasm. But she was startled by a sudden movement at the side of the bed and unwilling to turn her face away from Jhonny, she snuck a sideways glance. Standing boldly at the side of the bed, arms akimbo, looking over them in their moment of untamed rapture was none other than Jhonny's mother. Astrid watched in stunned wonder as, just beyond Jhonny's mother, the wall behind the altar suddenly burst into flame. She saw the sleeve of Jhonny's shirt rise up in the smoke, like the arm of a lost warrior.

All of this – Jhonny's rapturous and much too-human presence, the sight of his mother, and the flaming wall – was more than her heart could bear. The pain in her chest increased and she tried to cry out but she couldn't breathe. She gasped. Incredulous and focusing on the figure at her side, her eyes bulged and filled with tears. But then she remembered Jhonny, her lover, her soul mate, her eternal protector, and when she turned to look up at him, an overwhelming sensation of love and devotion washed through her stressed body and provided an ethereal calm. She smiled and exhaled her final breath.

Just when it occurred to Juan that he had selfishly allowed his pleasure to obliterate the vision of the woman he was with, and that he ought to have been a more considerate lover, he became aware of a sharp change in the atmosphere. His hair stood on end and he was suddenly filled with horror, not because he could sense his lover was having a heart attack – he wasn't even looking at her – but because he detected the familiar and detested scent of jasmine, which provoked him to turn and see Luisa Rocio, who was leering into his face.

He brutishly disconnected himself from the body of his lover to lunge at Luisa Rocio and he fell right through her to the floor. When he looked up, he saw the flames on the back wall and there were several images of his own face in their midst, curling, his smile distorting and turning black before disintegrating into ash and floating up in the smoke. He grabbed his shoes and ran out of the room directly for the street. He paused, suddenly realising that he needed to rescue Constancia but the ghost of Luisa Rocio was coming at him, fingers red and sharp as knives, ready to scratch his face off. Her own eyes reflected the fire, now roaring as the entire back of the house was in flames. Heavy smoke rolled out from the ends of her wild grey hair. In her fury, she momentarily lost both oversized pink Adidas. Hideous long toenails curled out like swords to cut him off at the knees. Her skeleton was visible through her cotton skirt and patched woollen sweater. He could hear the bones clatter as she raged towards him, arms outstretched, teeth gnashing. Piercing screeches erupted between her deep growls. Still naked, he turned and bolted down the street clutching his shoes. In his haste to cover his ears he dropped his shoes on the side of the road and he sprinted barefoot beyond Recoleta, across the bridge of the Rio Mapocho and didn't slow until he reached the silent metal kiosks of the booksellers on San Diego Street, where he huddled for several minutes to catch his breath. Snatching a couple of posters to cover up his nakedness, he continued at a wild pace along the deserted streets. Confetti from the New Year's Eve festivities stuck to the bottom of his feet. He kicked aside empty beer cans and avoided broken wine bottles at the curbs. Terrified, he looked over his shoulder at regular intervals, but the old ghost was nowhere to be seen. Luckily for him she had stopped to retrieve her pink Adidas and lost his trail. Finally he reached Franklin and found himself at the fringes of the Persa Bío Bío. He made his way to Slaughterhouse Square where he sank down onto the ground at the back door of Mario's restaurant, grateful for something cold and familiar. He leaned his head against the metal shutter and cried. Only then did he feel any remorse for leaving the scene and deserting Constancia, who seemed to have fainted from the anxiety caused by the same ugly ghost who had forced him to abandon the scene.

Only seconds after Juan had fled the scene and the house was engulfed in flames, Constancia, Hector and Jesica escaped out the front door. They huddled together coughing and crying, Constancia draped in a sheer black robe and Hector and Jesica wrapped together in a sheet. The volunteer fire department was helpless under the extremely dry conditions. In addition, it was New Year's Day and most of the brigade was still partying. It took awhile to rouse and ready those who were available because it was, after all, the first big holiday of the year. And when they finally arrived on the scene, under-staffed and disorganised, they discovered that the children had been playing in the fire hydrants again and there was not enough pressure to use the hoses. So the only thing they could do was stand and watch with the rest of the crowd, which had grown to more than two hundred people and included cameras and crew from three national television stations.

Constancia's drawn, tear-stained face pleaded into the camera for help and prayers for her mother and her boyfriend. Hector and Jesica stood at her side, heads lowered, unable to comprehend the tragic event. Surely it was not true that two people had perished in this fire, one of them a famous rock star. And surely it couldn't be true that the family was now destitute and that two loving children had to bury their mother, a well-respected cemetery caretaker, whose seasonal bonuses, which wouldn't have covered the cost of her funeral in any case, had gone up in smoke along with every other possession in the house. Such a sad state after they, like their neighbours, had only just begun to rebuild after the earthquake. Where was the justice?

Hogar de Cristo, Chile's biggest charity would be on the scene within minutes to provide basic clothing and shelter for at least a few nights. Hector did manage to say a few words about the boyfriend, because his sister who was far too distraught to carry on, had moved over to the curb where she squatted in her robe and was muttering, "Mamá, Jhonny. Jhonny, Mamá."

"Our dear companion and someone the whole country knows and loves for his gift of music, Jhonny Pretty from Jhonny Pretty y los Rockeros was the other victim of this terrible tragedy. We have lost our own mother and the country has lost one of its legends. These are profound losses, both on a personal and a national level, made worse by the fact that Jhonny Pretty was about to embark on a comeback."

Meanwhile, Astrid's charred, smoking corpse lay undisturbed on her bed, but it was still nothing compared to the sizzling passion she had felt just before she died. Later the coroner, known as Dr Death, not only because of his routine encounters with corpses but because of his grey-white complexion inherited from Scandinavian ancestors, would comment into the microphones that were shoved into his face, "I've never seen such an expression of satisfaction on the face of someone who has died under such cruel and tragic circumstances. This poor Señora suffered a massive heart attack, but by all appearances, it was kind to her." Constancia and Hector embraced this small comfort.

After chasing Juan Bonifacio down the street until she had to stop for her shoes and lost sight of him, Luisa Rocio returned to Astrid's side. It would take awhile before Astrid's spirit would realise she had moved to 'the other side.' Meanwhile, Luisa Rocio would be here to protect her and she contemplated whether it was in Astrid's best interest to know the degree to which the degenerate slime ball known as Jhonny Pretty had taken advantage and finally defiled her.

CHAPTER 30

New Digs for One and All

The cemetery newsletter 'Stiffs and Ash' published an article that read in part: "With the sudden and grievous loss of two of Santiago General Cemetery's long-time and best-loved caretakers, things will never be the same. Señora Astrid de las Nieves passed away in the early morning hours of New Year's Day in a tragic house fire that left her family homeless and destitute. Señora Ruby Oreno-Valdivia, her long time friend and companion decided to retire after hearing this sad news, saying she could no longer face Patio 35 without her best friend and valued co-worker." The article went on to detail information about the funeral arrangements and burial plans for Astrid de las Nieves.

Señor Rodriguez-Gomez, a patron of Patio 35 offered to construct a mausoleum for Astrid de las Nieves and her family in this same Patio 35 because it was familiar ground for Astrid. She will always be close to her beloved muertitos, and friends and family will have convenient visitor access.

Luisa Rocio was particularly thrilled with the plans for the new mausoleum because it meant she could move out of Mercedes de la Fuentes' depressing, low-class, unkempt niche and accompany Astrid to her new home. The plans were to complete the construction of the new family mausoleum within a couple of months. Meanwhile, Señor Rodriguez-Gomez had arranged for Astrid to be laid to rest in a three-month rental niche, which would have been occupied by his own son Adolfo Rodriguez-Rodriguez had they not cremated him instead and used the urn for a doorstop in his old bedroom.

Only a week had passed since the senseless tragedy and Astrid was still lost between heaven and earth. Once in awhile Luisa Rocio caught a glimpse of her, still dressed in the black baby dolls. She was concerned about running around barefoot since she had always been very protective of her feet and for this reason, when she walked, she avoided stepping on the daisies (which were plentiful on the path to heaven). At the same time, she was pleasantly surprised to find that her toenails and fingernails never chipped and the nail polish maintained its freshly painted finish.

Her funeral service was the most elegant the caretakers had participated in for years. Hundreds of mourners attended the outdoor affair to say goodbye and to support her two surviving children. Hector hadn't eaten since the night of the fire and as a consequence, he looked trim and fit in the new suit that Jesica had begged from a friend. Constancia threatened to revive the eternally dark Gothic style and wear it for the rest of her life, but Jesica talked her out of it, reminding her that her mother would probably not approve, and besides, it was a fad that had faded away, to be maintained only by the most stubborn of transvestites. In addition, Constancia's boss offered to let her choose several new outfits from the shop provided she remembers to tell everyone where they came from. It would generate sympathetic customers and such public relations opportunities were rare and valuable.

It was the cemetery manager, himself a retired pastor, who directed the service. "Astrid de las Nieves was a sister we shall never forget. She first worked as a child in these sacred grounds alongside her mother, who was also a highly respected and much loved caretaker. She was devoted to our muertitos and now finds herself among them." At this point, Constancia released a loud wail and Hector tightened his arm around her shoulder. "Let there be no doubt that she is among friends, the same friends she has taken care of, who she talked to and shared jokes with every day, whose tombs she washed and groomed. She is no stranger to these, the Lord's holy fields, where, today she walks hand in hand with the angels, and together with them and Jesus and the Virgin, she now looks down upon and protects each one of us." Constancia's knees were weak and she fell to the ground at the base of the wall, into which, on the fourth level from the bottom, her mother's casket had just been introduced and the cement worker, also her friend, was crying silently as he sealed it with fresh cement. The mourners looked on in silence.

"Let us pray for our beloved Astrid, may she rest in peace and may she watch over us poor sinners as she watched over those who went before her."

The crowd obediently bowed their heads and murmured "Amen" in the appropriate places. It was at this poignant juncture that the pastor nodded to Juan Bonifacio, known to those here as Jhonny Pretty, and he raised his voice to the heavens in song for Astrid.

Juan had become aware of the poor woman's demise two days after he fled from the scene. Because the house had been asleep when he arrived with Hector and Constancia, he assumed she was still out somewhere enjoying a New Year's celebration. He hadn't noticed Hector nudging Constancia and pointing at their mother's purse on the shelf.

He was so terrified by the unexpected intrusion of the ugly ghost during his moment of intimacy with Constancia, that it was only after he lay quivering at Mario's door, he realised he'd left her alone to burn in the fire. There was no doubt in his mind, by the way, that this deformed pile of bones that kicked about in her own foul air in the pair of too-big pink Adidas, had caused the fire. But that was beside the point. The problem was that he had shown himself and Constancia, the woman he loved (he dared to say it aloud to himself – "the woman I love") that he was nothing more than a selfish coward and he couldn't see how redemption would ever be possible. He agonised over the tragedy and his absence from the scene, made worse for not knowing the condition of Constancia, Jesica and Hector. What if they had all perished? If he had been horrified by that evil, clanking bag of wrinkles and her screeches from hell, how had they survived the demon's attack? What if all three of them perished? Even if they escaped the scorching heat, how had they eluded the sinister old spirit?

When Mario arrived to unlock the restaurant later that afternoon he encountered Juan, his hair singed, his naked skin dark as charcoal, on the ground, leaning into the door, hugging his knees. He lifted his haggard face and it was wet with tears.

Alarmed, Mario pulled him to his feet, shoved him inside and locked the door behind them inside, "What the hell happened to you, my friend? You're a wreck."

Juan's jumbled phrases did nothing to elucidate and finally Mario ignored his efforts, understanding only that he needed some clothes, a cup of tea, a sandwich and a bed. The tea and sandwich were easy, he found old trousers and a t-shirt stuffed into a corner shelf of the storeroom behind the kitchen, which is where he also convinced Juan to rest onto the flea-infested mattress until he could make some sense of his situation.

Juan slept until the next day. He didn't notice Mario locking the door that night, making him prisoner on the no man's land where cockroaches bustled between the greasy pots and cardboard boxes of unrefrigerated vegetables. Even if he had, he was too weak to protest.

When he heard the key in the lock the next day, he raised himself to his elbows and whispered hoarsely, "Mario, what day is it?"

After sponging off in the public bathroom next door, Juan returned to sit down and have a cup of tea with Mario. He recounted the tumultuous events of New Year's Eve, excluding any mention of the ghost. No point in creating questions about his sanity.

Theme music for the national news blared from the small television that hung in the far corner of the restaurant, followed by a montage of images to recap of the week's stories. Both men turned to stare up at it.

The colour drained from Juan's face when he saw Constancia and Jesica, each leaning into Hector, who was explaining to the world how they were devastated by the death of their mother, who they lost in a house fire along with all of their possessions. They were in the dark, at the curb, huddled together in a sheet. Jesica looked boldly into the camera but Constancia's eyes were lowered, her face swollen with grief. Hector was saying, "And we lost a friend too. They haven't found his body, but the fire fighters are still working to clear away the rubble." The reporter cut to some new footage, which showed Hector, Constancia and Jesica standing in the same spot they had been the night of the fire. Now, two days later and in the light of day, although fully clothed, they were still the image of tragedy itself. The reporter held the microphone in front of each of them in turn, but Hector was the only one with anything to say. "We are crushed by the loss of our dear mother, who we found in her bed, where we are told, she appears to have had a heart attack and died without feeling the torture of the flames and smoke. We thank God for this small mercy. But our good friend, who many of you may remember was one of Chile's most well known rockeros of the 70s, Jhonny Pretty, is missing. They're still trying to locate his remains, but we've been told that he disappeared like a ghost in the night. It's possible that he fell into one of the sinkholes left by the earthquake. After the quake, we covered those holes as best we could, given our poor situation but the fire would have weakened the repairs. The firemen are looking."

"And the cause of the fire?" the reporter wanted to prolong the interview for its sensational value. "No... I don't know. Our house was old... they're still investigating. Maybe it was an electrical short, again maybe faulty wiring from our recent repairs, perhaps a cigarette (my mother smoked), or maybe some candles that were left burning here and there, or the fireman said that, since it was New Year's Eve, it might have even been some stray fireworks." The three of them pushed their way past the reporter who persisted. "And do you have family with whom you are staying now?"

Jesica jumped in, "They're staying at my house. They'll live with me now." Hector and Constancia huddled close to her and they walked in unison into the wreckage to look for Jhonny Pretty's body and any valuables that could have survived the inferno. The reporter turned to the camera. "This was indeed a tragic night for this close family. And also a dark night for Chilean music-lovers who will remember that the last time

Jhonny Pretty y los Rockeros were in the news, it was a terrible bus accident that brought an end to the legendary band. We will follow up on this and report back with any new developments."

Now it was Mario who dropped a mouthful of rice when his jaw fell. He turned to Juan and raised his eyebrows.

Juan was shaking. "I have to go. Mario, can I borrow 300 pesos for the bus?"

Mario rose to his feet and emptied the contents of his pockets onto the table. "Take it all, my friend."

Juan scooped up the coins and left for Jesica's place.

CHAPTER 31

Newsworthy

Juan hadn't attended a funeral since the death of his own mother, God rest her soul, and although he had never been fortunate enough to have met Constancia's mother, he now felt that he knew her intimately.

When it was confirmed that all of the de las Nieve's family photos had burned in the fire, a friend named Susana came forward with a 30-year-old photo of a young Astrid. She had it enlarged and framed and set it on the casket during the wake. Later it would be enclosed behind the glass of the niche. Juan was surprised by the striking resemblance that Constancia bore to her mother, jovial and bright as she appeared in the picture. He felt a charitable sentiment towards, and a special bond with her. Susana insisted that Astrid's tomb be decorated with several replicas of her favourite San Expedito medallions (something she had grown extremely fond of during the past couple of months) and she offered to donate some El Ritmo magazines that she had scrounged because of Astrid's love for the 70s music of Jhonny Pretty y los Rockeros. It was with this knowledge that Hector and Constancia insisted there could be no funeral without Jhonny Pretty singing at least two of Astrid's favourite songs.

On cue, he began with 'Softly' and between songs he said simply, and with heartfelt respect for the newly deceased, "This one is for you, Señora Astrid – now and for every single time I sing it in the future. And for anyone who hears it from this moment on, they will think of you." He was certain he believed what he had just said, and he began, acapella 'This is the Moment of Forever.' Within no time the patio was converted into a symphony of uncontrollable sobs, punctuated at the end with the trumpeting sound of a crowd blew their collective noses. The song, which would forever after bear a funereal aspect, was suspended in time on the gentle breeze that circulated the cemetery, bowing at the tombs of presidents and war heroes and genuflecting before Holy Family icons and local saints.

With the ritual blessing and speeches drawing to an end, Juan allowed himself to venture a look down the path towards his family mausoleum. It was quiet there, the soft breeze not disturbing the peace. It all looked normal, and there was no sign of the wicked bag of bones who had disguised herself as his mother. He had half expected to see her perched smugly on his front steps, just waiting for his inevitable return. "Well, not today, you old bag. Not today, and maybe not ever." And the caretaker was nowhere in sight either.

That day, Patio 35 had also been home to a media scrum. Normally, as a follow-up to the more sensational fire story on New Year's Eve, one or two local television stations might have appeared to scan the crowd and then transmit a clip that would be edited down to five seconds. But the presence of Jhonny Pretty provided a whole new angle. Television and radio crews were elbowing each other for the best vantage point. A fight broke out at the edge of the crowd when a young woman reporter from 'The Voice' said she deserved a position in the front because the cult following of her paper appreciated Jhonny Pretty and what he represented more than any other population demographic. "Let me get for them what is expected," she insisted. She was immediately silenced by a brusque, "Get to one side, you ignorant little commie," as a large cameraman deliberately stepped on her toe. She wailed, "You son of a bitch. This is gender and political discrimination and you'll pay for it."

The story that ran in The Voice that week began and ended with the incendiary treatment their reporter had received at the hands of another reporter from a mainstream media giant, which was driven by corporate greed. It was accompanied by a photo of Jhonny Pretty standing amongst the crowd at the cemetery wall, microphone in hand, looking up to the heavens. The caption read, "Jhonny Pretty sings for el pueblo, raising his voice in support of victims of natural and man-made disasters."

The television stations, too, chose to focus on Jhonny Pretty. "The famous victim of a terrible tragedy more than two decades ago, singer, Jhonny Pretty re-surfaces in the face of another tragic incident. And now he sings in honour of the victim and her family." Preferring not to wrap the story in politics, their plan was to attract viewers who were sympathetic to a personal tragedy. It was a success. Tears welled up in the eyes of the television viewers who were glued to their screens with their cup of tea and sandwich. They would tune in again for the 9 p.m. edition so they could watch and weep once more. The story of the terrible death by fire of the otherwise anonymous cemetery caretaker was on the tongues of everyone who remembered and loved Jhonny Pretty. Thus Astrid de las Nieves literally became famous by accident.

'Stiffs and Ash' was the only publication that saw through to the heart of the disaster. The headline on the front page of its special four-page edition in ominous black type, "Our sister Astrid, victim of a sinister accident," replaced the usual table of contents which habitually announced cola bottle decorating courses, dry flower arrangements, advice about hygiene, and warnings about superstitious gothic transvestites. "We grieve the loss of our dear sister and companion, Astrid de las Nieves. Like the angel she was in life, she now watches over us as our celestial guardian from on high, coordinating her good works with Jesus and the Virgin to protect and guide you through the rest of your own earthly existence. Señor Rodriguez-Gomez, who asked to remain anonymous as the donor of her niche and the constructor of an entire Astrid de las Nieves y Familia mausoleum, in his wisdom encourages all of you to pray to Astrid de las Nieves for intercession. The Church will also accept donations towards a fund to beatify this good woman, for there is no question as to her saintly qualities." Susana provided Astrid's photo for this too, but it was overshadowed by a decision by the newsletter editor who also did the layout and considered himself something of an artist. He took the opportunity to demonstrate his talent by superimposing Astrid's face into the centre of a flower. Its petals radiating outwards, and like the sun itself, Astrid appeared to be lighting up the planet.

Before long, and because the Church and the cemetery chief administrator understood their own people, they would profit from the sale of candles to be lit at the foot of Astrid's tomb, and also from the beatification fund, which could never possibly reach the required amount for official saint-making. Therefore local administrators would inevitably spend it. Astrid's death would be indirectly responsible for the administrator's new suit, his wife's renovated living room, not to mention the exotic leather boots, tangas and long-sleeved satin shirts that he bought for himself and his boyfriend to enjoy on a Saturday night. The priest was able to buy expensive bottles of wine, lobster and foreign cuts of meat to be served for dinner with the archbishop and for when he entertained the occasional young, religious movie starlet in need of a shepherd.

CHAPTER 32

The Wake

Juan did not have to beg forgiveness for his cowardly behaviour the night of the fire. Contrite as he felt, he was not permitted to finish his first sentence, "Oh Constancia, my love, I was sick with grief and it was not possible..."

She lifted her puffy face and touched her fingers to his lips. "Shh, light of my life, no need for explanations. I just want you here with me. You can't imagine how utterly destroyed we all were. First with my mother's... her..." she faltered, unable to pronounce the word and had to blink back the tears. "Then we didn't know where you were. We were so afraid. No one could eat or sleep. We all sat at Jesica's house like zombies. No one talked, we just moved about in a trance. Our loss was too much to bear, Jhonny, too much." And she sobbed into his shoulder.

Juan had suffered on his way over to Jesica's, fearful of their reaction. But he had to tell them something, anything. He sat on the bus, praying they would accept him and understand, blind to each street the bus trundled past. He was deaf to vendors who jumped on board and yelled over the roar and rattle of the vehicle, and he was oblivious to the raucous activity of football fans who piled into the seats around him. He was exhausted and guilty and had no fight left in him. When a hooligan loomed over him, he gave him his seat like a gentleman abdicating to an elderly lady. Fortunately something in his numb brain nudged him towards the door when the bus reached the stop near Jesica's house, and he limped off.

He pushed the buzzer at her front gate and waited listlessly. Mourners turned their heads to look out the window. They began pointing at him and he saw their mouths moving. More heads turned and new faces, animated, appeared at the window. The sudden furore inside culminated with Constancia screeching and barrelling towards him with outstretched arms, Hector and Jesica on her heels. The four of them crying as they clung to each other. Constancia, who was hanging on Jhonny, fainted and Hector had to bundle her up in his arms and carry her inside, Jesica and Jhonny following, their hands on Hector's shoulders.

The charred body of their mother was lying in a closed casket in the living room. Strangers occupied the chairs that were lined up on either side. Juan nodded politely and stopped to touch the foot of the casket in a gesture of respect and mourning. He followed the other three into the kitchen where at first they sat in silence. Then as if awakened by the same electric prod, they fought to begin telling the story each from their own perspective.

Hector won out. "My friend, we thought you were nothing but a heap of charcoal, in a hole under the floor. You wouldn't have had a chance. The old house ignited so fast. It was like an explosion."

"But we looked for you, Jhonny." Constancia's face was testament to their efforts, which had been in vain. "The firemen told us that we couldn't get any closer because of the heat. The house is still smouldering. There was no water in the hydrants. We're lucky to be alive, any of us."

"Hector and I ran out after we heard Constancia screaming. But when we opened the bedroom door, the flames just blew all over. Jesica passed out and I had to drag her away. If ever there was hell on earth, that was it."

Unable to repress his own story, Juan interjected. "I know. It was hell on earth. I felt the bony hands of the devil grabbing for me, and that's when I ran out. A creature from hell chased me out of the house and I lost my senses. My God, I lost my mind. It came after me. I couldn't stop to think. I couldn't stop to breathe. I had to run. I had to escape the clutches of this monster that was this close to grabbing me by the throat and choking me. It was as real as the fire itself, and I swear it was the cause of the whole thing."

The three of them looked at him, jaws on the table. "I know you think I'm a coward. And I don't deserve your forgiveness. I'll get up and walk away right now if you want. But it was el diablo who was in those flames and whose fingers reached out from the smoke. I have no doubt about it. I don't know why it attacked me, but I do know that if I wouldn't have run, I would be nothing but a charred mass under your floorboards." He rose up from his chair and Constancia pulled at his sleeve.

"No Jhonny, don't say any more. Don't blame yourself. Don't go. If you say it was the devil, then it was the devil. And we all know that the devil waits for no one."

Hector jumped in again. "It was all so fast. The place exploded. It was an inferno, and there's no doubt it was set by the devil himself. We didn't even find Mamá until the next morning. It was just too hot. We were all praying that she was at Señora Ruby's house. We knew deep down that Mamá had been taken, but anyway, we prayed for her safety and willed her to be okay." He looked over at Constancia, who had dropped her head onto the table and whose shoulders were shaking with sobs. "Okay," he said, "That's enough. We're here now and we don't need to drag ourselves through the pain again. I say we pay respects to Mamá by celebrating her life and then make our plans to move forward. What do you say, Cona? Mamá wouldn't want us to live in the past, especially an agonising one. Besides, she's watching over us all right now. And she's serene and nothing else can hurt her. Just remember that."

CHAPTER 33

Life Beyond

Experience is embedded in the depths of each atom of energy, taking it beyond terrestrial and even universal matter, to re-emerge amongst the mysterious existence of the eternal beyond.

Every second of Astrid's life passed in front of her eyes and she relived them as exquisite sensual experiences, having the power to feel the poignancy of each event in a way that had not even been possible in the living moments, let alone later whenever she had called it to memory. It was at once excruciating and beautiful.

Not only did she recall the important milestones of her life, as one would do while alive – such as her first day at school, leaving her studies to work with her mother on Patio 62, her first kiss, her first night with the organ grinder, her wedding, the births of her children, the death of her parents, the first big earthquake, the second big one, her introduction to Luisa Rocio, and finally Jhonny Pretty's entrance into her life – but each minimal event of her entire existence reappeared to shape her soul and then to release her from these same past experiences.

As if emerging from a fog or a deep sleep, she gradually became aware of being in another world. Well, it could not be described as a world because worlds are finite. This existence was limitless in its beauty and freedom – no barriers, no props of any kind, not even any clouds to lounge on, tranquil lakes to wade through, or meadows to prance across. And time did not exist. Not only was the concept of time foreign, but nothing was governed by it. She was clearly somewhere beyond. Later, as she leisurely turned over the events of her life like a magician turning over the cards in his deck, she understood how she could manipulate an isolated moment in time, juxtaposing it with another, to build meaning and consequence. She could have played her cards differently while she was alive and it would have been an entirely different experience, resulting in a different Astrid – same name, maybe even the same deck of cards, but definitely a distinct outcome. She played with various combinations and stopped when she realised how infinite the possibilities were.

It was as if time was gravity, and she now lived in a weightless place with the ability to turn and tumble herself and the events of her life, to comprehend them in terms of the energy they generated. She could superimpose one event over one another. For instance, it was possible to contemplate her first day at school and her last day on earth simultaneously, each one weighing equally in terms of importance. This was also true of an instant where she recalled swatting a fly over the dinner table. She considered it in the same light as the day she packed the organ grinder's belongings and kicked him out. One event was as significant as the other. In life, killing a fly would have been of no consequence, but in this ethereal existence it was obvious that the energy that was knocked out of the fly had dynamic implications, not only at that present moment, but into the future. It was similar to a ripple effect over still water. The fly's death echoed throughout existence; the energy required to swat the life out of it, as well as the conversion of that energy from life to death, expanded and took on another form. For example, it could have flown up to the sun and became a beam of light that glinted back at her from Jhonny's eyes. So, if she thought it through to its logical end, it meant that if she had never killed that fly, which was a nuisance over her dinner that day, the glint in Jhonny's eye might not have appeared, or it might have been a different kind of glint. This then called into question the idea of destiny and just exactly how far back one went to trace the consequences of their own decisions, and if, in fact, they could really interpret or manipulate these consequences at all.

In addition, being only one of a great multitude of human and inhuman beings, all of whom were acting and reacting, one was not in control of the spin of the earth, so to speak. Because of the expanding effect of innumerable inanimate objects reacting with each other, the possible results of all of this activity were infinite. Mathematically impossible to calculate, numbers bulged to mind-numbing concepts and back on earth it was a huge mystery, but here, beyond life, it was of no consequence; existence was just recycled energy.

Given that the mind boggling possibilities were impossible to compute or predict human beings had to accept that they were capable of dealing only with day-to-day decisions or planning for the short-term. The expectation of anything more would have paralysed people with fear of universal reprisal. Paradoxically, it was this infinite lack of control that provided peace of mind.

Lounging about in a celestial blue space that she could not identify, Astrid understood all of this and, although she could see the events of her life and identify what she would have called mistakes, perhaps even going so far as to regret her decisions, she saw how they were at once both inconsequential and relevant, and she was able to forgive herself. In addition to being able to forgive herself, she saw that the energy from her mistakes collided with reactions of other individuals and, as the energy was released into the universe, the result was often pleasant. She was not privy to the events of the lives of others and they didn't interest her; they were only effects of energy as it evolved and dissipated into the universe. What would have been cause for curiosity on earth had, at this level, become complacent understanding. No struggles, no questions, only answers and unlimited knowledge and wisdom. She was in the Garden of Eden but this time the fruit was not forbidden. She realised that this place was very probably what people on earth referred to as heaven.

She was kicking back with something like a large mango milkshake (she discovered that props didn't exist unless one conjured them up at will, which appeared to be perfectly acceptable), admiring the condition of her virgin feet, when she saw Jhonny Pretty's mother approaching, her pink Adidas still flapping even though there was no surface to walk on. In her case, the pair of Adidas seemed to replace angel wings. Well, to each his own. We are in heaven. It doesn't matter.

Luisa Rocio had arranged with the powers that be to become Astrid's official guide throughout eternity. This appointment was something like putting a planet in orbit, impossible to knock it off its track except by a colossally unexpected event, the chances of which Luisa Rocio estimated to be zero. So she and Astrid would revolve around one another forever. With this eternal companionship, she lost the impulse to meddle in earthly events. In fact, she had discovered the power to remain absolutely unattached, and for the first time she experienced no temptation whatsoever to interfere with anything she observed. Whatever it was, it was not important; instead it was mere entertainment, a perk that comes with a broad, universal perspective.

For the immediate future (which was neither here nor there in heaven) Astrid and Rocio were planning a trip to Iquique because they discovered that they both shared a lifelong dream to walk barefoot in the sands along the open stretches of beach. Luisa Rocio said she knew the way and they set off, disguised as two wispy white clouds in an otherwise clear, blue sky.

"The plan," she said with confidence, "is to come in over the sea and then we can wander along the beach however and whenever we desire."

Astrid was delighted, and they set off.

CHAPTER 34

The Moment of Forever

In ten minutes Jhonny Pretty would be on stage in Studio B of TVN, Chile's state-owned television station. It had been several decades since he was last there, and things had changed dramatically. He felt like a rookie and his nerves were frayed. Constancia knocked on the door of his dressing room and entered before he responded.

"Mi amor, you look fabulous." Constancia had selected his suit and was now in charge of dressing Jhonny Pretty for his comeback tour. 'Jhonny Pretty, El Gran Retorno' His dark blue trousers had a wide satin stripe running the full length of the exterior seam. The lapels of his jacket were trimmed with the same satin. Silver threads glistened in vertical pinstripes over the fabric. His hair had been conditioned and trimmed but he didn't let the hairdresser mess with the length and style. He was, after all, Jhonny Pretty from the 70s. That's who everyone wanted to see and hear, and more importantly, that's who he was and the only way he knew how to be.

Since the band fell apart, Juan had been stranded in a time warp. Although still existing in opposing realities, he and Astrid shared the fact that, for each of them, time stood still. Neither of them now lived in the present, at least not in the way that the concept is generally understood.

Juan had not had a drink in several weeks. He leaned on Constancia for the strength to resist. She was the best thing to come along since his lucky blue eye. He thought about his collection of talismans that were still stored in the leather box, now safely high in the closet in the bedroom he shared with Constancia. Even she was forbidden to touch them. He still didn't know which of the items was his lucky one and he continued to guard them all with the equal care. He did not blame the talismans for the fire because, as he saw it now, it had been the necessary evil, the catalyst for a road to health and happiness. So they had not been derelict in their duties. If anything, they had been complacent, but more than likely, they had some influence on events as they evolved. In fact, things had turned out better than he could have ever imagined. Consequently the talismans had become invaluable.

Jesica made the decision that Constancia and Jhonny would live with her and Hector, all as one big family, in her father's house. She told the usual housemates to vacate the premises because her life had changed, and they all wandered off in search of another kind soul with some extra space. Her father's portrait still hung on the living room wall and she said he never missed a thing that happened, and in his own way he provided guidance. Sometimes through dreams, sometimes through signals that were reminiscent of a particular habit of his. He used to lock windows tight at night so now and then if she left one open before going to bed, she'd find it locked tight in the morning. Or if she threw a car dusting rag on the floor, she would find it rinsed and hanging over the rear view mirror the next day. She said it was her father who told her the New Year's Eve fire had been a warning; all four of them were to stop drinking. If not, it would be the downfall for the entire group. And from now on, whoever gave into temptation would be responsible for the consequences suffered by the other three. Jesica also said that it was her theory that 'Jhonny's ghost,' – as they had come to refer to the evil apparition of Luisa Rocio on that night – was a hallucination caused by too much drink. It had finally caught up to him and nearly drove him crazy. For that reason, she reiterated, he could not be held responsible for his cowardice.

As far as the other three knew, Jhonny had been living with family in a small house in Recoleta. This was not entirely untrue; it's just that he failed to mention the family members were all dead. Of course, Constancia's vision of Jhonny's apartment, which she had imagined was a swinging bachelor pad, was shattered, but she forgave him for that, especially since she could see potential with her new, reformed Jhonny and the amount of money Hector would demand just for a glimpse of his handsome face, to say nothing of listening to his velvet voice. Hector whispered that, for a start, the makers of Fisherman's Friends' throat lozenges had approached him with a proposal. Hector was concerned that Jhonny might not want to wear the fisherman's rain hat because it would mess up his hair. But Constancia assured him, "Don't worry Hector. I'll work on him."

Before he moved out of the cemetery with nothing but his box of talismans and a radio, he offered his mattress and small corner table to a group of squatters in Patio 76, otherwise referred to as Patio Británico. They drew straws and, to Juan's satisfaction, the eldest man won the prize. "I've never won anything in my life before. I feel ten years younger. My luck has changed." He grinned a toothless grin that he directed around to each man in the circle. "Yeah? Now let's see you get a good looking girl to share that new mattress of yours." "Well, that'll be in another lifetime." he said. "Or maybe the ghost of a desperate woman," someone else suggested. "I don't care. I'll take her."

Later, when a gatekeeper of the Santiago General Cemetery spread a rumour about Jhonny Pretty living the life of a squatter in Patio 35, no one believed him. But to officially investigate and put an end to such damning speculation, the administrator had the padlock removed from the Maluenda-Valdéz family mausoleum so that he could personally do a revision. When he found nothing there, the gatekeeper was given a severe reprimand and told to curb his imagination. "Rumours of this magnitude are unacceptable. Besides, whatever happens in the cemetery stays in the cemetery. It is meant to be an eternal vault. If the dead frolic around having orgies under palm trees, it's nobody's business. And by the way, the rumours about Gothic transvestites having wild parties in the cemetery are nothing but wicked stories aimed at blemishing the reputation of both the institution of the cemetery and respectable drag queens. I don't want this type of thing to reach my ears again."

The last month had been a whirlwind for Juan. Not only had the living arrangements changed, but he was no longer a swinging single. Constancia was attached to him at the hip, and he was surprised to discover that he liked it. She also had the temperament of a bulldog and whenever a young woman so much as looked at him, she sprung into action, eyes alight, an ugly scowl warning her off. No one got a piece of Jhonny Pretty anymore. She even monitored his autograph sessions, and he was not responsible for the disappointment when she suddenly held up her hand and said to those still holding pen to blank paper, "That's it for today. Thank you very much."

Hector, the manager of the newly created Jhonny Pretty Corporation, had arranged for the television special that would open El Gran Retorno tour. He actually had to fight off the other channels, and this gave him plenty of negotiating leverage.

Hector organised a tour, beginning in the northern-most city of Arica. From there, they would travel south, covering every major town, ending in Punta Arenas, Chile's most southern city. Hector's experience in tourism proved to be vital to the success of the corporation. Jesica's technical expertise provided the company with the background to contract the best equipment and roadies along the way. Musicians scrambled to form a backup band and offers came in from all over, begging to open the act and Jesica's suggestion that they support local musicians resulted in regional talent contests. These were profitable spinoffs, fun and popular. There was money to be made at the gate as well as from signing the young hopefuls. Everything was under the control of the Jhonny Pretty Corporation.

Shortly before the airing of the TVN Jhonny Pretty special, the foursome was up in Arica, preparing for the first live show; the venue was a huge outdoor stage on the wide-open beach north of town.

"Jhonny, you nailed it." Hector was so pumped on the success of the TV special and buzz of the business that he had forgotten to eat. He lost more weight and looked fit in the new suits that Constancia ordered from a tailor. He remained loyal to his glossy hair and moustache, but had allowed a professional trim.

"It felt good, Hector. It feels good." Jhonny, too, was enjoying a youthful vitality.

Constancia rose on her tiptoes and kissed him on the cheek. "You're marvellous, my love, simply marvellous."

Jhonny was in heaven. He was about to go on stage and this time he loved the nerves, loved the apprehension, was anxious to face the crowd and to give them what they wanted, to give them more than they expected. He listened to the grey murmur of the multitude. There were fans as old and older than he was, and they brought their children. Teenagers, too, lounged across the sand at the edges of the main crowd. They wanted to see what all the fuss was about.

As planned, when the band increased the tempo and the crowd had worked itself up to a feverish pitch, Jhonny ran out on stage. The beach came alive with cheers, whistles and roaring applause. A dozen coloured lights circled around him. The crowd went wild and grandmothers screamed out his name. The flourish of stage lights and flashes from cameras were blinding. He couldn't see the crowd but he could feel them, a giant energetic mass. The anticipation rose to unbearable levels (several women fainted) as he strode coolly back and forth along the front of the stage, microphone high in the air. Suddenly the lights went down and he stopped. He froze as a single yellow spot focused on him, obliterating the band in the background. Eventually a hush fell over the crowd. For a few seconds, Jhonny was the only man on earth, frozen in time.

When he sighed into the microphone, the crowd screamed with excitement. Then loudly, over the voices of the people who all wanted a piece of Jhonny Pretty, he said calmly, "This one's for you, Señora Astrid." and he led the band into "This is the Moment of forever."

Luisa Rocio, having never been out of Santiago before and admittedly not the best guide in the heavens, held Astrid's hand as they looked for the perfect spot to watch the sun go down on the beach.

"I'm not sure if this is the beach we had in mind, Astrid. I saw a sign for Iquique quite awhile ago, so maybe we overshot it. I am not accustomed to long-distance travel at the speed of sound, or light, or whatever it is that we've just done. But we're here, and it's lovely, wherever we are."

The sun had already sunk below the Pacific horizon and soft waves lapped in a steady rhythm as the sun passed them off to the moon. A fresh sea breeze cooled the night air, and stars hung in a net over the bed of sand. If either one of these feminine spirits had been able to read the stars, they would have realised that they overshot Iquique by about 300 kilometres and that they were now wandering along the northern beaches of Arica.

"Yes, Señora. It is. But I thought it would be quiet and peaceful. What do you suppose is attracting that huge crowd?" Astrid pointed towards the coloured spotlights that were brushing over the tops of thousands of heads, which were bobbing in front of a stage on the beach.

Without another word, they wandered over towards the concert. Astrid took great pleasure in the cool, wet sand between her toes. What a delight to walk barefoot after all the years of having her toes cooped up in heavy leather loafers.

They reached the edge of the crowd and stood in silence.

"That's Jhonny Pretty." Astrid said, both as a statement of fact and an expression of delight.

She allowed the memory of her last living night to wash over her, recalling with meticulous and vivid detail, the moments of deep desire and final exquisite rapture, as she heard Jhonny Pretty say, "This one's for you, Señora Astrid." and he led the band into "This is the Moment of fsorever."

Astrid was in heaven.

Made in the USA
Charleston, SC
15 July 2013